A Journey Through Fire

Rise of Shadow · Reign of Light

Volume II

L.R. Knight

A JOURNEY THROUGH FIRE

Editor: Lorna Albert

Copy Editor: Rebecca Aikman

Cover Design: Todd Toews

ISBN: 9798597960517

Printed in the United States of America

I dedicate this book to my editor, Lorna Albert. Lorna, you've been in this with me since the beginning. Thank you for believing in this story. Thank you for believing in me as a writer. Most of all, thank you for your friendship.

A Journey through Fire

"Clinging to hope while you are in the heart of the fire will result in you being refined, rather than burned."

- Dolan Thain
Heart of the Brave

CHAPTER ONE

PURSUIT OF FREEDOM

Mikiel ran.

Over root and under branch, trees blurred as he darted past them. The forest consumed him. It had been days since he exited the Mountains of D'aal, yet he was still hunted. Troy and Bernice weren't far behind; he could hear twigs snapping under their feet as they pursued him. He ached, his feet blistering from the relentless pursuit.

He didn't know how much longer he could resist the persistent Bishops. It had been weeks since he was with the rest of their troop; since he saw Kaldon, Anneya, and Tolek. It had also been weeks since Alden had been slain by his very own blade. The scenario of the Seer's death stormed through his memories like a beast clawing at his mind.

The only time he was able to hide for a short rest, was when he could widen his distance enough from the Bishops to do so. Opportunities to rest were becoming scarcer and his mind was suffering from the lack of it. He feared it was only a matter of time before they caught him, making him pay for taking the life of the old Seer.

"Mikiel!" Troy thundered in the distance from behind him. "You can't get away from what you did! We will never stop hunting you!"

Mikiel, panting with each stride, looked up into the air to see a smoky hue draping over the sky. The sight was both terrifying and alluring to him. He noticed the skies began changing around the time he took the life of the Seer. The subtle darkness filling the air mirrored the Shadow swelling in his soul. It was overtaking him; changing him.

With each stride, he watched tree branches in the distance shifting in the wind. The sound of the wind always eased his nerves, soothing him. It reminded him of when he was a child. He and his mother spent many days wandering through trees and bushes. She taught him about different herbs surrounding the Peak of Lore. As an herbalist, she knew every species of plant intimately. She worked with them; healed with them. Sorting through the assortment of growing herbs together, the stirring of leaves from the wind always caught his attention. It calmed his fears, giving him a sense of peace. His mother was now gone, killed by the carelessness of those who fought to advance the Kingdom of Light. Hatred boiled within him, fueling him as he ran.

"There is no escape Mikiel!" Bernice shouted. The Bishop was so close. He could hear her breathy exhales behind him.

Scrambling to gain distance from them, he felt a tug at his foot as it hooked on an outcropping root. Panic flooded him. He slammed to the ground, winded. He closed his eyes, panic overtaking him as he fought to breathe.

Around him, he heard the ground ruffling. They had finally caught him. The relentless pursuit coming to an end, Mikiel felt a boot press down upon his back.

Troy spoke through tired breaths. "We told you we wouldn't stop. You should have saved us the long journey back. If it was up to me, your life would end right here to spare us the burden. Even so, the Peak of Lore has an adequate number of dark prison cells. One of those cells will be your new home."

Mikiel struggled to move under the weight of the boot. As they handled him, he felt coarse rope being tightly tied around his wrists. It scratched him, irritating his skin.

With his face pressed into the dirt, he turned his head and opened his eyes; regarding the treed landscape around him. It was a place that was a pure expression of freedom, yet he was shackled. He didn't know how he would escape, but he swore in his heart that he would. He vowed that he would not grow old and die in the prisoned walls of the Peak of Lore.

Their trek back was by no means easy. Mikiel had hoped the Bishops would want to rest; however, they took little time. They were eager to imprison him. They journeyed days with few words spoken to him. There was no need to speak to him. In their minds, he was nothing more than a murderer and a traitor.

Step after weary step, they forced him to trudge on. The Mountains of D'aal dawned before him yet again. He knew that somewhere hidden within those mountains was the Peak of Lore. He cringed at the thought of going back to the place where his mother was slain. Worse, he had two Bishops urging his steps. It was still weeks of travel away, yet foreboding thoughts tormented him of the stale cell awaiting him.

Ropes restricting his hands cut further into his wrists. He felt Troy shove his back.

"Get moving, traitor!" the Bishop shouted as Mikiel stumbled forward.

He hadn't noticed he was faltering in speed; however, Troy was always quick to remind him with a shove or a kick when he slowed.

"We need to stop, Troy," Bernice said, protesting against her partner's persistence. "We have gone eight hours without rest or food."

Troy grunted as he stilled in stride, clearly preferring to continue. "Fine, let's take some time to rest and eat. We will leave again shortly."

Bernice nodded in agreement. Her tensed muscles eased. "If you can track down some firewood, I'll keep an eye on the prisoner," she said, motioning to Mikiel.

Mikiel couldn't help but notice that every time the two Bishops referred to him since his capture, they no longer used his name. He was only regarded as *the prisoner* or *the traitor*. It was as though his identity was discarded and forgotten. He truly was lost.

He watched Troy disappear into the forest, searching out kindling wood to start a fire. The moment the Bishop was out of sight, he felt Bernice's grip tighten on the rope around his wrists. He watched the ground. He had been on his best behaviour since being captured; hardly making a peep unless spoken to. He did so on purpose. His only chance of escape was to appear unassuming and to wait for the perfect moment. With Troy gone, he wondered if that moment had finally arrived.

Focusing on the tenseness of the rope around his wrists, he waited for Bernice's grip to loosen. All he needed was one moment where she wasn't paying attention and he could make his move.

They waited in silence for Troy's return. Watching Bernice's darting eyes searching the forest, he knew she was trying to spot wood for the fire as well.

Find something, Mikiel thought in hope.

Her eyes rested on a piece of scrap wood several feet away from where they stood.

"Come on, prisoner!" she quipped with a yank on his rope.

He followed unflinchingly. He waited for Bernice to bend over, reaching for the piece of scrap wood. The moment she did, her grip slightly softened. Mikiel didn't know if he could best a Bishop's grip; but this may be his only chance. Before she could rise, he hurled himself forward with all his might. He felt the strain on the rope as Bernice tried to hold on; however, her grip broke. Without delay, he bolted into the trees leaving the Bishop behind. He knew his chances were slim for escape. He couldn't pump his arms due to the rope, but he couldn't allow himself to falter. His freedom depended on it.

He could hear Bernice close behind him. "Get back here, prisoner!" she yelled.

Without warning, Troy barreled through the trees after him. He'd thought the Bishop was further away, heightening his chances of escape. As Mikiel ran, he felt the mixture of sweat and tears stinging his eyes. He longed to be free from the Bishops. He longed to rest.

His legs pumping, he knew he likely had only a few more moments left of freedom. Through the trees, his eyes were caught by a peculiar sight. An ominous darkness hovered between the branches of trees. Thick fog swayed through the air like a semi-transparent shadow. He watched it, still trying to pay attention to each step he took. He'd never seen anything like it. It looked unnatural — otherworldly, even.

Like a bolt of lightning, the dark fog shot through the sky over Mikiel's head. He ducked, flinching with a startle. Immediately, he heard shrill screams cutting into the forest.

Two *thuds* sounded from behind him.

It was a risk to stop running; but both curiosity and fatigue caused him to cease. Turning around, he saw the forest was still. Troy and Bernice were nowhere to be seen. He somehow knew that they were likely no longer alive. The thick, darkened fog quickly wove around Mikiel, lingering behind him. He cringed as the unfamiliar shadow neared him. Its cool touch wrapped around his hands, then quickly dashed into the trees in front of him. He felt the rope that bound him drop to the dirt floor. Lifting his hands, he saw that his wrists were bruised and stained in blood. They stung from dirt and sweat. He was no longer bound.

Looking up from his wrists, he saw the dark fog drifting around the shape of a tree trunk. Behind the tree was a shadowed figure.

"You heard my call," the soothing voice said, weaving throughout the trees.

Mikiel rubbed his eyes in exhaustion, not knowing whether what he was experiencing was reality or a hallucination. He spoke forth none-the-less.

"What do you mean, '*I heard your call?*'" he asked.

"My call to the Shadow," the woman said, stepping forward so he could see her.

Even though she seemed frail in stature, she by no means looked gentle. Smoky fog drifted over her black robe which stretched to the mossy ground. Her pale face was framed by ash-coloured hair cascading down her shoulders. Black tattooed markings on her brow travelled up her face to hide behind her hairline. What transfixed him the most were her eyes. They were pale blue, like a deep gaze into the soul of winter itself.

He looked down, avoiding eye contact.

"I am Furion," the Entity said, introducing herself. "At last, *the Door of the Dominion* being opened grants me the privilege to come see you like this."

Mikiel remained silent.

Furion watched him with an inquisitive gaze. "Child, speak and tell me why you embraced the Shadow. Why did you answer my call?"

Tears tumbled around down the young man's face. In a whisper, he pushed words past his sorrow. "Because my pain is far too great, and hatred is inside my heart."

Furion gazed at him. "Now that you are broken, I can rebuild you. You must embrace the pain. Embrace the hatred."

"I killed a man; a Seer," Mikiel confessed. "I don't want to go to prison."

The Entity's stare penetrated the shaken young man. "I know who you killed. Alden was a threat to Agadin; a threat to my Dominion. You followed my guidance excellently. You did well, Mikiel. I will help you to avoid the chains you fear."

"How? Even though Troy and Bernice are rid of, others will come. I will be forever hunted," he stated with strain in his voice.

A smile spread over Furion's delicate face. "I will help you by giving you power."

"Power?" he asked. He braved looking up to meet the Entity's eyes once again. "What sort of power?"

Furion walked closer, nearing him. Reaching out, she placed an icy hand upon his shoulder. "You don't see yourself for who you truly are. You see a shattered soul; I see something far greater."

"What do you see in me?" Mikiel asked, his eyes looking once again to the ground.

Furion brought her face closer. "I see a *Roek*."

His eyes widened. He thought about how he had once seen Locrian *Command Creation*. It stirred something in him as he watched the Seer using the ancient ability. The sight awakened a longing to wield power; to understand his authority over creation.

"You know Mikiel, men and women of old would endure training for their entire lives to carry the title of *Roek*. What some spend their entire lives training for, I can grant in a moment," Furion said, snapping her fingers. "Roeks specialize in mastering one of the four elements of fire, water, wind, or earth. Tell me, which element would you wield if you were given the choice?"

Mikiel didn't know if Furion was being truthful in her claim. He knew to be called a Roek was no small accomplishment. He longed for greatness. He desired power. Most of all, he wanted peace that only freedom could give him.

He looked up to the trees again where Furion's dark fog first caught his attention. The trees began to shake and tremble as the wind coursed through them. He thought of the peace he knew as a child. He thought of his mother.

Breaking eye contact with the swaying trees, he looked back to Furion, the Entity who could grant him unfathomable power in a split moment.

He replied, "I would choose to wield the wind."

Chapter Two

The Skull No Longer Sleeps

K aldon smoothed his hand across the ancient rock walls. Torches were brought into the caved room, lighting the forgotten abode. There was nothing extraordinary about the room; it was simply a cave hidden in the depths of a mountain. Still, as his fingers stroked the walls, he knew an artifact of great significance once slumbered here; the skull of the demon dragon, Marradus.

Anneya kicked a stone, the sound of it echoing as it bounced off a wall. "How did the Sovereign of Shadow get the skull out of here? There's no exit," she stated, looking around at the faces that filled the caverned room.

Kaldon, Anneya, and Locrian had come down to the cave several times already to look over the scene. Being without Fen in a place so close to the Depths felt odd. The Philosopher typically spent all of her time in the private library, but she was still seeing Master Healers for the injuries she endured from her interaction with the Sovereign of Shadow. Tolek had come down as well, but he was too busy pulling the Peak of Lore back together to keep returning. It had been nearly three weeks since the Dark Paladin, Geran Rule, was slain and the army of Shadow was disbanded.

Locrian ran his hand over his hairless head. "Distance doesn't exist between the Nahmen and Kreel. Even if one of the Nahmen's Kreel were all the way back in Gorath, they could transport entire objects to the Sovereign's homeland with them. I suspect this is what they did. There is no question that Tymas Droll now has Marradus' skull."

Anneya grimaced in frustration. Kaldon looked down at the sunken groove in the stone floor. The sheer magnitude of it was staggering. Such an indent would have taken thousands of years to shape. For so long, the skull was hidden and safe; but no longer. It was now in the hands of a man who could raise the dead.

"I still can't believe Droll is a *Shan-Rafa*," Anneya voiced, her words carrying a haunting tone. "Who would have thought that all this time such a gifted healer was hidden in Gorath."

Kaldon nodded in concern. "Locrian, could the Sovereign actually raise a creature like Marradus from the dead?"

The Seer leaned down, running his hand upon the indented floor. "I don't know for certain. I know history records say Shan-Rafas could pull the spirit of a human right from eternity back into its body. Still, I would think a beast like Marradus would be another thing entirely."

Kaldon could feel his golden sword, *Integrity,* strapped to his back. *Humility* hung from his waist. He knew that Tymas Droll wasn't someone he had the liberty of fearing. The Shan-Rafa was his responsibility; his mandate. The Sovereign needed to fall.

"Locrian, have you heard or seen anything in a vision concerning Mikiel and the rest of his group?" Anneya asked changing the subject.

"There has been no word concerning those missing," the Seer stated in short.

Kaldon couldn't help but notice that he darted around any questions concerning the missing group. It pulled at his nerves. He hoped they were safe.

"We need to get going," Anneya said, placing a hand on his shoulder. "You can't be late for your lesson with Brenton."

Kaldon smiled, pulling his thoughts back to the moment. "Are you coming?" he asked, looking at Locrian.

The Seer looked through squinted eyes at the sunken groove. "No, you two go ahead. I need to think for a while."

The two turned from the Seer to ascend back to the surface of the Peak of Lore.

Before they were out of earshot, Locrian called out. "Oh, and Kaldon, don't forget about our lesson tomorrow," he said instructively. "We need to figure out what you did to Command Creation."

"Of course," Kaldon said.

The moment still burned in his memory when he spoke to rising steam, commanding it to become flames of fire. The flames swirled through the air to engulf *Integrity*. He wanted to understand what he did. He wanted to master the skill so he could use it against the Sovereign of Shadow.

Leaving the dark cavern, they travelled up through the Depths, making their way to the surface of the ancient mountain. Approaching the top of the stairs to the first floor, Kaldon noticed it was uncharacteristically quiet. While the lower floors of the library were purposefully silent for studying, the top floor was usually the exact opposite; it was social chaos.

Rising to the top floor, he was surprised to see hundreds of students clustered together, watching the door from which they came. A library that was normally hectic, was still in anticipation. All eyes rested on Kaldon.

In the middle of the grouped students, stood a man wearing the customary armour of a Blade. "Kaldon!" Brenton shouted, holding two wooden practice swords.

"Come on, Brenton. Do we really need to do this here?" he pleaded with his instructor. "Why can't we spar in one of the private rooms?"

"You can't disappoint all of these people, Kaldon. They all know what you can do. They want to see *it,*" Brenton said, motioning to all the students watching.

The swarms of people clapped their hands; some cheered. Kaldon turned to Anneya who had her hand over her mouth, holding back a laugh.

Brenton continued, "Besides, you haven't beaten me yet. This is your opportunity."

The crowd cheered in laughter, egging Kaldon on to spar with the Blade.

The ceaseless attention was growing old for him. Word buzzed throughout the facility about him defeating the three Dark Bishops. Although that created a stir, the news carrying the most hype was that he delivered the final blow that killed Geran Rule. Kaldon knew the General's defeat was a joint effort between him, Tolek, Locrian, and Anneya; but people seemed to dwell on the fact that it was his sword that ended the Dark Paladin's life.

From Brenton's direction, a wooden blade whirled through the air. Reaching out, Kaldon caught it. The crowd cheered and hollered. Anneya took a step back, knowing this was a battle that wouldn't be discreet.

"I can't believe you're making me do this," he muttered under his breath.

"Just go along with it," Brenton said, his smile wide as he walked over to him. The Blade handed him a piece of black cloth. "They see you as a hero, Kaldon. Let's give them a show. Now, put this over your eyes."

He reluctantly took the cloth and began wrapping it around his head, preventing sight. He was growing accustomed to such lessons with his instructor. His *foresight* hadn't faltered since the encounter with the Dark Bishops. He was able to summon it whenever he had need. Brenton was now teaching him not only to use his gift, but to develop it into something greater; a skill he could depend upon.

The blinder secure, Kaldon could feel his foresight awaken. The moment went still, his senses became clear. His mind was alert, ready to receive. Breathing steadily, he waited for Brenton to attack. He listened intently hearing the Blade's breaths. Subtle visions of attacks that would be thrown his way flooded him. In his mind, he watched a vision of the wooden sword coming for his head. Moving based on what he saw, he lifted his wooden sword as it crashed against Brenton's, preventing a blow.

The crowd of students gasped. He could hear murmurs breaking out, asking how he could block the strike without being able to see. Through foresight, he saw Brenton's sword targeting his legs. In response, he jumped in the air, clearing the low swipe. The Blade coming in again, he listened to the man's footing. He responded to what he saw in his mind. The sound of wood colliding cracked around him as he blocked and deflected numerous attacks.

"Come on, Kaldon!" someone shouted from the crowd. The affirmation was followed by uproarious cheers.

Watching the evolution of visions, he began not only seeing Brenton's attacks; he saw holes in his defence. This allowed him to begin fighting back instead of only defending. Brenton was quicker than most; but with his foresight, Kaldon could see several attacks ahead of him. The ability made a formidable warrior such as Brenton appear predictable.

Kaldon drove in with force, wielding his weapon with precision. With each attack, he could hear Brenton's breath beginning to quicken. That was exactly what he wanted. If the Blade grew tired, he would become sloppy, giving opportunity for error.

Then he saw it. In his mind, he saw Brenton coming in with a jab to the stomach. He figured if he could spin, dodging the attempt, he would be able to bring in a strike that would end the spar.

Brenton stepped forward. Blinded by his surroundings, Kaldon spun around the wooden sword coming at him. He could feel the wooden sword graze his side.

Close, he thought. *Too close.*

Being free from Brenton's jab, he quickly brought his own sword up, pressing it against the Blade's neck.

Brenton gasped.

The Blade panting, Kaldon pulled off his blindfold. His wooden sword rested over his instructor's neck. Looking around, eyes watched him in quiet shock. None of these people had likely seen someone use foresight before. Not only that, but Brenton was a Blade; a Blade who he just beat blindfolded.

"Great Divinity, I won…" Kaldon muttered in wonder.

The silence was killed as claps and shouts that filled the library. He saw Anneya cheering as well.

Tension evaporating from Brenton, he let out a hard laugh. "Congratulations, Kaldon. I knew it would only be a matter of time before you could beat me. I was just hoping it wouldn't be in a room filled with people," he joked. "You've come a long way with your foresight. We need to find ways to keep pushing its boundaries."

Kaldon nodded in agreement not wanting to test his voice, being so short of breath.

"Great job, Kaldon!" one of the women from the crowd called out to him.

He looked over, seeing a small group of women watching him bashfully. He furred his brow looking away. He wasn't used to such attention, nor was it something he desired.

Anneya walked up to him, pulling his arm close to her. She glared at the staring woman. The scowl of the feisty Blade made each woman look away. He was thankful that she quickly took a role in becoming a barrier between him and the crowds craving his attention.

As mounds of students gathered around Kaldon, he resisted sinking into the expectations of the masses. He knew many could be seduced by popularity and fame, but he also knew he could never find fulfillment in them. Solitude called him. He needed to be alone. He needed to further train. A quick spar with Brenton wasn't enough anymore. After all, he didn't desire seeing adoration in the eyes of others toward him; he wanted to see fear in the eyes of the Sovereign of Shadow.

Chapter Three

The Training of a Warrior

———◆◆◆———

B rushing through the torch-lit halls of the Peak of Lore, Kaldon diverted his eyes from those passing by.

Passing room after room, he heard professors prattling on to students about history, science, and mathematics. He shook his head in frustration. Only several weeks ago, lives were lost. Most went on living as though nothing was awry. It wasn't only warriors who were killed, but residents who weren't conditioned for war. Mikiel's mother was one of them.

Reaching the entrance hall, he felt relief knowing he would soon be outside once again. He didn't have time to waste in a classroom. Instead, day after day, he burrowed himself deep into the forest — out of sight, for the sake of training. He didn't dare tell anyone what he did outside the walls of the Peak of Lore; not even Anneya. She wouldn't understand — no one would. Whenever he questioned his methods to push his limits, he would remind himself of a famous quote from his father.

"No one begins at their mountaintop, nor are they born into triumph. The journey begins in the valley — in the testing. No significant calling is attained without significant training and refining."

- Dolan Thain

The wise words of the dead General echoing through his mind, he couldn't imagine his father being anything other than the one who history remembered him to be. Even though many books were written of his achievements and exploits, Kaldon found himself wondering if the man ever doubted himself, as he so often did. All that he knew was that with his father deceased, Agadin's loved hero was gone.

Pushing the thoughts away, he stepped outside. As far as he could see, mountains reigned. Fresh buds were coating the trees. The melting snow was contrasted by the greenery dotting the landscape around the Peak of Lore. Spring had arrived. He breathed in the mountain air.

To his surprise, the wind was more silent than normal. It was midday, yet the overcast was dreary, a foggy hue masking the sun's light. He had noticed the faint drabness coating the skies in recent days; however, he thought spring would have dethroned it by now. While at first, the tint was so faint that no one would likely notice, now its distinct husk grew darker each day.

Kaldon ripped his eyes from the off-putting sight of the darkening skies, fixing his gaze on the forest that awaited him. He knew that deep in those woods was where he could push himself. Forcing himself to spur onwards, he set his feet into motion. Trailing through rocks and trees, he sought out his favorite spot to train.

Finally reaching his preferred place, he knew he'd need to wait. As he usually did, he plopped himself onto the ground — allowing his back to press against the man-sized boulder. With the cold rock propping him up, all that lay before him was mountain, forest, and the offset skies. He exhaled, thankful to finally be alone and free from being the centre of attention.

He pulled out his leather journal and began scratching his pen into the ivory pages.

"I have shared words with a renowned Seer; fought alongside a Paladin — one of the greatest warriors in all of Agadin. I have laughed with a Philosopher who is one of the most brilliant minds in all the land. As I walk alongside the great, I see a common trait in each; they understand that limitation is not measured by circumstance. It is measured by choice. It seems as though limitation is more of an internal battle, rather than an external fate."

Closing his journal, he looked onward into the mountainous land populated with trees, stone, and wildlife. He wondered if he truly believed the words he just wrote. He couldn't help wondering if the obstacles looming before them were too mighty to prevail against. Tymas Droll passed before his mind; his sneer marking him. The tyrant had slain thousands throughout Agadin. Emotions rising, Kaldon's hand began to tremble knowing his own father and mother were among those slain by the Sovereign of Shadow. He wondered if their forces were strong enough to stand against one so sinister. He wondered if *he* was strong enough.

Reaching into his travelling clothes, he pulled out the pendant he never went anywhere without. As the circular emblem swung from the chain, he watched its bronze-like features reflect the light. When he first received the pendant from his mother, he thought it was just a memoir; now he knew better. The pendant was a *Legacy,* a symbol worn only by those called as *Protectors of Agadin.* The five prongs protruding from its core symbolized the five types of Protectors appointed by Divinity to shield Agadin: Paladins, Seers, Philosophers, Roeks, and Shan-Rafas. His eyes traced the outer band of the symbol. The line symbolized a rare, sixth Protector: *Paragon;* one who could access the gifts of all five other Protectors. Tucking the Legacy back beneath his shirt, he pondered the mystery of it. He was a Paragon, yet he still had little idea what that meant.

Still reflecting about his unique calling, he finally heard the sound he was waiting for. A low, vicious growl arose from behind the hulking trees. Each time he came outside the Peak of Lore, it was only a matter of time before a Kreel found him.

Stepping out from the shadows, the creature stood tall at about nine feet. It wasn't the largest Kreel he had seen, but its size was daunting none-the-less. The menacing creature's barreling chest was puffed outward in predatory poise. Its reptilian tail writhed as its bat-like eyes took in Kaldon. The Kreel's blackened fur stood in contrast to the light of day; its wings were smoothed back positioned for a ground-fight.

The beasts were nearly everywhere throughout the mountain and forested terrain. The morbid creatures had infested the Mountains of D'aal.

Rising to his feet, Kaldon pulled forth both of his swords. At its sheer size, he needed to remind himself why he was training as he was. As he always did, he forced the creature's hulking image to flee his mind. He replaced it with the appearance of Tymas Droll. That was who he truly wanted to inflict judgement upon.

As the fabricated image of the murderous tyrant consumed him, Kaldon grimaced.

The Kreel lunged.

Swinging at him with its mighty claws, he had seen the attack moments before with his foresight. Sidestepping the attempt, he spun his elbow around cracking the Kreel's snout. The creature staggered back with a shriek.

Those at the training facility avoided the beasts by any means necessary. Considering how many there were throughout the mountains, he saw the creatures in a different light. To him, they were an endless opportunity to train; to mature in ability and skill. Without his foresight, he knew that he wouldn't stand a chance against something so formidable. Thankfully he hadn't come across more than one at a time. Even with his foresight, he knew facing more than one would likely result in him being killed. He had slain nine of the creatures so far in a matter of weeks. He vowed this one would be his tenth.

He had fought enough Kreel to learn what their weak points were. While most parts of the creatures were nearly impenetrable, he learned to target their eyes, wings, snout, behind the knees, and their lower abdomen.

The Kreel pursuing him, he responded to the visions in his mind, shifting around the beast. Kreel were fast, but they were not smart. Kaldon came in, pretending to bring his boot up into the Kreel's stomach. He stopped mid-kick to instead bring the hilt of his sword down between the creature's eyes. The Kreel's eyes blinked in confusion. He had learned that the best way to defeat a Kreel was to perplex it; to be unpredictable.

The beast recovering, he brought up *Humility*, cutting one of its wings. The Kreel let out a mournful screech. Seeing opportunity, he dove in with a final blow, bringing his blade into its lower abdomen. It was only a matter of seconds before the creature thudded onto the mountain floor, stretched out on the ground before him.

Sheathing his blades, Kaldon thought of how it wasn't long ago he'd been terrified of Kreel. He wondered what his father would have thought of him; if the Warrior General would have approved of his methods. It didn't matter; his father was gone.

The bested Kreel stretched before him, he knew it would likely be easier for him to kill one thousand of the creatures than it would be to kill a Shan-Rafa.

Even though he stood in the stillness of nature, his thoughts were as wild as a hurricane. *Is it possible for us to win? Will this be good enough? Am I good enough?*

Before he found himself too far down the vortex thoughts, he pushed the musings away. Even though he dreaded the thought, he knew he needed to head back to the training facility. He couldn't find a moment of peace within its walls anymore. Leaving the body of the Kreel behind, trudging through the trees, he could see the facility coming closer with each step he took. Reigning over the mountainous castle, the skies stole his attention yet again. Their dimmed light unnerved him. There was something amiss about it, yet he couldn't place why. It looked unnatural, unfitting for Agadin.

He heard a sound rip through the stillness. Kaldon stopped in an instant, looking to a stage of trees off to the side from where the sound came. He unsheathed his swords again, the resounding rings escaping into the forest. Knowing it could be another Kreel, he didn't know whether he should risk taking a look. To defeat a single Kreel was one thing; fighting two back to back may be another entirely.

From the assortment of trees, he heard the noise again. It didn't sound threatening or hostile. It sounded discreet — faint even — like a whimper.

He watched the shaded trees as he heard the subtle whimper again, yet louder.

Pushing past his caution, he slowly began weaving through the trees. Trailing between trunks and branches, he could feel strands of spiderweb catching on his face and beard, proving no one had been through these parts for quite some time.

"Please... Help me," a voice muttered weakly through the landscape.

Kaldon's hesitancy evaporated, replaced by alarm. Delving deeper into woods, he searched for what sourced the desperate plea.

He saw her.

A woman trudged throughout the landscape, struggling to stay standing. Her scarlet gown, which was clearly not suitable for travel, was torn and stained by both dirt and blood. She looked young in appearance; however, the few greying streaks in her dark hair showed she was older than she appeared.

Concern welled up in him. "Don't be afraid! I'm here to help you!" he called to reassure her that he wasn't a threat.

The women kept walking, seemingly aimless, without response.

He approached her slowly. Based on her behaviour, he knew she was clearly in some state of shock. He noticed that under her arm she carried a book, seemingly the only thing she had with her for her travels. Reaching her, he placed a hand on her shoulder. She stopped mid-step, slowly turning her gaze to him.

"I'm here to help you," he said. "What is your name?"

"My name…?" she responded in a daze.

Kaldon nodded, encouraging her to respond.

"My name… My name is Ceanna Brimnas," the woman said, as if recalling a forgotten memory.

Before he could reply, she burst into tears, falling into his shoulder. He held her, preventing her from falling over.

"It's alright. You're safe now," he said as she wept.

"Ceanna, I need you to tell me what happened," Kaldon said looking her in the eyes, trying to pull information out from her.

She regained her composure, looking back in the direction from where she first came. "I am from the city *Stone Hedge*, just beyond the Mountains of D'aal."

"Stone Hedge? I haven't heard of such a place," he muttered in thought. "How far away is the city from here? How long have you been traveling for?"

"Weeks…" Ceanna said, still watching the path from which she came. "Stone Hedge is a grand city. It has a sizeable army and holds much political power in Agadin."

Looking at the woman in her scarlet gown, he could hardly believe she had travelled for weeks. "Why do you keep looking back to that path?"

"I'm being hunted," Ceanne whispered. "I need to see Tolek, immediately."

"Hunted?" he asked, allowing his sight to trail down the path from which she came. "Who is hunting you?"

Tears began rising again in the woman's eyes. "Those who overthrew Stone Hedge. The Sovereign of Shadow's army came to the city nearly one month ago and overthrew it. Kreel were everywhere. So many lives were lost. Those who weren't killed were either forced to join the Sovereign's army or to become his slaves. Even those in our army who weren't killed were forced to join his. Stone Hedge is now lost under the Sovereign's reign…" she said as her voice trailed off.

"Great Divinity…" Kaldon whispered. He knew the Sovereign's army must have gone to Stone Hedge before attempting to overtake the Peak of Lore.

"How many from his army did the Sovereign leave behind once it was taken over?" he asked.

Ceanna rubbed her face. "Around thirty thousand were left behind to take over the city."

He shook his head in wonder. The part of the army he and his troop disbanded was fourty thousand. That meant the Sovereign originally brought seventy thousand warriors on their mission. He wondered how many the Sovereign actually had under his will. Those seventy thousand could very well have only been a fraction of the army of Shadow.

In her weakly state, Ceanne fumbled as she stood. He watched as the book she carried slipped out from underneath her arm. Reaching out, he caught the salmon-coloured book mid-fall.

Lifting the book, he read the title aloud. *"The Lion's Roar; The Raven's Call."*

He smiled as he gazed upon the cover. "'This was my favourite book as a child," he said handing it back to Ceanne.

"Mine as well," she said, tucking it under her arm, clearly happy to have it back. "This was the only thing I could retrieve before I left my home. I'm thankful to have it with me. It is a reminder of better times…"

He understood her connection with the book. He remembered reading it back in Rundle as a child, before his mother's life was taken.

"Kaldon?!" His name echoed throughout the trees. He recognized it as Anneya's voice.

Ceanna flinched at the sound of the shout, clearly still shaken. He placed a hand on the anxious woman's shoulder to steady her nerves.

"Don't worry, you're safe now. No one is going to find you," he reassured her before responding to Anneya.

"I am over here! Follow my voice!" he shouted back to the Blade.

Anneya materialized from the trees. "Kaldon, where have you…" the Blade's voice trailed off at the sight of Ceanna.

"Anneya, this is Ceanna Brimnas," he said, introducing the rattled woman. "She needs our help."

Anneya watched unblinking, staring at the woman who wore a scarlet gown stained in blood. "I am well aware of who this woman is," Anneya said. "Ceanna Brimnas is the Queen of Stone Hedge, one of the largest cities in all of Agadin."

CHAPTER FOUR
DAWNING LIGHT

———————✦◆◆◆◆✦———————

"Times are dire," the Paladin said cryptically into his abode.

Kaldon, Anneya, and Tolek each sat upon leather chairs waiting for Ceanne Brimnas, the Queen of Stone Hedge. A brick fireplace crackled and snapped as the burning logs warmed the Paladin's home. Bookshelves filled with ancient writing and artifacts added to the ambiance. What stood out most in the room was the trademark of a Paladin: weapons. They were scattered everywhere. Kaldon knew there wasn't a sword, axe, dagger, or spear in sight that Tolek didn't have complete mastery over.

He looked up at Tolek. The Paladin looked tired; fatigued from holding the Peak of Lore together under such circumstances.

"Do we have any word of what the Sovereign has planned?" Kaldon queried.

Tolek shifted his weight. "You mean other than his plans to resurrect a demon dragon that could tear apart all of Agadin?"

Kaldon and Anneya stayed quiet.

The Paladin looked down. "Unfortunately, we do. The prisoners are beginning to talk."

Anneya's brows raised at the comment. Hundreds from Tymas Droll's army were kept in the prison deep within the facility. Dark Knights, Blades, and Bishops were locked away for questioning in hope of discovering the Sovereign's strategy.

"What does that vermin have planned?" she hissed.

Kaldon watched the light of the flames illuminating the white teardrop scar travelling down her cheek. Its jagged appearance matched the ferocity in her tone.

Looking into the swaying flames, Tolek spoke. "We know that Droll has been methodically overthrowing cities throughout Agadin, taking his time dismantling them piece by piece. Based on what we have heard from the prisoners, his plans have now escalated. Since he has already claimed multiple major cities, he is sending a large portion of his army to quickly take several prominent areas by force, all at once. He apparently doesn't want even a small fraction of Agadin untouched by the Dominion of Shadow. Much of his army is marching out from Gorath as we speak. I can't imagine how many innocent lives will be lost," the Paladin said.

Anneya sunk into her chair. "When will this madness end?" she whispered under her breath.

Discouragement sweeping into the room, Kaldon sighed heavily. He knew the Sovereign had likely been planning his domination for years; possibly even decades. The Dominion of Shadow was advancing, and its momentum seemed too powerful to stand against. He looked out the window, his eyes once again resting upon the musky taint of the skies. The subtle darkness still unnerved him.

"Do you think the skies have something to do with this?" he asked, his attention distant.

Tolek and Anneya looked at him.

"The skies?" she asked, crossing her arms while leaning back in her chair. "What are you talking about?"

His eyes bounced between the two, watching their blank stares. "You haven't noticed? There is a faint dimness that has begun covering the skies. It started around the time the Sovereign's army came here. It has grown darker ever since. It can't be a coincidence."

Tolek looked at him through squinted eyes. "I think you might be reading into this a bit much, Kaldon. It's normal for the skies to dim from time to time."

"This is different," Kaldon said shaking his head. "There's something unnatural about it. I just can't put my finger on it."

Anneya reached out, placing her hand on his arm. "I don't see how the tone of the skies changing can be a part of the Great War. The Sovereign sending his armies is enough to worry about without us chasing things that aren't even there."

He looked over to Tolek, who was clearly already back to thinking about the Sovereign's army. He was surprised to see how quickly the Paladin dismissed his theory.

"Maybe you're right," he stated, humouring them. He was certain there was something amiss with the skies, but knew he wasn't going to get anywhere with the stubborn Paladin and the Blade.

The door stole their attention with a rigid creak. Looking into the dim room was Ceanne Brimnas. She seemed much more content after being able to take a warm bath and put on a clean dress. The borrowed grey dress was much less formal than her royal gown. Tolek had already sent out Bishops to seek those who were hunting the queen and to eliminate potential threat.

As she took a seat, Tolek didn't hesitate to begin. "Tell me what happened," he said, hoping the queen would be eager to give a full account of everything that took place.

Ceanne reached out, grabbing the warm mug from the table set before her to warm her hands. She sipped her tea slowly, then began. "It all started when I was sitting in my chamber hall. I was at my desk, signing documents for my kingdom, as I do every day. I was surprised when three of my advisors stormed into the room. The three of them dragged in Glaric, my Chief Messenger."

"Glaric…" Anneya muttered aloud the odd name. "What did he do?"

The queen's face soured at the mention of the messenger's name. "Glaric has been my personal messenger ever since I first took reign over Stone Hedge when I was still a little girl. My advisors told me what I would never have expected: Glaric had embraced the Shadow. I still don't understand how someone so close to me became so corrupt without my knowing. He had apparently been leading others in my staff to embrace the Shadow as well."

Tolek nodded. "Unfortunately, Droll is a clever man. He doesn't only use brute force. He understands politics quite well. He looks for key people who can give him immediate influence in a kingdom."

Ceanne, sat up straight at the comment. "Clearly. However, a queen should know better."

"We had something similar take place here at the Lore," Anneya said. "Many here embraced the Shadow without anyone knowing; some even in high positions of authority. Thank Divinity each of the traitors were stopped and displaced from the training facility."

"We weren't so fortunate," Ceanne said, taking another sip of her tea. "We spent much time weeding through who was loyal to Stone Hedge and who wasn't. What we didn't expect was that an army was on our doorstep. We spent so much time focusing internally, we didn't suspect open war was upon us."

"Open war?" Kaldon asked.

The queen nodded. "A swarm of Kreel attacked Stone Hedge. We have high walls of defence, yet they were useless against foes that can fly. I can still hear the screams of my people. I'm sure I will be haunted by them for the rest of my life."

"That's terrible…" Anneya said.

Kaldon and Tolek said nothing, waiting for more details to unfold.

"The Kreel tore apart homes and buildings. They stole so many lives..." Her voice began to shake as she sunk lower into her chair, tears emerging. She paused before continuing, regaining her composure. "Our soldiers weren't trained to fight such beasts. They have only fought men. The Kreel quickly brought my army into submission.

"I still remember when the General of the army followed the Kreel into Stone Hedge; Geran Rule. Upon his arrival, the General's eyes climbed the stone cliff on which my house stands. He looked me straight in the eyes, wearing a sneering smirk. He knew I had no chance to regain authority over Stone Hedge. He had won. My kingdom, once a place of refuge is now where the Sovereign's reign is enforced."

"It should comfort you then to know that Geran Rule is dead," Tolek said brashly.

Ceanne raised her brows. "That does comfort me — at least somewhat."

A chilling moment lingered at the mention of the Dark Paladin's death.

"Did you see the Sovereign of Shadow?" Kaldon asked.

She shook her head. "No, I didn't stay long enough to see him. Many of my advisors were killed — some right before my eyes. However, the few who remained loyal, helped me escape. They ushered me to a secret passageway that brought me into the Mountains of D'aal. That began my journey here."

"How did you make it all the way here?" Anneya asked, warming her hands by the fire.

"I walked. I ran," Ceanne answered. "I slept by the fire's warmth at night. I went to sleep so cold at times, I was surprised to awake in the morning, realizing I hadn't frozen to death. I have had many close calls with the men who hunted me."

The queen continued, "As terrible as my journey here was, nothing was as terrifying as the dreams I had while sleeping. Through many frosty evenings, I was tormented throughout the night. I had dreams of my people being harmed. I had dreams of the Dominion of Shadow in Agadin; dreams of death…"

Kaldon sat up in his chair. He knew from experience that dreams often carried significance. He had been an avid dreamer ever since he was a child. Before he could ask about the nightmares, Anneya cut in.

"I'm sorry about your home. I can't imagine what it would be like for a queen to see her kingdom fall," Anneya said in a soft tone.

Ceanne ran her hands over her dress, smoothing it as she spoke. "I have mourned a great deal for Stone Hedge; however, what happened to my home is just a scratch compared to what I believe is coming. I can't help but believe something terrible to about to happen in Agadin. I fear the Sovereign of Shadow has dreadful plans."

⬥⬥⬥

"To the left!" the site manager shouted as one of the bones for the colossal wing was shifted to its proper place. The last bone was finally aligned.

With hundreds of labourers surrounding him, Tymas Droll stood in the magnificent room. It was not a room magnificent in decor, but in size. The Sovereign of Shadow had it built for the uncommon event. The room was the only place large enough in all of Gorath for the work that needed to be done.

Tymas stood before the skeletal beast. It took the muscle of hundreds to place the bones into their right order. It took years to accumulate every piece of the demon dragon's remains; however, each piece, both the intricate and grand were collected and appropriately positioned. With him, hundreds of workers gathered around the remains of the ancient dragon. It was finally complete.

They were all fatigued after such work. They ached, though none would dare leave. To see a Shan-Rafa at work was a rare occurrence as it was. To see a Shan-Rafa raise such a creature from the dead had likely never occurred in the history of Agadin.

Tymas looked at the two gaping holes in the dragon's skull where its reptilian eyes once rested. He wanted the skull right before him as he performed his task. He desired to watch the menacing eyes of Marradus take shape right before his gaze. Over the years, he had risen many individuals from the dead; armies of individuals. Marradus would be another thing entirely. It would be his most prestigious achievement.

Rand walked up from behind the Sovereign. With white-wisps of hair and wild brows, the stocky-old man stood much shorter than Tymas. "Sovereign, I saw Marradus' spirit circling through the Dominion of Shadow in a vision. It grows restless, anticipating its physical form."

The Dark Seer was certainly gifted; a true asset. "Thank you, Rand. I am looking forward to meeting such a beast."

Rand stuttered. "Are you sure, Sovereign? In the vision I saw, Marradus looked ferocious. Do you truly believe such a creature can be controlled?"

He turned to look into the Dark Seer's eyes. "You question my leadership, do you?"

Rand fidgeted with his robes. "No! May it never be, Sovereign. You were clearly chosen by Furion herself to advance the Dominion of Shadow in Agadin."

The Sovereign looked back to the skeletal beast resting before him. *Marradus will indeed serve me,* he thought.

To have such a creature leashed by his command, he would see all of Agadin in his hand. He knew his armies were scattered throughout the land, overthrowing cities; however, the dragon would be another thing entirely. There wouldn't be a kingdom he couldn't possess; not a king or queen who wouldn't bow before him. He placed his hand on the skeletal snout. He could feel Marradus' spirit in the Dominion, the spiritual land of death and decay, proving that the Dark Seer's words were true. The Sovereign's heart began quickening. He preferred to work alone; however, he didn't want to wait for hundreds of men to exit before he could advance.

Tymas leaned over to Rand. "Dark Seer, you would be wise to leave right now."

The Dark Seer lifted his bushy brows. "You mean to move forward so soon, Sovereign?"

"Oh yes," the Shan-Rafa said gently. "The demon dragon has slept for far too long."

Rand nodded, leaving the grand room as quickly as he could.

Tymas felt the hundreds of eyes upon him, waiting in expectation. The Shan-Rafa, placed both hands upon the skull. He pressed his forehead upon the chilled bone. He knew it was an intricate task to perform. Marradus was a creature of the Dominion of Shadow, therefore, he needed to call forth the spiritual land of death. However, to give life by raising the dead, he needed to also access the Kingdom of Light; the Golden Land. He hated the place. The Kingdom was the Dominion's exact counterpart. It was everything he despised. This day, however, summoning the Kingdom was crucial to ignite the spark of life he needed to summon the dead.

When he first embraced the Shadow, he feared he would no longer be able to heal; that he would be severed from his link to the Kingdom of Light. Being cut off from the endless paradise would render his gift useless. Yet, Furion taught him otherwise. The Entity enlightened him to know his gift as a Shan-Rafa was irrevocable. Those who were born as Protectors of Agadin, Divinity graced with free will to either live for the Light or not. While those who embraced the Light partook of the Kingdom freely with thankfulness, for Tymas it was rather different. When he summoned the Kingdom, he was like a thief robbing what was no longer his. He stole that which was most pure, perverting its purpose to advance the Shadow in Agadin. Furion taught him that it was the grandest gesture of mockery; like a backhanded slap to Divinity.

"Marradus..." Tymas whispered in a hiss.

The Shan-Rafa could feel the dragon's spirit turning towards him from the Dominion of Shadow.

"Marradus, it is time for you to awaken. It is time to breathe flames again. It is time to taste flesh."

He could feel Marradus' spirit pursuing its body in a radical chase, desiring to fill the void of its bones. It rushed frantically to reach its physical form. The Shan-Rafa knew he needed to have perfect timing. As soon as the spirit reached its body, Tymas needed to summon the Kingdom of Light to spark life; to create, birthing what has been dead for nearly four thousand years. To miss his timing in summoning the Kingdom could be disastrous. Years of preparation could have been for nothing; however, Tymas was no amateur in healing, nor a babe in robbing from the Kingdom.

"It is time," he whispered.

Marradus drew near. With his eyes shut, the Shan-Rafa knew his body was beginning to glow with the glimmer of eternity.

Feeling the dragon's spirit reach its body, with all his might, he reached for the Kingdom of Light. He felt the essence of eternity. Opening his eyes, the Shan-Rafa threw his head back at the shock of experiencing the otherworldly force.

Crack!

The Kingdom of Light collided into Agadin. Immediately, the workers around him began screaming in terror. They pleaded, begging for escape, yet mercy would not befall them. The cries only lasted for a quick moment, as an eerie quiet rolled into the colossal room.

The pressure of the light continuing to grow around the Sovereign, he saw every one of the hundreds of workers laying on the floor, unmoving. He assumed it would happen. To experience the Kingdom of Light was something you needed to grow into. These men didn't have the privilege of such training. Experiencing the touch of eternity with such adamant force had stopped their hearts. The light did not falter; it continued to increase. It swelled into the grand room. The fallen workers around him quickly became lost in the otherworldly glow. The walls and ceilings were hidden by divine light. All that filled his sight was the light of eternity. Beyond the room, cries ascended. The light of eternity shone so bright that he assumed everyone in Gorath would feel its touch. He wouldn't have doubted that Gorath shone like a torch on a hill, burning bright for all of Agadin to see.

With the intensity of eternal light around him, Tymas dropped to the ground panting. He could hardly fathom the sensation of the Kingdom of Light, the perfect force dancing upon his skin.

He waited. He listened, hoping he would hear the sound of a monstrous inhale.

As Tolek, Ceanne, and Anneya talked about the events of Stone Hedge, Kaldon looked out the window. Night blanketed the Mountains of D'aal. Looking at the black canvas of evening, his attention was pulled in. Beyond the mountains was a stirring. Through the dark, light began cresting upon the horizon. His eyes widened.

The light was far off, yet its brightness did not pale. He knew that whatever the light was, it was so powerful that it could likely pierce through even the Dominion itself. At the sight, he felt a familiar tingle on his skin. At its touch, he knew that he was having a glimpse of eternity from the Kingdom of Light. He had never before seen such a grand manifestation of eternity; he never knew such a thing was possible. What he didn't understand was why he felt so uneasy. His nerves quaked. His foresight blared. Something was horribly wrong.

His eyes taking in the illuminated glory of eternity, quiet words escaped from his mouth. "Great Divinity… what is happening?"

The attention of the others turned to the light that shone in the night sky. Tolek rose instinctively. Kaldon and Anneya sat still in a stunned gaze. Ceanne spilled over in tears.

The queen's voice trembled in fear. "This confirms what I saw! I knew it wasn't just my imagination."

Kaldon placed his hand on her shoulder. "What does it confirm?!"

"My dreams!" she wailed through her cries. "On my way here, I saw the death that would come upon Agadin."

He released his grip on the woman's arm, slowly sinking back into his chair. He feared to ask, yet knew he had no choice. "Ceanne, what did you see in your dreams?" he asked.

Light from the skies pouring into the Paladin's abode, she paused as she looked up to blank faces awaiting her response. She said, "In my dreams, I saw a great light shine over Agadin. It was the beginning of the horrors that would inevitably befall us. After the great light came... I saw fiery death blazing throughout the skies."

CHAPTER FIVE

SECRETS OF SEERS

K aldon's fingers bumped over the inscribed quotes chiseled into the walls throughout the Peak of Lore. Walking through the torch-lit halls with Anneya, he read the words penned by Philosophers from throughout history. Each step took him closer to his training session with Locrian. He was eager to learn about Commanding Creation.

The spitting torches decorating the ancient walls brought to mind the blazing white light that illuminated Agadin's skies. Between professors, staff, and students debates and conversations were flooding throughout the Peak of Lore. The mystery of it consumed the training facility.

Kaldon could still feel the faint tingle of the Kingdom of Light from the night prior. Concern ate away at him. He hoped there wasn't truth to Ceanne's dream.

"Kaldon, look at this," Anneya said, breaking his anxious thoughts.

She stopped in the middle of the hall. Her fingers smoothing over a quote from the famous Philosopher, Etticus Thawler. She read aloud.

"To esteem vision before individuals is a path to greatness. The disregard of the human need is a quality that a leader must possess to embrace heightened potential."

- Etticus Thawler

Before the last word even left Anneya's mouth, she laughed in annoyance. "I don't know who would believe something so ludicrous. Can you believe this?!" the Blade blurted out.

While he personally enjoyed hearing the musings of brilliant minds, he knew Anneya had a strong distaste for philosophy. However, as she read the quote, he shook his head in frustration along with her. The quote sounded to him like something Tymas Droll would teach.

"It's mindsets like this that Agadin needs to be rid of," he replied, turning towards her. "We need to convince Tolek to take this nonsense off this wall."

The Blade nodded adamantly in agreement.

The two walking down the sagely hall, taking in endless proverbs of old, his mind bounced from place to place. He thought of the great light. He thought of Ceanne Brimnas and of the group that was still missing in the Mountains of D'aal.

"What's wrong?" Anneya asked, gently placing a hand on his arm.

He realized there was strain on his face. "I'm worried for Mikiel."

She pressed her lips together in thought. "I'm sure Mikiel is fine. He had a Seer and two trained Bishops to protect him. You shouldn't be worried about him."

"How is it possible for four people to go missing with no trace at all? It doesn't make sense," he said.

Before she could respond, he continued, "Locrian knows something. He dodges my questions whenever I bring it up."

"I've noticed that too," she admitted, looking at the wooden door that was only a few steps away. "You are going to try and find out what happened from him right now, aren't you?"

He squeezed her hand. "I need to."

She nodded. "Alright, but don't intimidate the Seer too much," she teased, letting go of his hand.

He smiled at her sarcasm. He knew that him intimidating the Seer would be like a mouse intimidating a lion. Locrian was likely one of the most famous men in all of Agadin. He wielded unfathomable ability; however, famous of not, Kaldon needed answers.

As he reached out to open the door, Anneya snatched his wrist. "Kaldon, you haven't forgotten about later, right?"

He looked over, seeing her sheepish look; an uncommon expression for a Blade to wear. He knew exactly what she was referring to. Shortly after his session with Locrian, a ball was being held. It was customary, considering a queen was visiting the Peak of Lore.

He smiled. "Don't worry. I haven't forgotten about our first dance."

"I'm a lucky woman. I get to show off my date tonight; the famous *Kaldon Thain*," she said in a laugh turning down the hall. "Enjoy your lesson."

Kaldon laughed under his breath, shaking his head as he watched her walk away. As excited as he was for his dance with her, the door before him pulled him into the seriousness of the moment.

Turning the handle, it resounded in a squeak. Looking into the empty room, he saw it was similar to the one he and Brenton sparred in regularly. The white rooms were scattered throughout the training facility for the purpose of tutoring warriors for battle. Locrian figured it was as suitable as any to train someone to Command Creation. In the centre of the room upon the floor, sat the renowned Seer, awaiting his pupil.

They shared a silent stare. Before the Seer could greet his student, Kaldon spoke up. "Locrian, I need to know what happened to Mikiel, Adlen, Troy, and Bernice."

The Seer looked upon the resolute young man. "So much for small talk…" he muttered in a sigh, trying to make light of Kaldon's direct approach for answers.

Kaldon could feel determination rising within him. "I deserve to know," he said.

"You are right, Kaldon," the Seer said in a gentle tone. "I shouldn't keep such things from you. Come in and shut the door."

Gripping the handle, as soon as he felt the door click shut, the Seer spoke. "Alden is dead," Locrian said plainly, not coating his words.

Kaldon's eyes widened. "Dead?! Are you certain?"

"He was killed," Locrian said, speaking into the empty room. "I saw his death in a vision; although the one who took his life is veiled from me."

Kaldon looked away. "Locrian, I'm sorry," he said knowing the Seer's relationship was strained with his former mentor. "Are the others alive?" he asked.

"The *River of Time* hasn't revealed that to me. It's possible that they still live; however, it's equally possible that they were killed with Alden," he said with reserve.

Kaldon ran his hand through his hair, not knowing how to respond.

"Come, sit," the Seer said, pulling his attention back. "There is nothing we can do about it right now. Tolek still has scouts out looking for the remaining three."

"But, what about Mikiel?" he asked.

An instructive expression spawned over the Seer's face. "Kaldon, you can only help others to the extent that you help yourself. You need to learn about your abilities if you want to help those like Mikiel. Your training to learn about you Commanding Creation is essential. Now, sit down."

He reluctantly sat on the wooden floor. All that was between them was a still glass of water. He pushed his thoughts of the three away from his mind. The Seer was right.

"Before we begin, I have one final question," he said, his eyes resting upon the teacher-like Seer.

Locrian lifted his eyes. "Let me guess, you want to know what I think about the light that shone through Agadin last night? I can honestly say, I have no solid theories yet."

He could tell by the Seer's response that he had likely been hounded mercilessly by those wanting to hear his thoughts about the strange phenomenon.

"Could it be a sign that Marradus is alive?" Kaldon asked.

Looking at him through squinted eyes, Locrian spoke quietly. "It's possible. Tolek told me about the queen's dream."

He nodded his head in agreement, looking up to the Seer again. "I was actually wanting to ask you about something else."

"Oh?" Locrian cocked an eyebrow.

Kaldon shifted upon the hard floor. He said, "Other than the light that shone through Agadin last night, the skies have been changing; becoming darker. Gloomy. I think it has to do with what's going on in Agadin. I believe it has to do with the Great War. I mentioned it to Tolek and Anneya; but they looked at me like I was crazy."

A smile spread over Locrian's smooth face. "Well, aren't you perceptive. I assure you; you aren't crazy. You are beginning to think like a Philosopher, looking at things from angles that others don't even think to look. You are more like your father than you think."

Kaldon shifted uncomfortably at the comparison.

"Then is there something wrong with the skies?" he asked, pulling the conversation back on track.

Locrian nodded. "There is. They have been defiled. Do you remember the message Alden gave when he first came to the Peak of Lore?"

He thought back to the chilling moment. He remembered sitting in the Peak of Lore's entrance when the old Seer stormed into the training facility, speaking about a vision he had. In the vision, he saw the *Door of the Dominion* opening.

His eyes widened in realization. "No… the dimming skies is because the Door of the Dominion has been opened?"

The Seer wore a sad smile. "Unfortunately, it is. The darkness in the skies isn't mist or fog. The Door of the Dominion has been opened for quite some time now. It has become a gateway for the Dominion of Shadow to come to Agadin. The darkness in the sky is the essence of the Dominion. It is eating away at the skies, corrupting it with death."

Kaldon shivered at the thought. "What will happen if it isn't stopped?"

The Seer shrugged. "I haven't the slightest clue. Not only do I not know what could happen from it, I have no idea how to prevent it from spreading."

Kaldon felt sick to his stomach. Here he was, sitting before the smartest man alive, yet even *he* was baffled on how to save Agadin. The Door of the Dominion was open, stealing the skies from them. The meaning of the mysterious light from the night prior was left unexplained. One after another, impossible circumstances piled before them.

"Locrian, what can we do to stop all of this?" he said, the words falling from his mouth.

With nothing but the still glass of water between them, the Seer said, "We can start by raising you up to be who you are destined to be."

He slid the glass closer to Kaldon. "To begin, we are going to see how you do with commanding this water to obey you."

Chapter Six
Commanding Creation

The indigo water was still in the cup before him.

"Tell me again what you did when you first Commanded Creation," Locrian said, his hands poised upon the robe stretching over his knees.

Kaldon knew that Locrian had a mind that was unmatched in all of Agadin. With his smooth head and charcoal robes, the man looked wise and sagely. The only thing that wasn't fitting was his age. An individual wasn't typically advanced enough in training to carry the title of a Seer until they were much further advanced in years.

"I saw strands of steam rising from a stone," he said. "I spoke to the steam in my mind, commanding it to become fire. When that didn't work, I spoke the command aloud. Then the steam evolved into flames."

"Fascinating," the Seer said, shaking his head. He leaned in closer. "I don't think you understand the significance of what you did."

Kaldon sat back, waiting for him to elaborate.

The Seer instructively lifted a finger into the air. "To simply command fire is admirable; but to *create* it like you did is extraordinary."

"What do you mean? I didn't create fire," Kaldon remarked.

"You don't understand," Locrian said, shaking his head again. "Let me put it this way: if you were sitting by a campfire and commanded the fire to sway from side to side, that would be Commanding Creation. You did much more than that. Essentially, you took the heat rising from a stone and made it transform into flames. In doing so, you did more than command the fire to obey you; you *created* an element. Quite impressive, indeed. That would have even made a Roek proud."

"I never thought of it that way before." He leaned back placing his hands upon the cold stone floor. He looked at the glass of water sitting between them. "So Commanding Creation would be making this water rise into the air; whereas, creating an element would be causing it to overflow with more water."

"Exactly!" the Seer said, snapping his finger. "You are doing more than manipulating an element. You are birthing it, giving it life."

Kaldon appreciated the man's passion for knowledge. He seemed thrilled to be teaching someone about the lost ability. "So, how did I manage to create an element?" he asked.

Locrian laughed holding his hands up. "I haven't a clue."

He frowned, wishing the Seer could offer more insight. "Could Roeks of old create elements?"

"Oh, yes," the Seer replied. "They were masters of the elements."

Locrian pushed the glass of water closer to Kaldon. "Now, show me how you do with trying to command this water to obey you."

"I thought it was only possible to command one element?" Kaldon asked, watching the glass of water.

Locrain pressed his lips together. "Oh no, a Roek could likely command every element: fire, water, wind, or earth. They would, however, master only one of the four, knowing every detail about it."

He continued, "You may be entirely different, Kaldon. You are not a Roek. You are a Paragon; likely the only who has ever lived since Dawntan Forlorn was alive. I can assure you; I'm determined to understand how a Paragon Commands Creation."

He felt uncomfortable having the title *Paragon* placed on him. It was a title of great weight; shrouded in mystery.

"Focus on the water," Locrian stated in an instructive tone. "Remember, Divinity has created all of Agadin and mankind was given authority to reign over it. You *can* control this water."

Kaldon focused on the water in the glass.

Locrian continued, "Remember, you need to use authority to Command Creation. Authority comes from not doubting: *Don't* doubt. Believe in your reign-ship over creation."

Kaldon allowed all thoughts to leave his mind. All that existed to him was the glass of water before him.

Water, rise, he thought.

The water was steady; unmoving.

Water rise, he thought again more adamantly.

The water was still without sway or ripple.

Locrian interjected. "Speak. Step into authority. Don't try to convince the water to move, *command* it to move."

"Water rise!" he said, with force in his tone.

The two watched as the water remained steady in the cup. "I can't do it, Locrian," he said, running a hand through his hair in frustration.

"Keep trying," the Seer said in encouragement. "It will take time to learn this ability. Roeks of old took a lifetime to perfect the craft."

Obliging, Kaldon focused. He spoke to the water in thought and in word. He tried speaking with force, as well as in a whisper. Over-and-over again he tried to summon the water, yet the liquid rested. He would have thought that Locrian would come and go as he practiced; however, the Seer simply sat before him. Every so often, he would give a recommendation, but the Seer mostly sat observing.

Kaldon sighed in frustration. His body was beginning to stiffen from sitting for so long. For hours, he laboured, trying to move the water; yet, it continuously slept, unchanging.

"Alright, let's give it a break," the Seer finally voiced. "I know the water didn't move at all, but did you feel any breakthrough?"

Kaldon stretched out, testing the tenseness in his muscles. Wiping his hand over his face, he saw the shimmer of sweat on his hand. "My belief in my link to creation ebbed and flowed. There were times I could feel the link, while other times I felt nothing at all."

"It will take time, Kaldon," Locrian said, affirming him. "Tell me, how is it that you summon your foresight?"

Kaldon turned his head in thought. "I look within myself. I find a steady peace. Once I've found it, it feels like everything becomes slow."

Locrian smiled, giving him a knowing look. "Perhaps this is what you need to do in order to learn to Command Creation."

"Perhaps," he said.

He didn't understand how he could create fire from nothing in one moment; yet the next, he couldn't even make a subtle ripple in a cup of water. He hadn't even seen a hint of the ability since the incident with the fire.

Looking up, he saw the Seer watching him. A question rose within him.

"Is that what you do to see visions as a Seer — look within yourself?" he asked.

"In a sense, yes," the Seer said. "However, visions that a Seer experiences are much more intense. Foresight is subtle, like a quiet spark. Visions that Seers have are like a storming river crashing through your mind."

He stared blankly. "That sounds terrible. How often do you have these visions?"

Locrian laughed. "I think a more accurate question is, 'how often do I *not* have them?' I've trained myself to continuously see into the River of Time. I have also been trained to withstand the intensity of visions. I hardly notice the pain inflicted by them anymore."

"The pain?" Kaldon asked, never imagining that visions would come at such a cost. "I can't believe you stay sane."

Locrian's eyes turned sad. "Unfortunately, some don't keep their sanity. Many slip into what is called *the fall of a Seer.*"

Kaldon could hear the empathy in his tone. Considering the Seer's immediate change in countenance, he hesitated to ask, yet decided to anyways. "What is the 'fall of a Seer?'"

"That is when a Seer descends into madness," Locrian stated with strain on his face. "Seers have a weakness. Their weakness is isolation from those who don't share the gift of visions."

Kaldon looked down instinctively, feeling uncomfortable at the mention of Seers going mad. "That seems like an odd weakness for a Seer."

"That's because it is," Locrian said. "Seers are gifted and trained to continuously see the River of Time. They are consumed by past, present, and future simultaneously, seeing from an eternal perspective. Someone who isn't a Seer sees through a temporal lens. They remember the past and anticipate the future; however, they live only in the present. That is why Seers need to be around those who don't carry the gift. Community keeps a Seer grounded so they don't become lost in the River of Time."

Kaldon sat silent, not knowing how to respond.

Locrian continued, "Alden once told me that in the past, this is how Seers were tortured. They were locked in a room, isolated for months at a time. Slowly, the River of Time would take them, pulling them into insanity."

Kaldon closed his mouth, realizing it was agape. Silence lingered between the two as he watched the Seer. "Has a Seer ever escaped the River of Time after falling into insanity?" he asked.

Locrian looked up at him with unease in his eyes. "Never. They are forever lost in madness."

After a brief silence, the Seer spoke up. "Shall we try the water again?"

Kaldon could tell that he was trying to change the subject, clearly growing uncomfortable. Although hungry to learn, he didn't know if he could still his thoughts enough to make the water obey him — he wondered if he would ever be able to. He didn't have a lifetime to learn; he needed to be ready immediately.

"How do you know I can learn this ability, Locrian?" he finally asked, revealing his doubt in himself. "Me summoning the fire could very well have been a one-time occurrence. Roeks are long past; it makes sense that the ability to Command Creation may be as well."

"That is exactly what Alden used to say," the Seer said, looking away. "I always told him that those who could Command Creation would walk Agadin again to command the elements. Mark my words: Roeks will rise once again. Alden always called me a fool, but I know their time will come."

"You truly believe that?" he asked.

Locrian nodded his head. "I do."

"How do you know?" he voiced.

Locrian looked up to Kaldon with conviction in his eyes. "I know the Roeks will rise again, because I know of one who lives."

Kaldon's eyes went wide. "How... Where...?" he asked, fumbling over his words

"Far from here. His name is Orin," Locrian replied. "He is the first Roek born in thousands of years."

"How did you meet him?" he asked in shock.

"I stumbled upon him in my travels," the Seer said with the flick of a hand. "He is by no means a flashy man — older, liking to keep to himself. I doubt any know of his ability other than myself and his wife. That said, it is hard to keep hidden from a Seer."

Lost in the thought of an actual Roek roaming Agadin, the Seer spoke up again. "Orin's existence is how I know you can learn to Command Creation."

Kaldon fixed his eyes on the still glass of water. After hours of attempts, the liquid was still disobedient to his commands.

The Seer looked at him with serious eyes. "I have a sense that Agadin has need of your ability," he said.

He breathed heavily, trying to force his discouragement to cease. He watched the liquid blue, knowing he couldn't give up. Stirring his confidence, words fell from his mouth.

"Water rise."

CHAPTER SEVEN

DESIRE FOR AUTHORITY

———◆◆◆◆———

"Sovereign, several factions of the army have already left Gorath," Rand said, walking at a steady gait upon the grassy ground.

Walking throughout the courtyard, Tymas slowed himself to a stop. Looking at a section of flowers adorning the boisterous garden, he replied, "I am looking forward to expanding my reach of influence. I need more children to guide to truth. It shouldn't be long until they reach the cities Aramil, Baindin, and Tainsman. Overtaking them will be an easy feat for us," he said in a smooth tone. Reaching for a rose, he stroked its silky peddles.

"It will be especially simple with Marradus," the old Seer said in agreement, watching the Sovereign, who appeared lost in thought.

A smile curled onto the Sovereign's face. "Yes, Rand — especially with Marradus. I used to send in the Kreel first; however, something as terrifying as Marradus will be much more effective. The demon dragon will cause kings and queens bow before me."

Tymas continued walking, brushing past flower beds scattered throughout the courtyard. He looked up to his ebony-coloured tower that loomed over Gorath. The tower was menacing, designed to intimidate with its cryptic designs. The grand piece of architecture stretched high into the sky, ending in a distinct point that looked as though it pierced the heavens. He knew whoever looked upon it cringed from fear. He knew that from here on forth, it would be no longer only Gorath who would kneel before him; all of Agadin would.

Tymas and Rand neared their destination. It had been several days since he resurrected the dragon. The Sovereign hadn't yet visited the creature, giving it time to readjust to its material form. The building dawning closer, they could hear Marradus' heavy breaths through the cement wall.

At the sound, Rand stopped.

"Rand? Aren't you coming?" the Sovereign asked, turning to the old Seer.

Rand gazed upon the arched doorway, leading to the dragon's place of rest. "Um, Sovereign, if you don't mind, I would prefer to not look that creature in the eyes."

Tymas knew exactly what the old Seer was referring to. Seers had the innate ability to read the scroll over individuals. Rand's complexion continuing to pale, he understood that the man would prefer to not read the thoughts of a creature from the Dominion of Shadow.

"Fine, stay behind," the Sovereign said, moving towards the entrance door.

Rand's hand came forward, snatching his arm. "Sovereign, are you sure you should go in there? I know you are a Shan-Rafa; however, I doubt anyone could be safe from such a beast."

The Sovereign's face twisted in annoyance. He knew what the dragon was capable of. He also didn't doubt that he could tame the dragon. He didn't have the luxury of fearing the creature; Marradus would serve him — he had great plans for the beast. All he needed to do was prove his dominance over it.

He ripped his arm out of the Seer's grip. "Touch me again and you will no longer have a hand to grab with," he hissed.

The old Seer backed away timidly. "I apologize, Sovereign. Your courage is truly admirable."

Tymas grimaced at the attempt of flattery. "Go and prepare the remaining armies, Rand. Don't disappoint me again."

Rand nodded in adamant devotion, immediately obeying.

Tymas looked into the entrance maw that held the horrid beast. Ducking under the sturdy archway, he left the cowardly Seer behind. At the end of the hallway, he could only see a small portion of the creature. With each step he took, more of the dragon came into the full scope of sight.

He finally stepped into the large expanse of space crafted specifically for one purpose: housing a creature of unimaginable stature. The looming dragon peered at him with reptilian eyes, full of life. Even though the room they were in was extraordinarily large, it felt cramped and void of space due to the creature's size. The grand room had no ceiling so the dragon could come and go as it pleased. He wanted to make sure such a beast was comfortable under his rule.

Tymas gazed over the onyx scales that encased Marradus, like thousands of shields assembled to protect the ancient dragon. Its teeth hung like stalagmites protruding from inside a cave. From its head came two horns as mighty as mountain peaks. Its eyes were a pale yellow, with a black streak down their middle — as dark as the Dominion of Shadow itself. The dragon's expression was ravenous.

Marradus' head hanging low, the Sovereign placed a hand on the dragon's snout. As it breathed outward, he could feel its scathingly heated breath on his hand.

The Sovereign retracted his hand quickly at its sting. He held his hand before him to quickly heal the burn. The pain numbed immediately.

"Marradus," Tymas stated. "It is an honour to have you in my service."

The Sovereign flinched as Marradus unexpectedly stomped one of its colossal claws to the ground like the descent of lightning. He felt a rumbling beneath him at the mighty blow. Cracks spiderwebbed up the walls encasing them.

"Such power..." he whispered.

He looked at the menacing dragon, surprised at how quickly it grew agitated. Marradus' tail swung, lashing the air in jagged strokes. The dragon curled its elongated neck, stretching its gaze to the open skies that hovered above it. It then corkscrewed its long face back downward, its reptilian eyes resting upon Tymas Droll.

Peering at the creature, he felt echoes beginning to swell throughout the confines of his mind. He took a step back in confusion at the unexpected sensation that was erupting through him. Voices awoke, singing throughout his thoughts. Some voices were as loud as an avalanche; others were as faint as the rustling of leaves. At their sound, he could feel vibrations coursing throughout his conscience. He didn't know what Marradus was doing; however, there was no doubt the dragon was causing the internal chaos in his mind. The voices slowly quieting, a primary voice began to ascend above all others.

"Tell me, why would I serve a man such as you?"

The smooth voice cooed throughout Tymas' mind like silk caressing his thoughts. Even though the dragon's mouth was still, the voice raged in the Sovereign's inner core. He never would have imagined such a creature would have the ability to communicate in such a way. As inviting as Marradus' internal voice was, Tymas could feel his face beginning to flush in fury. He hated when his authority was questioned.

He looked at the beast unflinchingly, refusing to be intimidated. Hands poised behind his back and his chin held high, the Sovereign spoke. "You will serve me because I am the one who created you. I am your *father*. I am the Sovereign of Shadow, chosen by Furion herself to bridge the Dominion of Shadow to Agadin."

Marradus pulled its scaled lips back, revealing its monstrous teeth. Tymas was convinced it was the creature's attempt at a smile of mockery. Amidst the dragon's morbid grin, its echoing voice shook the Sovereign's core.

"Furion told me no such thing. She knows I am my own authority. Even Furion's demands, I perceive as mere requests."

Barring its teeth again, echoes screamed throughout Tymas' mind, this time with more heated aggression.

"The only request Furion made for me in coming to Agadin was to spare your life. That is a request I haven't decided whether I will fulfill or not."'

Tymas screwed his face in disgust. "You will serve me, you vile reptile! I worked for years to bring you here!" the Sovereign shouted.

Marradus stretched its mighty wings in rebellion; the first time it had done so in thousands of years. The girth of them brushed against both walls on each side of the sizeable room. Pulling its neck back, the dragon's head arched to the skies above it, letting out a soulless roar.

Tymas took a step back as the creature betrayed its full size. Hot wind coursed around the Sovereign, the violent breath from the dragon's roar. Marradus' words pounded throughout the Sovereign of Shadow's mind.

"You are not my master. You are no leader, only a puppet. A puppet who will watch as all of Agadin bows before me. I will reign from my throne in the skies of Agadin."

With a jolt, the demon dragon waved its jagged wings, thrusting itself into the open expanse of sky above it. The Sovereign looked up at the beast as it jerked throughout the fading blue canvas. There was nothing graceful about the demon dragon as it flew. It thrashed about like a nightmare in the flesh.

As the dragon ascended to impossible heights, Tymas felt the creature's whisper rip through his mind. He closed his eyes as Marradus' declaration rung throughout his being.

"I am chaos."

CHAPTER EIGHT

COMING REVELATION

K aldon brushed his hand over his pale blue jacket, missing his forest-green cloak. He knew he would be stuck spending his evening feeling uncomfortable, clothed in what others deemed fashionable. He hated such clothes, preferring what was comfortable and functional; however, he also knew that dressing up was a small price to pay. After all, attending a ball meant he and Anneya would finally have their dance.

At the front of the ballroom, to the side of the grand stage, were several instrumentalists ready to perform. String players lined themselves up in an orderly fashion, awaiting instruction to lead those at the ball in song and dance. Tolek sat on the other side of the grand stage with his advisors. He was wearing his maroon jacket and white cape that traced down his back. No one would dare approach the Paladin.

Kaldon watched Ceanne mosey through the crowd in a scarlet gown very much befitting her title. The dress was no doubt tailored specifically for the queen by the staff of the Peak of Lore. He noticed she wore thick paint on her face, amplifying her features. The queen laughed in conversation with several of the guests. He was surprised at how quickly she involved herself with those at the facility. He heard rumours that she was befriending many of the staff and warriors throughout the castle.

Even though the dance was about to begin, he found himself distracted feeling an itch in his mind again. He crunched his face, trying to ignore it. He was never one for headaches; but he'd felt the itch on and off since finishing his session with Locrian. He wondered if it was due to trying to Command Creation but couldn't be certain. He spent hours with the Seer trying to move the water, but to no avail. The discovery of a living Roek still ran through his thoughts.

He felt a tap on his shoulder. Turning around, he saw Anneya.

Looking at her, he almost forgot about his headache. She wore an elegant blue dress, matching his assemble. Before he could say anything, she leaned in, pressing her lips against his. As she pulled back, his eyes were wide.

"Anneya…" Kaldon said, his face flushing red.

She threw her head back in a laugh. "What did you expect? Tonight, is the night we are finally having our first dance, isn't it?"

"Absolutely, it is," he said in a stammer, still caught off guard from how forward she was. Something about Anneya was beginning to feel like home to him; safe even. The sight of her still made him both nervous and excited at the same time. He grabbed her hand, holding it in his own.

From the grand stage, a woman's voice arose. Looking over, he saw Ceanne Brimnas standing on the marble platform, her hands held before her.

"Thank you for welcoming me into this great facility," the queen said, drawing the eyes of every guest as she waved her hand to the pristine room surrounding them. "As many of you have likely heard, my kingdom, Stone Hedge, has been overrun by those who have embraced the Shadow."

"I inherited my throne as a young girl after my father's death." Ceanne's voice began trembling in emotion. "He was a great king, a noble king. His life was taken by poisoning. Nearly all of you would have heard of his fall. It is a prominent part of Agadin's recent history. My father's death sparked war. After discovering the assassins who took his life were from neighbouring cities, Stone Hedge attacked."

Kaldon watched guests nodding in sympathy as they listened. Several shed tears. The king's death was clearly common knowledge to those at the Peak of Lore. Being from Rundle, he hadn't heard of such events.

Wiping away tears, the queen hid her mourning with a smile. "Everything that was handed to me has now been taken away. Everything I have built was torn down. This is why I want to give you my sincerest gratitude. Thank you for helping me and for honouring me with this wonderful ball."

Cheers erupted for the queen and her strength to give a speech when she was clearly in distress. She bowed in gratitude, then backed away from the attention of the crowd. Replacing her, a sound suddenly ascended from the stage. Strings began singing, rising to engulf the room in song. Kaldon looked over, seeing musicians wielding their instruments in perfect pitch. Around him, he watched the slow melody pull men and women together to dance. He noticed that Tolek stayed seated. He couldn't imagine such a man dancing.

He looked over to Anneya, who watched him with expectation. As people swayed around them, he reached out his hand inviting her to dance. Accepting his invitation, she came in close to him. His hands rested on the hollow of her back, her arms wrapped around his neck, her head upon his chest. Swaying to the rhythm of the music, they took in the long-awaited moment together.

"I can't believe we had to defeat an army and kill a Dark Paladin for this dance," Anneya said to him.

He laughed lightly. "It was worth the wait."

He could feel her face stretch into a smile as it pressed against his chest.

"Excuse me," a voice said, rising above the sound of instruments.

Kaldon and Anneya eased their hold on one another, looking towards the source of the voice. Standing before them was Ceanne Brimnas. "I hope you don't mind, Anneya. May I cut in?" the queen asked politely.

Anneya's brow furrowed. Kaldon knew she wanted to object; after all, so did he. However, they both knew there would be dire consequences to reject a queen's proposal to dance.

Anneya let go of his hands in frustration. He could feel her angst. He sighed quietly, trying to hide his disappointment. He knew this was likely Ceanne's way of trying to thank him for saving her life. To dance with a queen was quite the honour, although her timing was tremendously inconvenient.

"Of course," he said, holding out his hand.

"I am greatly honoured you would accept my request," the queen said, taking his hand.

She moved in closer to Kaldon. He felt uncomfortable sharing a moment so intimate with anyone other than Anneya. As he and the queen slowly spun to the rhythm of the stringed instruments, he watched Anneya pass through the crowd on the dance floor and move towards the set of stairs. The Blade climbed to the second floor of the ballroom without turning back to look at him and the queen.

"Kaldon, I want to thank you for finding me," the queen said, pulling his attention back to her. "Since my kingdom has been taken from me, I don't have anything to offer you but my sincerest gratitude."

"It was my privilege to help you," he responded kindly, secretly anticipating the dance's end.

The queen looked him in the eyes. "I need to know — what were you doing out in the mountains on your own? It is terribly dangerous out there. There are Kreel nearly everywhere."

Holding her, he could feel something pressing against his stomach. The sharp and stern feel contrasted Ceanne's form. Looking down, he could see a squared imprint in the pocket of her gown. Seeing the shape, he knew it was the book she had with her when he found her throughout the Mountains of D'aal, *The Lion's Roar; The Raven's Call.* He watched the book, wondering why she kept it so close to her. It seemed to never leave her side.

"I go to the mountains to think and to be on my own," he said in distant thought. The itch in his mind began stirring again. At first, he wondered if it were his foresight; however, quickly decided otherwise. His foresight differed, feeling like an alarm churning through him. The itching pressure was different.

Ceanne looked up at him. "You have a tendency to think in dangerous places, Kaldon Thain."

Kaldon stayed quiet. The music finally quieted, which permitted the dance to come to its end. He knew she would want to chat, but he had a more important task at hand. He needed to make sure Anneya was alright.

Turning to leave, Ceanne placed a hand on his shoulder. "Thank you for the dance, Kaldon," she said with a smile.

"The honour was mine," he replied, thankful to be ending the interaction.

With Ceanne walking away, he slipped through the crowd to the stairwell to find the Blade. He climbed the stairs to the second floor of the ballroom. The higher he climbed, the more the music faded, becoming distant and lost from his ears. On the second floor, no torches or candles lit the room. The only light that shone was from the radiance of the moon peeking through a window hollowed-out from the stone wall. No one occupied the room other than the Blade looking out the window into darkened skies.

"I'm sorry," he said, approaching the Blade.

Standing beside her, she didn't turn to him as she spoke. "I'm not upset with you, Kaldon. I know you had to dance with her. She's a queen. It would have been incredibly insulting to deny her; punishable, even."

"What's bothering you then?" he asked, placing a hand on her back.

She sighed. "Don't you ever get tired? We just stopped an army. We killed a Dark Paladin; something that is no small feat. Yet, it doesn't seem like we are any closer to stopping the Dominion of Shadow from invading Agadin. Geran may be dead, but now we are awaiting a demon dragon to rule the skies. I mean, we can't even enjoy a simple dance with one another."

"I know," he sighed. "I wish there were no wars taking place, no Sovereign of Shadow. I wish there was no Great War."

"I wish there was no Ceanne Brimnas," Anneya said turning to him with her eyebrows raised. "I don't trust the woman."

Kaldon smirked, not knowing if Anneya was jealous or if her concern was valid. Looking out the window, he noticed the Mountains of D'aal looked darker than usual.

Without shifting his eyes from the grim skies, he said, "Do you remember when I asked you and Tolek if the darkness in the skies could have something to do with the Great War?"

She looked distantly in thought. "Of course. I'm going to be honest, at first, I thought your theory was ridiculous. But even now, they look gloomier than before. Even the stars look a bit dimmer."

Kaldon nodded. "Locrian told me it's because the Door of the Dominion is open. He said that the darkness in the skies isn't fog or cloud; it is the Dominion of Shadow coming to Agadin."

Anneya's face began to pale. "Is he sure?"

He looked over to her. "I can't help but think that the times we are in are far more dire than we think. Agadin is in great danger. What's worse, is that none of us know what to do about it."

Her response to the hopeless news was silence as she reached out grabbing his firm hand. At the feel of her silky touch, he rolled his thumb gently over her knuckles. Before he could speak words of comfort, he crunched his face as the itch in his mind began increasing. What was once subtle, was beginning to feel more like a claw scraping against his skull.

"Why are you making that face?" Anneya asked, her grip loosening from his hand.

He didn't respond as the feeling amplified. The scrape was like a stab of pain piercing through his mind. Staggering back, he brought his hand to his head in a moan.

She placed a hand on his shoulder. "Kaldon, what's wrong?"

He let out a shout as his mind began flooding with images. When he saw images in his mind with his foresight, they were often so discreet that he might miss them if he didn't pay close attention. The images now rushing through his thoughts were like an ocean crashing against the screen of his mind.

He no longer saw the walls of the Peak of Lore around him. He didn't see the second floor of the ballroom. Even though he couldn't see Anneya, he could hear her muffled screams in the distance. He couldn't help but avoid her pleas, watching a vision in his mind unfold.

Kaldon saw himself leaving the Peak of Lore. He saw himself journeying great distances alone, far past the Mountains of D'aal. He saw the end of land where the ocean roared and crashed before him. He had never seen the ocean before that moment — the blue azure tumbling in waves. In front of the ocean, he saw a great city; mighty in size, surrounded by at black wall. Ascending from the city was a dark and jagged tower that stretched high into the skies. There was no doubt in his heart as to what city he gazed upon. As his sight remained on the menacing tower, words shot through his mind like an arrow piercing through his thoughts:

"The Roek must rise. The Seer will fall. The Paladin needs to obtain the impenetrable shield. The Paragon must soar."

Kaldon gasped in air, panting.

He was on his hands and knees upon the stone floor. Running his hand over the calloused stone, he was thankful to be awoken from the vision. The pain he endured at seeing such an oracle was excruciating. The mysterious words quaked through him.

"Kaldon, are you okay? What is happening?" Anneya said, leaning over him in a panic.

The ominous tower still loomed in his mind. The image wouldn't leave him. It was as though he were marked by it. Once he was able to still his breaths, his words came like a hammer, shattering his and Anneya's hopes for peace or comfort.

"I had a vision," he said through staggered breaths.

"A vision? Are you sure?" the Blade asked, taking a step back.

He nodded his head adamantly.

"What did you see?" she asked.

Kaldon looked up to her. "I saw that I need to leave the Peak of Lore. I saw the ocean… I saw a mighty tower…"

"A tower?" Anneya asked. "Do you know where this tower was?"

"Yes." Tears wet Kaldon's face. What he saw was unmistakable. He said, "I need to journey to Gorath."

CHAPTER NINE

SEPERATE ROADS

The demon dragon soared through the skies above the city of Edmont. Arrows soared, ricocheting off its mighty scales. Swords, axes, and spears were rendered useless. The army of men had no chance against the beast. Marradus opened its mighty jaws, a spark of flames igniting. Through the dimmed skies, fire reigned with wrath. Buildings were torched; homes reduced to ash. A city once filled with laughter was draped in sorrow and screams. As the city was devoured, Marradus lifted its head to the skies, releasing a raging roar.

Locrian flinched as the dragon's roar echoed throughout the vision in his mind.

"What do you see?" Tolek asked, leaning in.

The Seer's eyes snapped open as he panted in shallow breaths. In the Paladin's abode, the fireplace crackled before them. Among the collection of books and weapons, the Seer sat as visions passed through his mind. For hours on end, he had been in search of anything that may help them.

"It is as we feared," the Seer said, his face covered in sweat. "Marradus has awoken. The Kingdom of Light that shone throughout the skies must have been summoned by Tymas Droll. The creature looks more menacing than I ever would have imagined."

Tolek took in the information, showing no emotion. "Is it as large as Dawntan Forlorn described in his writing?"

The Seer hung his head, still recovering from the terror of what he saw. "Its size is like no creature I have ever seen. Edmont has been destroyed; Marradus has torn apart the entire city. I can't imagine how many lives have been lost."

"Great Divinity…" the Paladin whispered.

"It is worse than we thought," Locrian said, running a hand over his bald head. "Edmont wouldn't have been on the Sovereign's mind just yet to conquer. He is more calculated than this. I didn't see any of the Sovereign's warriors in the vision. Marradus was devouring the city on its own."

Tolek squinted his eyes in thought. "What are you saying?"

Locrian held out his hands. "What is worse than having a demon leashed?"

Tolek paused, then said, "One without restraints?"

The Seer nodded. "I don't believe the dragon is obeying the Sovereign of Shadow. It is moving by its own will."

"That should help us then," the Paladin replied, sitting up straight. "The Dominion of Shadow will be divided."

The Seer shook his head. "No, you don't understand. While Tymas is precise and strategic in his planning, Marradus will be the exact opposite. It will be like terror itself coursing through Agadin. The dragon will be unpredictable."

Tolek looked away. "We need to act now, Loc. We don't have time to wait around any longer."

The Seer sighed. "I am leaving, Tolek."

"What do you mean you're leaving?" the Paladin asked. "We stand a better chance sticking together."

"I know my place," the Seer responded. "My strength is not in my brawn. I need to fight a creature like Marradus with my mind. I need to seek information."

"Where would you find information to defeat a demon dragon?" the Paladin asked.

Locrian ran his hands down his charcoal robes. "I will go to *Noriden*."

"Noriden," the Paladin repeated, leaning back. "The house of Philosophers. Do you think there will be information there?"

"I can't be certain, but I must try," the Seer replied. "If there is a place that holds information that could aid us, Noriden would be it."

Sitting in thoughtful silence, Locrian fidgeted with his robe. "Tolek, please tell me you have a plan."

Before he could respond, the door suddenly opened.

Anneya walked in, exuding agitation in her stride; Kaldon walked in behind her. Both Tolek and Locrian rose from their chairs. The four looked at one another, each feeling the unspoken words communicating that something was terribly wrong.

Growing more impatient than she already was, Anneya stepped forward. "It's alive, isn't it?"

Un-swayed by her abruptness, Tolek spoke. "Marradus has been risen from the dead. It has already begun devouring cities."

Before either could respond, the Paladin looked to them with a stern gaze. "The three of us need to leave, immediately."

At the mention of them leaving, Kaldon began shifting uncomfortably. Anneya crossed her arms, looking over to him. "Well, should you tell them, or shall I?"

Kaldon wished she were more supportive of his decision. However, as he felt the weight of *Integrity* strapped to his back, he was reminded that he was an appointed Protector of Agadin. That meant he needed to do what he felt was best for Agadin. He needed to trust what he saw in his vision.

Tolek crossed his arms as well. "Tell us what?"

"If you are passing north through the Mountains of D'aal, I can travel with you for a time. But I will eventually need to branch off on my own. I need to travel to Gorath," Kaldon explained.

At the mention of such dark lands, Locrian brought his hands up to clench his hairless head. "Gorath! What do you mean you are leaving for Gorath?!" the Seer said in alarm.

Tolek stood still, looking at the young man with strain on his face. "You can't be serious... You can't expect to take on an entire kingdom on your own. You will be killed."

"I had a vision," Kaldon said, standing strong under the scrutinizing gazes.

"A vision?" Locrian stopped pacing. "No... it can't be. What happened?"

He eyed the Seer who seemed to be on the brink of panic. "I experienced what felt like a dull headache for several hours. I didn't think anything of it; but then the vision stole my sight. I saw that I needed to travel to Gorath."

The Paladin looked over to Locrian. The Seer held a contemplative look upon his face. "It started as a headache, you say?"

He nodded. "At first the vision began like an itch in my mind, then it evolved. It felt like rushing waters pressing against my skull; like a mountain trying to squeeze itself into my head."

Locrian rubbed his chin in thought. "That's a vision alright. What did you see? Tell me everything."

Rubbing his hands together, he tried to recall the entire vision. "The vision was quite scattered, coming in different waves. First, I saw myself travelling on my own past the Mountains of D'aal. I saw the ocean. I have never seen anything like it."

Locrian prompted, impatiently. "Then what?"

He continued, "I saw Gorath. I saw the Sovereign of Shadow's black tower looming over the land. Then, I heard words being impressed into my mind."

The Seer crunched his face in thought. "Words? What words?"

Kaldon quoted the prophetic message from his vision: *"The Roek must rise. The Seer will fall. The Paladin needs to obtain the impenetrable shield. The Paragon must soar."*

At the look on Locrian's face, Kaldon knew the Seer was meditating on specific words in the prophecy; *the Seer must fall.* Considering there was likely only a handful Seers alive, he hoped the oracle wasn't referring to him.

He turned to look at Anneya who was uncharacteristically quiet.

The Seer looked deep into Kaldon. "The River of Time showed me a long time ago that you have a unique part to play in the Great War. This means your path will be unconventional. I may not like it, but you need to do what you feel is best for Agadin. You best obey your vision and go to Gorath."

"What?!" Tolek said, raising his voice.

Anneya threw up her arms. "You have *got* to be kidding me!"

"The River of Time is guiding Kaldon," the Seer stated mater-of-factly. "He *must* go."

Kaldon spoke up. "I know you both don't agree with my decision, but I know that I need to leave. Gorath is the last place I want to be. I can still feel the essence of the vision coursing through me, as though it's instructing me. There is no doubt in my mind that I need to follow through with what I saw."

All that laid behind Anneya's scowl was silent disapproval. Tolek rubbed his brow in frustration.

The Paladin looked to Anneya. "Blade, are you going with Kaldon as well?"

The Blade bit her lip in frustration. "No. Kaldon said he needs to go alone. He won't allow anyone to go with him."

Tolek spoke directly to her. "Journey with me then, Blade. We are heading north, so Kaldon can come as far with us as he can before he needs to leave."

"I will come with you," she said in a quiet voice.

"What is your plan, Tolek?" Locrian asked.

The Paladin spoke with a tone refined to certainty. "The moment I heard about Marradus' skull being missing, I sent messengers throughout Agadin. We are about to see something that hasn't taken place in quite some time."

Kaldon wanted to know that Anneya would be safe but knew that a Paladin's missions were never without chance of death.

He looked at the stoic Paladin. "What is going to take place?"

Tolek's determined gaze shifted from face to face. "I have summoned all of the Paladins scattered throughout Agadin to unite. We are going to hunt a demon dragon."

CHAPTER TEN

SHADOW CALLS

L ocrian ran his hand over rare books sitting on stone shelves throughout the Depths. Dust coated his fingers as he scoured over titles only the most brilliant minds in all of Agadin would ever have the privilege of reading.

"The Evolution of Paladins," he whispered, reading the title aloud. "This won't do," he said, shaking his head in frustration.

He was growing weary, searching through the endless books. Book after book he roamed, like a voyager scouting forgotten land. Finding information about Marradus was proving to be more difficult than the Seer had hoped.

"I told you, you won't find anything here, Locrian," Fen said gruffly.

He looked over, seeing the Philosopher arched over numerous books as she sat upon the floor of the library. With frayed hair and simple robes, she had a pen in each hand, writing in two notebooks at once. He knew she was fractioning her mind, an ancient ability used by Philosophers. He was glad to see her alive and well after her interaction with the Sovereign and his Kreel. The Master Healers did a thorough job healing her broken bones.

"You're sure there is nothing here about Marradus?" he pressed.

She put down her pens, looking at him. "Seer, I have gone through all these books dozens of times. I've told you, there are no books here that even mention Marradus, other than the book Kaldon brought here from his hometown, *The First Paragon.*'"

Locrian sighed. "That is disappointing."

"You're a Seer, can't you just look into the River of Time to find the information you're looking for?" she questioned.

"I wish it worked that way," he said. "I can't always choose what I see. The River often decides what visions I see."

Pacing in thought, he continued, "There must be a way to kill the dragon. If the Sovereign can raise such a beast from the dead, then we should be able to eliminate it."

"Have you thought of going to Noriden?" Fen asked. "They have one of the most extensive collections of knowledge in all of Agadin. If anywhere held information that you seek, it would be there."

"I have," Locrian smiled in thought. "In fact, I've already told Tolek I will be leaving for there once I am finished here. Have you been to Noriden?"

Fen cleared her throat. "Oh yes. In fact, I was trained there for a time. In my opinion, Noriden has the cleverest minds in all of Agadin."

"You mean, other than yourself?" the Seer teased.

Fen let out a raspy laugh. "It's interesting hearing that remark come from the man who is renowned as the smartest man alive — that is, since Dolan Thain's death of course. That is no small achievement considering you aren't even a Philosopher."

Locrian laughed with her. "People say I am the smartest man alive because of my imagination and intuition. I have the ability to imagine; to create. However, any Philosopher alive could best me in knowledge; there is no doubt about that. That's why Dolan was so remarkable. He was a perfect blend of imagination and knowledge."

"True," Fen replied, thinking about her brilliant pupil, now gone. "You will love Noriden. Every resident of the small town is required to ascend to have the knowledge of at least a Scholar."

"Are there many Philosophers?" Locrian asked.

"There are a few, yes," she said, lost in nostalgia thinking about the renowned town.

He looked at the hunched-over Philosopher. "Fen, why don't you come with me?"

She looked up with a dazed look.

"As you've said, you have read every book here in the Depths dozens of times," the Seer said. "There would be limitless knowledge for you to research in Noriden. More importantly, you would have many around you like yourself. You wouldn't have to be alone any longer."

Fen waved a hand. "I don't mind silence, Seer. I like my own company."

The Seer smiled sadly. "Somehow, I doubt that. Know that those from Noriden would greet you openly. At least consider making the journey."

"I certainly won't be joining you now," Fen stated. "However, if it means that much to you, I'll consider journeying there at some point."

He smiled at the Philosopher, who was clearly trying to hide emotions. He could see the sadness shawled over her; he could see the unspoken longing for companionship.

It was drawing late, and he knew it was still a several hours climb back up to the surface of the Peak of Lore. He needed to begin his journey to Noriden.

"Well, Fen, I won't be seeing you for quite some time," he said to the crouched over Philosopher.

She smiled at him. "Thank you for your words. I will think on what you've said."

He nodded, saying, "Hopefully I will see you there. Maybe you can teach me a thing or two."

The Philosopher beamed proudly, turning back to her work.

Leaving the Depths, he began his journey up the stone-chiseled steps. Reaching the second level of the library, he saw several Scholars seated at study desks. Men and women, advanced in age, were immersed in the contents of prestigious books, reading information that was permitted for their eyes alone.

Amidst the Scholars and books, something stood out like a snowflake in summer. Before a door leading deeper into the library were two Bishops. With pale blue capes hanging down their muscular backs, each stood militantly. Such brute warriors in a study hall of Scholars were unfitting. Locrian had seen one of the Bishops before with Tolek — his name was Klassen. The other Bishop was unknown to him.

"We were sent by Paladin Tolek to find you," Klassen said, looking at Locrian. The Bishop's voice whisked throughout the study hall. Scholars flinched at the burly voice breaking their concentration. Each pretended not to be distracted in their studies, considering they wouldn't dare tell a warrior such as a

Bishop to quiet.

He weighed the Bishop's words. "I was just with Tolek before coming down here. Why does he have need of me?" Locrian asked annoyed. He needed to leave. Time was dire.

The Bishop didn't hesitate to respond. "The Paladin didn't tell me why he needs to see you. He asked me to escort you to his whereabouts."

He rolled his eyes. "Fine, let's be done with this quickly," he said complying.

"Follow me," the Bishop said turning down one of the corridors.

Following the Bishops through what seemed like endless halls and corridors, the Seer was surprised to find that he wasn't heading upstairs to the library's surface, instead being led to an older wing of the mountainous castle. The deeper he delved into the mountain, the barer the walls became. No books covered the walls in this place. He watched the steady stride of the Bishops; however, the more he watched the warriors, the more uncertain he became. He had never heard of Tolek spending time in the library, let alone in a section so secluded. Something was amiss.

The Bishops turning a corner, Locrian hung back. The Seer held still, clinging to the wall. He listened intently.

He heard the Bishops stop. Noticing he wasn't with them, they began retracing their steps. He waited for them to round the corner; his timing would need to be perfect.

As the Bishops came around, Locrian spun his metal staff up into the air, striking Klassen under the chin. The warrior stumbled back, falling to the ground unconscious. Before the second Bishop could respond, the Seer leapt at the oversized brute. Locking the metal staff over his neck, he pinned the Bishop against the wall.

"Tell me where you are actually bringing me!" the Seer demanded. "Tell me who sent you!"

The Bishop strained his neck against the Seer's staff, chuckling through coughs. The man placed a beefy hand against Locrian's chest, thrusting him aside. He knew he could never best a Bishop in strength. The only reason he could take out Klassen was because he had surprise as an asset — now he had no such luxury. He lifted his staff again to strike the Bishop, as a voice arose from a nearby room.

"Locrian…" the soothing voice called.

At the sound of his name being called, he let his staff drop to his side. The Bishop scowled at him. Locrian frowned, turning his back to the warrior. He walked down the forgotten hallway as the remaining Bishop followed behind. He sought the room from where the voice came.

Stepping into the quaint room, before him was what he did not expect to see. A woman in a scarlet gown stood before him.

"Clearly it wasn't Tolek who wanted my attention," the Seer quipped.

"Very perceptive of you," the woman in the scarlet gown said.

Locrian took a step toward her. "You must be Ceanne Brimnas, the Queen of Stone Hedge. Am I correct?"

The queen smiled cordially. "It is good to finally meet you. I have heard much about the renowned Seer of Agadin."

"Why did you bring me here? If you want to cause me harm, you should know your Bishops are no threat to me. A Seer has weapons greater than swords."

The queen waved her hand in a laugh. "Oh, I know all too well of your intimate knowledge of time." She looked at the Seer with a questioning gaze. "By the way, why would you assume I want to harm you?"

He looked around to the hidden room in which he stood. The plain room had nothing in it, except for a cot and two troughs laid upon the cold floor. One had scraps of food, while the other had water. The room was so deep into the forgotten wing of the mountain that it was possible people hadn't walked this ground for decades. It was so isolated that no sounds or pleas could be heard. Any cries would be snuffed out by distance.

"From the looks of it, you plan on imprisoning me," the Seer remarked.

A sneer spread over the queen's face.

He looked deep into her hazel eyes, reading the scroll of her life.

Ceanne took a step toward him, not shifting her gaze. "Tell me Seer, what is it that you see in my soul?"

His eyes widened. "I see that Shadow has stolen your heart a long time ago."

"You truly are gifted," she said, running a hand down his cheek. "I have known the Shadow ever since I was a young girl. One of my father's staff introduced me to the way. Not long after, Furion herself began visiting me in my dreams. She was the one who guided me."

"You took your father's life…" the Seer said as his eyes glazed over with tears. "How could you poison your own father? Wars began because of his death. So many lives were lost. It was you the whole time…"

She looked away. "Don't be so shocked, Seer. My father was a weak man; one ruled by his compassion. You know that Furion targets those with influence. Who is more influential than an uprising queen?"

"Tolek will be told of this immediately. You will not get away with what you've done," Locrian voiced.

"Tolek doesn't suspect a thing," Ceanne replied. "He is too consumed by his mission to see clearly. He sees me only as another victim needing to be rescued."

Without reply, he turned around to the room's exit to be met by the brutish Bishop. Filling the frame of the doorway, the Bishop stood with sword in hand. Ceanne came forward, standing beside him. The queen patted her hand on the iron door to the room.

"You cannot leave, Locrian. This door here is so strong, it could halt a small army of men."

"Watch me," the Seer said raising his staff. He had taken out one Bishop already, all he needed to do was disarm one more.

Ceanne lifted an arm. With her hand stretched toward him, he watched in wonder as black void began drifting over her delicate skin. Shadow danced around her hand and between her fingers.

"What is this?" the Seer asked, taking a step back.

The blackened smoke thrusted forward toward him, pressing against his chest. Like a hammer slamming against him, he flew to the ground, landing on his back with a grunt. He tried lifting himself from the ground; however, the shadowy fog held him to the stone floor. Struggling against the sinister force, the black void felt like ice against him.

"What is this?!" he shouted in a strain.

"It is darkness and shadow," the queen laughed in amusement. "Furion knows how to give good gifts to her children, doesn't she? She said that since I am a queen, I should have unique privileges. Who would have thought I would be given the ability to wield the essence of Shadow?"

"Witch…" he muttered. "You will not harm me! Free me at once!" he declared.

Ceanne smiled. "You are right Seer; I will not harm you. You will harm yourself. I know that isolation is the weakness of Seers. How long will you be able to hold onto your sanity before the River of Time washes it away?"

Locrian writhed under the icy shadow's grip. "Ceanne!"

"Goodbye, Locrian," the queen said closing the door. "Enjoy your descent into madness."

Locrian laid upon the floor. The only sounds he heard were his racing breaths and the sound of a lock clicking shut.

Chapter Eleven
The Measure of a Man

It had been nearly a week of travel since they left the Peak of Lore. An army of men and women pressed onwards through seemingly endless landscapes of rock and trees to the meeting place of Paladins. It was only a matter of time before Kaldon would need to leave his friends, venturing out on his own to the homeland of Tymas Droll: Gorath.

Kaldon, Tolek, and Anneya walked together, the sound of clopping boots coming up behind them. It was Klassen, one of the Bishops from the Peak of Lore.

The Bishop stilled his panting breaths before speaking. "Paladin Tolek, I had the overseers of smaller factions of the army give me their final numbers," he said militantly.

"And?" the Paladin pried.

"We are still strong in number, at five thousand warriors. None have been lost to the Kreel," the Bishop said.

Tolek nodded, expressing his approval. "Thank you, Klassen. Keep me updated if anything changes," he said.

The Bishop nodded in compliance.

As the Bishop began turning to leave, Tolek spoke up again. "Hold on."

The Bishop stopped.

"What did you do to your chin? It's completely bruised," he asked.

Klassen brought up his hand to his blackened chin. "Some of the warriors got in a squabble. I was punched while breaking up the fight."

Observing the interaction, Kaldon knew the Bishop was lying. His bruise was already beginning to yellow. The strike wasn't recent. From the looks of it, it must have happened a little over a week ago while still at the Peak of Lore. Tolek's face betrayed that he was thinking the same thing.

The Paladin weighed his heavy gaze upon the Bishop. "Must have been some punch to leave a bruise like that."

Klassen stayed silent.

Tolek lifted a hand towards the Bishop's chin; he flinched, not knowing the Paladin's intentions. Kaldon and Anneya watched as his hand began to faintly glow with the Kingdom of Light. Pain was erased from Klassen's expression. The black and yellow colouration of the bruise quickly dimmed, being removed from his paling face.

"Thank you, Paladin Tolek," the Bishop said with a stutter, clearly unnerved.

"Be more mindful next time, Klassen," Tolek said in a nod, dismissing him. The Paladin's advice was clearly more than mere words; they were a warning, telling the man he knew something was amiss.

As the Bishop disappeared into the array of warriors, Kaldon nor Anneya voiced their concerns about Klassen. Both knew that the Paladin was a more-than capable leader.

Kaldon's looked at Anneya. Through the swarm of soldiers, she watched with a hawk-like focus as Ceanne Brimnas struggled at a distance. As the queen pulled up her dress to step over a fallen tree trunk, the Blade shook her head.

"I know you don't trust her, Anneya, but she's a queen. That must amount to something with you," Tolek said, raising an eyebrow. "On top of that, even if there was something off about the woman, an army of five thousand is more than capable of taking care of any threat from her."

Kaldon watched the interaction, curious to see how she would respond to the Paladin. He knew she disliked the queen; however, he still didn't know if her concerns were valid or not.

"I don't know what it is about her. Something just doesn't sit right," she said with agitation in her tone. "Something other than her ridiculous choice of travelling clothes."

Tolek chuckled.

She looked at him with a scowl. "You know it's true. Look at her!" she said waving a hand.

Unaware that she was under scrutiny, Ceanne let out a frustrated sigh as a Knight came up to her, unhooking her dress from a protruding twig.

"She's pathetic," the Blade said, rolling her eyes.

Tolek shook his head, entertained by the impatient Blade.

Ducking under a branch, Kaldon spoke up. "Tolek, where is it you are meeting the Paladins?" he said, changing the subject.

Pulling his eyes from the Queen of Stone Hedge, the Paladin replied, "We are meeting them at a place called the *Courts of Light*.

Then we will head out in search of Marradus."

"I've never heard of such a place," Kaldon whispered in thought.

Anneya stopped. "Wait, I've heard that name before."

Kaldon and Tolek slowed their pace, taking in the flustered Blade. She gave them both a blank stare. "The Courts of Light was a place in a nursery rhyme I heard as a child. Staff at the Peak of Lore used to sing it to me when I was a little girl, before I would go to sleep."

She began quoting the song:

> *"Though evils rise and shadows dawn,*
> *though demons shriek, imposing plight,*
> *to the fall where visions spawn,*
> *the courageous seek the Courts of Light."*

Tolek smirked. "That's the place."

"I had no clue it actually existed," she said in wonder.

He nodded his head. "The Courts of Light have been a meeting place for Protectors of Agadin for thousands of years. It may be one of the most hidden destinations in all of Agadin."

"Are the Courts of Light more hidden than the Peak of Lore?" she asked.

"Oh, yes," the Paladin stated. "Only a handful of people alive know of its whereabouts. The army we have with us won't even be allowed to follow."

She ran her hand through her hair. As words escaped her mouth, her face paled. "Is it true what I was told as a child, that it is guarded by the *Valley of Blood?*"

A somber look spawned across the Paladin's face.

"The valley of *what?*" Kaldon asked.

"The Valley of Blood," she said quietly. "I was told as a child that the Courts of Light are guarded by bowed plains where visions torment those who try to pass through."

He looked to the Paladin, waiting for him to laugh at such an absurd idea. Tolek instead met them both with a dark gaze.

"The Valley of Blood is a real place," the Paladin said, resting a hand upon his hilt. "The Plains of Morah — where the Courts of Light are hidden — are for the most part peaceful. But the Valley of Blood is a dreadful place. It protects the sacred land from those who try to find the courts by plaguing them with visions."

"Visions?" Kaldon asked skeptically. "How is it possible for someone to receive visions on a plot of land?"

Tolek elaborated. "Legend says that thousands of years ago there were several hundred Seers summoned to meet at the Courts of Light. Some came with ulterior motives; to eliminate those who served opposing kingdoms. Before the entrance to the courts, war broke loose. It was a massacre. As the blood of Seers was spilled throughout the valley, so was their gift to see visions. It defiled the land, cloaking it in the *Curse of Seers.* It is said that since the battle was so treacherous and the Seers died in such horror, those who walk through the valley are taken by visions of their worst fears coming to pass."

He continued, "As terrible as such a battle was, it worked to the benefit of keeping the Courts of Light hidden. The courts hold secrets that have been kept hidden since the foundation of Agadin was laid. Since those who dare to walk through the valley are confronted by their worst fears, only the bravest succeed in passing through. Most turn back, never the same again. Others who have attempted have been filled with such terror and sorrow that the visions take their lives before they even make it through. Only those undivided in heart and courage can go through unscathed. It is a terrible place."

"You have passed through the valley, Tolek?" Anneya asked, wide-eyed.

"Several times," he said stoically.

Anneya shuttered.

"What sorts of secrets do the Courts of Light hold?" Kaldon asked, his mind reeling at the thought.

Warriors darting around them throughout the mountain terrain, the Paladin looked to him with a heavy gaze. Waiting for men and women to be out of ear shot, the Paladin said, "Legend says that Divinity will at times shine his light in the courts; he does so to instruct those who he deems worthy of his wisdom. My hope is that he will find the living Paladins of Agadin worthy of his instruction. Considering the events taking place, he would know that we are in dire need of it."

Kaldon quieted at the thought of being in the presence of the one who created all things. He didn't know Divinity visited those who walked Agadin. Such a thought was both alluring and terrifying to him.

"How far away is the journey from here to the Courts of Light?" Anneya asked.

"A little over a month of travel," he said, keeping his eyes on the mountain road.

Kaldon wished he could go with them. As a Protector of Agadin, he would have likely been permitted to enter the courts; however, he knew that he wasn't mandated to go. There was a far more dreadful place he needed to visit.

"How much longer will I be travelling with you before I need to go on my own?" he asked.

"Your road leading to Gorath isn't far, Kaldon. In fact, it's only several hours up ahead," the Paladin said, pointing up their trail. "Once you see the cliff with stone overarching its edge, you will need to head out on your own. There is a path along the cliff that you will follow."

At the mention of Gorath, Anneya picked up her pace in stride, leaving the two to walk by themselves.

At the sight of her leaving, Kaldon sighed. "I don't know what to do with her, Tolek. I don't want to leave, but I don't feel like I have a choice in the matter."

Tolek turned his gaze to him. "Has anyone ever told you that you don't know anything about women, Kaldon?"

"Brenton tells me frequently," he admitted.

"He's right," Tolek said pointedly. "Anneya is afraid for your life; so am I, for that matter. She isn't only afraid for your life; she is afraid of losing you."

"Losing me?" he questioned.

Tolek looked at the young man. "It's no secret that Anneya is tough, Kaldon. She is one of the most stubborn people I have ever met. That said, it means a lot when she allows herself to care for someone like she does with you."

He looked forward, seeing Anneya making her way deeper into the sea of warriors. "I really care for her; I want her to know that. I also know that I need to go to Gorath," he said.

The Paladin put a hand on Kaldon's shoulder. "I know. I won't pretend I've been fond of your decision. I haven't been. But I believe that there must be a reason for you going. Locrian said you are being guided by the River of Time. I trust his opinion."

Kaldon nodded, thankful for the Paladin's approval. He looked forward, past the warriors. He appreciated the company of friends but found himself thinking of how he would soon be journeying on his own.

"Don't doubt yourself, Kaldon."

He turned to the Paladin at the unexpected remark. "Why would you say that?"

"Because I know you're afraid," Tolek said. "Just remember that Divinity wouldn't give you a vision for no reason. You can overcome whatever will be set before you."

"At times I have trouble believing that," Kaldon said in honesty, his voice coming out quieter than he expected.

Soldiers rushing around them, Tolek kept his eyes forward. "Do you know why we often struggle to believe in ourselves?" the Paladin asked.

Kaldon looked to him, waiting for his answer.

Tolek continued, "It's because we have a tendency of measuring ourselves against those who have gone before us."

The remark cut him, knowing exactly what he meant. "You're saying my father is a hard man to live up to?"

Tolek nodded. "Dolan Thain was a remarkable man. He had the most gifted mind I've ever come across." Turning his gaze to Kaldon, he said, "Comparison stunts our perception of ourselves. You need to remember that there was a time when your father wasn't known as the *Warrior General* or as the *Great Philosopher*. There was a time when he was just *Dolan*. Your father didn't first choose greatness when he was mantled with titles; he chose greatness long before, when no one even knew his name. He understood that seeing your own potential is a choice."

Kaldon was quiet at the words. It was hard to imagine his father before he was revered throughout Agadin.

Tolek continued, "All I'm saying is that it's fine to be inspired by your father, but your true mission is to discover who *you* will be."

He breathed in the words, knowing they would take time to fully sink in.

Eyeing the renowned Paladin, a question stirred within him. "Tolek, have you ever battled with measuring yourself to another?"

"I used to compare myself to my former mentor; the man who trained me to become a Paladin," he said hardening, clearly not expecting the question. "The man who trained me was a warrior like no other. There isn't one alive who would be able to best him."

Considering the man's expertise in warfare, Kaldon was having troubles wrapping his mind around the idea of Tolek holding another warrior in such high regard. Watching the Paladin, he saw pain in the man's eyes that was uncommon.

"Who was it who trained you? Is he still alive?" Kaldon asked.

Tolek was quiet at the questions.

Finally, he spoke up, ignoring what Kaldon said. "Your safety isn't guaranteed on the mission before you," he said, shifting the subject completely.

Caught off guard by the Paladin's abruptness, Kaldon wished he could prod him more. In many ways, Tolek was still a mystery to him. The agitation in the man's stride told him not to press the subject.

Tolek continued, "Anneya needs to know that you won't gamble your life foolishly. You best prove to her that you are going to try your best to come home to her. She deserves at least that."

Kaldon looked around, wishing she were still in sight. He longed to stay with her but knew he didn't have a choice. He hated the thought of leaving, with her not knowing she held an important place in his heart.

He said, "Thank you, Tolek. I will do just that."

Chapter Twelve

Lonely Road

The group trudged onward through the Mountains of D'aal. Kaldon's eyes scoured through the endless warriors. He spent a significant amount of time looking for Anneya, yet she escaped his sight.

His eyes bouncing from face to face, he saw men and women who had left the comfort of their own homes to pursue a demon dragon. Warriors marched onwards, armed with swords, axes, and shields that would presumedly be useless against such a creature. Admiring their courage, he wished he could fight alongside them. Yet, as the nearing cliff came into view, he knew his turnoff had come.

He wished Anneya wouldn't have kept her distance from him. He had things he needed to say to her. He had something he wanted to give to her.

Just as Tolek said, the path was narrow and right along a cliffside. He knew the drop would be thousands of feet into the deep chasm. He also knew the narrow path was likely far safer than the rest his journey to Gorath would be. He hoped he would survive to see Anneya's face again. As warriors dashed past him, he looked at every face, hoping it would be her; yet it was not. She clearly found it easier to disappear, rather than to say goodbye to him.

He breathed in the light mountain air, attempting to summon the courage to move his feet forward onto his isolated path.

It was time. He took a step forward.

"Kaldon, we need to talk," Anneya's voice said from behind him.

At the sound of her voice, relief swept through him. Turning around, he saw her face wet with tears.

"I've been looking for you everywhere!" he said.

"I've been avoiding you," she replied through sniffles.

He stayed silent, waiting for her to continue.

"I'm sorry, Kaldon," she said, running her hand through her golden hair. "I just know I won't be seeing you for at least several months. Worse, since you are going to Gorath, I may not see you again at all…"

He could feel the sting of emotion rising in him at the thought of never seeing her again. "I don't want to leave, Anneya. I need you to know that."

He reached out, placing a hand on her upper arm. "All I want is to be with you. I don't understand it; but, somehow, I feel that the fate of Agadin rests on my willingness to go right now. Locrian said the River of Time is guiding me. Everything in me wants to fight what he said, so I can be by your side, but I believe there is purpose in me leaving."

"I know. I wish it weren't true, but I understand," she said in a trembling voice. She reached into her armour. "I have something for you. I grabbed it from the Peak of Lore before we left."

Materializing a small-leather book, she held it before him. The leather was stained a midnight-blue, holding a look of elegance. His eyes traced the rivets on its cover. He read the title aloud.

"Heart of the Brave."

"What is this?" he asked, reaching out to grab the old book.

"It was written by your father," she said, quietly. "It's filled with some of his proverbs of wisdom. Apparently, it was penned to encourage people to persevere into who they were destined to be. I figured it would be fitting for your journey."

He smiled, thinking of his conversation with Tolek. He tucked the precious book into his cloak.

"I have something for you as well," he said, looking up into her tear-filled eyes.

She watched him in anticipation. He reached out, grabbing her soft hands. As he did so, he placed something in the centre of her palm. At its feel, her face turned curiously. Upon opening her hand, she saw his Legacy. The five-pointed pendant rested in her hand, catching the sun's light.

"Kaldon, I can't take this. This was your father's. Your mother gave it to you…" she said in a whimper, trying to hand the priceless pendant back to him.

"Keep it safe for me," he said as his hand cupped hers, closing her grip on the rare symbol. "It's my promise to you that we will be together again. It's my promise that one day we won't have wars to fight or dragons to slay. It's my promise that my heart belongs to you and no other."

Anneya tried to stutter out words, but before she could, he leaned in, kissing her cheek. His lips lingered upon the teardrop scar that descended her cheek. He wished he could erase her pain;

to ease the sting of them being separated.

Loosening his grip from her, the path along the cliffside called to him. After taking one last look at the woman who was more than a Blade to him, he turned to the path that would lead him to Gorath.

Leaving his beloved, his feet met the lonely road he was destined to travel.

Chapter Thirteen

Lies Coated in Honey

————◆◆◆————

Warrior by warrior, Anneya wove through the army scattered throughout the open Plains of Morah. She had dedicated hours to the endeavour. Her boots winding through the matted grass, she thought about the mountains. She hadn't seen them in what felt like weeks. Growing up in the mountains, the yellow and green fields surrounding her felt disquieting. The mountains were also where she had last seen Kaldon.

Looking from face to face throughout the army, she secretly hoped she would stumble upon him; to see his eyes amidst the emerald fields. She knew it wouldn't happen. He was gone. She spun his Legacy between her finger and thumb. She felt each bump of the five protruding lines digging into her skin. Catching herself, she tucked the pendant back underneath her silver armour, realizing she had been playing with it again.

Even though the thought of him weighed on her, she couldn't allow herself to be distracted on her mission. Twilight protected her from being spotted as dusk began veiling over the army. She sighed in frustration wishing she knew where Shar was. The

Bishop would have proven helpful in her self-imposed mandate; however, one easily became lost amongst five thousand. Anneya knew she didn't have time to delay. She needed to follow Ceanne Brimnas.

The queen went from person to person; men and women alike, interacting with each. Anneya considered herself to be social, but she quickly realized that Ceanne was another thing entirely. For hours, the queen moseyed to different warriors, building connection and rapport. She was shocked at how quickly people took to her. It would only be a matter of minutes before whoever she talked to was in fits of laughter or moments of tears, opening their hearts to her. Even though the queen's efforts looked innocent — considerate even — the Blade saw what was behind her actions.

Standing behind three bulky soldiers who were socializing, she knew she was shielded from the queen's sight. Listening intently, she tuned her ears to the sound of Ceanne's voice while she interacted with another one of the female Knights.

"How long have you been in the Paladin's service?" the queen asked in a soothing tone.

The Knight stood proud in her onyx clad, the customary clothes of a Knight. "For nearly five years now. It has been an honour to serve a man such as Tolek."

"He truly is a wonderful man, isn't he?" Ceanne asked pleasantly.

The Knight nodded in agreement. "One of the finest."

The queen tilted her head inquisitively. "So, you know the Paladin, then?"

The Knight distorted her face. "Um, well no. I don't know him personally."

Ceanne tisked, shaking her head. "Oh, that's a shame. A formidable warrior such as yourself deserves attention. After all, you are laying down your life to serve him."

"I never thought of it that way before," the Knight said, wiping her hair from her face. "But Tolek is a busy man. I understand that he can't take time with everyone."

The queen let out a light laugh. "Oh, my dear, you are so gracious. You clearly don't think as highly of yourself as you should."

She placed a hand upon the Knight's shoulder. "Look at me, for example: I'm a queen, yet I know you deserve my attention. You aren't just anyone; you're a Knight of Agadin. You are a warrior of the people. You are worth my time."

A smile spread across the Knight's smooth face. "Do I really?"

"Oh, yes, my dear. You certainly deserve recognition. Never forget that," the queen said, squinting in a smile as she walked away.

Anneya felt her face heating as she watched Ceanne walk up to another one of the warriors, initiating another twisted conversation. From person to person, she watched her target countless warriors throughout the plains. Anneya had heard enough. She was convinced that the queen was trying to turn people from Tolek's leadership to her own.

As the queen was busy prattling on with a new warrior, the Blade's gaze widened in realization. Ceanne didn't have anything in her hands. She wasn't carrying the book she went everywhere with. She bit her lip in frustration with herself for not noticing it sooner. This was her opportunity.

Her eyes darted about, looking for the only place the mysterious book could be. She had been in its presence for nearly three quarters of an hour, without even thinking to look there:

the queen's tent.

The queen lost in conversation, Anneya quickly made her way to the beige tent that was cloaked with an array of looming trees set behind it. Moving between soldiers, she didn't worry about being discreet. The warriors would be used to Blades not being courteous. She touched the rough linen, looking around, making sure no one was aware of what she was doing. She knew that entering a queen's tent would be punishable if she were caught. She knew it would be hard to justify her actions to Tolek, but she had no choice.

She slipped in.

Anneya looked around the pristine tent. It wasn't large per se; however, it was sizeable considering it was a temporary dwelling place for travel. As her eyes rested upon furniture and a large bed, the Blade rubbed her eyes in frustration. She assumed a queen would have fine things; however, she also knew the cost of travelling with such pieces. She must have convinced some of the warriors to carry the furniture for her during their travels. These men and women were likely walking to their deaths, yet this woman was ordering them to pamper her so she could have her impractical comforts.

She found herself already wanting to leave the elite dwelling place, yet she needed to find what she came for. She pulled open drawers and sorted through clothes. She looked behind cabinets and under the throw rug, all to find nothing. Then she saw the queen's bed.

Anneya remembered when she was a young girl; she would pen notes to herself, writing her emotions upon paper. Since she wanted to keep her thoughts private, she would hide them underneath her bedding. She wondered if the queen thought similarly to her.

The Blade slowly walked toward the bed of a queen, stuffing her hands underneath the mattress. Running her hand through, she felt something hard. Pulling it out from its hiding place, she found Ceanne's book.

She held the children's book before her eyes. "The Lion's Roar; The Raven's Call," she read the title aloud, running her hand over the bronzed cover.

She opened the book, skimming through its ivory pages. As she sifted through the words, a chill grazed across her skin.

"Some fear the Shadow, as they should. However, Shadow is not the most dreadful of things. Shadow is but a precursor to what Furion's true objective is. Once Shadow is established throughout Agadin, the most terrifying of forces can take shape. Void. All that once was will be reduced to nothingness. Shadow will consume all, until there is nothing left."

- Tymas Droll

"This is no children's book..." she whispered, as goose-pimples rose upon her flesh.

She could feel that the paper-like cover felt unfitting against the book, almost as though it were loose. Using her fingernail, she began picking at the book's cover as it began stripping off. She unraveled the fake-paper cover, seeing black-leather binding underneath.

Her eyes widened at the black book. In gold lettering, the title was written: *"The Law of Shadow."*

She closed her eyes at the horror of such literature. Through the stillness, she heard the ring of steel. With the book in hand, she looked back to see Klassen standing in the doorway of the tent.

"You aren't permitted to be in Queen Ceanne's tent," Klassen said, pointing his sword at her.

The Blade stood tall, not faltering under the Bishop's gaze. She knew any Bishop alive was capable of killing her; however, she didn't have the luxury of backing down.

"Tell me, how is it that you became Ceanne's henchman?" she quipped.

Klassen's face was as hard as stone. "The queen has offered things to me that others cannot," he said.

"Like what?" Anneya pressed.

"Eternal rewards," the Bishop said. "No one else alive can offer me that."

She knew that when the Bishop said, *no one,* that he was referring to Tolek.

"Ceanne is manipulating you, Klassen. She's been doing this with countless warriors throughout the army. You should know better!" she spat.

"You're wrong!" Klassen shouted. "I've served Tolek for years and never been offered the recognition that the queen has given me. She has power that even he couldn't comprehend!"

Anneya took a step back, seeing how quickly the Bishop grew hostile. "She's trying to turn the army against Tolek. She's been lying to you!"

She held out the *Law of Shadow* before the Bishop's sight. "Look at this!"

He looked at the black leathered book as strain grew upon his face. The Bishop lifted a hand, smacking the book from Anneya's hands. "I don't care what the queen reads. I only care about what she has promised me."

She flinched at the Bishop's reaction, distancing herself to the back of the tent. Reaching behind her back, she summoned her bow, nocking it with an arrow.

With the arrow's point directed at Klassen, the Blade snarled a warning. "If your hand touches me again, you are going to get an arrow through your heart."

She watched his breaths begin quickening. He released a shout as he began filling the gap between them. Not hesitating, the Blade fired the arrow at Klassen. Lifting his sword, he effortlessly cut the arrow from the air. He jumped into the air swinging his sword down at her. She dodged the attack, whirling her bow around to crack against the Bishop's ribs. He moaned, holding his side. The Bishop pulled out a second sword, breathing heavily as he watched her.

Anneya took several panting steps back to gain distance between her and the rage-filled man. She knew she wouldn't be able to beat a Bishop in hand-to-hand combat. She needed to think of something.

Holding her bow forward, she pulled out two arrows. As she placed each upon the bow's string, she angled each so one would target his upper body, and the other his lower. Both arrows fired. She knew two arrows would be easy for a Bishop to deflect; however, she hoped he wouldn't expect them as a diversion.

As the two arrows soared toward the Bishop, she saw him swinging his swords accordingly to deflect them. Before either one reached their marks, she summoned a third arrow; firing it at the Bishop's midsection.

The first two arrows were cut from the air, each spinning in opposite directions through the tent. In the same moment, Klassen released a sudden grunt. Looking down, he saw the third arrow protruding from his abdomen. As blood sprayed from his mouth, he crumpled to the ground.

Anneya let her bow drop, placing her hands upon her knees in a pant.

"I see you found my book," a calm voice said before her.

At the icy tone, Anneya could feel the hair on her arms begin to rise. Turning around, she saw the woman in the scarlet dress.

Ceanne walked into the confines of her tent. "It isn't the most pleasant feeling to walk into your abode of rest to find an intrusive Blade and a dead Bishop," the queen said dourly.

Anneya took a step forward, looking the queen head on. "You may have been able to fool the others, but I know you've embraced the Shadow. You serve the Sovereign."

Ceanne raised her eyebrows. "The Sovereign? I'm sorry my dear, but I'm afraid you are mistaken. I didn't lie when I said the Sovereign took Stone Hedge from me. He feared the political power I carry. Tymas Droll's influence has gotten to his head. He has power in Agadin, there is no doubt, but he is not my authority. I serve the Entity, Furion."

"Why do you have his book then?" Anneya challenged.

Ceanne raised one of her brows. "Isn't it wise to learn from your enemies if they understand what you do not? Seems like you need a lesson in war, *Blade.*"

She scowled at the queen. "Whoever you serve, your work here is done."

The queen smiled courtly. "Anneya, you don't know what you're saying. I can offer you more than the Paladin can. I can give you your heart's desires. I can…"

Before the queen could finish, Anneya brought her fist up, slamming it into Ceanne's face. The queen staggered backwards at the blow, falling onto her back.

"Sorry *queen*, but I don't take well to offers from traitors," she said, looking down at her.

Ceanne let out a faint laugh, bringing her eyes up to meet Anneya's. "I'm sensing a bit of tension from you. Perhaps you are just upset by the fact that Kaldon Thain preferred to dance with me, rather than you?"

She could feel the words stinging her heart. The insult hurt her more than she would have cared to admit. Grabbing her bow, she pulled forth another arrow pointing it at the queen.

"Anneya! Stop!" a booming voice called.

The Blade heard the tent's fabric at the entrance begin to ruffle. Through the doorway, Tolek walked into the entrance, his white cape tracing behind him.

"What's going on here?! Lower your bow!" he commanded.

"No," Anneya objected, vengeance filling her tone.

She watched Tolek's tough demeanour soften at the sight of Klassen, his former pupil, lying dead upon the ground.

Ceanne slowly stood up, beginning to whimper. Tears coursed down her cheeks. "Oh, Tolek, I was communing with the warriors when I heard clamour coming from my tent. When I came to look, I was shocked to see that your Blade was sneaking through my personal belongings!"

The queen gave Anneya a tear-filled glare, holding her hand toward Klassen's body. "This brave Bishop tried to stop her. It was then when she shot him with an arrow killing him!"

Anneya watched the Paladin's expressionless gaze. She could tell he was masking his emotion at seeing one of his students dead before him. Amidst the tense moment, she heard steel colliding from outside the tent. Aggression was stirring. The three ignored it, unmoving at the sudden rouse.

Tolek looked past the queen. His eyes took in Anneya.

"Anneya, tell me what *really* happened," he stated.

She could see the queen's look of shock, learning that Tolek didn't believe her story.

"Ceanne Brimnas has embraced the Shadow," Anneya said. "I've followed her nearly all day without her knowing, listening to her trying to convince the army to betray your leadership. Unfortunately, Klassen gave into her lies and tried to kill me."

She reached down, picking up the ebony book that Klassen knocked out from her hands, *The Law of Shadow*. "I found this. The book of the Dominion of Shadow, penned by Tymas Droll, himself."

Without taking his eyes from the black-leather book, the Paladin spoke. "Ceanne Brimnas, get on your knees," he said unsheathing his sword.

Anneya caught herself holding her breath, realizing she was about to see the queen executed right before her eyes. Quietness reigned between the three.

The tense moment was pierced as Ceanne let out a laugh. "You two are fools. Don't you hear what is happening outside? I have more of a shield than you would think. Tolek, you should be ashamed of how quickly some of your warriors turned against their beloved leader. All it took were a few empty promises."

Anneya watched the Paladin's hand tightening over the hilt of his blade. Before he could even approach the queen, Ceanne lifted her hands, one pointing at Tolek and the other at Anneya. Thick darkness swelled over her hands, hiding them in shadow.

As the black fog drifted around the queen's delicate skin, Anneya could feel her heart fluttering in anxiety at such an otherworldly sight.

"Great Divinity, what is that?" she asked.

Ceanne laughed. "My dear, it is the Dominion of Shadow coming to Agadin."

CHAPTER FOURTEEN

THE DIVIDE

Anneya fired the arrow.

In the confines of the queen's tent, the arrow soared towards Ceanne Brimnas. Her hand shrouded by dark void, she stood unmoving. The arrow touched the void, disappearing into nothingness.

"No… How is that possible?" Anneya asked, her voice trailing off.

The queen let out a shrill cry as darkness shot from her hands towards the Blade and Paladin. Anneya winced as the dark fog knocked her back, pinning her against the hard floor. Tolek dove out of the way, avoiding the attack.

"Tolek! *Do* something!" Anneya shouted.

Still on his knees, the Paladin pulled forth several knives, hurling them toward the queen. Considering his expertise, every knife was aimed to perfectly target a fatal organ. Out of nothing, shadowy mist grew before Ceanne — like a wall between her and the Paladin. Shadow ate the daggers, leaving her unharmed.

Realizing weapons wouldn't work against the queen, Tolek knew they would need to do something different to overwhelm her. As cloth from the tent brushed against him, he felt around for the pegs that kept it standing. Feeling a wooden peg, he pulled it loose. Immediately, the cloth was caught by the wind, tearing it from its place. The linen was stripped, leaving the three under the glow of the moon and dimming stars.

Around the three, several warriors were beginning to act out, attacking others in the black of night. Anneya knew the warriors were those who had been swayed by the corrupt queen. As Ceanne watched the warriors lashing out around her, Anneya felt the shadowy hold on her slightly loosening.

Tolek stood to his feet, speaking to the army. "Kill this woman!" he said, pointing toward the queen.

The Paladin's shout echoed throughout the hilled fields. Thousands of eyes watched, seeing Ceanne wielding unthinkable power. Bishops, Blades, Knights, and common warriors unsheathed their weapons. The ring of steel was like a shout, piercing through the night.

Ceanne's face turned to dread as warriors all began approaching her. However, as the bulk of men and women came, cries began popping up from within the army. Warriors suddenly fell to their death, their peers against them; those who betrayed Tolek.

Seeing the numbers of those who were rebelling, Anneya's spirit shrank.

Ceanne laughed at the sight of warriors turning against one another. Even though many of the soldiers were occupied, nearly fourty warriors pursued the queen. At the threat approaching, she lifted both her hands toward those approaching.

Anneya gasped, feeling the icy force fully lift from her. She could still feel the cold touch lingering throughout her body. The

Blade watched as a wall of darkness launched from the queen. Like a wave, the black void hit the fourty warriors, taking their lives on impact. Their lifeless bodies laid upon the green pastures.

With Ceanne distracted by the scene before her, Anneya crept behind one of the queen's oak dressers. She watched as Ceanne took in the chaos she'd created.

The queen's eyes darted about, resting on the assortment of trees behind her. She was aware that once the Paladin found his bearings with the traitors, he would come for her. She had done her part in dividing the army. She also knew her followers who survived the battle would find her. She now owned them. The queen sunk into the trees.

"You aren't getting away that easy, traitor," the Blade whispered into the night.

Looking back, Anneya saw Tolek taking out traitors from every direction. Knowing the Paladin was more than capable of pulling the army back together, she slipped into the woods, following the queen.

Her heart pounding against her chest, she could barely see as her eyes slowly adjusted to the darkness. The moon beaming between branches and twigs was the only source of light to guide her through the thick forest. Each tree she passed could have been a hiding place for Ceanne Brimnas. Anneya knew that at any moment her life could be taken from her. Instinctively, she reached behind her armour to hold her Legacy. The five points poked into her skin as a reminder of who she was; a Blade of Agadin. She was the one who held Kaldon Thain's heart.

"Anneya Padme," Ceanne's voice sailed, being carried by the wind.

The Blade spun around, trying to discern what direction the voice came from. All she saw was darkness.

"How does it feel to be all alone with no one to rescue you?" the voice sang, followed by a sinister laugh.

"Show yourself, coward!" Anneya shouted, still clenching the Legacy in her fist.

She heard rustlings from a nearby bush. Emerging from the shadows came Ceanne, her scarlet dress looking black in the dead of night.

"Why? Why go through all this trouble to tear apart an army?" the Blade asked, her voice trembling in anger.

Ceanne stopped, surprised that Anneya was voicing anything other than a plea for her life. "I admire your bravery, Blade. I have my reasons for dividing Tolek's army. Mark my words, death will inevitably win. There is no hope for Agadin."

"That's a lie," Anneya said raising her tone.

"Is it? Dominion cloaks the skies!" the queen said, waving a hand to the dimming stars. "You all march on an impossible mission to kill a demon dragon. Even if you did succeed — which you won't — you'd still have the Sovereign of Shadow and his armies to contend with. What you don't know is that Marradus is just the beginning. The Dominion of Shadow has no shortage of monstrosities. Furion has no shortage of puppets to manipulate. This was a war that was lost before it even began."

Anneya scoffed at the queen's words, although she could feel the weight of them tempting discouragement to settle in.

Before the Blade could reply, Ceanne cut in. "Look at your own life. You are one whose overcome impossible odds. I have never met such a young Blade. It truly is impressive. Yet, you are journeying to your death. You will not kill Marradus. You can't. Not only that, but the one thing you actually desire is completely out of your grasp."

"And what is it that I desire?" Anneya snapped.

The queen spoke in a soft tone. "To belong."

Anneya could feel tears beginning to sting her eyes. She knew the queen was trying to manipulate her; to use her. She needed to stay strong.

Ceanne continued, "I've seen the way you look at Kaldon. You try to appear strong, but I've seen the longing in your eyes. And, where is he?" she said, gesturing her hand. "He's left you, just like everyone else. You are alone, Anneya; forgotten."

Anneya spilled over in tears. She could feel the lie seeping into the tender places of her soul. She remembered her childhood, how her father and mother left her. She thought about the time she was forced to spend alone and neglected without her true parents. She remembered her adopted father who quickly became her abuser; the man who gave her the teardrop scar. All of this was because she was abandoned. Now, Kaldon had left her as well.

The queen stepped forward. "I can give you everything you could ever need or want, Anneya. I can give you a home; a place to belong. Follow me, and you can forever be by my side. You will never again have to feel like the broken little girl who was rejected and abandoned."

Through stifled sobs, she fought the emotions that were trying to persuade her to fall into the queen's hand — into the Shadow.

"What is your answer, Anneya?" the queen beckoned. "Let me show you who you really are. Let me show you how strong you can become."

Anneya looked up to Ceanne. Through the sting of emotion, she forced her voice to rise, taking the reins of her life. "Never."

Ceanne's face turned dark. "I despise when people so pathetic refuse me."

Darkness began surrounding the queen. Shadow engulfed her. As she stretched out her hands, Anneya watched thick darkness course towards her. She reached up, holding onto her Legacy. She took a deep breath, accepting her defeat.

All that Anneya saw was Shadow until everything went black.

CHAPTER FIFTEEN

FALLEN CITY

G laric clenched his hands around the iron bars. Looking down from the prison tower to the open expanse of the impressive city, shards of rust from the metal pressed into his skin. The city of Stone Hedge was the place he once called home; now it was corrupted by those who had embraced the Shadow. Groups of warriors marched down overrun streets. Most common folk were already killed or recruited into the Sovereign's army. Looking up to the skies, he saw the most terrifying of sights. Kreel flew about, their screeches filling the air. Stone Hedge was no longer a place suitable for peace or belonging; it was an abode of death.

He ran trembling hands down his blackened clothes. He could feel the clammy dirt worked-into what he wore. A Chief Messenger by profession, he preferred to appear well-kept. Considering he was one who delivered messages of importance to people of influence, appearance was important. Letting out a sigh, he reminded himself that he was no longer a Chief Messenger. He was one accused of embracing the Shadow.

He could still remember the look in Ceanne Brimnas' eyes when she heard he had embraced the Shadow. There was a look of carelessness, as though it didn't matter to her what happened to him. He would have preferred an outburst of rage; however, her indifference told him just how little she cared for him. Her look hurt him far more than what the prison guards had done to him; her apathy, more wounding than the beatings and ridicules he endured. Glaric had served the queen for decades. Still, she clearly didn't care for him, nor for all his sacrifices. Even so, he would never betray her. He never had. Despite his sentence, he knew he would never embrace the Shadow. He had been framed.

Looking over the simple and reclusive cell, he still couldn't believe how he ended up in such a place. He didn't know who'd framed him. It could have been numerous people working for the queen. Many coveted his position of influence. Faces of the queen's staff tumbled through his mind, as they had for the entire month of his imprisonment. In the end, he knew it didn't matter who had done it. He knew it wouldn't change the fact that he was a prisoner. Ceanne had decreed his execution, but the city was attacked before it could be followed through. He was forgotten in his cell; left to fade away, as though he didn't exist at all. It had been well over a month of him being locked in the cell. He knew he had withered to nearly nothing, nourished only by the occasional vermin scurrying through the cell. Thankfully during his time of imprisonment, spring had arrived. The melting snow permitted liquid to seep in through the window, offering water.

He sat down, leaning his head back against the cold wall. He was a prisoner for a crime he'd never committed.

Click.

Glaric turned his head, his heart quickening at the sound. In nearly an entire month, no noise at all had filled the cell hall.

He shuffled over the floor in a panic. He knew that the only ones who would have access to the prison hall would be those who embraced the Shadow. Everyone else from Stone Hedge no longer had the freedom to venture through the grand city. Within the four walls of the cell, the only furniture was a cot, tucked away in the corner. There was nowhere for him to hide. Knowing there was no other option, Glaric quickly laid flat upon the ground, forcing himself to breathe shallow breaths. His only hope was to play dead.

He heard boots clopping upon the cement floor, coming his direction.

"Look at that sap," a voice said as the steps came to a halt.

Another man grunted. "It's a good thing he died in this cell. He's too scrawny to be trained for war. Better he loses his life from starvation, rather than by my sword."

Glaric listened as the two men laughed. From the dim of the shadows, he held his open eyes steady to fake no sign of life. He saw the men's dark boots, encircled by black capes that stretched to the ground. He dared not look higher in fear of being found out. Based on the onyx cloaks, he knew two Dark Knights stood over him.

"Let's get his body out of here before it begins to rot. The Sovereign will have need for these cells," one of the Dark Knight's said.

Glaric heard the prison door click open. He couldn't count how many hours he sat watching the iron door, wishing he held the key to his freedom. He felt the Dark Knights grab his arms and legs. As the two men hoisted him effortlessly, he fought letting out a grunt. Hanging as limp as he could, he swayed from side to side as the warriors descended back down the tower of prison cells.

It didn't take the two men as long as he would have thought to carry him to the tower's bottom. Glaric was just thankful he wasn't dropped during the descent of stairs. Being carried through the arched doorway, he could feel the heat of the sun touching his skin. At its feel, a tear fell down his cheek. It was the first time he felt the direct warmth of the sun in over a month's time.

"Let's throw him with the rest," one of the Dark Knight's commanded. "The fire should be starting soon to get rid of all the remains."

Glaric tried not to panic at the mention of bodies being burned. That would mean he would only have a small window of time to sneak away. He felt the Dark Knights beginning to swing his limp body to throw him. He knew it would be difficult to remain still as his body slammed upon the ground.

Don't move. Don't move, he thought adamantly.

The Dark Knights released him as he briefly soared before impact. Glaric slammed onto the stone floor. Though he ached, he laid as still as possible. He hoped none of his bones were broken. With his face pressed into the ground, he was thankful he hadn't landed on his back. He knew he wouldn't have been able to hide his straining grimace.

The sound of the boots of the Dark Knights growing dimmer, he waited in stillness. Allowing a few minutes to pass, he slowly moved each of his limbs to test to see if anything was broken. A smile spread across his bearded face realizing he was still intact. Amidst the doubtful chances of survival, he knew Divinity was shining upon him. Even though everyone in Stone Hedge believed he was a traitor, he knew that Divinity saw his innocence.

He listened as soldiers skirted past him. He needed to find a place where he could be hidden. The clamour of warriors ceasing, he flipped onto his back.

Focus, he thought to himself. To delay would mean death.

Slowly, he turned his head to see if anyone were about who would spot him. All warriors were far away or distracted for the time being. It was likely his only chance. Slowly rising, he saw the bodies of the slain that surrounded him. Hundreds were scattered all around.

His countenance tightened. This wasn't the time to mourn. He could mourn once he fled the overthrown city.

In the distance, away from the warriors, he saw an alleyway between buildings. It would be the perfect place to shield him from the eyes of those who had embraced the Shadow. Quickly, he hurdled around the bodies. Crouching as low as he could, he ran.

The shadow of the alley draping over him, he exhaled in relief. His body felt worn and tired, but he needed to move onward. Looking through the alleyway and into the distance, he saw where he needed to run; the Mountains of D'aal. He could keep hidden there.

"Hey, you!" an abrupt voice echoed between the buildings.

Glaric, not even looking behind him to see from whom the voice came, bolted deeper into the alley. He knew if he were caught, he wouldn't even have the shallow privilege of being a prisoner again. He would be slain on sight.

Hearing men shouting from behind him, he pumped his legs as hard as he could, but he was weak from malnourishment. Before him, the straightway of the alley was cut short by a building made of brick. The alley turned either right or left. What direction he turned could very well determine his fate. Nearing the building, he quickly turned left.

Upon turning the corner, Glaric saw a man standing before him. Before he could slow himself, he crashed into him, hitting the oversized man like slamming into a secure wall. Before he could even process what was taking place, he was on his back panting. He looked up to see a man wearing silver armour with a pale blue cape that traced down his back.

Glaric gulped.

"Well, well. What do we have here?" the Dark Bishop asked with a violent sneer upon his face.

"Uh, I'm, uh…" Glaric stammered.

The Dark Bishop reached behind Glaric's neck, pulling him to his feet. "Come with me. The Sovereign of Shadow wanted no escapees, and we aren't making an exception for you."

The Bishop pulled him out of the alley, back into the light of day. Mounds of warriors scurried about the cobblestone streets of Stone Hedge.

"Attention!" the Bishop demanded.

Warriors throughout the streets of Stone Hedge stopped whatever it was they were doing, looking over to their superior.

"I don't know how, but some of you let this civilian slip past. Don't let it happen again!" The Bishop looked to Glaric. The scrawny man trembled under the gaze of the man.

The Bishop unsheathed his sword. "Now, let's show this man what happens to those who try to escape the hand of the Sovereign of Shadow!"

Warriors cheered in a cry for blood.

The Blade's sword raised into the air. Glaric looked to the skies one last time; skies that were dirtied by the filth of the Kreel. Even beyond the beasts, the sky looked different; dimmer than he remembered it once being.

Just then, he saw a black spot in the distance. This mark differed from the Kreel that soared. Whatever it was, wasn't casually flying; it flew with purpose.

It was coming towards Stone Hedge.

"Look!" Glaric said, pointing into the sky.

The Bishop stopped, mid-swing at the odd reaction, looking to the skies.

The creature drawing closer, the Dark Bishop's grip on him loosened. Glaric took a step back. He thought the Kreel were dreadful; however, this beast was monstrous. Its size was nearly unfathomable. The dragon's wings were jagged, like chiseled stone; it's tail thick like the trunks of several trees bound together. The dragon thrashed about in open air. Kreel darted about, fearing the beast. Glaric watched as the dragon snatched Kreel right out from the sky, devouring them in a single bite.

Warriors began running, trying to find shelter from the creature; however, Glaric knew there was no place one could hide from such a beast. As it opened its mighty maw, the dragon drew closer to Stone Hedge. From within the creature's mouth, he saw a spark which ignited into flames. Fire tumbled throughout its reptilian jaws.

Glaric's eyes glazed over in tears. All that could escape his mouth was a whisper. "Great Divinity, no…"

All watched as fire began blazing through the skies of Agadin. Glaric knew it was coming to devour Stone Hedge. The grand city would be no more.

Marradus had arrived.

Chapter Sixteen
Smoke and Rubble

"Insecurity is a fascinating concept to me. It can shape both the passive and the arrogant. It can mould the downtrodden and the proud. It cages individuals in fear and anxiety. It limits them. The only way insecurity can be dethroned from a heart is when true confidence takes shape. Confidence matures an individual from a flapping leaf, to a mighty oak: unshakable by even the strongest of winds. Once confidence is forged, limitations cease to exist. Confidence is a door to the extraordinary; a gateway to the remarkable."

- Dolan Thain
Heart of the Brave

Kaldon closed the book of wisdom, tucking it back into his cloak. It was brimmed with many of Dolan's musings and teachings. With each step he took, he allowed quotes from his father to sink into his understanding. He meditated on them, attempting to memorize the proverbs. He did this not only to encourage himself on the journey, but because the book was the only thing he had to remind him of Anneya. He reached up, rubbing his chest, feeling nothing but his flesh beneath. Usually he felt his metallic pendent pressing into his skin, but his Legacy was far away; kept safe by the woman who held his heart.

As wise sayings flowed through his mind, he wrinkled his nose again at the potent smell filling the air. The farther he travelled from the Mountains of D'aal, the more the smoky scent increased. Flames were raging somewhere; he just didn't know what could create such a putrid smell.

His eyes roamed the land which grew hillier with each step he took. Trees were beginning to thin, leaving vacant space for grass and shrubbery. The air was filled with more substance in contrast to the hollow mountainous air. Seeing an ensemble of towering trees ahead, he knew they were a natural barrier establishing an end to mountain territory. He didn't know how far Agadin stretched before him; however, obligation pressed him onward into the unknown.

Watching the nearing barrier of trees, he did what he often did to pass time. He allowed the vision he'd had at the Peak of Lore to wash through his memories. It was a vision that completely changed his course of direction, rendering him alone. He didn't allow his mind to dwell on the tower of Gorath; instead, he thought of the ocean. The mighty body of water moved him. The waves crashing through his memory inspired him, affirming his quest to the Sovereign's hometown. As blue azure soothed him, the words he heard booming through his vision circled through his mind.

"The Roek must rise. The Seer will fall. The Paladin needs to obtain the impenetrable shield. The Paragon must soar."

Even though he didn't know what it meant, the words stirred his soul. He knew everything was connected somehow; the prophecy, the ocean, the smoky scent…

Nearing the group of towering trees, his nose became more agitated by the distinct aroma. The odor was growing to be overwhelming. With his eyes glued upon the barrier of trees, he watched as branches began trembling. He curiously watched the disturbance, as nearly two dozen trees shook. From the barrier, thousands of small birds bolted out from trees, soaring past him.

Kaldon jumped at the sudden change. He watched the panicky birds flustering around him, like a grey cloud quickly darting through the air. Several foxes and vermin scurried from the barrier. Each ran in his direction from whatever dwelled on the other side of the trees.

"What is going on?" he whispered, knowing that the animals were clearly fleeing from something.

Then he heard it. Through the quiet of the day, shrill screeches pierced through silence, filling his ears. He sighed heavily at the sound, realizing what the animals were running from.

They were being chased by Kreel.

Kaldon unsheathed *Humility* and *Integrity*, one in each hand, he kept his gaze upon the treed barrier. The ring of steel sung throughout the hilly land. As the shrieks amplified, he could hear that there were multiple Kreel coming his way. He braced himself for what would inevitably come.

Twenty Kreel emerged from the barrier. Darting through the air, they wailed into the daylight. Holding his swords forward, Kaldon knew his foresight was a formidable ability, yet doubted it could protect him from so many of the creatures.

The Kreel nearing him, he held his breath. As the rotting smell stung his nose, the shrieks caused his head to ache. He lifted his swords, preparing for a fight that he knew could very well cost his life.

The first Kreel nearing him, Kaldon readied himself to swing his swords; however, as it reached his vicinity it flew right over him. He stopped, eyeing each of the beasts. One by one, they ignored him, flying around him like the fleeting birds. He listened to the distinct tone in their cries, as understanding swept over him. They weren't hunting. They were running from something just as the other animals were.

A question dawned on him. *What would Kreel run from?*

The scent of flames stinging his nose, his eyes widened. "No..."

He began picking up his pace, running in the direction from where the Kreel were fleeing. As he passed the line of towering trees, he watched as smoke ascended into the dreary skies. Amidst the lush land, he saw a grand city in the distance. Upon seeing it, he knew the identity of the city even though it had fallen to mounds of rubble. It was engulfed in flames, smoke, and ash. It now resembled a cemetery rather than the renowned city, Stone Hedge.

Looking at the fallen city, he heard cries ascending to the skies. The chaos hadn't yet stopped; suffering hadn't settled. As flames touched the air in writhing licks, Kaldon knew what was behind Stone Hedge's demise. As a roar echoed from the broken city, he felt it rumbling throughout his core. It was like nothing he had ever heard.

Before even realizing it, he was in a full-on sprint toward what was left of Stone Hedge. As smoke assaulted his lungs, he coughed violently as he ran. Stepping under the stone archway entrance of the city, he could feel the scraps of destroyed buildings and houses under his feet. Screams and cries surrounded him from every side.

A mother was crouched in a pile of rubble, weeping hysterically. She held her daughter in her arms, attempting to shield her from the death that surrounded them. Kaldon shook his head in shock. What chance did they have against such chaos? His mind blurred at the havoc. Scenario after scenario, he saw those who he knew would likely die. His stomach soured at the very thought.

Through the waves of smoke swooning through shattered buildings, it wasn't only civilians running in terror. Warriors from the Sovereign's army were not immune from such terrors. His breaths were becoming staggered; his lungs pumping to fight off the effects of the smoke.

His foresight flared within him; alarm wrenching through him. He looked around to pinpoint what his foresight might be warning him about. Then he saw it. A crack shot up a colossal building beside him.

The crack resounded in a snap. Kaldon looked to the foundation as the mother holding her daughter screamed in terror.

"Great Divinity…" he whispered, seeing that the woman and child would be crushed by the faltering building.

As stone began to fall, he ran at them, scooping up the child and grabbing the mother's hand, forcing her to move from where the building would land. He ran them to safety as the stone fortress crumbled to the ground. Upon impact, he felt the vibrations of the earth underneath him. He panted, placing the child in her mother's arms.

Looking into the young girl's tear-stained face, he ached that one so young needed to endure something so terrible. He spoke to the mother, his voice coming out as a raspy wheeze; the impact of the smoke startling him.

"You need to leave! Now!" he shouted, forcing the words out.

The mother spilled over in tears. "You don't understand, this is our home…" she said through hysterical weeping.

Kaldon cut her off. "It's either you leave, or both you and your daughter will die."

The mother summoned her composure. She looked into his eyes, nodding her agreement. Lifting her daughter, she fled to find the city's exit. Watching the mother running to save her daughter's life, he felt his body already throbbing. He brushed the warm debris from his cloak. He wished he could go with them to ensure their security; however, he needed to burrow deeper into the fallen city.

The deeper he went into the remnants of Stone Hedge, the more manic people were. He found himself in an open courtyard. From the looks of it, it was once a market. Business carts were scattered everywhere, proving it was a place where folk once shopped and socialized. Those who served the Sovereign of Shadow had swords drawn, cutting down civilians, trying to navigate their way out from the turmoil. Through the haze of smoke, Kaldon saw the rage that lingered in the eyes of those who followed the Sovereign of Shadow.

As his sight bounced around, he saw four Dark Blades eyeing him. His anger stirred, not having time for distractions. He wanted to find the source of the mayhem. From the look in the eyes of the four Blades, he knew they were intent on his blood being spilled. Kaldon unsheathed *Humility*.

Taking in the four, his foresight began to guide him. Subtle visions whispered throughout his mind, betraying their now predictable attacks. He smiled, knowing he had already seen the end of the fight before it even began.

Without delay, he bolted towards the four. Jumping into the air, he drove *Humility* down with staggering force. Following what his foresight revealed, he targeted one of the Blades, aiming for the area of defence he knew would be left unguarded. *Humility* cut in. As he landed, the first Blade slammed to the ground, no life left in him. The remaining three didn't hesitate to come in.

Kaldon ducked, avoiding the swing of an attack. Lingering low, he used *Humility* to slice one of the other Blade's legs. The man cried out as he dropped to the ground. As another came in at him, he took the defence, blocking potential blows. With a

Blade on each side of him, he used *Humility*, spinning about to block each attack.

Then the moment came. As he spun around an attack, he used his other hand to unsheathe *Integrity*. *Humility* and *Integrity* twisted and jabbed like a wild wind, cutting down the foes.

Kaldon paused as the final two Dark Blades hit the rubble floor.

He breathed in the victory. He knew there were enough of the Sovereign's warriors throughout the fallen city to fight endlessly; but attempting to kill the swarms of warriors would do little good. Afterall, he wasn't here to fight warriors; he needed to find a dragon.

Looking down at the fallen Blades, he heard a roar.

CHAPTER SEVENTEEN

THE MEETING

Through the ascending cries from the broken city, a bone-chilling roar pierced the air of the crowded streets. Marradus leapt into the air through stale smoke. Its wings held it in place above the fallen city. At the sight of the onyx creature, Kaldon stepped back, realizing that Dawntan Forlorn's writings didn't do the creature justice. It was a monstrosity. With its extended wings, he couldn't fathom its size. He stood marveling at the surreal creature.

As Marradus' head writhed back and forth deciding where to focus its attention, its reptilian eyes took in the only person who wasn't running in panicked fear.

It saw Kaldon Thain.

He watched the raging dragon focus in on him. Even though fear rattled through him, he chose to stand, unmoving. Marradus tucked in its reptilian wings, allowing itself to drop to the ground. Landing on its four claws, Kaldon felt the quake beneath him. With unfathomable speed, the serpent-like dragon crawled towards him. Reaching him, the demon dragon stopped.

Kaldon and Marradus regarded one another. Taking in the most horrifying beast he had ever seen, he knew that in one movement the dragon could end his life. One breath of flames could incinerate him into nothingness.

Looking into the reptilian eyes, what he least expected began to occur. Echoing swells flared within his mind. At first, he thought it was a spark of his foresight; yet as he saw the dragon's pensive stare, he knew better. Marradus was communicating with him. The dragon's voice screamed throughout his mind.

"Are you so arrogant, not to fear me?"

Despite the scorn of dread inside him, Kaldon spoke through the tension. "I don't fear you," he lied.

Marradus swung its colossal tail, striking a nearby building. He watched as stone cracked at the blow, causing rock to rain from the sky. Chips and debris filled the air as the building crashed to the ground.

"And who are you?" the slithering voice asked, booming into Kaldon's core.

Marradus, brought its head closer to him. As the dragon's long neck arched around Kaldon, he turned in circles, keeping his eyes on the creature.

He swallowed, forcing himself to rise into confidence. "I am Kaldon Thain; Paragon of Agadin," he answered, the title feeling foreign rolling off his tongue.

The dragon's lips curled up into a sneer. *"I don't care what title you bare. There isn't a warrior alive who could dethrone me from Agadin. There isn't an individual alive who can best me. Even the Sovereign of Shadow is reduced to nothing before me."*

The dragon's voice hissed through his mind.

At Marradus' declaration, the dragon stomped down upon the city floor, causing structures to creek and crack. Kaldon took a step back. He reached behind his back, summoning *Integrity* from its scabbard. He held forth the sword that was forged by the very scales of Marradus. The golden blade held the very essence of the Kingdom of Light. As it pointed at the dragon, it was like a shining star amongst death.

At the sight of the blade Marradus let out a haughty roar. *"Am I so mighty that you crafted weapons from my remains?"*

Before he could respond, Marradus opened his deadly mouth, arching its head back. He watched as flames began tumbling over its ivory teeth. Holding forth *Integrity*, he knew he had authority over the flames that the dragon conjured. He hoped his ability to Command Creation would cooperate. He had controlled fire in the past; more than ever, he needed to again.

As fires raged towards him, he shouted, speaking to the flames.

"Fire, you will not harm me!"

The flames roared at Kaldon.

"You will stop, now!" he commanded.

Seeing that the flames weren't ceasing, he grunted in frustration. Diving out of the way, he landed upon the rubble floor as fire sailed over him. Feeling heat upon his back, he writhed, scrambling to escape its bite.

"You cannot escape me! No one can!" Marradus' voice taunted, pressing into Kaldon's mind.

He rushed to the creature, vowing that *Integrity* would touch the dragon's onyx scales. With all his strength, he drove in with the golden blade. *Integrity* met the onyx scales with a clash. The sword awkwardly bounced off Marradus' scales. Regaining his composure, again and again he slashed at the dragon, yet the scales were never marred or scratched.

Marradus, swung its head around, barring its man-sized teeth. Kaldon dove out of the way again, hearing the dragon's jaw snap closed in its attempt to devour him.

Frantically trying to keep hidden from the massive creature, he looked at *Integrity,* frustrated that the sword was completely useless against the ancient dragon. The smoke was growing thicker, making his head spin. He was growing dizzy as Marradus grew more aggressive. If the dragon didn't kill him, the fumes of smoke certainly would. Fighting blacking out, he knew he didn't stand a chance against the dragon under such conditions. He searched for a place of fortitude to hide away.

His eyes found an open sewer hole down the street. He knew if the dragon saw him jump down, all it would need to do was breath a blaze of fire down after him to end his life. Seeing an old cart beside the manhole, he saw his one chance at escape.

Racing to the cart, he tried to draw the attention of the dragon. Stopping before the cart, he faced Marradus. Agitation grew on the creature's face, releasing flames of fire towards him. As tumbling reds and yellows neared him, he ducked behind the cart as it became submerged in flames. As thick smoke began ascending from it, he knew it was his opportunity to escape.

Kaldon felt the sting of heat. Looking down, he cried out as he watched fire dancing up his arm.

Shawled by thick flames and smoke, he knelt into the manhole, leaving the surface. His arm scorched by flames, he panted in agony. Looking to his forearm, he saw that some of his flesh was eaten away. His strength giving out, he laid down on the stone floor in the sewers. His arm felt like knives were stabbing his flesh over and over. He fought letting out moans of pain. He didn't know if Marradus knew of his whereabouts. If it did, he knew he wouldn't be alive much longer. He needed to remain quiet.

Laying his back in the filth, Kaldon looked up through the manhole into the thick skies. His entire body ached; his arm was in agony. He listened as cries began to ascend. Marradus was breathing its wrath, stealing lives.

Many of its victims were the Sovereign's warriors; however, many were not. Civilians who were dominated by the Sovereign's army were woven throughout the fallen city. Yet, Kaldon knew there was nothing he could do. He cursed himself for failing.

As he fought losing consciousness, he heard the mayhem from above slowly quieting. All that meant was that there likely weren't any more lives for the dragon to steal. All of a sudden, he heard a loud jolt, feeling it shake the ground floor. He knew it could have only been one thing; Marradus was finished. Everyone was either dead or too well hidden for the dragon to find them. As he looked out the manhole, in the distance he saw Marradus soaring over a city that was no more.

At the sight of the demon dragon in the sky, tears came to Kaldon's eyes. He remembered the first time he saw the legendary Owl soaring throughout Agadin's skies back in Rundle. The eternal bird of fire inspired him, invoking hope. He laid in a sewer then; he laid in a sewer now. The difference was that hope no longer reigned in Agadin; the skies were now dominated by death.

His eyes slowly closing, he listened to the silence in hope of hearing even a single whimper, yet nothing came. Homes were broken. Families were lost. Thousands were killed. They were all victims of the horrid beast.

Chapter Eighteen

The River of Time

With each step, Locrian felt the plush grass beneath his feet. Pressing his metal staff into the ground, he walked throughout the bright grasslands. The sun smiled upon him as he was taken in by the perfect weather. It was neither too hot, nor too cold — it was perfect — timeless. As a violet butterfly fluttered past him, the Seer appreciated its casual flight as it flitted through the wondrous world. Crickets chirped, their songs echoing over hills. Trees swayed in perfect rhythm. Each boulder and rock seemed to be placed both purposefully and perfectly. It was a paradise.

Even though peace engulfed him, he could still hear the subtle pounding in his mind. Sounding far off, water crashed through his consciousness. He dug his staff into the ground, pausing at the realization. He was lost in another vision; misplaced yet again in the River of Time.

Taking in the paradise around him, he reminded himself it wasn't real. It was a mirage. As time went by, he found it harder and harder to remind himself of that. In reality, he knew he was sitting in the hidden room at the Peak of Lore, imprisoned within the confines of Ceanne Brimnas' trap.

Looking over the flawless land, he watched as three more butterflies bearing an array of colours danced through the air past him.

"This isn't all too bad though, is it?" the Seer whispered, holding a relaxed smile upon his face.

He stopped, catching himself. "Locrian! That's insanity speaking," he reprimanded himself.

His mind was fleeting away, being stolen by the River of Time. Listening to the river rushing throughout his consciousness, he remembered the rigorous training he'd endured since childhood. As a Seer, he'd dedicated his entire life to learning how to wield his gift. Now, that gift was his prison. It had turned against him, making him its victim; forcing him to endure the torturous descent into madness.

Watching the swaying trees in his vision, he understood he wasn't too far gone yet. It would likely only be a matter of time before he awoke from the vision. The illusion would fade away, as it had in times prior. He cast his eyes up at the blue canvas of the sky. Beyond the clouds, he watched images take shape, like paintings being created in the air. He was thankful at the very least that he could use his gift to watch what was taking place from eternity's perspective.

Visions spawning over the day-lit sky, Locrian took in the sight. He saw Tolek marching with his army through grassy terrain. The group of warriors was fewer in numbers than when they first left the Peak of Lore. Taking a closer look at the vision in the sky, he saw that two Knights carried Anneya on a linen stretcher. The Blade's eyes were shut. Her chest was shielded in armour, preventing Locrian from seeing whether she was breathing or not. He knew very well they could have been carrying her simply because she was injured or unable to walk.

For all he knew, they could also have been ushering her to her grave.

The Seer felt emotion rising at the sight of seeing the stubborn Blade laying so still. Considering that Ceanne was nowhere to be seen amongst the crowd, he knew what had taken place. He didn't need to see a vision to know why the Blade laid prostrate. The queen was no doubt to blame. He wished he'd had the chance to warn Tolek before he was captured.

The vision in the sky began shifting, changing its tone. Locrain clenched his fist, wanting to know if Anneya was alive. She needed to be. He ripped his eyes from the vision in the sky, loathing the fact that he couldn't always control what he saw.

As the vision took on a new form, he was drawn in again. Deeper discouragement set in as he saw Marradus storming through the skies of Agadin. The demon dragon killed mercilessly, devouring whatever it saw. It raged throughout the land. From amidst Marradus' imposed ruin, a face then began materializing in the vision. The Seer saw the child-like face; he knew exactly who it was. Tymas Droll shouted to armies, commanding them to demolish cities; to kill innocents. His armies ravaged the land, stealing lives, dethroning kings, and queens. He manipulated the helpless to embrace the Shadow.

The Sovereign's sinister smirk pressed into Locrian's core. With a shout, the Seer hurled his metal staff as far as he could throw it. Agadin was falling.

The vision taking on a final form, the Seer dropped to his knees. His demeanour faltered at the sight. He saw Kaldon laying in a damp sewer, unconscious. Tears tumbled down Locrian's face as he saw the young man with a scorched arm. Ash and soot covered him, shawling him in defeat.

The Seer's voice trembled as he wept. Considering the number of prophecies he spoke, it was rare for him to remember a particular one. The first prophecy he'd spoken about Kaldon was cemented in his mind.

"You were created for more than the depths of the sewers. One day you will soar with the stars. One day you will be someone great."

"Oh Kaldon, don't forget who you are," the Seer pleaded.

Disrupting his sorrows, Locrian watched as the vision evaporated from the sky. He sighed, allowing his sight to drop. Looking upon the grass, his face churned as he saw the emerald green fading. Through the veil of his tears, he watched as colour washed away from the trees and sky. Crickets no longer chirped, and butterflies no longer fluttered. The vision was coming to its end.

Locrian gasped, the world of vision felled from his eyes. With tears streaking his face, he looked around frantically, no longer seeing the paradise land. All he saw was the isolated room and the locked door. Coming from the elaborate world of visions, the small room felt suffocating. With his back pressed against the cold wall, he thought on how he was beginning to prefer fantasy, rather than his current surroundings.

Maybe insanity is a gift, meant to free me from the cruelty of what is taking place in Agadin, he mused, staring at the wall before him.

With nothing to do but gaze forward, he waited for another vision that would inevitably take him. He waited for what felt like hours. The visions had become more frequent with time. He knew if he stayed in that room for much longer, there would be a moment when he would no longer be able to return to reality. He would be lost in the River of Time. He may have been too far gone already. No one in history had ever escaped the *Fall of a Seer.* Why would he be any different?

At that thought, a declaration from Kaldon's vision ran through his mind. The words terrified him.

Into the hollow room, he muttered the cryptic words. *"The Seer will fall."* He looked forward. "And, indeed, I am."

Images passed before his sight. Another vision was already pulling him in.

Chapter Nineteen

Dragon Fire

Pain shooting through his arm, his eyes snapped open. Letting out a cry, sweat dripped down his bare chest. His arm rested beneath his blanket, hiding the wound. Agony coursed through his arm like lava erupting from a volcano.

"Easy there. You need to rest," a woman said, placing a hand on his naked shoulder to still his nerves.

Kaldon realized he was no longer on the sewer floor in Stone Hedge; instead, he was laying upon a soft bed in a generous sized room. He looked up to the woman who was leaning over him. She seemed only slightly older than him, bronze-coloured hair tumbling over her shoulders in subtle curls. Several other women of different ages scurried in and out of the white room, performing different tasks and duties. Each wore identical beige robes hanging loosely from their bodies. The robes stretched downward, nearly touching the floor as they scurried about.

Feeling the woman's hand still resting upon his skin, he shifted his weight, forcing her hand to move.

"Where am I?" he asked, fighting off his disorientated state.

The woman brushed her hand against her robes, smoothing them. "We found you in Stone Hedge. You had nearly no life left in you," she said. "We are in a small town called *Gilead* not far from where the dragon attacked."

Kaldon closed his eyes. He remembered the devastating silence that had filled Stone Hedge. The memory almost hurt more than the raging burn storming across the skin of his arm.

"Don't be sad," the woman said in a smooth voice, seeing his expression. "You're safe now, here with us. We will protect you from the terrors of Shadow."

He brought up his hand that was free from the pain of burns. He rubbed his finger and thumb over his eyes, trying to brush away the blur in his sight. He didn't care about being safe; he wanted the fallen to live again. Shifting on top of the bed, he felt uncomfortable without his cloak and shirt. Then he noticed it: the absence. He stiffened in alarm. The familiar weight that he normally felt against his body was missing. He was used to feeling the rectangle object pressing against his chest; now it was gone. At the void weight, his eyes scrambled throughout the small room in search.

"Are you looking for this?" With a smile, the woman pulled forth the book. "Don't worry. We have everything you had with you here, including your swords."

He saw *Humility* and *Integrity* resting upon a nearby table. He looked at the book. As the words, *Heart of the Brave,* beamed at him from the rough leather, he sighed in relief.

"Yes, thank you," he said reaching for it, grateful to have it in his hands again.

She wore a smooth smile. "You seem to care a great deal about that book. What's so special about it?"

He pulled the book closer to him. "It was given to me by someone who is very important to me."

He could feel the woman's smile radiating on him, clearly thankful that she was the one who got to return his prized possession to him.

He looked up to the woman. "Who are you?"

The woman looked away, her cheeks blossoming in a rose-red hue. "I'm sorry, where are my manners? My name is Joy. I'm a Matron of Gilead."

He nodded, as the blur in his eyes slowly lifted. He found himself thinking more clearly. "A Matron of Gilead?" he asked.

Joy grinned. "Gilead is a town of healers. We have hundreds of healers here, all varying in skill and ability. *Matron* is another term for *Master Healer.* I am one of many here."

For the first time, he noticed that his throat didn't feel as hoarse as it did while being in Stone Hedge. His breathing felt clear. "Did you heal me?" he asked.

Joy twisted her face. "Well… partially. I used my ability to remove the smoke from your lungs. Smoke from a dragon's fire is toxic. If we hadn't gotten rid of it, we wouldn't be having this conversation right now. Your arm, however, is another story."

"Thank you for saving my life," he said distantly, trying to process the fact that he came so close to death so early into his journey.

The bite of fire still rivered up and down his arm. As he tried to pull off the sheet to see the wound, Joy reached down, placing her hand on his bare shoulder again. She pressed him against the bed. He flinched under her soft touch.

Brenton always told him that he knew nothing about women; however, Joy was seeming more interested in him than he would have preferred. There was no doubt she was attractive. Any man would be proud to be seen with her; but she had one glaring flaw he could never overlook. She wasn't Anneya.

"I still don't know your name," Joy said in a bubbly tone.

He sighed, reluctant to share too much. "My name is Kaldon," he said in short.

When his response was met with silence, he looked up, seeing her face paled to stark-white. The other women stopped their work, staring at him.

"What's wrong?" he asked, his gaze looking from face to face.

"You're him… You're the one who killed the Dark Paladin?" she whispered.

"Excuse me?" Kaldon stuttered. Surely word about him hadn't travelled this far past the Peak of Lore.

Joy continued, her mouth agape. "You are Kaldon Thain, the one destined to be the hope of Agadin…"

"The hope of Agadin?" he asked.

She wrapped her hands over his unscathed knuckles. "Oh, yes. People throughout Gilead have been talking about you; that you have come to rescue Agadin from Shadow. Yet, here you are, in Gilead. I give you my word that I will personally take care of you until you are in good health again."

As Joy's vibrant eyes glowed at him, Kaldon nearly laughed aloud at the claim. Wounded arm or not, he didn't have time to sit around being pampered.

"Thank you for your, help, but I need to leave," he said.

He grabbed the blanket, pulling it off his arm.

"Kaldon, no!" Joy protested.

As the blanket was pulled back, he saw that his arm was blistering in red; gnarled, by dragon's fire. It looked far worse than when he was in Stone Hedge, as though his flesh was being eaten away. His stomach twisted at the grotesque sight.

She pulled the blanket over his arm again. "I may have been able to vacate the smoke from your chest, but your burn is something beyond my skill to heal," she said with empathy in her tone. "You can't leave. You need to rest. Over time, we may be able to restore your arm to some degree, but it will take time."

His head spun as he fought blacking out from the sight of his arm. "I don't have the luxury of time. A Master Healer can't heal burns?" he asked, his frustration evident.

Joy shook her head. "A Master Healer can heal burns, but a burn from dragon's fire is another thing entirely. I've read historical books about when dragons once roamed Agadin. Their fire is nothing ordinary. The hottest and most deadly flames are conjured from within a dragon. It doesn't only lick flesh, it burrows straight to the core of where the burn took place. Even when the flames are put out, the burn continues to eat away at the flesh; this is why your arm looks worse than when you were first inflicted. In fact, there's a good chance it will still get worse yet."

Stretching his fingers out, he felt the burn deep within his arm. He could feel it in his bones. He had never felt anything like it.

"When will the pain stop?" he asked.

Joy bit her bottom lip. "I've read that the pain inflicted by a dragon's flames could last years."

"Years…" he muttered without realizing. He couldn't imagine enduring such pain for such a long and extended period. He would be nearly useless, unable to even lift a sword.

She shifted uncomfortably. "We can take care of you until you are fully recovered. We have had many needing extended stays until they were fully well," the Matron said in a light tone, trying to infuse optimism into him. "It will be my honour to take care of you, Kaldon Thain."

He looked at her blankly. "I can't sit around waiting for this to stop. I need to leave, immediately. Surely, there must be someone here who can heal my arm."

Joy's forehead creased, irritation wrinkling into her brow. "Now, now, Kaldon: there isn't anything we can do. Only the *Head-Matron*, would potentially have the ability to perform a healing so intricate. She is our leader; one marked by divine wisdom. She is by far the most skilled healer among us in Gilead. In fact, many wonder if she will one day rise to become a Shan-Rafa," she said with reverence in her tone. "However, we of course have no way of knowing that for sure."

Kaldon nodded his head. "Then I need to see this *Head-Matron*. I don't have time to sit around while Agadin falls apart."

At his words, he saw the three women running errands cringe at his remark. Joy's eyes went wide. "No one sees the Head-Matron unless they are summoned by her. We may put in a request for you to see her, but it would likely be months before she even hears such a request."

He looked from face to face, bewildered. "You can't expect me to sit here helpless when you all have the means to aid me. You said it yourself; you believe I am the hope of Agadin. I can't help if I'm confined to this bed for the next several years waiting for a burn to heal."

Joy cleared her throat. "I understand you are frustrated, but the rules are…"

"I don't care what your rules are," he said, cutting her off. "I need to see your Head-Matron. Now."

He rose from the bed, grabbing his shirt and cloak. The women looked at him, baffled that he was blatantly rebelling against their rules. He winced, pulling his traveling shirt over his arm, feeling the rough fabric brush against his blisters and gashes. Using his good arm, he sheathed his swords.

"Kaldon, no one sees the Head-Matron unless she chooses," Joy said, her hands shaking as she slowly approached him.

He looked deep into her, his gaze stopping her in mid-step. "You have no way of stopping me."

He strode out of the room.

Walking the length of the hallways and past countless rooms, there didn't seem to be anything glamorous about the building. The walls, clearly painted white years ago, were now yellowing from time. Exiting the building, he felt the paling sun graze over his skin, Dominion cloaking the skies. The town of Gilead seemed as undressed as the building he just left; each structure devoid of colour. Surrounding the town were several outcrops of rock and greenery, hiding the small town from sight. Healers of all sorts made their way through pebbled streets. Every man and woman who he passed wore the same beige robes, striding along roads with seemingly no worry or concern. Considering he just witnessed a grand city being destroyed, the sight of their apathy made him boil.

His eyes scaling a pathway, he saw a simple building that sat upon a grassy hill. Other than a few characteristics, this building looked similar to others spread out through Gilead. Red trim was painted over the door posts with words written in them. He recognized the language, being *Old Agadin*. What made this building differ most from the others were the two guards who stood on each side of the entryway. Seeing they were dressed as everyone else was, he knew they weren't common guards; likely stationed for show, rather than function. He watched the peaceful expressions sprawled over each of the guard's faces. He knew that the building must be a place of importance.

Kaldon made his way to the path. With each step he took, his arm throbbed. Pain writhed through him. Determined, he didn't slow his pace as he neared the building. The calm demeanour of the two guards evaporated at the sight of him.

"I am here to see the Head-Matron," Kaldon said directly, hoping it was in fact the right place.

The two men eyed him nervously, clearly not accustomed to conflict. One of the men looked at his arm, seeing the sleeve of his shirt marked in blood that was seeping through.

"You mustn't be thinking clearly with a wound like that," he said. "You best go and rest until someone can tend to you. No one sees the Head-Matron without first being summoned by her."

"No," he replied. "I need the help of your Head-Matron, and I won't leave until I have it."

The guards flinched at his stubborn directness. As he eyed them, something odd stuck out to him about the guards; they were weaponless.

"Where are your swords?" he asked.

The other guard spoke up, his eyes lingering upon the swords strapped to Kaldon's hip and back. "Here in Gilead, we don't believe in using weapons. We are here to bring peace and healing to Agadin; not war."

"Good luck dethroning Shadow with nothing but your hands. Passivity will get you nowhere against the Dominion of Shadow," he said, his remark surprising even himself.

He could feel the men wilting under his scowl. The more confident man spoke again. "Nonetheless, you cannot see the Head-Matron. The *wise one* cannot be approached whenever someone pleases. There are rules here that everyone must abide by. I don't know who you are, but that includes you."

Kaldon hoped it wouldn't come to this. He could tell they were good-hearted people, yet they didn't understand the greater battle taking place around them. They didn't understand that it was of dire importance that his journey continued. If he didn't get the healing he needed, he would either need to stay in Gilead until he was better or leave marred ineffective by the dragon's flames. Neither were an option for him. He knew he would never hurt anyone as harmless as those who stood before him; however, he knew he needed to convince the guards to let him move onward.

As quick as lightning, he brought his good hand up, pulling forth *Integrity*. The sword unsheathed with the sound of ringing steel. The metallic chiming was foreign in such a town. Its golden blade whirled throughout the air with surprising accuracy, halting before the guard's throat.

"My name is Kaldon Thain and I will see whoever I please. Step aside," he said in a snap, hoping the empty threat would be enough to disarm the guards.

Both guards' eyes went wide. He could tell by the expression on their faces that they had heard rumours of him, just as Joy had. Having no choice, both stepped aside, leaving the door unprotected. Neither were willing to stand their ground against a man who held the reputation of killing a Dark Paladin.

With his sword in hand, Kaldon reached out, twisting the doorknob. As the plain door swung open, he looked inside of the Head-Matron's abode. His gaze widened at the unexpected sight.

Similar in expression to the rest of Gilead, the room was barely adorned. On the wooden floor, feet clomped about as men and women in simple robes rushed about in duty. Many sorted through fabrics and filled out paperwork as several prattled on about matters of their small town. It felt hectic, other than one aspect. Upon the floor, in the middle of everyone was a young girl, barely ten years of age. Her ebony hair framed her young face. Her gaping eyes watched those who performed tasks around her. He knew the poor girl must have been utterly bored watching everyone executing their monotonous tasks.

Kaldon stepped into the room, disappointed that no one in the room looked as though they fit his vision of what he thought the Head-Matron would look like. All seemed to be servants and workers. At the sound of his heavy boots hitting the ground, several people stopped, their eyes resting upon him. One by one, each stilled, stunned by the fact that someone would dare enter the Head-Matron's abode. The young girl watched him curiously.

"I am here to see the Head-Matron of Gilead," Kaldon said, amplifying his voice. "Where is she?"

His voice echoing throughout the large room, whispers immediately broke out at the audacious request. The only one who didn't seem rattled by the unexpected interruption was the young girl who sat upon the floor.

She slowly rose from the ground, lifting a hand. At her motion, a hush was established in the room. Everyone quieted in wait. The girl's eyes were filled with innocence; her demeanour with purity.

In a gentle tone, she said, "I am the Head-Matron."

Chapter Twenty

Head-Matron

K aldon eyed the young girl. *"You're* the Head-Matron?"

"I am," she replied. Her delicate face was stoic in expression; unreadable.

A woman bearing streaks of grey in her hair stepped forward. Her fists tense in anger, she said, "The Head-Matron doesn't need to answer your questions!"

Kaldon could tell by the authority in her tone that she was likely an advisor of sorts to the Head-Matron. As the older woman interceded for the young girl, he watched the Head-Matron's eyes fall to the golden blade he carried.

"You are him, aren't you? The hero everyone is talking about," she asked in a meek tone, ignoring her advisor. Her eyes were filled with wonder.

"Yes," he answered, his tone softening. He knew a girl of her age should be outside playing with other children, not leading a town of healers; yet here she was. He felt for her — for how others imposed an adult role upon her. He sheathed the legendary blade.

"My name is Kaldon. What is your name?" he asked, a smile growing on his face.

Men and women began looking around at the question. The same advisor spoke up again. "You have no right to ask the Head-Matron her name!" she said in a growl.

The Head-Matron looked to the scowling advisor. "This man isn't a threat to us, Shandra. I believe he is a friend to Agadin. I can sense the purity in his heart." The girl turned to him, saying, "My name is Olivia."

Shandra quieted at the remark. Kaldon was surprised at how the girl conducted herself. He knew better than to belittle someone simply because they were unassuming; yet, gifted or not, she was still a child.

He stepped forward. "Olivia, I need your help. I've been told you are more skilled than even a Master Healer. I heard that you may even one day become a Shan-Rafa."

A childlike smile spread over her innocent face. "You've heard correctly. I am from a lineage of extraordinary healers. My gift showed itself much sooner than what is common. We believe in Gilead that whoever is strongest in the ability of healing is who Divinity has appointed to lead." Olivia looked over to her advisor. "Shandra held the position of Head-Matron until I recently came into leadership."

Looking towards the frowning advisor, Kaldon empathized with her angst. Once revered by everyone in Gilead, she was stripped of her authority by a prodigy child.

"I am on a dangerous mission; an important mission," he said to Olivia.

"And what mission would that be?" she asked.

He noticed that her advisors had trained her well to be diplomatic. He weighed his next words. "It has been revealed that Tymas Droll, the Sovereign of Shadow, is a Shan-Rafa. He is the most formidable healer in all of Agadin. I am currently journeying to Gorath to take his life."

Olivia's eyes grew wide. "A true Shan-Rafa... I thought they had all died out ages ago."

He didn't want to frighten the girl, yet he knew it would do little good to hide truth from her. "I assure you he is a proven Shan-Rafa. He has armies so grand in size that they are nearly unstoppable. Based on what I've seen of Gilead, you have great compassion for those in need; but you are ill-prepared for the war taking place. I would advise arming your healers with weapons."

Shandra took a step forward. "Weapons have been forbidden in Gilead for over a century. We are a people of peace. There will be no weapons here."

He ignored the former Head-Matron, keeping his gaze upon Olivia. "Shadow is rising throughout Agadin. Every one of us needs to take a stand against it. This includes you. Agadin needs Gilead to rise. Your people need to be prepared for what is coming."

Olivia's eyes began swelling with tears. Kaldon expected her to pool over in fear, yet she didn't.

The young girl said, "If Agadin needs our help, then we will summon the blacksmiths from neighbouring cities and towns. Weapons will be crafted for everyone who is capable of wielding one."

Shandra's face began reddening. "Head-Matron, you can't listen to this man's blasphemy! We play our role by offering healing and hope to those in need!" she said with a wave of a hand.

Olivia watched her calmly. "We will continue to offer healing. We will be a source of peace to Agadin. The Dominion of Shadow will be by no means timid, and neither shall I. As of today, tradition will bow to reason."

Before Shandra could object, the Head-Matron looked over to Kaldon, her serious tone demanding silence from those around her. "How do you plan on killing a Shan-Rafa?" she asked.

The words felt morbid coming from the mouth of one so young. He could feel Shandra's eyes burning into them, but they both ignored it. He found himself grinning. He was beginning to like this girl.

"Considering you may be one of the most skilled healers in all of Agadin, I was hoping you could tell me," he stated.

A smile curled onto the girl's face. "Legend tells us that Shan-Rafa's can heal as quickly as they are wounded."

He nodded, knowing the legend was true. He remembered Tymas Droll once healing himself right before his eyes.

The Head-Matron continued, "That being said, I doubt a sword could kill Tymas Droll. You would need to get creative."

"Creative? How so?" he asked, his face turning in thought.

"Think about it," she said. "Shan-Rafas are so skilled in healing that all they need is a split second to heal themselves. But what if you took that moment away from them? What if, say, one fell from a cliff? Upon impact, their life would be taken from them instantly. They wouldn't have time to heal themselves."

"I never thought of that before," he admitted, running his hand through his hair in thought.

"That's because you aren't a healer," Olivia let out a faint laugh. "If I do rise to become a Shan-Rafa, it is wise to be aware of the ways people may try to take my life."

Kaldon shook his head in wonder. "No offense, but you are much wiser than most would expect from someone your age."

"So, I'm told," the young girl beamed. "Now, how can I help you for your journey to Gorath?"

Pulling up his blood-stained sleeve, he grimaced as it scraped over his skin. "I've been burnt by dragon's fire. One of your Matrons told me it could be years until it is fully healed. Agadin may not have years. She said you may be able to help me."

Olivia slowly walked over to Kaldon, her eyes taking in the gnarled wound. Her small fingers glided over what looked like chewed up flesh.

"I've never seen a burn from dragon's fire…" she whispered.

Kaldon's hope sunk at her words.

As her hands danced over the marred flesh, she spoke. "I can feel the burn eating away at you; even in your bones, corrupting even the marrow. The Matron you spoke to was wrong about it healing in years." She looked up to Kaldon. "If this isn't healed immediately, then your arm will likely have to be amputated."

His eyes widened. "Can you heal it?" he asked, hardly able to believe the fate of his arm was in the hands of such a young girl.

"Maybe," she said, squinting her eyes as she examined the wound. "Let me try something."

Men and women surrounded them trying to get a glimpse of the healer at work.

Her hands began glowing with the radiance of the Kingdom of Light. He was surprised how effortlessly she summoned the eternal force. He could feel it tingling his flesh. It breezed over his skin like a cool touch.

The Head-Matron looked up to Kaldon with hesitance stricken upon her face. "This is likely going to feel odd. I need to manifest the Kingdom straight into the bones of your arm."

He nodded his head at her words, bracing himself. As her hands lit brighter, the familiar presence of perfect peace came, the force of paradise invading Agadin. Closing his eyes, he breathed-in, the distinct atmosphere engulfing him. Flawless utopia spilled over his arm and into his pores. It coursed through his veins; massaged his muscles. He felt the light growing brighter as the Kingdom punctured his bones with a *pop*. The sensation felt both awkward and wonderful. Radiant light shone in, caressing even marrow with its wondrous touch. Toxins evaporated from inside his body. Opening his eyes, he watched his gnarled arm begin reshaping, normalizing. Blisters subsided. Bleeding halted. Flesh stitched itself back together.

As the light began to still and settle, Kaldon held up his arm. What was once useless and marred was, for the most part restored; nearly perfect, other than a few components. A hue of crimson red stained his arm. He was marked with the colour of fire. Scars stretched over his forearm and hand, like bolts of lightning engraved into his skin.

Olivia sighed; perspiration matted upon her smooth forehead. "This is as good as I can do for you. I'm afraid dragon's fire is far too abrasive to be fully rid of. I'm hoping over time, the remaining pain will vanish."

Stretching out his hand, Kaldon felt the lingering after-bite of fire. The pain was nothing like before, yet still distinct enough to notice.

"This will do just fine," he muttered as his eyes traced his lightning bolt scars.

The young Head-Matron pulled his attention back to her. "Remember, not even a Master Healer can heal scars: Only a Shan-Rafa can. Scars are left behind as a reminder of what we've overcome."

He remembered Anneya telling him that very thing when he first asked about her teardrop scar. He pressed his lips together in thought as he stared at his new scars. He remembered why his arm was wounded. He remembered the lives that Marradus stole; those who he failed to save.

"These scars aren't a reminder of what I've overcome," he stated. "They are a reminder of what I failed to do. I will not make the same mistake again."

The room shifted under his weighty words. In the silence, he could feel the pull from the door behind him; the door leading him onwards to Gorath. He had been delayed for long enough.

"I will not forget what you have done for me," he said to Olivia. "If you are ever in need of my aid, find me and I will help you. Guard your wisdom, Head-Matron. Keep in the Light."

Turning to leave, he could feel Olivia beaming at him. The young Head-Matron watched him as he was about to embark again upon the dangerous journey.

As he stepped outside the door of the building, he heard her young voice ringing in his ears one last time.

"Even though Shadow rises, I trust that you will free us from the Shan-Rafa. Stay strong, hero of Agadin."

Chapter Twenty-One

New Weapon

———◆◆◆———

With a shout, the warrior swung his sword at the Sovereign of Shadow. Tymas Droll lifted his elongated sword upward, deflecting the slice. In his private training room, he poised himself for attack. Sweat dripping down his bare chest, five trained warriors surrounded him with swords in hand.

Tymas thrashed about, wielding the curved sword against the soldiers. He knew honing his skills for combat was necessary. Not only was the spar purposeful in refining how he wielded a blade, but it also gave him the opportunity to exercise his ability to heal. He ordered the men to come at him relentlessly.

Purposefully allowing the hit, Tymas felt one of the swords trace down his naked back. He watched his blood spray across the maple floor. Instantly, the wound stitched over with new flesh. Not allowing his pace to falter, he pressed in against one of the warriors. He knew his body glowed with the Kingdom of Light as the remnant left from his healed-over wound. He had allowed dozens of similar attacks to make their mark during the spar. In the last hour alone, he healed himself from countless life-threatening wounds.

Through the blur of ceaseless strikes, something caught Tymas' eye. Other than a chair and couch in one of the corners for quick rests between spars, the room was void of distractions. No one was to enter uninvited, and never was he to be disturbed during a session. He paused at the oddity of such a sight. A figure cloaked in black stood at the door's entrance. At first, anger was roused from within him at the thought of someone entering during his session without his approval. When he realized who the cloaked figure was, he let his sword drop to the side.

All five warriors looked around, confused until their eyes caught the ominous sight as well. Each warrior lowered their weapons.

"Furion," he whispered as his chest heaved in exhaustion.

The warriors looked over to the woman draped in black. Shadow drifted around the Entity. There was no doubt in Tymas' mind that the warriors had heard myths about Furion. As the woman's ice-coloured eyes took in everyone in the room, he realized he was holding his breath.

"All of you, leave," the Sovereign said with an exhale. The five scurried out without hesitation, thankful to leave the Entity's presence.

Furion's soft voice arose. "Hello, Tymas."

"How are you here right now?" he asked, trying not to allow his voice to quiver.

A subtle smile curled onto Furion's face. "You mean, how am I visiting you in the material realm?"

"Yes," he replied, not pulling his eyes from her. "You have only ever visited me in my dreams."

She drew closer to the Sovereign. "This was your doing, Tymas. You opened the Door of the Dominion. Its effects are blooming. While the door remains open, the Dominion of Shadow will continue to expand in Agadin."

He cringed at the thought. He longed to bring the Dominion of Shadow to Agadin; however, the thought of Furion being able to visit him whenever she pleased unnerved him.

Before he could respond, she spoke up. "Thank you for resurrecting my pet, Marradus."

The Sovereign lifted his chin, his face snaking into a frown. "Speaking of your pet, that reptile refuses to obey me," he said.

Furion raised a brow. "Obey you? Marradus was never meant to obey you."

His fist tightened over the hilt of his sword. He knew he couldn't allow his anger to swell against the Entity.

"I've spent years of my life working toward bringing that reptile back from the dead and it's completely useless to me," Tymas said, with the wave of a hand.

Furion eyed him. "Irrelevant. It is far from useless to me. It has torn apart entire cities throughout Agadin. It has already destroyed Edmont, Drant, Stone Hedge, and many more."

As the words left her mouth, Tymas felt his face beginning to heat. His voice trembled. "Stone Hedge! Stone Hedge was already under my power! Why would that creature destroy a city already devoted to me?!" Tymas hurled his sword to the floor.

As the sword clanged upon the wooden floor before her, the Entity snarled in anger at the outburst. He grimaced at her expression, feeling an unexpected pressure forced against his chest. The Sovereign grunted as he lifted from the ground, flying backwards, hitting the wooden wall with a *crack*. He heard his bones pop against the impact of the wall.

Pinned against the wall, he cringed as he hung with his feet lifted from the floor. His head spun as he summoned the Kingdom of Light. The Sovereign knew that anyone other than a Shan-Rafa would have died from such a violent impact. Light began glowing upon his skin, healing the numerous broken bones the hit had caused.

Furion stood before the trapped Sovereign. "You may be a Shan-Rafa, but I could kill you in a breath if I chose to," she said, snapping her finger. "This is the very reason I needed Marradus here. You are far too calculated, Tymas. You may be able to lead a movement throughout the land; however, Marradus could very well end Agadin. That is something you could never do. You play a part in my plan — but never forget — you are only part of it."

He felt her invisible grip leave him as he dropped to the ground. Laying on the wooden floor, he willed himself to pull in a breath. Everyone who knew he was a Shan-Rafa thought him invincible; but he knew what Furion said was true. She could end his life in a moment if she chose.

Furion turned, walking away from him. "I do, however, appreciate you. Even though you don't see the grand picture I am orchestrating. You have served me faithfully since you were a child. Because of that, I brought you a gift."

He looked up. "A gift?"

"Yes. I know you desired for Marradus to be your pawn, but I have different plans for my pet. Therefore, I brought you a new toy to use at your leisure."

He intentionally suppressed his once again rising anger at Furion's implications to his work being a game. "What is this *toy* you are referring to?"

Furion looked to the training room's door. "Mikiel, come join us," she said.

Tymas watched as a gangly-young man walked into the training room. In the garb of travelling clothes and a messy mop of hair, Mikiel stood with his shoulders slouched, looking at the two menacing tyrants before him.

"What is this *joke?*" the Sovereign said in a laugh, rising from the floor.

Furion ignored the sarcasm, not turning her gaze from the young man. "Mikiel here is from the Peak of Lore. He knew Kaldon Thain; the one you failed to kill, yet again. The one who killed Geran Rule."

He scowled at the mention of his fallen General. "So, what of it? Why is he here?"

She nodded her head to the young man. "Show the Sovereign what you can do. Show him what I taught you."

He watched as Mikiel eyed the leather chair tucked away in the corner. Stretching his arms awkwardly toward the old piece of furniture, a gentle whistle crept into the room. The whistle grew as a caress of wind coursed in. Tymas could feel the wind swooning over his flesh as it made its way to the chair. The chair was carried by the wind, twisting into the air, obeying the young man's silent command.

The moment his arms dropped, the chair gave way, rushing to the wooden floor. With a loud *clap,* the chair smashed upon the ground, rendering it cracked and dismantled.

Tymas could feel his heartbeat beginning to quicken at such a sight. "You brought me a Roek?" he asked, his gaze turning to Furion.

"A Dark Roek. Mikiel has embraced the Shadow," the Entity said, correcting her pupil.

He walked over to Mikiel, looking him up and down. "You have quite the ability."

"Thank you," Mikiel said, anxiously fidgeting with the sleeve of his traveling clothes.

"Excuse me?" the Sovereign said, his gaze piercing into Mikiel. "When you address me, you will call me, Sovereign of Shadow. You haven't earned the right to excuse my title."

Mikiel gulped. "Yes, Sovereign of Shadow."

"That is more like it," Tymas said to the young man. "Tell me, Dark Roek, can you command the wind whenever you choose?"

Without responding, Mikiel looked back to the chair that he once lifted into the air with the wind. Reaching out a hand, wind swirled into the room again, engulfing the chair; however, this time, the wind did not lift it. Instead, it entered its cracks and crevices. A low whistle filled the room as the wind expanded within the old piece of furniture. Within seconds, the chair exploded; splinters and fabrics wafting throughout the room.

The Sovereign laughed heartily in amusement. "You have outdone yourself with this gift, Furion. He is remarkable!" he clapped his hands in delight.

The Sovereign began walking over to the room's door with excitement in his stride. "There is no doubt about your ability, Mikiel."

Peeking outside the door, the Sovereign of Shadow called, summoning the five warriors he'd sparred with only moments ago. Without delay, the five warriors hurried into the training room. Each stood, watching Tymas, Furion, and Mikiel.

Tymas held his hands behind his back as he spoke to Mikiel. "In order for you to serve me, Dark Roek, you need to have more than ability. You need to be ruthless."

He paused, looking to the five warriors. "Now, show me how ruthless you can be towards these men."

Mikiel's eyes opened wide at the extreme demand. As his foot shuffled uncomfortably upon the floor beneath him, he looked at Furion; the one who saved him from a lifetime in a cell. The one who gave him the ability to Command Creation.

The Entity looked deep into the Dark Roek. "It's alright. It is time to use what has been given to you. Embrace who you are. Show us how great you can become."

Mikiel looked to the five men whose eyes were darting from person to person in panic. Pushing hesitation aside, he lifted his hands toward the five men. Each closed their eyes, embracing their fate.

As shrill silence reigned, all they heard was the rushing of wind.

Chapter Twenty-Two

Footprints and Nursery Rhymes

A nneya felt her body bouncing. Side to side she swayed. With the sound of multitudes around her, she let out a groan that was lost in the booming chatters. Realization struck her: she was being carried.

With her eyes shut from the weight of exhaustion, she laid, gazing inwardly into darkness and shadow. She watched as something began to emerge from the deep places of her mind. As features took shape, a figure began to form. At the sight of dark hair framing a face painted in makeup, she knew immediately who it was. The sight of her blood-red dress made her heart quicken. Her eyelids began fluttering at the sight of the Queen of Stone Hedge. She looked at the queen's face and heard her voice in her mind.

"He's left you, just like everyone else has. You are alone, Anneya. Forgotten."

Anneya's eyes snapped open.

Quickly sitting up, she shouted in fury, drawing her bow and an arrow. "Where is she?!"

Beside her, Shar jumped, startled by the Blade's sudden outburst. Panic dissipated from the Bishop's face, turning into delight.

"Anneya! You're awake!" Shar shouted, her brown curls bouncing in her excitement.

Anneya looked around frantically, seeing her friend beside her. Both Knights who carried her stopped, placing the stretcher upon the ground.

"Where is Ceanne Brimnas!" the Blade snarled.

Shar paused, then said, "She's gone. No one could find her. The last we saw of her was over a week ago. She stole nearly one thousand warriors from the army, convincing them to follow her."

Anneya's jaw dropped. "One thousand…" she whispered, her voice trailing off.

The Blade shifted, feeling the grass beneath her. Her eyes roamed over the lush land before her. Looking up, she was taken aback when she saw the skies. A strange darkness blanketed the skies. The sight made her stomach twist in knots.

"Where are we? Where is Tolek?" she asked Shar.

"We are still in the Plains of Morah," the Bishop said, pressing her lips together. "Tolek had to leave."

"What?! Where did he leave to?" she asked, rising from the ground. As she stood, her legs wobbled. She could tell it had been a while since she stood upright.

The Bishop spoke softly. "Tolek didn't leave your side for nearly the whole week of you being unconscious. We didn't know if you would awake or not. He stayed as long as was possible, then he needed to leave for the Courts of Light. The army was ordered to stay here until he returns."

Her eyes widened at the thought of the Paladin being so concerned for her. She fought down the emotion that threatened to show in her voice. "How long has he been gone?"

Shar pointed north, up the grasslands. "He went on his own that way almost a day ago."

"Only a day…" Anneya whispered to herself as she strapped her bow to her back. She readied herself to walk in the direction that Shar pointed out to her. Stepping forward, her legs felt weak.

"If he only left a day ago, I should be able to catch up to him if I hurry," she said.

The Bishop stood in front of Anneya, planting both hands on her shoulders. "Woah, there. Where do you think you're going? You just woke up. You need to rest."

Looking sternly into the Bishop's eyes, Anneya spoke. "I'm following Tolek. If the Courts of Light are going to offer insight on how to protect Agadin, then I need to go."

The Bishop let out a somber laugh, clearly frustrated with the stubborn Blade. "You don't understand. Tolek told me that if someone enters the Courts of Light who isn't mantled as a Protector of Agadin, that the penalty is death. Even if you do find him, you could literally be handing over your life by leaving."

Anneya allowed her eyes to drift into the distance, in the Paladin's direction. "I need to follow him. I'm not going to sit by and watch Agadin fall apart."

"What about the death sentence?" Shar pressed.

She shrugged her shoulders. "A death sentence is only a threat if someone sees me."

Shar smiled sadly, clearly uncomfortable. "Anneya, I think you're forgetting about something."

She took in the Bishop, waiting for her to continue.

"To find the Courts of Light, you will need to pass through the Valley of Blood."

The Bishop's words cut into Anneya's courage like a sword. She shuddered inside at the thought of a place where hundreds of Seers were killed in battle, defiling the valley. The land was cursed, and those daring to pass through were tormented with visions of their worst fears and greatest sorrows.

Anneya breathed in deeply. "Even so, I must go."

She could tell Shar disapproved of her decision. She looked away, knowing this was how Kaldon must have felt. She felt a pang of regret, wishing she had been more supportive.

"Shar, I know you don't want me to go, but I need your help. Do you have any insight on where I will find the Courts of Light? Considering how secret the place is, I'm assuming Tolek is going to be diligent in covering his tracks."

The Bishop cleared her throat. "I honestly wish I could help you, but I only know of one thing that may offer guidance. While Tolek was watching over you when you were unconscious, I heard him mutter something under his breath."

"What did he mutter?" the Blade asked in hope.

"Something about how he needed to go to the *Stone of Agadin;* that he would find answers there. But I have no clue what that means," she said, shrugging her shoulders.

Anneya stood straighter at the mention of the Stone of Agadin.

"What's wrong?" Shar asked resting her hand upon the hilt of her sword.

"I've heard that name before in a nursery rhyme that was sung to me as a child," Anneya said.

She began quoting the song:

> *"Like a carpet for the feet of kings,*
> *the valley greets those seeking lore.*
> *To the Stone of Agadin,*
> *in hope to find the secret door."*

Shar's eyes widened. "You mean this place that Tolek went to is from a nursery rhyme?"

Anneya looked away in thought. "It seems this story is far more real than I would have ever imagined. All I know is that I need to find this *Stone of Agadin.*"

She reached out, placing a hand upon the Bishop's shoulder. "I need to leave now, Shar. Thank you for watching over me, my friend."

The Bishop's eyes were glazed over. Anneya leaned in, giving her a hug goodbye. "Take care of the army here. All these men need a woman to keep them in line."

Shar smiled. "Consider it done, my friend. Please, be safe."

***

Anneya brushed her fingers through the thick grass. Tracking wasn't her forte. The problem was that the Paladin was proving difficult to follow. There were times when his footing would trail off into three or four separate directions. She knew he made different paths for diversions, backtracking his steps before he travelled onward. She found herself lost in the scattered patterns, like an endless maze she had been navigating for almost three days with little sleep.

As her hand bumped a small rock in the grass, she groaned. She wished she knew what she was looking for. The Stone of Agadin could have been anything. For all she knew, it could have been a small pebble or a colossal boulder. Making matters worse, the deeper she journeyed into the plains, the more fog crept in, making it hard for her to see far into the distance. Picking up the fist-sized stone, she threw it into the distance. As it bounced down rolling hills, she felt weariness throughout her body. She was exhausted.

In strands of grass, her eyes rested upon three sets of footprints going in different directions. Anneya pressed her hand upon each step. She felt the soil's depth on each of the three paths of prints, feeling the dirt sink deeper in one more than the others. The Blade smiled, knowing the Paladin put more weight on that step, proving he was running on it, rather than walking. She knew it wasn't a diversion, but the actual trail the Paladin took.

"Not as smart as you thought, Tolek," the Blade said with a smirk.

She ran down the path, chasing the Paladin's trail. The nursery rhyme she'd heard as a child about the Courts of Light rang through her mind. She searched through the song in search of keys to the mystical destination.

"Though evils rise and shadows dawn,
and demons shriek, imposing plight,
to the fall where visions spawn,
the courageous seek the Courts of Light.

"Dark and shadow one must abhor,
to glimpse upon the sacred Light.
Secret place, hidden door,
through emerald fields, cloaked from sight."

Anneya knew she was in the right place; however, the Plains of Morah were vast. One could travel weeks through them and not reach their end. Her eyes wandering over hills, she followed the imprints that Tolek's boots left. If she followed his prints, she believed she would find the legendary place. She mused at the thought of finding a hidden door that led to the courts. She knew if she weren't careful, she could miss it entirely. Her eyes scaling up a nearing hill, she could see the Paladin's prints ascending with it.

Letting out staggered breaths, she climbed the inclined hill. Her legs burned. Its dampness upon her skin, the fog grew thicker as she ascended. Reaching the top of the hill, she watched as the fogged skies broke. She looked forth to a stunning sight: a valley bowed through the green plains, like a walkway leading to a lonely mountain. A single mountain towered into the skies. From the pale mountain, a light-blue waterfall descended, ending in a pond. Fog rolled around the whole circumference of the mountain and valley like a protective shield.

"The Stone of Agadin," she whispered.

She was moved by the majestic sight. The mountain reminded her of the Mountains of D'aal; however, there was something unique about this one. The rocky mountain was shaped completely of pure-white stone. Nearly everything about the sight looked heavenly, like a reflection of the Kingdom of Light: The Golden Land. That is, all looked heavenly except one thing: the bowed valley that led to the mountain. While the rest of the Plains of Morah exuded peace, the valley before her was shrouded in darkness. Looking at the valley was like peering into a cave. She knew it was the Valley of Blood. Her legs began to tremble.

As a cool breeze stroked her skin, she remembered her most hated verse of the nursery rhyme. It was the one that frightened her as a child, giving her terrors in the night.

She whispered it aloud.

"The darkened valley steers away,
shielding with the curse of Seers.
Heroes only find their way,
persisting through their greatest fears.

"Abode of light sleeps in peace,
protected by the darkened bite.
Visions claw; the bravest cease,
as courage dies by threatening night."

Gulping, she forced her feet to step forward. Even in her descent down the grassy hill, she felt the darkness of the Valley of Blood creeping up her skin. Would she be strong enough to live through it? Through the darkness, she fixed her eyes upon the Stone of Agadin, the mighty mountain that reigned in the Plains of Morah. The mountain held the secret door to the Courts of Light.

As she breathed in, the Valley of Blood engulfed her.

CHAPTER TWENTY-THREE

THROUGH FEARS

A t the bottom of the valley, Anneya took in the still pasture around her. Cradled in the middle of two hills, the grass was dull and lifeless, its vibrance stolen by the curse of Seers.

Darkness pulled her in as though she was in the centre of a misty storm cloud. She watched as what looked like a black-floating fog swooned around her. She knew it was the visions taking her mind. Breathing in, the fog pulled into her mouth, its icy touch dancing into her lungs.

Her eyes darted from place to place, anticipating her greatest fears and sorrows coming to life. Walking forward, she reached up, grabbing the Legacy that she wore around her neck. The touch of its firm metal gave her courage; it made her feel as though Kaldon was right there with her.

"Turning back isn't an option. Just keep moving forward," she voiced quietly to herself.

Squinting through the fog, she followed the Paladin's footsteps, frustrated she could no longer see the Stone of Agadin. The sight of it was obscured by the murky air. The mist darkened and Anneya stopped. Her heartbeat quickened as an image took shape before her.

"Nothing here is real. Nothing here can hurt me," she reminded herself in a faint whisper.

A low growl rose, echoing through the enclosed valley. She drew her bow and an arrow, waiting to see what would emerge from the shadows. She gasped, as the largest Kreel she had ever seen stepped toward her. At nearly twelve feet tall, the creature puffed out its chest. With its bat-like face and reptilian tale, the black fog was befitting for such a ghastly creature. The Kreel let its wings stretch wide, revealing its intimidating size.

Anneya nocked her arrow on her bow, aiming it at the creature. The Kreel let loose a piercing screech as it launched from the ground directly at her.

As she looked down the shaft of her arrow steadying her aim, she took in the oversized Kreel raging toward her. "You aren't real," she muttered aloud.

Snarling ravenously, the Kreel drew closer.

"You aren't real!" she shouted, letting her bow drop to her side, choosing not to fire.

The moment the Kreel reached her, it vanished into nothingness.

She exhaled in relief. Taking deep breaths, she was shocked at how lifelike the vision was. The Blade walked onward, following Tolek's footprints. As her eyes chased the flowing fog, she waited to see what visions would come next.

Slowly, the world of Agadin began to take shape before her. Materializing from nothing, land emerged. She saw Gorath and the Plains of Morah. Her eyes wandered over cities and towns, as though she were soaring above the unfolding landscapes. The vision rested on an image of the Peak of Lore. The facility stood tall like a guardian watching over Agadin. She ached, longing for her home. Around the mountainous castle, blue skies faded to greys and purples. A menacing darkness swirled around it as if death itself had shrouded it.

"No!" she shouted.

Like a mighty hammer striking the colossal mountain, a crack ascended the stone. Rock began to fall. Anneya watched as the mountain castle shattered, falling to pieces. The renowned facility avalanched into scrap and debris. Such an occurrence would leave thousands dead.

"Nothing here is real," she murmured faintly, convincing herself that the Peak of Lore was still safe.

Keep moving, Anneya. Don't give in to the lies, she thought, forcing her feet to move through the valley.

Looking up, she noticed that the vision faded to nothing. She was beginning to see the outline of the Stone of Agadin up ahead. She was getting closer. The white mountain was beginning to shine through the darkness. As she approached it, waves began emerging from the depths of darkness. Another vision was materializing.

Just keep walking.

The waves growing, she knew she was looking at the ocean. Blues crashed together. She'd never had a fear of water, so didn't understand why she was seeing the waves. Remembering Kaldon's vision, she stopped in her tracks. She may not fear the ocean, but she did fear that the restless pursuit of his vision could lead to his demise.

Before raging seas, she saw him standing on a stage. Instead of holding *Humility* and *Integrity*, he held a sword that she had never seen before. She knew he would never go anywhere without the blades. On the stage with him was an isolated, dead tree. Under its branches stood Tymas Droll. In beige robes, the Sovereign of Shadow held his arched sword before him. The Sovereign drove in, swinging in wrath.

"It's time for you to be with your father and mother in death, Kal Wendal!" the Sovereign mocked.

"Kaldon!" she yelled reaching out an arm, watching him attempting to block each strike.

At the sight of the man she loved, fighting the most dangerous man alive, she could feel her palms start to sweat. As Kaldon whirled his swords about, the Sovereign swung his blade, cutting away his weapon. She covered her mouth. Tymas drove in, piercing his blade into Kaldon's chest.

The ocean roaring behind him, Kaldon laid still upon the ground, dead.

She closed her eyes as she listened to Tymas' sadistic laugh. Tears covered her face. She wept bitterly as she fought to not believe what she saw.

Keep walking, Anneya. This isn't real. Kaldon is alive.

Forcing herself to press on, her chest throbbed with each sob that came out. She wailed at the image of seeing Kaldon killed, but still she pressed on amidst the wrenching sorrow threatening to overwhelm her. She shut her eyes from the vision, stoically trudging on for what felt like an insufferable amount of time. She felt a shift around her; the atmosphere changed. Opening her eyes, she saw the Stone of Agadin before her. The white mountain pierced through the darkness.

"I made it." she said, tears pouring down her face. She followed the Paladin's footprints, moving closer to the mountain that was home to the Courts of Light.

Stepping closer, she watched as a final vision began to manifest around her. As she was touched by the light of the Stone of Agadin, she watched two figures emerge.

The previous visions were dark and terrifying, but this time, the sun shone brightly. Every detail was distinct. Her senses were heightened. As the two slowly drew closer, she watched curiously. It was a man and a woman. Even though they were unidentified, she felt a pang of sadness well up from within. Through the silence of the vision, she heard the cries of an infant rising. Taking a closer look, she saw that the man and woman held a baby girl, swaddled in cloths.

Through mountain terrain, the two carried the baby girl to a small wooden house. The wood was worn and ragged, unfitting as a place of shelter. The sight of the familiar home felt like a thorn piercing into her soul.

The sight paralyzed her.

"No… Please, no," she begged.

The man reached out, knocking on the wooden door. As it creaked open, Anneya watched an older man with a balding head emerge. The stout man was her adopted father. Tears spilled from her eyes at the sight of him. She remembered the horrors of what he did to her growing up; the pain he inflicted. As she tried to wipe away her flowing tears, she felt her thumb bump over her teardrop scar that ran down from her left eye; the scar *he* gave her.

The man and the woman — her father and mother — held the baby girl toward the older man. "We don't want her. What will you give us for her?" her father asked.

The words cut into her like a thousand knives. She dropped to her knees weeping uncontrollably.

The older man looked at the small child. Reaching out his arms, the mother handed over the baby girl. A vile grin spread over his face. Reaching into his pocket, he pulled out a silver coin, placing it in the mother's hand. The man and woman nodded their agreement, turning away from their daughter.

Watching her father and mother walk away broke something deep inside of her. Anneya fell to her side holding her knees sobbing. Crouched in a ball on the ground, all the times as a little girl when she was neglected and abused flooded her mind. She remembered what that man had done to her.

Through wails and cries, she pleaded. "Papa, Mama, please, don't leave me! Don't leave me by myself! Please!"

Rocking back and forth upon the matted greens, her sorrow took her. As her body shook in emotional agony, she was sure the pain in her heart would take her life.

She wailed into the valley. "Please, don't leave! Please, don't leave me!"

With every tear she shed, she was sinking deeper into her trauma; deeper into her greatest sorrows. The Stone of Agadin was so close, yet she hadn't the motivation to move onward. Her pain was too great. She wanted to die.

Trembling, she felt hands reach down, lifting her from the ground. She writhed against whoever had grabbed her, frantically trying to get free. Looking up, all she saw was a blurred image wearing a white cape. The man pulled her up into his arms, carrying her closer to the Stone of Agadin. Sobbing uncontrollably, she wrestled, not knowing whether the man was another vision.

Nearing the isolated mountain, Anneya heard the waterfall thundering against the white rock. In the dazed fog that confused her mind, she reached out, allowing her fingers to stroke the wet stone.

She looked up, seeing that the man carried her under the waterfall to a hidden cave that dwelled behind. As he sat them down upon the cold and damp rock, she whimpered in her broken state. Being out from the valley, she realized this man wasn't a vision. He was real. She knew she had made it through the Valley of Blood; however, at the same time, she didn't care. All that passed through her mind were the father and mother who never wanted her. Ceanne Brimnas was right. She was alone. She was forgotten; unimportant.

Looking towards the man who carried her, her eyes shifted into focus. She saw the frame of Tolek's face; his blonde hair, whisked with greys. Hidden behind the waterfall, she listened to it pounding upon stone. Gazing upon the Paladin, she spilled over in tears.

"Please don't leave me… Please don't leave me alone," she shut her eyes, pleading in sobs.

Tolek pulled Anneya close, cradling her in a fatherly embrace. Her tears soaked his shoulders. As she wept, he kissed her forehead to comfort her.

He whispered over her, saying, "Anneya, I don't know what you saw in that valley; but one thing I do know for certain is this: I am not going anywhere. I am going to protect you. You are important and remembered. And above all else, know that you are never alone."

CHAPTER TWENTY-FOUR

UNDERCOVER

———————◆◆◆◆◆———————

Watching the pale blue water crashing against stone, Anneya was surprised at how long it had taken her to calm her emotions. For a time, Tolek held her so she wouldn't endure the trauma alone. After a while, he let her be. As she regained her strength, he focused on what he had been toiling at for nearly an hour straight. The Paladin was at the back of the cave running his hands over the clammy wall, lost in thought. The rock in the cave was airtight, leading nowhere. Yet, there he stood, transfixed upon the wall.

"Thank you for rescuing me," she said quietly, testing her voice.

"You risked your life following me, Anneya," he said without turning around, his hands pressing against the stone wall.

"I'm aware," the Blade said, her voice echoing through the quaint cave. "It was a risk I had to take. I will not sit by watching Agadin fall."

"It was a foolish decision," he said bluntly.

She shifted uncomfortably at his disapproval, wishing she hadn't needed to come. She wouldn't wish what she experienced in the Valley of Blood on anyone. Her abdomen ached from sobbing. Her eyes were puffy and swollen.

"I'm sorry you had to endure the Valley of Blood," Tolek said looking back. "Truly, I am."

As he turned back to the wall, she swallowed, forcing cries to suppress that were threatening to rise again. She changed the subject. "We've made it to the Stone of Agadin. Where are the Courts of Light? I expected more than an empty cave."

Ignoring her question, he pressed his forehead against the wet stone. She watched as he rested his hands purposefully upon the rock's face, each finger intentionally positioned.

"I think I remember..." he whispered in thought.

She twisted a strand of hair between a finger and thumb. "Remember what? What are you doing?"

Once his hands found their proper placement, the Paladin whispered into the white mountain. *"Door, make way to the Courts of Light."*

At his words, the cave wall cracked. She watched as a stone door swung open before him.

"The hidden door," she stammered.

He wiped sweat from his face. "Yes. As if the Valley of Blood wasn't enough protection, they had to have a nearly invisible door."

She gazed in wonder at the door that hung open, leading into the Stone of Agadin. Through the stone entry, she could feel the atmosphere emanating from inside. It was thick with substance. She closed her eyes at the undeniable presence.

"Why is it that I feel the Kingdom of Light right now coming through that door?" she asked, being taken in by the blissful sensation.

The Paladin looked back to her. "The Courts of Light are a place where the Kingdom and Agadin dwell together. The presence of eternity rests here."

She realized her eyebrows were raised. "You mean, the Kingdom of Light never leaves here?"

"Exactly," the Paladin said, gazing through the door. "This mountain is a dwelling place for the Kingdom of Light."

The Blade rose from the ground, approaching the mysterious door. Looking through the stone archway, she saw a beige stairway leading up into the white mountain. Not only did she feel the essence of the Kingdom of Light coming from up the mountain, but she heard murmurs of people talking.

Tolek reached out, placing a hand on her shoulder, stopping her from ascending the steps. "I'm still not happy with you for following me, Anneya. If anyone discovers you aren't a Protector of Agadin, things aren't going to turn out well for either of us."

She bit her lip. "I can't explain why, but I believe I am supposed to be here."

He nodded. "I don't doubt your heart; however, you are about to meet some of the most formidable warriors in all of Agadin. I need you to follow my lead. Got it?"

She forced a smile. "Got it."

Following him up the stairs, the chattering increased in volume. Sweat broke out on her forehead at the thought of meeting a group of Paladins. The only one she had ever met was Tolek; and although she felt safe with him, she knew he was undeniably the most dangerous man she had ever met. She expected no less from those at the top of the stairs.

With each step, she felt the cramps in her stomach dissipating. The puffiness in her eyes lessened in swelling. It was the Kingdom of Light healing her. She could feel the essence of eternity wrapping around her. Feeling the heat of the Kingdom growing upon her hands, she opened and closed them, reveling in the sensation.

"Fascinating," she whispered into the stairwell.

Ascending to the upper room, they entered the cordial space. The walls of the entrance to the Courts of Light were constructed from the white stone of the mountain. The marble floor was pristine with mahogany furniture resting on it. Similar to the Peak of Lore, the walls were covered in writings. The lost dialect of Old Agadin was carved into the walls. There were several windows looking out to the Plains of Morah. She knew she was in a place where only a handful in history had stood; only the most elite in all of Agadin. As profound as the room was, it almost paled in comparison to the nine Paladins who stood before her.

Each watched Tolek and Anneya.

Taking in the Paladins — three females and six men — she knew each was a master of combat. There wasn't a single weapon that they couldn't wield with excellence; not a fighting style they hadn't perfected. Even though there were only ten Paladins in total around her, she didn't doubt that they could defeat an army of ten thousand.

"Tolek!" one of the Paladins yelled in a gruff voice.

Looking at the man who shouted, Anneya's eyes widened. She had never seen a man so large in all her life. His chest looked to be twice the size of an average man's, his arms the size of tree trunks.

Tolek let out a laugh of relief. "Henry, it is good to see you, my friend. I'm glad you were able to make it."

The two men came together, clasping one another's forearms in a greeting. Henry gazed at Tolek from behind his furry brow. "I would never miss an opportunity to fight alongside *Tolek the Brave*," the large Paladin said lightheartedly.

Even though the man was clearly brutish, there was a jovial spirit to him. Henry's moustache was grown out, braiding down past his chin. Anneya thought to herself that the obscene amount of hair on his face made up for the lack of it on his head. Then she noticed his choice of weapon. Strapped to his tremendous back was a silver war-hammer. The weapon was nearly as tall as she was.

She watched Henry's eyes shift to her. A smile spread over his face. "And who might this be?"

The large Paladin walked up to Anneya, grabbing her hand. He brought it to his lips as a welcome. Her hand felt like a child's in his meaty grip.

Before she could respond, a woman emerged from the back of the room. "Yes, Tolek, that is exactly what I would like to know. Who is this?"

Henry's smile evaporated from his face, realizing that Anneya may not belong in such a place.

Anneya's eyes didn't leave the woman who was likely almost two decades older than her. Her scarlet hair was tied back, kept from being in her face. Clothed in brown and silver armour, she looked as though she would be a blatant threat to whoever pressed her.

Tolek addressed the female Paladin. "Dianne, this is Anneya Padme."

The female Paladin with the cherry-coloured hair, eyed her up and down.

Before she could begin drilling the Blade with questions, Tolek continued, "Anneya is a Philosopher."

At his claim, the Blade stayed still, trying to hide the shock that pounded through her.

"A Philosopher!" Henry exclaimed, looking to the other Paladins. "Quite impressive."

Dianne cocked an eyebrow. "She looks quite young to be a Philosopher. Tell me, where have you trained?" she asked.

Forcing her breathing to steady, Anneya replied, saying, "I trained in Noriden under several Philosophers. I took a liking to the topics of strategy of war and prophecy. Once I memorized a significant number of Dolan Thain's books, I began venturing out to master several streams of science and mathematics."

She unwaveringly looked head on at the Paladins who were scrutinizing her. She may not have been a Philosopher; however, she knew that she was smart. She just hoped she was smart enough to trick them.

Henry looked over to Dianne. "She sounds like a Philosopher to me, Dianne."

The female Paladin looked to Henry. "That's because you are made up of all muscle and no brain."

The other Paladins laughed at her feisty remark. Even Henry slapped his knee, balking out a laugh. Anneya and Tolek were the only ones who didn't, discerning the severity of the situation.

Dianne squinted at the Blade. "Tell me Anneya, why then do you wear the customary armour of a Blade? I'm sure you are aware that if you aren't appointed as a Protector of Agadin, that you have forfeited your life coming here."

Out from the corner of her eye, she saw Tolek staring at her crimson shoulder spikes. She knew he was likely internally mulling over at how to respond to the incessant questions. As he began opening his mouth to answer for her, Anneya cut him off.

"In my spare time, I acquired my rank of warrior as a Blade," she responded. "Since the philosophy of war tactics fascinates me so, I felt it would be beneficial to my learning if I knew battle firsthand. Too many Philosophers spend too much time hiding behind their books. Knowledge needs to be experienced, not just read about."

Silence lingered throughout the room. "From the sounds of it, you are a unique type of Philosopher," Dianne said sarcastically.

"You don't believe me?" Anneya asked, wanting to end the prying woman's suspicions. Reaching behind her armour, she pulled forth the Legacy that hung from her neck. She knew every one of them in the room carried the rare symbol. At the sight of the Legacy, Tolek's gaze grew.

Tossing it to Dianne, she watched an expression of surprise dawn over her face. The Paladin looked up at Anneya, her eyes wide.

"Maybe now I won't have to tolerate the nonsensical suspicions of a skeptical Paladin," Anneya snapped.

A smile spread over Dianne's face. "I admire your bite. I get the feeling that you and I are going to get along, Philosopher."

Tolek cut in, taking attention from Anneya. "That's enough from all of you. I didn't summon you all here so that you could argue with one another."

"My apologies," Dianne said with a nod.

In a soft tone, Henry spoke up. "Why did you summon us?"

Tolek paused, knowing the weight of his words. "Marradus has been risen from the dead by the Tymas Droll."

At the words, every Paladin fell quiet. Anneya watched as Tolek took the attention of everyone in the room. She could tell he held their tremendous respect.

Dianne stepped forward. "Does this mean that he is a Shan-Rafa?"

Tolek nodded in confirmation. "It does."

His gaze wandering over the greatest warriors alive, Tolek spoke. "We may be formidable as a force, but the demon dragon has engulfed entire cities. I doubt an entire army could slay such a beast. Marradus is a creature from the depths of the Dominion of Shadow. We may be Paladins, but we might not live through this mission. We need to step into the Courts of Light immediately to seek direction."

Tolek then looked to Anneya. "We need wisdom that not even a Philosopher can conjure. If Divinity doesn't answer us, I fear that Agadin will be no more."

Chapter Twenty-Five

The Courts of Light

W

alking through the white halls, Anneya felt the presence of the Kingdom of Light dancing all around her, tingling her flesh. Walking amidst the Paladins, her eyes took in the Old Agadin written across the ancient walls. She longed to know what the words said; what secrets and wisdom they contained.

Through hallways and corridors, she saw rooms for lounging and bedrooms scattered throughout the fabled mountain. The sun's light lingered upon the marble floor and a soft breeze swept into the hallway.

"This way," Tolek said, taking a left turn down a marble path.

Following, each Paladin turned the corner. As Anneya followed, she nearly gasped, realizing they'd entered the Courts of Light. The fairytales she heard as a little girl were real; right before her eyes.

Several pillars stood in a circle, holding the mountain rock securely in place above the sacred room. Vines blooming with flowers wove up the mighty pillars. Encased within the pillars were approximately twenty marble chairs, placed in a circle, to seat those who would wait for Divinity's council. In the centre of the circle was a bare stone table. Beyond the room, she saw the expanse of Agadin. The white mountain was so tall, it gave her a breathtaking aerial view of the land. Through the dimming skies, the persistent light of the sun smiled upon the room.

Stopping at the stone archway, Tolek unsheathed his sword, leaning it against the wall. Turning back to the warriors, he said, "Leave your weapons at the door. Instruments of death are not welcome in this place."

Approaching the stone table, he reached around his neck pulling forth his Legacy. Carefully placing it upon the table, he then sat in one of the marble chairs. Each Paladin followed doing the same.

Reaching the stone table last, Anneya pulled forth Kaldon's Legacy. Bringing it to her lips, she kissed the ancient symbol, then carefully placed it upon the stone.

Sitting in the marble chair, she flinched at its cold touch. Her heart pounded, not having yet grown accustomed to the renowned warriors surrounding her. She glanced from face to face, each one of the most formidable warriors in all of Agadin.

The warriors were focused on the centre of the room, awaiting in expectation of the great light of Divinity to shine. Anneya didn't know what to expect. Would the light start off subtle, gradually growing? Would it crash in like lightning? Would Divinity speak audibly to them? Her mind raced with the unknown.

In silence, the eleven waited. Every time a bird passing by would caw, Anneya sat up straighter, wondering if it were a spark of the great light; however, each time she was disappointed. As an hour passed, she watched as agitated glares began sprouting on the faces of the Protectors of Agadin.

Surely, Divinity wouldn't deny giving wisdom and counsel to such an important group of warriors, she thought to herself.

"What is taking so long?" Platius asked, shifting with irritation in the uncomfortable chair. "We've been waiting for over an hour. Are you sure this isn't just folklore, Tolek?"

She eyed the outspoken Paladin. Wearing simple armour, his hair was longer than she was used to seeing on a man. He looked to be much smaller than the others; however, he possessed confidence that only a Paladin could bear.

"I am sure." Tolek's expression was unmoving. "I've been here within the Stone of Agadin several times. I have seen the great light of Divinity. It is the furthest thing from folklore."

"So, you've actually seen Divinity's light?" Henry asked in wonder, leaning forward. "How many times have you seen it?"

Tolek's serious gaze rested upon the large man. "I've only seen it once. It was like nothing I have ever experienced."

"Only once?" Henry asked, slouching his shoulders.

Tolek nodded. "I have been here several times, but Divinity is selective when he chooses to show himself."

Platius stroked his chin that was barren of hair. "So, you mean it isn't guaranteed that Divinity's light will show?"

"No," Tolek admitted.

Anneya watched discouragement wash over the room.

"When you saw Divinity's light, did you come alone?" Dianne asked.

"I saw the great light about eighteen years ago. I wasn't alone." Tolek replied. "I came with Dolan Thain."

At the mention of the renowned Philosopher, a quietness hushed over the concession of Paladins.

"Dolan Thain…" Henry whispered, his gaze wide. "You knew the Warrior General, the Great Philosopher?"

"I knew him quite well. I can assure you his mind was as remarkable as you've heard," Tolek said.

Dianne leaned in. "Is it true what I have heard about his son; that he walks Agadin? Is it true that he carries the title of a Paragon?"

Anneya felt butterflies in her stomach at the mention of Kaldon.

"Yes, it's true that Kaldon is a Paragon," he replied. "However, he is quite young in his ability."

Carrying a pensive look upon her face, Dianne spoke. "How then do you know he is a Paragon?"

He looked up to the adamant Paladin. "I know because he has taught himself to use *foresight,* an ability that takes a lifetime to master."

Anneya saw the looks of shock grow upon each one's face. She knew there wasn't a Paladin in the room that didn't know how to wield the ability of foresight. Each understood how tremendously difficult it was for one to learn the skill.

Tolek continued, "Not only that; he has also summoned the Kingdom of Light to heal with barely any training. He has even Commanded Creation."

"He has Commanded Creation? You mean, like a Roek?" The words escaped Henry's mouth.

Tolek's steady gaze confirmed the question.

"Fascinating," Dianne said, leaning back.

Each Paladin faded into thought. A Paragon being in Agadin was no small matter. Each looked onward waiting for the great light to come, weighing the events taking place in Agadin. For hours they waited in silence. Anneya looked onward. Weariness was beginning to drape over the impatient group; darkness was beginning to dethrone the day. Yet, nothing came. Not a glimmer; not even a spark of the great light.

She could feel her eyes growing tired; heavy. She fought her eyelids closing, not wanting to miss the great light if it came. Exhaustion was taking her. The moment her eyes closed, she basked in the peace of the Kingdom of Light around her.

Through the still, she began feeling a low rumble from within her core, disrupting her rest. What started off subtle, grew rapidly like a roar. Deep within the centre of her being, a low voice quaked through her.

"When the Paladins sleep, come alone."

Anneya opened her eyes, sitting up in a startle. Gasping, she looked forth to see ten Paladins watching her.

"Are you alright, Anneya?" Henry asked in concern.

She had never heard such a strong and alluring voice in all her life. It was fused with authority; endowed with power she never knew existed. The only thing she could make sense of was that it was the very voice of Divinity.

"I'm fine, Henry. I just drifted to sleep is all," she said, trying to slow her breaths as she sunk back into the chair. She could still feel the rumbling of the voice vibrating through her body, yet she didn't dare share what she'd heard.

Silence lingered in the court. Through the quiet, Platius stood abruptly, agitation streaked across his face. "We are all falling asleep!"

The impatient Paladin looked to Tolek. "I'm a Paladin, not a sluggard. I came to defend Agadin. We are wasting our time here. The demon dragon is terrorizing Agadin, we shouldn't be sitting here waiting for fairytales to come to life. We should be fighting."

Tolek raised his voice. "Platius, it would be wise for us to wait."

"For how long? A week? A month?" Platius asked, waving a hand. "Agadin will have fallen by then. I say we leave now, traveling by night to track the dragon."

Dianne stood. "Tolek, I agree with Platius. We need to fight. Divinity clearly isn't coming."

Tolek looked around the room at the tiring Paladins. Each looked weary from waiting. Then his eyes rested upon Anneya.

Trying to gain her composure, she still felt the booming voice lingering in her core. She believed more than ever that Divinity could speak. How unnerved she felt was proof enough to her. Once everyone was asleep, she needed to return on her own.

"What do you think?" Tolek asked her.

She looked from Paladin to Paladin. She saw how weary they were, but she knew she couldn't leave.

"I don't think we should leave the Stone of Agadin. I believe Divinity will come. We should sleep for the evening and begin waiting again in the morning," she said, trying to buy time so she could come back on her own.

Tolek smiled. "It seems that it was wise for me to bring a Philosopher with me," he said.

He looked to the rest of the warriors. "We will rest and then begin waiting again in the morning."

Platius didn't hide rolling his eyes. Dianne rubbed her forehead in frustration.

Tolek continued, "If you are so adamant to leave the Stone of Agadin, then you are dismissed; but Anneya is right. I believe the great light will come."

Chapter Twenty-Six

A Touch from Eternity

L aying upon her bed, Anneya looked out the window as faded stars flickered in the sky. She waited several hours in the grand bedroom, fighting to stay awake until all the Paladins were asleep.

She sat up, still watching the stars, as the internal voice she heard in the Courts of Light whispered through her memories.

"When the Paladins sleep, come alone."

Placing her feet onto the ground, her toes were warmed by the richly carpet masking the floor. Grabbing her boots, she strapped them around her feet.

It was time.

Making her way out of the room, she slowly closed the door behind her. Peering down the white halls, the glimmering moonlight lit the way. Walking soundlessly towards the Courts of Light, she was thankful the room wasn't far off. With each step, she felt her nerves rising higher and higher.

Passing the doors of each Paladin's private room, she listened to their snores, stilling her worries of being found out. Taking a final turn, she walked into the empty room lit by the moon's glow.

Slowly walking, she felt a deep reverence. As she did earlier with the Paladins, she pulled the Legacy from around her neck and kissed it. She placed it upon the stone table once again. Looking to the empty chairs around her, she thought the courts felt much calmer with no one else there. It was like her personal shrine: her place of peace.

Rejecting the hard seats, she chose to kneel before the centre stone. The floor was hard against her knees as she waited in the quite room. Anticipation fluttered in her heart, yet she didn't feel to be in a rush. She knew she wasn't waiting for just anyone; she was waiting for the creator of all things.

In the cool of the night, a heat began pressing against her face, flushing her cheeks. Opening her eyes, she watched as light materialized from the centre of the room, above the table.

The great light shining before her, she gasped. She squinted at its brightness as though she were peering into the sun itself. The heat on her face began to move over the rest of her body, wrapping around her like a blanket. She inhaled deeply, feeling the tangible light coursing into her inner-being.

"Your courage is something to be greatly admired, young one."

The mighty voice sounded around her from every direction, engulfing her. It resounded not only around her, but from the depths of her heart. Inside, outside, and all around it consumed her. She trembled hearing Divinity's words. It was the very voice that summoned the mountains into being; the one that called forth the ocean, giving it its power. It was the voice that created all of Agadin.

Anneya lifted her head, shaking before the great light. She looked around, expecting to see a figure of sorts, yet all she saw was light. It was as though Divinity was all around her, as though he was everywhere all at once.

"You risked your life coming here."

Tears began running down her face. "I did," she stammered. "You know then that I am not actually a Philosopher. I am not a Protector of Agadin."

"I know everything about you," the great being said. *"There isn't a thing about your life that I haven't seen."*

She felt naked at the comment. "Will you then take my life for coming here?" she asked.

At her question, the light shone brighter. It thickened around her like an embrace. It felt like a warm affirmation smiling over her.

"Certainly not. I do not punish such bravery; I reward it."

Her entire body shook with each word Divinity spoke. She trembled under his mighty power. "We have come seeking counsel from you, Divinity. Please, tell me how we can protect Agadin from the Dominion of Shadow."

Anneya expected an answer right away; however, a silence lingered as though Divinity were gathering his thoughts.

"I have already revealed that secret."

"What do you mean? Please, tell me," she pleaded.

"I revealed the answer within the prophecy given to Kaldon Thain."

He then began quoting the prophecy: *"The Roek must rise. The Seer will fall. The Paladin needs to obtain the impenetrable shield. The Paragon must soar."*

She shivered under the weighty prophecy.

"The fulfillment of this prophecy is the way to protect Agadin from Shadow. In fact, it has already begun. The Seer has fallen; he is lost in the River of Time."

She didn't understand what Divinity meant; however, she felt a pang of sadness. She hesitated, but her curiosity drove her to find answers.

"Is Locrian the Seer that the prophecy speaks of?" she asked.

"He is."

Anneya gulped, feeling her face growing wet again. "Is he alive?"

"Barely," Divinity replied. *"He is hanging onto his last strand of sanity. If he lets go, he will be forever gone."*

Her voice began to shake. "Divinity, you know all things. Will Locrian survive?"

Compassion emitted from Divinity's tone. *"I cannot say. His destiny will be determined by his willingness to persevere. It is up to him whether he lives or dies."*

Preventing herself from breaking out in tears, the Blade decided to ask another question. This wasn't the time to mourn; she needed answers. "I know Kaldon must be the Paragon in the prophecy, since he is the only one who lives. Please, tell me who the Paladin is who is spoken of in the prophecy."

"You were with him today. I have revealed myself to him in the past. The Paladin is the one who is called, 'Tolek the Brave.'"

"What is the impenetrable shield?" Anneya asked, trying to pull out as much information as she could. "As far as I know, no such shield exists. Even the strongest of metals can be penetrated. Where would he find such a thing?"

"You are wrong. There is a shield that cannot be penetrated. Tolek the Brave has the potential to find it as you hunt the demon dragon."

Potential, Anneya thought. She wished Divinity's words were more definitive, rather than conditional. Knowing she wasn't going to fully understand the prophetic riddle, she tried taking a different approach.

"Where is Marradus now?" she asked.

"The dragon is currently flying to the city called 'Flank.'"

She'd heard of the grand city, knowing it was only one week of travel from where their remaining army was stationed. "How many has Marradus killed so far?"

"The onyx dragon has taken nearly three hundred thousand lives since its resurrection."

The words drove discouragement directly into her. "Three hundred thousand…" she whispered, her voice trailing off.

She looked up into the great light. "We will go. We will kill the dragon."

"Defeating Marradus is essential for Agadin's survival. You must leave tomorrow; any later and your opportunity will be lost. Waste no time."

She nodded in a vow to fulfill the request. Before she could speak, Divinity's voice pierced through the light once again.

"Never allow yourself to overlook the Great War between Light and Shadow, young one."

She furrowed her brow, confused. "I know of the Great War: the war between the Kingdom of Light and the Dominion of Shadow. I have dedicated my life to advancing the Light. It is the very reason why I am a Blade."

"Then you would be wise to remember that even Marradus is a small part of this war. The Sovereign of Shadow is a small part of it as well. They are dangerous, yes; however, the Great War is much grander than what has already occurred in Agadin."

She was caught off guard as she felt offense rising in her heart toward the creator of Agadin. She stood to her feet. "Marradus taking nearly three hundred thousand lives is no small occurrence. The monstrosity needs to be stopped."

"You are correct. Marradus must be destroyed. It cannot remain; however, there is more at risk than hundreds of thousands of lives. All are at risk. Agadin as a whole is falling apart."

"I don't understand," she said quietly. "How can there be a greater threat than the demon dragon?"

"With the Door of the Dominion open, Shadow is eating away at Agadin. It is stealing the very skies. You will understand. Once 'Death's Snow' falls, you will understand."

"What is *Death's Snow?*" she whispered, fearing the answer she would receive.

"The beginning of nothingness. The sign of 'he' who is coming."

The words terrified her, sending tremors throughout her body. "Who is coming? Who are you referring to?" her voice said in trembling fear.

At Divinity's silence, Anneya shuffled her feet uncomfortably. All she really knew was that they all must leave for Flank at daybreak.

Standing before the great light, she could feel a final question stirring within her. "Divinity, why did you choose to speak to me alone, rather than to all of the Paladins?"

Instead of answering her directly, Divinity asked her a question. *"Tell me, what do you respect most about, Tolek the Brave?"*

She rubbed her hands together uncomfortably, surprised that the creator turned the question back onto her. She thought for a moment.

"Tolek is the greatest fighter I have ever met in my life. His skill is unmatched by anyone I have ever seen," she said. "But the quality I respect about him the most is his ability to lead others. Many of the other Paladins here are only warriors. They make a difference through simply fighting. Tolek is another thing entirely. Not only has he mastered battle, but he also oversees the Peak of Lore, training uprising warriors. Even here, all the Paladins look to him to take charge. People look to him to lead."

At her answer, the great light shone brighter, warming her skin.

"You admire his quality as a leader because you have a similar calling in your life. Your story is only at its beginning. Not only do you have the potential to lead, but you are called to lead some of the most important individuals in all of Agadin. They will look to you as their leader; then you will have to make a decision."

She held her breath waiting for Divinity to continue.

"The decision is whether or not you will choose to be brave, to step into who you were always destined to become: a leader. Never belittle yourself, young one."

Looking down, she didn't know how to process the eternal words. She could feel tension growing in her heart; strain spreading over her face. As profound as such a declaration was, her mind began being pulled back to the image she saw in the Valley of Blood. It was the image of her mother and father leaving her; the image of her abusive stepfather holding her. The man had terrorized her, binding her to a broken past by inflicting her teardrop scar.

Deep down, she knew that broken-young girl was no leader.

Reading her thoughts, Divinity's powerful voice spoke again one last time.

"Never belittle yourself. Remember, I reward bravery such as you have shown, young one. Receive freedom from the shackles of your past."

At that, she began feeling the heat of the great light amplifying upon her face. It began tingling in the presence of the *great one.*

At its touch, she reached up to run her fingers over the skin on her face. As her fingers glided over her cheek, she expected to feel them bump over her teardrop scar; however, all she felt was her soft skin, unmarred.

Falling to her knees, she laughed in ecstasy at the sensation of the Kingdom of Light. For the very first time, she felt her tears cascade down a face that was no longer marked or scarred.

For the first time, she knew without a doubt that she was free.

Chapter Twenty-Seven

Forin Woods

L ooking past the hood of his forest-green cloak, Kaldon watched the guests in the run-down tavern. Safely enclosed within the wooden walls, men and women danced about in a frenzy. He felt the warmth of his tea-filled mug. From his place, tucked away in the corner, he felt grateful to be able to rest his body from his travels. It had been almost four months since he had seen Anneya. In the quaint city, Bailsbur, he was drawing closer to the hometown of the Sovereign of Shadow; Gorath. He was likely only several weeks away from the city. The ominous-black tower he saw in his vision called him, beckoning him onward into the unknown.

He looked at *Humility* and *Integrity* which were resting on the oak table. Running his fingers over the leather bands disguising *Integrity*, he felt confident that it was concealed well. The legendary blade's identity needed to be hidden. To carry a sword in Agadin was expected; however, the unique appearance of such a sword would raise too many questions.

Looking down to his reddened forearm, his eyes traced the lightning bolt scar that marked him. He had experienced burns as a child, but nothing like this. Even though Olivia's healing restored his arm for the most part, it still burned. He had hoped the pain would have subsided by now, but the lick of fire still scraped through his arm.

Placing his hand upon the burn, he needed to dim the pain raging through his arm. Doing what he always did while summoning the Kingdom of Light, he brought the image of the fiery bird from eternity to his mind. As the Owl's flames tumbled through his mind, he called the Kingdom to Agadin. A smile grew on his face as he began feeling tingling on his forearm. The burning pain began to dim.

He exhaled in relief. He knew it was only a temporary reprieve but was thankful for it. He'd tried to heal his burnt arm many times since his time in Gilead. Sometimes it would come, while other times it wouldn't. He was growing in his ability to call forth the Kingdom but had yet to master the skill.

He rested, regaining his strength before setting forth to travel once again, when his thoughts were interrupted by one of the tavern's peddlers.

The brightly dressed peddler jumped onto a table in the centre of the tavern, adding to the clamour of the night. He wore vibrant clothing of reds, blues, and yellows. Kaldon knew it was a strategy to draw the eyes of crowds as he entertained. He was used to seeing peddlers coming and going through the tavern. He watched several share stories and songs, trying to squeeze out as many coins from the listeners as possible.

The man projected his voice, hamming his tone for theatrical effect. "You have all heard stories of Kreel! You have heard of the tales of Dawntan Forlorn and Tolek the Brave! But I have come today to tell you a new tale."

Guests in the tavern quieted at the peddler's words. All leaned in to be engrossed by whatever tale the man had to offer.

Pausing to ensure their attention, the vibrantly dressed peddler continued, "I will share with you a story of victory: a story of hope! I will share with you the story of Kaldon!"

Kaldon's eyes widened and he almost forgot to breathe.

"Tell us!" one of the guests shouted.

The peddler lifted a hand into the air as he began. Kaldon tensed, wondering what the obnoxious man had to say about him.

"Kaldon grew up far past the Mountains of D'aal, in a small city no larger than our own. He had a humble beginning, growing up on the streets. But little did those around him know that he had a deep secret... No one knew who he really was."

The peddler paused, taking in the curious eyes that watched him.

"Who was he!?" one of the guests begged.

"Tell us!" another shouted.

"Ah, ah," the man said waving a finger. "You know the rules."

Several guests walked up to the man, throwing coin down at his feet, urging him to continue with the tale.

The peddler smiled in gratitude. "Are you ready to hear Kaldon's secret?"

The tavern guests roused in cheers.

Kaldon held his breath.

The peddler leaned in. "He was the son of Dolan Thain."

Men and women throughout the tavern gasped. Murmurs and whispers spilled throughout the group. As guests began rushing to the table throwing more coin on the table, Kaldon realized his mouth was agape.

The peddler continued, "Kaldon left his hometown to chase greatness. He learned an ability which allowed him to see events before they even take place. They say, he is like a Seer of battle. He even bested a fully grown Kreel; a feat difficult for even a Bishop."

As the peddler paused, one of the women shouted. "Tell us more!"

A smile spread over the dramatic man's face, knowing that his audience was captivated. He continued, "Kaldon Thain found himself at the Peak of Lore, the renowned training facility, where he befriended Tolek the Brave. He played a role in stopping an entire army from capsizing the facility. He wielded the final blow to kill the army's General; Geran Rule, a Dark Paladin."

Guests stood, cheering at the epic tale.

The peddler hushed the crowd, forcing their excitement to simmer. "Kaldon Thain is a Protector of Agadin, but he is not a common one. He is rare, indeed. While we have heard of Paladins and Seers, he is something altogether different. Although I do not know the meaning of his title, the word spreading through Agadin is that Kaldon Thain is…. a Paragon."

An awe-filled silence filled the tavern at the mention of Kaldon's title as a Protector of Agadin. Most had likely never heard of it before it escaped the peddler's mouth.

Before the peddler could expand further on his tale in an attempt to make more coin, Kaldon stood, strapping *Humility* and *Integrity* to his hip and back. He had heard enough of his personal story becoming a petty bar tale. Making his way to the door, he left the clamour of the tavern behind him. Grabbing the wooden handle, a weathered voice arose.

"Excuse me, young man."

Kaldon turned around to see a man, matured in age, behind him holding a stick for walking. Seeing the elder's bald head, other than for a few spindles of stark-white hair, he concluded that he was likely in his early-eighties in age.

In a worn voice, he continued, "Would you mind grabbing the door for me, my boy?"

Kaldon watched the man, appreciating seeing someone growing to such an age. In Agadin, it was uncommon to see such a thing. Most lives were often taken much earlier by the effects of weather or war.

"Of course," he said, pulling open the door.

As the sagely man walked out of the tavern into the black of night, Kaldon called out to him. "Could you please direct me, sir?"

The old man turned around. "Well, that depends. Where are you going?"

"Gorath," he responded.

"Ah, Gorath." The sagely man's auburn eyes looked upon him with concern. "From the looks of those swords you carry, you likely won't heed the warning I am about to give you, but no one who journeys to Gorath is safe. You would be wise to keep your distance."

Seeing that Kaldon wasn't wilting after his word of caution, the old man sighed. He said, "Unfortunately, the quickest path to Gorath is the most dangerous. You will need to go through Forin Woods. Dark things live there: dreadful things. But it is only one week's travel through. To go around the forest, it would add a full month to your journey if you don't know the right paths."

"Then I must go through Forin Woods," he said, determined.

The old man nodded. "Ah, well then, best of luck to you, young man."

He patted Kaldon's shoulder as he turned to face the streets of Bailsbur. "Wield your swords true," he said as he left.

He watched the old man as his walking stick carried him into the dark of evening. *Wield your swords true,* he thought to himself, the odd words running through his mind.

Kaldon stepped into the night. Walking through the empty streets, he breathed in the hot wind around him. He wasn't used to such a climate change. Growing up so close to the Mountains of D'aal, he was accustomed to the cold. The closer he came to Gorath, the more heated the air became. The swell of humidity felt damp on his clothes.

Making his way through the town, he could already see Forin Woods in the distance. Walking closer to the body of greenery, he thought of the peddler's tale concerning his life. It was odd for him to hear his story summed up in only several minutes. People of Agadin were beginning to see him as a hero; though it wasn't how he perceived himself. He was simply trying to do what he could for Agadin's sake.

Standing before Forin Woods, he paused taking a deep breath, tasting humidity on his tongue. Exhaling deeply, he stepped into darkness as the trees engulfed him.

He trudged for what felt like hours through the still forest. He heard the cracks of wood around him and the movement of trees in the wind. As peaceful as the treed land seemed, Kaldon couldn't ignore the increase of angst in his nerves. He knew it was his foresight flaring. Something was amiss. There was no way around a forest of such magnificent size. To go back and around wasn't an option. He felt the increased incline as he climbed a hill that led deeper into the woods. With each step he took, the words of the elderly man from the tavern cautioning him about travelling through Forin Woods rung throughout his memories, urging him to turn back.

Nearing the top of the hill, his foresight swelled, making his stomach turn. Pine trees surrounding him, he stopped, catching his breath. His foresight told him that something deadly dwelled on the other side of the hill, but he needed to persevere. For all he knew, it could simply be a few of the Sovereign's warriors or a Kreel. He had killed his fair share of men and Kreel; still, he also knew it could be something far worse.

Taking a step forward, peering over the hill. He nearly gasped aloud. Thousands of trees were stretched out before his sight, strung with darkened blotches hanging from the solid branches. Nearly one thousand adult Kreel swung from the trees — asleep, like bats in a cave.

Knowing the only path through the dark woods was to travel onwards, all that escaped his mouth were the words, "Great Divinity…"

CHAPTER TWENTY-EIGHT

UNDERSTANDING STARTS AS A SEED

K aldon felt himself trembling at the sight of so many Kreel. He knew he could kill one or maybe two; but one thousand would be a massacre. Taking in the sight, he gulped, knowing that the only way to Gorath was to go through.

He slowly crept over the hill, descending to where the Kreel slept. Before him, he looked at an upside-down Kreel that hung at nearly ten feet tall in size. With each breath it took, it released a raspy snarl as a snore. Carefully brushing past the beast, he prayed its eyes wouldn't snap open. Weaving between trees, he fought accidentally brushing against the drooping Kreel. He knew if they awoke, it would only be a matter of seconds before he would be torn apart by the creatures. With each step, his foresight stormed through him, shouting warning.

Kreel by Kreel, he made his way through the labyrinth of creatures. Following the patterns of the snores of the beasts, he stepped only when a snarl would sound to mask his steps. He'd already counted over two dozen of the beasts on his way through yet knew there were hundreds more. He knew it would likely be hours before he would be safe and free of the creatures.

Snap!

Anxiety slammed into him upon hearing a dead branch break underneath his foot. He waited in stillness as he watched the closest Kreel.

Don't wake up. Don't wake up, he thought in panic, looking at the creature hanging nearly eleven feet in height.

The nearest Kreel's eyes fluttered for a moment, then suddenly popped open.

No, Kaldon thought. With seemingly boundless Kreel surrounding him, he knew there was no way out.

The Kreel let out a wretched shriek, waking the others around it. He watched as hundreds of Kreel dropped from the trees, landing on the forest floor. He breathed heavily as endless eyes looked upon him, lusting for his blood to be spilled.

He unsheathed *Humility* and *Integrity,* holding them out to his sides. The gold and silver blades shimmered in the moonlight. He could feel his arm burning from Marradus' flames as he held *Integrity.* His foresight blared as a multitude of different scenarios raged through his mind; however, he knew the ability would do him no good. There was no way he could dodge every attack that his visions promised would come. In that moment, he knew he wouldn't live throughout the night. From every side of him, Kreel growled and shrieked, ready to feast.

Preparing himself for certain death, he began to feel a subtle vibration from under his feet. The sensation climbed from the ground and up his legs. Adrenaline pumping through him. He was ready to fight to the very end, while the vibrations continued to grow into a rumble coursing through the forested floor.

Trees began to shake, then violently sway from side to side. The Kreel looked from right to left, confused. Kaldon's legs shook. He tried to keep his balance as the earth quaked violently beneath him. The Kreel began screeching into the night, their wings extending as the intense vibrations forced them from the ground.

Each leapt into evening skies, forsaking their prey, fearing the sudden earthquake.

As nearly one thousand Kreel cried in wails, Kaldon covered his ears at the high-pitched screams. He watched the creatures fading into night skies. The rumbling slowly ceased. The trees stilled; the sound of havoc gone.

Kaldon panted as lingering anxiety rivered though him. With the Kreel gone, all he saw was the empty forest. He allowed his breathing to steady. Thankfulness washed over him for the earthquake, though he couldn't help feeling the timing seemed *too* perfect.

Peering into the empty forest, the rustling of branches sounded in the distance. Looking into the mass of trees, all he could make out was a shadowy image of a shorter man, hunched over with a walking stick. He immediately recognized the old man from the tavern.

The residual vibrations still shaking through him, he pondered the timely earthquake. His eyes were fixed on the old man. Kaldon followed him.

Keeping his distance as much as he could, he hid behind trees, bushes, and boulders so he wouldn't be spotted. Considering the man's age, he was surprised how little he needed to take time for rest. There were a few times when he would pause, taking in his surroundings. In these times, Kaldon worried that he might be discovered, but it wasn't long before the man went on his way again, burrowing deeper into the woods. Following him for what felt like several hours, he finally reached his destination.

Looking over the hedge of bush, Kaldon watched him walking steadily towards a small house tucked away in Forin Woods. Most of the forest was dark and gloomy, but here, strands of light pierced through tree branches, illuminating the home. It was surprising how well-hidden the house was. Trees stretched hundreds of feet into the air, like a shield preventing sight. He doubted he would have been able to find it if he hadn't followed him.

The old man ran his hand over the worn door, brushing off old chips of paint. Constructed by stones nearly the size of a man's head, the house seemed to be held together with sturdy clay. It was clearly a well-used place, looking as though the man may have spent decades in it. Surrounding it were plants, flowers, and shrubbery. All looked to be properly tended to; cared for. The old man stepped away from the door, making his way to the backyard.

Keeping his distance, Kaldon followed.

Hiding behind surrounding trees, he saw the old man tending to plants and herbs in the backyard. He had never seen such a garden in all his life. Flowers of all sorts adorned the backyard in vivid colour. The old man walked to specific plots of space, using a finger to press seeds into the soil throughout the garden.

Kaldon stepped out from the shadows of the trees. The old man had his back turned to him as he nipped away at shrubbery with gardening tools.

He spoke in a soft tone, as not to unintentionally startle the man. "It is good to see you again, friend."

The man paused, slowly rising from the grassy floor. He turned to face Kaldon. "It's good to see that you finally chose to emerge from the shadows."

Kaldon raised his eyebrows. "You knew I was following you?"

The old man laughed weakly. "Of course. I know these woods better than anyone. Living in such a dangerous place, you learn to know when you are being followed."

The old man picked up his bag from the ground rummaging through it. "You must be hungry. I must have some food here somewhere. You probably haven't eaten since you started following me, am I right?"

"No, thank you. I'm not hungry," Kaldon lied. He was starving. As hungry as he was, more pressing things weighed on him. "I'm sorry if I startled you. I didn't have a choice."

"And why would that be?" the man said, resting his bag on the ground again.

"I needed to follow you because it isn't every day that I meet a Roek. It is good to finally meet you, *Orin,*" Kaldon said, keeping his eyes on the man.

"A Roek..." the old man said, shaking his head in a wheezy laugh. "What makes you think I am this *Orin* you speak of?"

Kaldon rested his hand upon the hilt of *Humility.* "You scared off a swarm of Kreel by creating an earthquake. It must have been you. You saved my life. I'm grateful for what you did for me."

The old man tensed his face. "I don't know what you are talking about. I was simply hiding from the Kreel. The earthquake had nothing to do with me. It was a coincidence; a lucky coincidence for the both of us."

Kaldon ran his hand over his beard, tilting his head. "You can pretend if you want. Locrian told me about you. He said you like to stay hidden, keeping to yourself. He said no one knows who you really are, other than you and your wife. Where is she? Maybe she will tell me who you really are," he pressed.

The old man's eyes turned sad. "My wife died three years ago. I am here alone."

"I'm sorry," he said, wishing he had chosen his words more wisely. Looking at the tucked away home, he realized how lonely the man must be.

"Agadin needs your help, Orin," he said, with determination in his tone. "The Sovereign of Shadow has servants everywhere throughout Agadin. Worse, the demon dragon, Marradus, is causing chaos throughout the land, tearing apart entire cities."

"I've heard rumours of this dragon," the man said, quietly. "I wouldn't be surprised if it will bring Agadin to its end."

Kaldon stepped forward. "Then help me. Help keep Agadin safe."

The old man pressed his lips together, looking away. "Even if I were this man you speak of, I couldn't stop a dragon. What would you expect me to do?"

"I would expect you to train me," he said with his gaze stuck on the man.

The old man let out a faint cough, clearing his throat. "And who are you? You seem to have a lot of assumptions about me for someone who is so secretive about himself."

Kaldon waited in the moment, weighing his next words. "I am a Protector of Again."

"Ah, I see," the old man said, lifting his chin. "And what is your name, Protector of Agadin?"

Stirring up his confidence, he said, "I am Kaldon Thain, the son of the Warrior General, Dolan Thain."

He watched as the old man's eyes slightly widened.

"Kaldon Thain. I've heard of you," the man said. "You are the Paragon everyone is talking about…"

He nodded, hating to admit his life was such topic of conversation. "Orin, I need you to train me how to Command Creation. I doubt there is anyone in all of Agadin other than yourself who can," he said.

Within the confines of his personal garden, the old man looked at Kaldon with conflict marking his face.

"Please... For the sake of Agadin," Kaldon said.

The old man looked to the garden enshrouding them. He took in the vast array of flowers, shrubs, and plants. As time passed between them, the man opened his worn hand, looking at a single brown seed he carried in his palm. He sighed, slowly kneeling onto the forest floor beneath him. He placed the seed in fertile soil, using his thumb to press it deep into the ground.

Kaldon watched as the old man simply kept his eyes on the small patch of soil. A thin green strand poked out from the dirt. He could feel wonder taking him as he saw new life birth right before his eyes. The leafy strand slowly twisted into the air, growing in both height and girth.

His eyes grew wide — the plant was already half the size of the old man's body. The stem that stretched from the soil, began taking a mahogany colour. What looked like coarse bark began coating the trunk. Higher it grew, until it towered nearly twice the size of Orin.

Speechless, Kaldon watched as branches stretched from the tree's trunk, giving life to forest-green leaves. Stems took shape from the branches. Red fruit, the size of a man's fist swelled from nothing right before his eyes. Once the ruby apples took form, Orin reached up to pluck one of the pieces of fruit, holding it out to him.

Kaldon reached out hesitantly, grabbing the apple. He could feel its firmness in his hand. He examined the piece of fruit and the grand tree before him, astounded at how all of this came from a tiny seed in mere moments. All he could get out were a few faint words. Little did he know, those words would shift his perception of everything he thought he knew.

With wonder in his tone, he said, "Orin, teach me everything."

CHAPTER TWENTY-NINE

PERFECT SOIL

———◆◆◆———

Kaldon looked around the confines of the quaint home, seeing what he would have expected from the old man. The furniture spread throughout was mature and well used. It wasn't messy at all, but instead well-ordered. Every pot and pan had its place; every decoration was purposefully positioned. Sitting at a kitchen table, he looked upon the unassuming Roek.

"Orin, how did you first learn about your ability?" he asked, eager to learn about the man.

Orin took a sip of his tea. Looking at the young man before him, he was clearly weighing whether or not he should answer the question.

"I know you can Command Creation," Kaldon sighed. "I just watched you grow an entire tree from a tiny seed. I'm not going to tell anyone about your secret."

Rubbing his hands together, the man mused aloud. "I'm sorry. As I mentioned before, the only ones who have known of my ability were Locrian and my wife, Mary. But I suppose if it will benefit Agadin, I will tell you."

"It truly will," Kaldon said, reassuring the man.

Taking a deep breath, he began. "I was eleven years old when I first used my ability. I grew up on a farm on the outskirts of the Plains of Morah. My parents were farmers. My older brother was digging a rather large hole, when the dirt walls gave out on him. I remember the horror, watching my brother being buried alive. I screamed, stretching out my hands, reaching for him. Then it happened."

"What happened?" he asked, leaning in.

"The dirt halted, being held in place," Orin said in a raspy voice. "I was astounded by what I saw. It was as though the dirt was defying gravity. It gave my brother the opportunity to climb out, unharmed."

"So, from this point on, you could Command Creation?" he asked, intrigued.

The old man let out a rough laugh. "Oh no, it wasn't that simple. When my brother's life was spared, I didn't even know I was the one responsible for the dirt not crushing him. It was an enigma to me. I spent night after night, running the scenario through my mind. It wasn't until five years later that I realized the only explanation was that *I* was the one who stopped the dirt."

"Unbelievable," Kaldon whispered.

Orin nodded. "It was then when I began practicing commanding the earth. I spent countless hours with a bowl of dirt before me, trying to convince it to move. I felt like a fool doing so. Even as I tried, failing over and over again, I knew the truth; I was the one who saved my brother. After what felt like an eternity of practice, it finally happened; the dirt obeyed me.

After I saw it happen once, I was unstoppable in my pursuit. Day and night, I practiced. At first, I exercised my ability on dirt, then stones. Once I grew comfortable with stones, I began challenging myself with commanding shrubs and trees. It took several years before I was able to make the earth quake."

"Your ability reminds me of stories my mother told me as a child," Kaldon said, shaking his head in wonder. "I've only Commanded Creation once, with fire. I haven't been able to since. Locrian has the ability to command wind; however, it is nothing like I've seen you do."

Orin laughed lightly. "I taught him how to do that, you know. Locrian is a good man; that said, his true gift isn't in Commanding Creation."

He nodded in thought. "Can you command the other elements then? Fire, water, and wind?"

The old man rose, walking to one of his cupboards. "Oh yes, but to a much lesser degree. Earth means more to me than the others; almost as though it's an extension of who I am," he said, rummaging through cabinets and drawers.

"What is it you're looking for?" Kaldon asked.

"Come on, where are you?" Orin complained, speaking into the cupboards as objects tumbled about — ignoring the question.

"Ah, there you are," he said, holding out a dated clay bowl. "It even has some dirt in it still."

He placed the paled-red bowl upon the table. "This, is the bowl I used to teach myself how to command earth," he explained.

Kaldon saw that inside the old clay bowl, only a thin layer of dirt was matted on the bottom. "Don't I need more dirt than this to practice?" he asked.

241

A patient smile spread over the man's wrinkled face. "Of course you do."

Stretching his weathered hand over the old bowl, Kaldon's eyes popped as the dirt began to multiply, building upwards, nearly reaching the rim.

Orin reached his hand in, smoothing out the dirt. "Now that, my boy, is perfect soil. When I first taught myself to Command Creation, it was challenging to draw even a line in this dirt. But, with practice, there are no limits to what you can do."

The Roek's eyes intimately watched the soil, as his gaze flicked up. Following his stare, dirt ascended above the bowl. Kaldon watched as the soil spun throughout the air, making patterns and intricate shapes of all sorts. It was like a dance of creation performing right before him.

"What do I need to do in order to learn how to do this?" he asked, his gaze following the complicated designs.

The dirt dropped from the air, landing back in the bowl. He looked in, seeing that the wondrous patterns were once again lost in the ordinary bowl of soil.

Pushing the bowl closer to him, the Roek said, "You must learn to draw a line before you can orchestrate a design. Now, get started."

Orin stood, grabbing a broom from the pantry, and made his way into the living room to begin sweeping. The Roek moseying about, Kaldon fixed his eyes on the dark-brown dirt. He longed to see the elaborate designs again yet sighed at how even writing one single line in the soil felt impossible.

In his mind, he imagined a line taking shape in the dirt. He meditated on it moving from left to right. Over, and over again he did so. At the sound of Orin's broom brushing upon the wooden floor, he thought of when he once commanded fire to wrap around his sword *Integrity*. If he did it then, he could do it now.

"Earth, move," he whispered to the soil.

Unresponsive, the soil sat still.

He tried standing and sitting. He attempted whispering and shouting, yet the soil did not obey him. It simply sat still, disobedient to his command. Each minute passing, frustration swelled within him. He didn't have time to speak to a bowl of dirt. Lives were at stake.

After nearly three hours of strenuous striving, he finally gave into discouragement. He slouched into his chair, pushing the bowl of dirt away.

Orin looked up from his household tasks, walking back into the kitchen. "What's wrong? You'll never get anywhere with an attitude like that."

"I don't have time for this," he said, looking up at the calm Roek. His peaceful demeanour fanned his frustration into greater flames. "I don't understand. Locrian told me that Commanding Creation has to do with understanding authority; that it has to do with our link to creation. I believe in my link to creation, but this soil won't do anything," he said, waving a hand in frustration.

"Yes, Locrian is correct," Orin nodded. "Your understanding of authority over creation is what will give you the ability to Command Creation. However, that statement is greatly simplified. It's true that we need to have a belief in our link to creation; however, it is also accurate that true authority doesn't come from that belief."

Kaldon rubbed his tired eyes. "What do you mean?"

"True authority comes from knowing who you are," Orin said.

As Kaldon sat in thought, the Roek continued, "Tell me, why is it that you want to learn this ability?"

"So I can kill the Sovereign of Shadow. He is destroying Agadin, just as he did my father and mother," he responded directly.

"That answer alone reveals your weakness," Orin said, keeping his gaze on Kaldon. "You have more trust in learning this ability than you do in yourself."

"I don't understand what you're saying. I need this ability to defeat Tymas Droll," he said, looking away.

Orin nodded. "That may be true; but, think about it this way: If a man is crippled by his insecurity, yet he somehow manages to build a thriving kingdom, he will be content with what he has built. However, if he, for whatever reason, loses his kingdom, what will he be left as?"

"He will be left as nothing, because he had nothing to begin with," Kaldon said, trying to follow the Roek's analogy.

"Exactly," Orin said, with an instructive finger pointing in the air. "Now, if a man builds a kingdom who is already confident in who he is and then loses it, he can simply build again. He isn't crushed by failure. He is refined by it, because his confidence is found not in what he can do, but in *who he is*."

"True," Kaldon nodded. "But how does this apply to me?"

"It applies to you because you place far too much importance on learning your gift. You think *you* learning your gift will make you a hero, but it won't. Don't get me wrong, learning your gift is important; however, a frail heart cannot properly wield a weighty gift. Only a confident and whole heart can. If you believe you're not capable without your ability, then you don't deserve to have it."

Leaning in closer to the young man, he continued, "Kaldon, with or without the ability to Command Creation, you can be the hero that Agadin needs."

Doubt twisted Kaldon's face.

Orin cut in before he could object. "You can! Until you believe that, your insecurity will be the barrier preventing you from Commanding Creation. You need to learn to believe in yourself more than in your abilities."

Kaldon tried to let the words to sink into his heart.

Orin looked deep into the young man. "I'm sorry, my boy. I know that you want to grow quickly, but your mindset is your true obstacle. In order to be built up, you first need to be torn down. We need to take care of the intricate, before we can perform the magnificent."

Orin slid the bowl to Kaldon. "Now, let's fix your perspective. Draw a line in the soil."

CHAPTER THIRTY

MARY

Hearty flames swayed inside the stone fireplace. Feeling the warmth, Kaldon watched strands of heat ascending in the still air. He thought back on his previous week. Day after day, Orin unpacked the concept of Commanding Creation. It was proving to be more complex than he expected. He learned very quickly that, as impressive as Locrian's ability to wield wind was — compared to Orin's, his understanding was extremely limited. The Roek was like a storehouse of revelation concerning the lost art.

He had lost track of the hours he spent trying to take authority over soil, ushering it to move at his command. He attempted to summon the wind, to manipulate fire, to stir waters. He had no success. Creation rebelled, rejecting his command.

There was something comfortable about the home. Growing up on the streets, he was never granted something so consistent and unchanging. His swords *Humility* and *Integrity* leaned up against the wooden wall. He hadn't touched them since he arrived, allowing them to become draped in dust. It was a shame for him to know that he would need to take up the swords again the following day. Whether he learned the ability to Command Creation or not, the time had come for him to leave and continue his journey to Gorath.

Stretching his hand out toward the flames, he meditated on the flames moving. He imagined them obeying him. Yet, as coals popped, the fire simply flicked steadily, ignoring him.

"Stop striving. You are trying too hard," Orin's voice bellowed from the kitchen, followed by the sound of pots and pans clanging about.

The Roek was cleaning again.

"Striving can only take you so far," he said from a distance. "You need to enter a posture of rest if you want to Command Creation. There is insecurity in striving; there is confidence in rest. You must believe in yourself more than in your abilities."

Kaldon dropped his hand looking onward into the flames. He'd heard him say the words over and over again, yet they still hadn't penetrated. He thought of Marradus and its flames. He thought of Tymas Droll. As each hour passed by, restlessness grew within him. He had wasted one full week doing nothing but fruitless training.

He could hear Orin tidying behind him. The man incessantly cleaned, dusting the same spots every day. He washed the same dishes, continually keeping his home in order. He knew the man was entrenched in routine, yet he must have experienced the restless that he himself felt. When the world around you is falling apart, you can only ignore it for so long.

His eyes looked out the window, seeing that nightfall was setting in. He observed the apple tree that Orin had grown right in front of him. The Roek wielded unfathomable power; yet here he was in self-imposed isolation. He was pushed aside from the rest of Agadin; forgotten.

"I need to know something," Kaldon spoke into the lonely home.

Orin put down the old mug he was washing. "What is that?"

He turned around so as to see the old man. "Once you learned your ability, what did you do with it? There's no point in learning an ability simply to let it fall to the wayside."

A sly smile spread over the Roek's weathered face. "Oh, believe me; I used my abilities."

He waited in silence, inviting the Roek to continue.

"Throughout my twenties and thirties, I tracked armies," Orin said.

Kaldon's brows raised. "Tracked armies?"

The Roek nodded. "Once I began understanding my ability, I wanted to use it to advance the Kingdom of Light in the Great War. I was always on the move, traveling in pursuit of those who followed the Dominion of Shadow. I remember countless times pursing armies who served the Dominion. Many of them sought to kill innocents and to destroy cities. I would prevent that from happening."

"How would you stop entire armies?" he asked, leaning against the armrest of the chair.

Orin made his way to the window. He smoothed his hands over the leaves of one of the plants perched upon the windowsill. "I would open up the earth to devour them."

Kaldon's eyes widened. "Entire armies?"

Orin nodded. "The most I swallowed at once was thirty thousand."

Kaldon took in the Roek, hardly able to process what he'd just said. "Why did you stop?"

The old man let out a wheezing cough. "Excuse me?"

"You said you tracked armies during your twenties and thirties. Why did you stop?"

Orin paused, taking in the young man. "I met Mary."

He quieted at the mention of the Roek's deceased wife. He talked about her frequently during their time together.

"I first saw her when I was visiting Bailsbur," Orin said. "During this time in my life, I was so focused on my mission that I didn't have eyes for anyone. But there was something about her I had never seen in anyone else. There was a kindness that is rare: a gentleness. We fell in love. When I eventually told her about how I could Command Creation, she didn't believe me."

Kaldon listened as the man reminisced about his wife.

The Roek laughed, lost in thought. "I still remember the look on her face when she first saw me command a tree to move. She was mesmerized. I eventually told her how I'd tracked armies; how I had saved countless lives. Mary admired my bravery for how I used my ability, but she knew what would happen to me if people knew what I was — what I was capable of. I would no doubt be recruited for war. I would be used for my abilities. Mary and I would never be able to truly be husband and wife. I would be a slave to those with power and influence. I needed to choose between my mission and Mary."

Kaldon nodded, understanding.

"Tell me, my boy. Is there a woman in your life?" Orin asked.

Kaldon looked away, the question catching him off guard. "There is," he admitted. "Here name is Anneya."

A creased smile grew upon Orin's face. "I knew it."

The old man walked closer to Kaldon, placing his hand upon the chair on which he sat. He gazed into the graceful flames. "If you care for her that deeply, you should marry her."

He could feel his cheeks beginning to flush red. "Marry her?!"

"Absolutely," Orin said. "I will tell you something you won't hear from many. One of the marks of a true man is his ability to keep the heart of a woman for a lifetime."

Kaldon considered the words. "Those sound like wise words."

"That's because they are," Orin said in a laugh, patting him on the back as he began making his way back to the kitchen to clean.

He watched the Roek retreating into his routine. His heart broke for the old man; his loneliness was evident. He knew Orin was entrenched within his own comfort.

"Orin," Kaldon called from the chair.

The old man turned around.

Kaldon spoke softly. "We could use your help to defeat Marradus; to fight against the Sovereign of Shadow. I may not learn how to Command Creation. Even if I did, I likely wouldn't be able to do anything enough to present a threat to the Dominion of Shadow. You can. I have never seen power like you have. You can do what you once did, advancing the Kingdom of Light. You can still make a difference in the Great War."

Orin looked away.

Kaldon rose from his chair, hearing the floor creaking beneath him. "Come with me to Gorath. Help us save Agadin."

The old man looked around his home with glazed eyes. To Kaldon the house looked vacant; lonely. However, to Orin it was a library of memories. It was a place that reminded him of what once was. It reminded him of Mary.

The Roek's mouth opening, Kaldon leaned in to hear what he would say.

"Never," the Roek whispered.

As the word echoed throughout the comfortable home, Kaldon stopped himself from taking a step back at his blatant unwillingness.

"But you could be a part of saving Agadin…" Kaldon stuttered. "Lives are at stake. How could you refuse?"

Orin turned away, making his way deeper into the house to his bedroom. "No one can know of my ability, Kaldon. I will not leave. I simply want to be left in peace," he muttered.

With Orin retreated to his bedroom, Kaldon again took a seat in the fabric chair. As sad as he felt for the man, he could feel anger swelling towards him. Agadin needed heroes to rise, not those who would cower in complacency. As far as he knew, Orin was the only Roek alive; that meant he was likely one of the most powerful people who currently walked Agadin. Yet, here he was imprisoned, crippled by his apathy.

Sinking into the chair, he looked into the fire once again. If Orin wouldn't help, he couldn't allow that to become his own excuse to not fight. He held out his hand again before the fire. He could feel his hand tensing, his veins bulging in attempt to Command Creation. As soon as he felt strain growing upon his face, he stopped himself. He remembered what the Roek said to him.

"There is insecurity in striving. Confidence in rest. You need to believe in yourself more than in your abilities."

Heeding the words, Kaldon flipped his hand over, his palm now facing the ceiling. He wasn't going to strive; he would invite the flame, expecting it to come.

His eyes lit as he saw the fire flicker. A strand of flame slowly grew out from the fireplace as though it were being sucked toward him. He watched as the small remnant of fire, no larger than a coin, sailed toward him to rest in the centre of his palm.

His heart raced within him as he watched the translucent fire that danced in the palm of his hand. As fire tumbled in his hand, he could feel flames burning hot within his soul, affirming him onward in his mission.

Resting his head back against the chair, he watched the flame slowly dim. He wished it would last longer. He felt himself losing grip on the subtle flame. It had taken him a week to accomplish what he'd just done. As remarkable as it was, he knew a small flicker of fire wouldn't stop Shadow from reigning in Agadin.

The fire slowly evaporating from the palm of his hand, his head sunk deeper into the chair. His eyes growing heavy, he relished in the small victory. Knowing he would leave the following day to Gorath, sleep took him.

Chapter Thirty-One
Quiet Betrayal

O pening his eyes, Kaldon saw that the flames were barely alive in the fireplace. The room around him looked far drearier than a moment ago. He could no longer feel the heat of fire lingering on his hand. Looking about the room, something seemed amiss; otherworldly.

Realization swept over him. He was in a dream.

From behind him, a smooth voice spoke, filling the humble home.

"Oh, Kal Wendal, it really has been far too long since we have seen one another," the voice cooed.

At the sound of the voice, he immediately knew who it was. He shut his eyes in frustrated dread. Rising from his chair, he looked upon the sinister face. He hated the man.

"Tymas Droll," Kaldon said, tilting his head upwards.

The Sovereign let out a light laugh. "I'm glad to hear you still remember me. After all, we have had some intimate moments together, haven't we?"

Kaldon remained silent, knowing he was looking upon pure evil.

At his silence, Tymas stroked his smooth skin. "Do you really need me to remind you? I still remember my favourite moment with you. You should have seen the unforgettable look on your face when you discovered that I was the one who killed your mother."

Tymas shook his head in thought. "What a priceless moment that was."

At the mention of his mother, Kaldon felt sorrow trying to well up from within him. He used his rage to suppress it.

Stepping toward the Sovereign he spoke. "I wish I could have seen your face when you first heard that I killed your Dark Paladin. Wasn't he your best friend?"

Tymas' face soured, then quickly calmed. "You stopped a small fraction of my army, that is true. However, I have armies all throughout Agadin. Cities are being dominated as we speak. Innocent blood is being spilled. Shadow isn't simply coming; it is here."

The Sovereign looked him up and down. "And here you are, a helpless man who thinks he can save Agadin. You can't save anyone, Kal Wendal. You are still a broken boy, the sewer rat from Rundle. Don't think I've forgotten. I rivaled against your father, eventually taking his life. I can confidently say that you are only a shadow of a man compared to him."

The words stung, but Kaldon looked deep into the Sovereign's eyes. It wasn't long ago when such words would make him turn on himself. No more.

"I'm coming for you," Kaldon said pointedly. "I will hold you accountable for everything you've done."

A cryptic smile grew over the Sovereign of Shadow's face. "Now, that is where you are mistaken, Kal Wendal. In fact, *I* am the one coming for you."

Crack!

At the sound, Kaldon's eyes popped open, awakening from the dream. Looking around, his foresight was blaring. Tymas Droll was nowhere to be seen.

The noise came again, this time more aggressively.

At the pounding sound, he looked back as pieces of wood from the entrance door exploded into the air. Rising from his chair, he watched as several warriors clothed from head to toe in armour charged in. He counted twelve in total. He knew that before him were twelve Dark Bishops.

He reached to his side to pull forth a sword. Grunting in frustration, he felt nothing but his waist. He was weaponless, *Humility* and *Integrity* leaning against the wooden wall.

"What is going on in here?!" Orin voiced in concern, rushing down the worn hallway.

At the sight of twelve Bishops in his living room, the Roek stopped, taking in the sight.

"We aren't here for you, old man," one of the Bishops said in a gruff voice. "Stay where you are, and your life will be spared."

The Bishops slowly walked toward Kaldon; weapons drawn. His foresight was spinning within him. Visions coursed through his mind, yet without a weapon he was defenceless. He could feel sweat beginning to streak down his face. He looked at the wide-eyed Roek who was trembling at the sight of such barbaric men.

"Orin! Help me!" he called to the old man.

The Roek's gaze darted back and forth from Kaldon to the Bishops. He breathed quick breathes, terrified. They drew closer to Kaldon.

"Orin! *Do* something!" he hollered.

Watching the old man standing still and silent, his demeanour sunk. Orin wasn't going to do anything. The cowardly Roek was going to let him be captured to protect his secret. Kaldon felt tears stinging his eyes as he watched him. The man was betraying him by doing nothing.

Dark Bishops reached for Kaldon. He dodged the vice-like hands that grasped at him. As visions passed through his mind, he followed them like a compass guiding him. Ducking underneath a threatening blow, he brought a fist up, connecting it under one of the Bishop's jaws. The man sprawling to the ground, he brought a foot to the side of another man's knee. He heard it snap on impact. The second man fell. However, he knew he had no chance. There were too many.

An eager hand grasping his arm, Kaldon felt one of the Bishop's knees explode into his stomach. A fist slammed into his face making his sight blur. His head spun. The men pummeled him over, and over again. He let his body go limp, losing his will to fight. There was nothing he could do. As much as his body ached from the strikes, it didn't hurt nearly as much as the betrayal from the elderly Roek.

When the Dark Bishops grew tired of beating him, two held him up from underneath his arms. He felt his feet dragging upon the tired floor. He could feel his eyes beginning to swell shut. He didn't doubt that it would only be a matter of minutes before he wouldn't be able to see anymore.

Taking his last opportunity, he lifted his eyes to see the comforting home for the last time. He took in the orderly abode.

He saw *Humility* and *Integrity* leaning against the wall.

It took all his courage to look at the old Roek. Orin's weathered face was matted in tears.

Being dragged out from the once peaceful home, he mustered the only words he could. "Orin… Please, help me."

Through raspy sobs, he heard Orin speak words that were like a sword through his heart. "I'm sorry, my boy. I just can't. I'm so sorry."

CHAPTER THIRTY-TWO

THE HUNT

It was midday; however, Shadow dimmed the skies. Anneya was beginning to loathe how each day it grew darker. As her eyes roamed over the Plains of Morah, she thought on Divinity's words which he'd spoken to her in the Courts of Light. They felt like a eulogy spoken over the beloved land.

"With the Door of the Dominion open, Shadow is eating away at Agadin. It is stealing the very skies. You will understand. Once Death's Snow falls, you will understand."

She knew it was true; Marradus was horrifying. Still, with or without the dragon, Shadow was prevailing. Marching on through the plains, she looked at the remaining army of four thousand. They persevered onward to the city of Flank, in hope of preventing the demon dragon from demolishing yet another city.

Out of the corner of her eye, she caught Tolek watching her again. She knew he was looking at her face; where she was once marked by a teardrop scar. The remnant of her childhood was gone. Running her fingers over her now smooth cheek, she mourned leaving the Courts of Light behind. She missed the white mountain.

She watched all ten of the Paladins amongst the army, their slight advantage in an impossible mission. At first, the Paladins didn't believe her when she told them that the great light came to her, or that Divinity had spoken to her, telling her to come to the courts alone. For most of them, their ego clouded their judgement rendering them unable to accept that Divinity would choose her rather than a Paladin. Her healed scar was all the proof she needed. Everyone knew that not even a Master Healer could make scars vanish. Only a Shan-Rafa could — a Shan-Rafa or Divinity himself.

"What was it again that Divinity spoke to you about me, Anneya?" Tolek asked, interrupting her train of thought.

The Blade tried to hide her irritation. Tolek asked her the same question over and over again, as though he expected her to have a different answer each time.

"Divinity said that you were the Paladin spoken of in Kaldon's prophecy. He said that you need to obtain the impenetrable shield. You have the potential to find it, when we hunt Marradus."

"You're sure that is all he said?" he pressed.

Anneya fought off scowling at the Paladin. "As I've said before, Divinity didn't have anything else to say about the matter."

Tolek ignored her blatant annoyance, already lost in thought once again. "Where would I find such a thing?" he muttered in thought.

She rubbed her nose again, leaving the Paladin to his pondering. The burnt smell grew with each step their journey took. She hoped it was a forest fire, yet knew better than to be so optimistic.

"Tolek!" the shout came from the distance.

Looking back, she saw Henry running in a steady gait toward him. As the colossal man ran, it was a sight to behold given the sheer size of him.

"The men are all in order, Tolek; readied to fight when we find the beast. They listened to every order I gave. You have trained them well," Henry said in a deep tone.

Tolek nodded his gratitude.

"I'm sure there isn't a person alive who wouldn't listen to you, Henry," Anneya teased, trying to lighten the mood. "The soldiers seem terrified of you. They can't stop staring."

"You think?" Henry asked, looking back to the surrounding warriors, seeing their attention stuck on him. "Considering they are used to seeing Tolek all the time, they are clearly just shocked at seeing someone so good looking around."

She barked out a laugh. Considering their circumstances, she was surprised to see a slight smile stretch over Tolek's face.

"How is it that you can get away with poking fun at Tolek? Everyone else just gets a Paladin's scowl," she said.

"Tolek has endured my teasing for many years, my dear. Since we were still young boys," Henry replied, patting Tolek's shoulder. "We trained together. I still remember when we were both Knights."

Tolek nodded, confirming the man's claim. As Anneya looked at him, she could tell the Paladin was lost in thought. His mind was already in the battle before them; on Marradus. Even though she considered him a mentor, he was still a mystery. She knew nearly nothing about his past, or about his training.

"Who trained you both as Paladins?" she asked.

Henry looked at Tolek seeing if he would reply. When he didn't, the large Paladin spoke up instead. "A Paladin being trained is rare, not common by any means."

The Blade furrowed her brow. "Couldn't a Paladin simply train another?"

Henry shook his head. "It isn't that simple. Only one Paladin in this century had the gift to train other Paladins. In fact, not only has he trained every one of us here, but he has trained every Paladin who walks Agadin today."

Anneya's eyes were wide. She had no clue there were different types of Paladins, nor that one needed to be uniquely gifted to raise up others.

"Where is this man now?" she asked.

Henry continued, "He disappeared almost two decades ago. Considering Paladins rarely live to old age, most believe he died on a mission. Some of us Paladins here were the last he ever trained. He was called a *War Lord*; a special breed of Paladin, appointed by Divinity to raise up others. Throughout Agadin, he is known as the *King of Paladins*."

"The King of Paladins…" she whispered. The title felt foreign coming from her lips. Her mind raced at the revelation. "What was his name?" she asked.

Tolek surprised her, speaking forth. "His name was *Rederick Rule*."

She could hear contempt in the Tolek's tone, his countenance hardening.

"Rule… That names sounds familiar." Her eyes went wide. "Wait, was he Geran's father?" she asked.

Tolek didn't respond.

Her mind was a whirlwind of questions. "Where is he now? How did he just *disappear?*"

"Easy there, Philosopher. You are going to give yourself a headache," Henry said, snorting a laugh. "No one knows where Rederick is. As I said, most believe he is long dead. That man was like nothing I have ever seen. He was faster than any Paladin alive, able to summon more force than even the mightiest. It isn't for no reason he carries the title, War Lord. The Paladins followed him without question. Then one day without a word, he was gone."

Anneya shook her head in wonder. She looked at the Paladins that surrounded her, realizing why each were scattered throughout Agadin. Their leader was gone; the King of Paladins, lost.

Before she could ask another question, she watched as one of the Paladins rushed through the multitude of soldiers towards them. It was Dianne. The Paladin halted before Tolek, unapologetically breaking up their conversation.

"Tolek, we are approaching Flank. The demon dragon has beat us there," she said.

He breathed in through his nose, taking in the smell of fire. "I assumed as much," he said.

"It gets worse," Dianne said directly.

Tolek tilted his head at Dianne's claim. "How so?"

She sighed. "I've been told some of the Sovereign's soldiers are there."

"I thought Marradus doesn't serve the Sovereign?" he stated. "Why would his warriors be there?"

She shook her head unknowingly. "The dragon doesn't serve the Sovereign. I'm assuming he is trying to reap the benefit of

Marradus' mayhem. I think he is sending soldiers to lay claim to what remains of cities and their people once the dragon is finished."

Tolek stretched his hand around the hilt of his sword. "That's smart of him to use Marradus' recklessness to his advantage. Do you know how many soldiers are stationed outside of Flank?"

She shook her head reluctantly. "I'm not sure. I heard at least one thousand."

Tolek unsheathed his sword, its metallic ring muffled by the noise of the army. His jaw clenched. "I'm going to make sure they don't see the end of day. Spread the word: none of them live, unless I say otherwise. We go, now."

Dianne and Henry both nodded, immediately rushing to the overseers in the army. War was about to begin.

The Paladin's command echoed throughout the ranks. The pace of soldiers quickened as they began running in the direction of the city. Anneya was surprised at how quickly the army of four thousand picked up in pace. She began quickening in her stride as well. She had fought in many battles, yet this was the part she hated the most; running into the unknown. She knew that at the peak of any upcoming hill, opponents could come into her line of sight. On all sides, Paladins surrounded her. Each time her feet hit the ground, she felt the weight of the Legacy bouncing around her neck, affirming her onward.

Reaching the top of an emerald hill, her heart faltered at the sight. In the near distance, she saw scarlet flames ascending from within the city walls. The sight made her immediately stop in stride. As warriors stopped alongside of her, they hushed in unison, eyes agape. All watched what hung above the city of Flank. It was so terrible that she nearly forgot to breathe. The onyx dragon hovered, flapping its monstrous wings. From its mouth raged reds and yellows, engulfing the city. Even the most formidable of armies wouldn't be capable of defeating it.

"Anneya! Come on!" Dianne yelled back to her.

Refusing the shock that threatened to settle in, she began running again head on into a battle she knew was going to be a massacre. Out of the corner of her eye, something caught her attention.

"You've got to be kidding me…" she mumbled. "Tolek!"

The Paladin stopped, looking back to Anneya. The Blade pointed into the distance to the mob of warriors who weren't their own. The numbers were far more staggering than Dianne first said. Standing far off from the city, they waited for the dragon to be finished with its purge so as to take what was left of the city. Nearly five thousand soldiers of the Sovereign of Shadow waited. Kreel soared above the army, awaiting to feast upon the dragon's leftovers.

Tolek's body tensed at the sight. The Paladin rushed through his ranks of men, ordering that they take out the imposing threat. Anneya knew the warriors were well trained; however, the numbers were a stab of discouragement.

"Henry!" Tolek shouted.

The large man turned his attention.

"We are four thousand versus five thousand! They need a Paladin to lead them. Show them how it's done!" he commanded.

Without hesitation, Henry let out a shout as he summoned his war-hammer from his back. Anneya knew that even the most confident would cower before such a man. As the large Paladin charged, the army followed him. Bishops, Blades, Knights, and warriors stormed toward the waiting army. In the collision of steel, blood immediately began to spill. Kreel began to feast. Watching Henry wield his war-hammer was like watching a tornado in battle. He spun the hammer around his body, slaying whatever came in his path.

The battle raging, Anneya found herself jealous of those fighting men and Kreel. She knew she at least stood a chance against them; but with the remaining nine Paladins, she ran head on toward the dragon.

Even through the sounds of war, she was surprised that she could hear the dragon's mighty breaths. Its exhales sounded like an avalanche crashing down mountain terrain. With Tolek at the lead, the Paladins ran alongside her. Each was unshakable in their pursuit. She supposed each carried the confidence to believe they could single handedly slay the beast; yet here she was doubting they would last even minutes before falling to their deaths. The Paladins summoning their weapons of choice, Anneya didn't bother drawing her bow and arrows. She knew no one could shoot an arrow such a distance to hit the dragon.

Taking in the gargantuan creature before her, she flinched as an arrow shot past her head. The arrow sailed high-ward to impossible heights. Considering how far away the archer was, it took several moments before it ricocheted off the dragon's thick scales. She had never seen someone gain so much distance with an arrow before. Looking back, she saw Platius nocking another arrow to his bow, firing with unfathomable accuracy.

The second arrow rebounded from the demon dragon. Marradus turned its attention from the city to the concession of Paladins. The creature roared in wrath at the sight of Agadin's finest warriors. The dragon writhing closer, Anneya could feel her adrenaline pumping.

"Come on, Philosopher. Grab your bow!" Platius shouted.

Not use to being referred to as a Philosopher, she finally realized he was talking to her. "Our arrows won't harm it!" she shouted back through the clamour.

"I know that!" Platius snapped. "We aren't trying to hurt it; we are trying to distract it. Now draw your bow!"

She watched as the other Paladins rushed to the dragon's side, outside of its focus of sight. It hovered in the dreary air. Following Platius' command, she drew her bow, knowing the dragon was now close enough for her to hit. Firing an arrow, it flew high, deflecting off Marradus' midsection. Its attention was stuck on Anneya and Platius. The dragon's reptilian eyes pierced into her, shattering her peace.

"Great shot!" Platius said, drawing another arrow. "Now, watch this!"

Anneya frantically watched, knowing the dragon's scales were too tough to penetrate. As Platius released his arrow, it soared toward the dragon's head. The beast carelessly turned its face to the side, knowing such a small projectile wouldn't harm it.

The arrow bouncing off its cheek, a smile grew on Platius' face. "I have you right where I want you, you beast…"

The Paladin fired a second arrow at the dragon's face; however, this time Anneya's gaze widened as it shot directly into the creature's snout, right into its nostril. Marradus snorted in annoyance. At the puncture, the dragon arched its neck back, roaring into the sky. Marradus' gaze looked down upon Platius and Anneya once again. Its eyes were like death. Marradus dropped from the sky in anger.

Landing on its feet, Anneya felt the ground shake beneath her.

"Yes!" Platius shouted, shooting a fist into the air.

Anneya was stunned. "How did you…"

The Paladin gave Anneya a cocky stare. "You will learn, Philosopher. You will learn."

Marradus snarled at the two archers. With its attention on them, she knew the other Paladins were nearing the dragon for closer combat.

"What do we do now?!" she asked, the dragon ramping up to charge at them.

"We wait," the Paladin said.

The Blade watched as the other Paladins rushed to the side of the dragon. Marradus' tail stroked the air at the disturbance. She kept her focus on Tolek to see what he had planned.

"Don't you dare, Tolek…" she whispered, covering her mouth in shock.

The dragon distracted by Platius still shooting arrows, Tolek gripped his hands onto the scales on the dragon's tale, climbing his way atop the dragon. The other Paladins followed his lead, using its tail and legs as means to mount the creature.

As the Paladins scaled the creature, each used their weapons to slash and jab. Anneya thought to herself that it looked like ants scurrying along a fierce bull.

"I can't believe it…" she voiced. It was absolute madness.

Platius smiled. "Clearly you haven't seen Paladins fight together, Philosopher. They don't call him *Tolek the Brave* for no reason."

With the Paladins on its back, in a jolt, the dragon shot into the air, letting out a dreadful roar. Anneya's eyes ascended with the beast. She couldn't believe what she was seeing. The Paladins were going to try to tear the dragon right down from the sky.

CHAPTER THIRTY-THREE
TREADING UPON SCALES

The dragon flew through clouded skies.

Tolek felt the wind pushing up against him. Looking down at the dragon's lengthy body, he saw Paladins scattered about trying their best to penetrate the beast with weapons of all sorts. He saw Dianne with her weapon of choice; the long-metal staff with razor-sharp blades on both ends, thrashing against the soaring dragon. Metal clashed against the mighty scales, bouncing off, not even leaving the faintest of marks.

The dragon began to jerk in the sky, trying to shake them off. Tolek took his sword, wedging it between two of the dragon's scales for stability. As the dragon twisted throughout the skies, he felt his body lift from its back. Clouds drifted past him, their coolness stroking his skin. He gripped the black hilt of his blade, knowing if he let go, he would drop to certain death.

A sharp yell erupted.

Tolek watched as one of the Paladins swords loosened from the between the dragon's scales. He knew the man well; his name was Clint. He was one of the greatest swordsmen alive. The Paladin flew from the dragon's form, being sucked from sight. His shout quickly dissipated into the sound of the wind. He knew Clint was falling to his death. No one could survive such a fall.

He remembered meeting Clint when he was much younger; another pupil of his former mentor, Rederick Rule. He knew Clint had a family. Rederick always said it was better for a Paladin to be unmarried, since they often didn't survive to experience old age. Though he despised the man, he found wisdom in his words. They were words he personally chose to embrace.

The dragon steadying, Tolek pulled his sword from between scales. Wasting no time, he rushed up Marradus' form, nearing its neck. Sensing the Paladin was making his way to its face, the dragon looked back, opening its mouth. Tolek saw a spark of flame ignite within its gaping jaws.

Shouting, he dove to the side. Clasping a hand on one of the scales, his body hung over the side, nearly tumbling off. At the sudden jerk, he felt his sword tug out from his hand. He watched the weapon as it fell through Agadin's skies. He shook his head in frustration. Dreadful flames scaled the dragon's body, engulfing one of the Paladins.

"No!" Tolek shouted as the fire-licked Paladin fell off the dragon's side. Her screams were piercing as she was eaten by flame, falling to her death.

Another gone, Tolek thought.

Hoisting himself back up onto the dragon's neck, he rushed against the wind to the dragon's head. Diving forward, he latched onto one of its ivory horns. He cursed himself for losing his sword, no longer having anything to attack with.

Holding on for his life, one of Rederick's lessons stormed throughout his mind.

"Even though a Paladin must master every weapon, they shouldn't become dependent upon them. They must become a weapon."

Tolek grimaced. Being at the dragon's head, the wind was fiercer than before. The constant gusts threatened to throw the Paladin from his grip. Fighting against the current, he slowly climbed up the beast's face. Marradus snapped its bite in agitation as Tolek shifted from side to side, avoiding the human-sized teeth.

His eyes watered from the sheer force of wind. Through the blur, his mind raced at seeing an arrow lodged in the dragon's snout. He nearly laughed aloud at the sight. He knew that only Platius could execute such a shot, hitting one of the very few places that wasn't cloaked in scales.

The Paladin leapt to the snout of the dragon, grabbing the arrow in his fist. Turning his head, he saw the two reptilian eyes watching him, both nearly the size of him.

He knew he only had one chance. Pulling the arrow from the nostril, Tolek loosened his grip from the snout. The force of the wind pushed him back toward the dragon's eyes. Shouting, he drove the arrow into the right eye of Marradus.

The dragon wailed in a wild roar. Flames shot from its mouth in a multitude of directions as its head writhed wildly. Without letting go, he tried to cover his ears from the deafening wail. The dragon began descending in a hurry to the ground below. Spiraling downward, he lifted from the dragon's body due to the momentum. He tried to grab ahold of a scale, but his grip wasn't firm enough. He crashed over the dragon's forehead, skidding down its neck and onto its mighty back.

While straining to reach for anything that would prevent his fall, he felt a hand grip the back of his jacket. In a halt, he felt his body stop. He breathed heavily, looking up to see that Dianne was the one who saved him. Tolek reached out, clasping his hand in between two of the dragon's scales, giving the Paladin who saved his life a nod of gratitude.

Marradus descending to the ground, he braced himself for impact.

The dragon's claws hit the ground, the impact forcing the Paladins to explode into the air. Each flew off, landing on the grassy ground. Tolek grunted at the impact. As he laid upon the Plains of Morah, he panted feeling his head spinning. He ran his fingers through the silky grass, thankful to be upon ground once again. He laughed aloud, hardly able to believe he was still alive. Looking back, he saw Marradus roaring in agony as the arrow protruded from its eye.

Next to him, Dianne sat up. She was watching the dragon. "Tolek, even for a Paladin that was remarkable," she voiced in wonder.

He ignored the compliment. "Were you able to get through any of the dragon's scales?" he asked, testing his voice.

Dianne shook her head. "No. The scales are too strong. They are impenetrable."

Tolek's frowned in thought. "What did you say?"

She looked over to him, confused. "The scales, they can't be broken. They're impenetrable."

His gaze widened, immediately shooting to his feet. He watched the dragon still writhing in pain upon the ground. "Give me a sword!"

Without hesitating, Dianne pulled forth a backup blade she kept strapped to her waist, giving it to him. "Tolek, what are you going to do?" she asked hesitantly.

Without responding, he bolted running at full speed toward Marradus.

"Tolek! No!" he heard the cry in the distance.

He recognized the voice. It was Anneya. He knew she feared for him; however, he didn't have a choice. Marradus needed to be stopped and he knew he had a prominent role to play.

The dragon, catching sight of him, spit fire in his direction. Tolek dove out of the way, avoiding the scorch. Without losing velocity, he was still on the move. Reaching the dragon, he jumped onto the beast's leg, hoisting himself higher and higher up the dragon. Targeting Marradus' abdomen, he jumped from its leg, catching a scale on the dragon's stomach.

"Don't you try and fly again, you stupid dragon," Tolek whispered through gritted teeth. Pulling forth his sword, he wedged the blade between scales.

Your scales may be rock-solid, but there must be a way around them, the Paladin thought, digging his sword in between them.

"Come on!" he yelled, as he twisted and applied pressure to the blade.

He knew if it took too long, Marradus would simply finish him off by either fire or bite. He needed to be quick; precise. Then it happened. The scale began to loosen. Allowing the sword to drop to the ground, he clenched the onyx scale with both hands, pulling and twisting with all his might.

"Come on!" he shouted, his muscles straining; veins bulging.

The scale ripped away from the dragon's body.

Holding the onyx scale, Tolek fell, plummeting to the ground. The impact was sharp. He ached, not doubting that he had likely broken a bone or two. He would no doubt need to take time healing himself.

Marradus let out a final roar, hoisting itself into the air, clearly having enough of the incessant Paladins. As the dragon retreated, Tolek watched the reptile soar, quickly becoming hidden in the darkness of the skies. He sighed, seeing that it was flying in the direction of Gorath.

Tolek slowly rose.

He knew all eyes were on him. He ached but wouldn't show it in front of the Paladins. They needed him to be strong. He made his way over to the remaining Paladins who stood with Anneya. When they left the Courts of Light, they started off with ten Paladins; now there were only eight. Losing two was no small price to pay.

Henry stood with them, the large man's clothes and face were streaked in crimson red. The Sovereign's soldiers and Kreel laid lifeless throughout the plains of Morah. Henry had succeeded. By his leadership, four thousand had killed five thousand, as well as a handful of Kreel. Still, Tolek could tell it came at the cost of nearly two thousand of their own warriors' lives. It was a weighty cost, indeed.

Anneya marched up to him. Based on her scowl, he wasn't expecting a hug from the Blade.

She held a finger before his face. "Don't you ever do anything like that again! You are a mad man!"

He breathed heavily. If she only knew all the life-threatening things he had done in the span of his lifetime. This would simply be another story to be told.

Her tone softened; tears streaked her face.

"Why did you do something so stupidly outrageous?" she asked.

Stupidly outrageous. Tolek smirked at the term.

He lifted the onyx scale, surprised by its weight. It felt good in his arm, being large enough to almost cover his entire back. In a refined tone, the Paladin spoke.

"Divinity required my help, and I was happy to oblige. It's not every day you come across an impenetrable shield."

Chapter Thirty-Four

Lost

"Papa, I don't want to go to sleep," Hayley whined.

"Me neither!" Haddy shouted, smacking her arms down on her cotton blanket.

Brenton crossed a finger over his lips. "Shhh! You two girls quiet down or you're going to wake up Honey," he said, looking over to the drooling toddler who was fast asleep.

He pulled up Haddy's blanket and kissed her on the forehead, then turned to Hayley to do the same. "Now, you girls need to go sleep."

"Fine," Haddy said, popping out her lower lip.

"Goodnight, girls," he said, stifling a laugh.

"Goodnight, Papa," they said in unisons.

Closing the door, he smiled. Walking down the hallway of their simple home in the Peak of Lore, he made his way to his bedroom hoping to finally get to rest for the evening. Looking at the wooden walls of their home, thankfulness washed over him for everything he had in life. He loved his family and they loved him. Entering his bedroom, he saw Flor laying under the white covers of their bed.

"Thank you for putting them to bed," she said, beaming at her husband. "Did they put up a fight?"

"Always," he said, letting out a tired laugh.

Flor laughed with him. "How about you? Are you going to sleep right away?"

"I'm going to try," Brenton said, sitting down upon the bed. "I've been waking up the last several nights. Every time I fall asleep, I have the same reoccurring dream."

Frowning, she smoothed her hand over the white blanket. "What have you been dreaming?"

He rubbed his face letting out a yawn. "I've been dreaming of a river; a river mightier than I have ever seen before. Floating on it are thousands of books, disappearing into the distance."

Flor furrowed her brows. "That is an odd dream. Any idea what it could mean?"

"Not a clue," he confessed, shaking his head. "It may be just nonsense. I haven't been thinking clearly recently. Kaldon and Anneya have been gone for several months. I worry they are in danger. I feel like it's nearly all I think about."

She ran a hand over his arm. "I'm sure they are all fine, Brenton. Every one of them is more than capable of taking care of themselves."

"Very true," he said laying down beside his wife. "I suppose a Paragon and Blade should be fine without me worrying about them."

She smiled at her husband's obvious attempt to still his anxiety. Running her hand through his dark hair, she spoke. "You rest up. You need it. Goodnight, my love."

Brenton leaned up, kissing his wife. "Goodnight, Flor."

As soon as his head hit his pillow, he felt sleep pulling him in. His eyes slowly shutting, he watched as images began passing through his mind.

Brenton saw he was no longer in his bed with his wife. He was dreaming again. Standing on a dry brook, his eyes were taken in by the crashing river; the same one he had seen every night in his dreams. Looking deep into the waters, images passed through the strands of liquid. He saw faces in the water. He saw places and events. It was like watching one of the theatre productions at the Peak of Lore, but here the scenes were translucent and fluid. The water held what felt like millions of different stories, like visions coursing through the water.

Thousands of books floated on the surface, bobbing up and down the magnificent river. Every colour and size of book he could imagine whisked away, disappearing into the distance, into the unknown.

"Where are they going?" he muttered to himself, watching knowledge sail away.

He followed the books walking along lush banks. Taking in the wondrous sight, he thought he heard something being muffled by the low thunder of the rushing waters.

He stopped, listening more intently.

"Please…" the whimper sounded from the distance.

Brenton's ears perked.

Following the quiet plea, his legs began pumping. As fast as he could, he ran down the stream following the books. He hoped he would find the source of the numb call. Through the vast array of floating literature, he saw something else barely floating above the water's surface. As soon as he saw the hairless head and wet-charcoal robes, there was no doubt to who the man was.

"Locrian!" the Blade shouted.

As soon as he put his feet in the water to go rescue the drowning Seer, he felt the river pulling him. He could feel it tempting him to venture out further; to go deeper.

He stopped. Something didn't feel right. He knew in his heart that if he went into the coursing waters that he wouldn't be returning. He would be lost, just as Locrian was. He watched the struggling Seer.

"Locrian! I'm here!" Brenton called out.

The panicking Seer flipped his head to gaze at the Blade who stood upon the brook. His eyes grew large. He moved his mouth, trying to speak.

"Locrian! Tell me what to do!" Brenton yelled, as water splashed over the Seer's head.

Waters raging and smashing against Locrian, he shouted with all his might. "Brenton! Find me!"

Brenton gasped, sitting up; choking back breaths.

"Hunny, what's wrong? What's going on?" Flor asked in worry, startled by his outburst.

All he could see in his mind was the image of the drowning Seer and the floating books. He looked to his alarmed wife.

"Locrian is in trouble," he said into the night, springing out from the bed. He clothed himself as quickly as he could.

"What?!" Flor asked perplexed. "What are you talking about? Locrian left the Peak of Lore months ago. You're being paranoid."

He kissed his wife on the top of her head. "Keep an eye on the girls. I need to follow the books!" he said in a panic.

"You need to *follow books?* What does that even mean?!" Flor asked, scrambling with her words. "Brenton, where are you going?!"

Making his way to the door, he shouted loud enough for her to hear. "I'm going to the library!"

Without giving his wife a chance to respond, he was out the door. Running as fast as he could, he made his way down the halls to the library. The quotes written on walls blurred in his sight as he rushed past them. He unapologetically darted past students who jumped out of his way. He didn't have time to be courteous.

Reaching the first level of the library, he peered in, seeing students lost in their late-night studies. He knew there would be no place on the first level for the Seer to find trouble. It wasn't private enough for such danger to take place. He thought about how much time the Seer had spent in the Depths since Marradus' skull was found. Rushing to the staircase, he began his descent.

Racing down the stone stairs, his feet finally met level ground as he reached the second floor. As soon as he arrived, the eyes of Scholars showed their disapproval. He didn't care. He scoured the elite library, seeing numerous corridors. The Seer could be down any hall; in any room. All he knew was that his friend was in danger and in need of him.

"Have any of you seen the Seer, Locrian?" Brenton asked in a panic, interrupting the studies of Scholars. "He would have been here several months ago passing through."

One of the Scholars, only slightly older than Brenton, slammed his hand upon the study desk, approaching to the Blade. "I've had enough of these incessant interruptions! I don't know why you think you can come here disrupting our studies!"

Watching the Scholar walking toward him with his pretentious finger pointed, he felt fury rising within him. As the Scholar neared him, Brenton reached out, clenching the man's robes in his fist. Lifting him from the ground, he slammed the Scholar against the wall.

"Tell me if you saw him!" he barked. "Otherwise, you will be held responsible for the Seer's life!"

The Scholar panted in fear. He lifted a finger pointing down a hallway. "Several months ago, I saw him go that way with two Bishops."

Brenton looked toward the hall. "Why did they go there?!"

"I haven't a clue… It's an abandoned wing of the library. No one ever goes there," the Scholar trembled. "Please, let me go…" the frail man begged.

The Blade dropped the Scholar, dashing into the hallway. Delving deeper, he heard men and women rushing to the Scholar to make sure he was fine. He knew they would likely be talking about such violence on the second floor of the library for quite some time. Brenton didn't have time to give the man any more thought.

With each step he took, he noticed books thinning; becoming scarcer. Instead of literature, cobwebs dressed the forgotten walls. Every room he passed, he checked, finding nothing but vacant space.

"Locrian!" he shouted over and over again, his voice resounding in echoes.

He was beginning to grow sore from the endless search. For over an hour, he delved further into the forgotten wing of the library. It sunk much deeper into the mountain than he ever would have thought.

His gaze scouring the quiet hallways, his eyes rested upon an iron door. While dust coated each door in the forsaken hall, this one looked as though some was brushed away in more recent months. He then saw that the bolt on the outside was locked.

"Locrian…" he whispered, dashing over.

With a forceful jerk, the bolt budged. He turned the door handle. As he swung it open, he saw what he feared he would. The broken Seer — his friend — laid up against the stone wall, unconscious.

"No, no, no," Brenton pleaded.

Rushing over to the Seer, he nudged his shoulder. "Wake up, Locrian."

The Seer sat limp.

"Wake up!" Brenton shouted, shaking his shoulders.

Seeing the Seer lost in a forced slumber, he hoisted the man onto his shoulders. "Don't worry, I'm going to take care of you," Brenton said. "We are going to make sure you wake up. You aren't lost anymore. There's only one person I know who might know what's going on with you. We need to find her. We need the help of a Philosopher."

CHAPTER THIRTY-FIVE

WHISPERS OF REALITY

Fen sat upon the hard floor, stroking her pens across paper. With nearly sixty books scattered around her, she read and wrote at the same time. She scratched her head, feeling her fingers getting tangled in the knots of her hair.

Thump. Thump. Thump.

She smiled at the sound of feet pattering upon the stone stairs. Someone was coming to see her. She had been hearing the awkwardly paced footing coming down the stairs for almost an hour. She had no clue who it could be. Based on the inconsistent steps, it was either someone with a hobble or someone carrying something heavy. She wished they would hurry up.

She thought back to before she met Kaldon and Anneya. The thing she had hated most was being interrupted in her work; meeting them changed that. She missed the company. Regret rang through her every time she thought about how she should have left for Noriden with Locrian. She looked around to the shelves of books that surrounded her. They once felt like her companions. They kept her content as time passed by and age crept in; however, they didn't feel like enough to her anymore. She longed for more.

Hearing feet scraping the stone floor, she smiled. Her mysterious guest had arrived. Her eyes riveted on the arched door. Her smile fell when she saw Brenton carrying Lociran.

Fen rose in a panic. "Oh no! What happened?"

She rushed over to the unconscious Seer.

Brenton said, "I found him locked in a room on the library's second floor. He's been trapped in there since everyone left the Peak of Lore. I don't know why, but he's not waking up."

Fen stopped. "Was he alone that whole time?!"

"I think so. Why?" he asked, placing Locrian on top of a cot against the wall.

Fen's hands began trembling as she reached for something to lean upon.

Brenton furrowed his brow. "What's wrong?"

Looking up, her eyes began to fill with tears. "Then he is already lost. He has been taken by the Fall of Seers."

"The *what?!*" Brenton asked, amplifying his voice in concern.

"The Fall of Seers," Fen said, quietly. "Seers descend into insanity if they are isolated for too long. For Locrian, several months alone would be the same as you spending nearly a lifetime by yourself. He is lost. He will not wake."

"How can you say that?" Brenton asked, his thoughts scrambling. "There must be a way for him to wake up."

Fen shook her head avoiding looking at the prostrate Seer. "There has never been a Seer in all of history who has come back from this fall into insanity. How did you find him?"

"I had a dream," Brenton said.

"A dream?" the Philosopher asked.

Brenton nodded. "I saw Locrian drowning in a rushing river. I have never seen anything like it before. There were pictures coursing throughout the waters. He asked for my help. He asked me to find him." He looked to the Philosopher. "I think Locrian gave me the dream."

Fen rubbed her head in thought. "That can't be possible. It's not possible for someone to project dreams into someone else's mind."

"Are you sure about that?" Brenton provoked. "Tymas Droll is able to. He's done it with Kaldon. Maybe Locrian found a way. If anyone could, it would be him."

Fen looked over to Locrian. "If what you say is true, then when you saw him in the river, he was drowning in madness. As we speak, he is being taken by the River of Time."

Brenton looked at her blankly. "I knew a Seer's gift works to allow them to see into the River of Time; I didn't know it could drive them insane."

Fen nodded sadly. "Indeed. If he truly did manage to do something so remarkable as give you a dream, then he must be in dire need. From the looks of him, I doubt he has much time left, if any."

Walking over to Locrian, she knelt at his bed placing her hand on his. "Are you still in there, Seer? Can you hear me?"

Struggling through the River of Time, he heard a familiar voice murmur throughout the vast skies above him. He remembered the raspyness in her tone. It was Fen.

Fighting the powerful current, he didn't know if the voice was a part of a vision or if it was real. If it was real, then that meant Brenton got his message. The Blade had found him. If not, he knew his time was short. He couldn't hold on much longer.

Water sprayed into his face. The mighty river pounded around him. The Seer saw images swimming through the swells of liquid surrounding him. He pulled his eyes from the visions; resisting being pulled into them. He knew that if he sunk below the waters, that he would be gone, forever lost in madness.

"Wake up, you fool. Wake up!" Locrian shouted at himself, his head submerging underneath the water again. He bobbed back up, breathing in with force; gasping for air.

He heard a voice again storm throughout the skies, like a crack of lightning. This time the voice came from a man.

"Fight, Locrian! Don't give up!"

It sounded like Brenton. He knew that if the voices weren't real, then they would lead him further into deception; deeper into insanity. If they were in fact real, they could be his compass guiding him back to reality. It was his only hope.

Water crashed into him, forcing him to tumble in the current. As he rolled throughout the waters, another voice called.

"Wake up, Locrian!"

The voices were growing louder. He needed to follow them. As water violently coursed around him, he waited for another voice to call.

"Locrian!"

At the sound of Brenton's voice, Locrian didn't reject it. He threw his belief into it with all his might. He could feel it. Taste it. See it. It felt like reality.

Speak again, the Seer thought.

"Wake up!"

Fen's voice wove into him. Even though the river was pulling him deeper, the voice calling him back to reality was powerful. The war between sanity and insanity was agony.

A swift swell of water washed over Locrian's head, fully submerging him. With his eyes open underwater, he watched the boundless visions swimming through the River of Time. He was fully submerged. Waving his arms and legs, he tried to project himself back up; yet the river pulled him deeper. He knew he didn't have the strength to rise again to the surface.

Please speak, the Seer thought, as the waters pulled him deeper.

He reached up, trying to feel the surface but didn't find it. Water filled his ears, everything sounding muffled and numb. He felt himself losing strength; his thoughts were drifting away. He felt his feet touch the bottom of the river, grooving into the sandy floor. He had sunk into the depths of madness. He looked up, seeing the sun trying to shine through the barrier of water. Its rays were lost in the thick swell of liquid. It was too late for him.

Looking around, he watched visions swimming around him; visions that would engulf and consume him. He tried to move his feet out from the sand-filled ground, yet they were matted in; stuck. He didn't have the strength to fight anymore. He was lost, felled by his own gift.

To his left, a vision began evolving, He was tired of resisting. It was too late for him to fight any longer. He had lost his will to try. Giving in, he took in the image. He watched as Noriden materialized before him; the ancient abode of Philosophers. At its sight, he forgot about the river around him, as though it were lost to him. His sight narrowing towards Noriden, he saw a scroll tucked away in a forgotten bookshelf. Its paper held a yellowed glare, tarnished by time. The scroll opened. As his eyes scaled the words, he felt his curiosity peaking.

"Furion's goal is both grand and terrible. She doesn't only desire death to cover Agadin, she longs for nothingness to take it."

As the Seer read the ancient words, he heard a distant call shouting through the vision.

"Locrian!" the raspy voice beckoned.

The Seer grew annoyed, brushing away the incessant voice that tried to pull him away from the vision. He took in the scroll again, further reading its words.

"I have seen Death's Snow in a vision. It is terrible. The descent of Death's Snow is a sign of Agadin coming to its end. If the snow falls, then I fear it may be too late, for it is a sign of he who is coming."

The words *"Death's Snow"* gave him shivers. And who was it referring to when it said, *"He who is coming?"*

The Seer was looking forward to studying such a scroll. It clearly held important secrets; secrets reserved for grim times. His gazed wandered to the bottom of the scroll to see who had authored such a piece. He smiled at seeing Dawntan Forlorn's name written.

"Locrian!"

He heard it again; the sound wanting to rob him of his vision. To deprive him of studying Dawntan Forlorn's words. Yet, when he heard it, the familiar tone was alluring to him. It gripped him. He turned his attention to the muffled voice that called him by name.

"Locrian! Wake up!" the man and woman's voice cried in unisons.

Fen and Brenton's voices crashed into the river, hitting Locrian's core like a surge of life. As much as he longed to read the scroll laid out before him, the Seer ripped his eyes from the vision. He could feel his feet still locked into the sandy ground as the River of Time coursed around him. He needed to leave.

Reaching behind his back, Locrian pulled forth his metal staff. He threw himself into the voices; into reality. His teeth ground together as he slammed the staff into the sandy floor. At its impact, the water responded by rippling out from him. Liquid retreated from the renowned Seer. Looking from side to side, he watched as the River of Time parted, splitting in two. To his right and left were two watery walls holding steadily. The River of Time was unable to touch him. Water dripped from his linen robe. He gasped in air once again. Before him was a clear path, leading him back to reality.

With each step, he looked into the river walls, seeing visions treading throughout them. The watery walls held, unmoving. He was free from their insanity. He stripped his eyes from the images coursing through the liquid walls. He had no need to look at them. He was no longer a slave to visions; nor a slave to his gift. He was the master.

His staff patting the ground with each step, he followed the path out from the River of Time and straight into sanity.

Upon the old cot, Locrian sat up gasping in air.

Brenton, who was sitting on the bed jumped in a startle, falling to the floor. With a thud, the Blade grunted.

"Locrian!" Fen shouted, diving into the Seer. The Philosopher wrapped her spindly arms around him. "You're alive. You're alive!"

From the ground, Brenton smiled seeing a man who had come back from madness. He shook his head in wonder.

"Remarkable…" the Blade whispered.

"Locrian, you did it!" Fen cried. "You did the impossible. You overcame the Fall of a Seer!"

Brenton sat staring up at him, still mesmerized. "You truly do have a gifted mind," he whispered.

Hearing their voices, Locrian didn't give the flattery attention. He simply stared blankly, taking in reality once again; a place he feared he would never again gaze upon. He realized he was in the Depths. As much as being in the cave-like room comforted him, his mind lingered upon the final vision he saw while in the River of Time; the scroll written by Dawntan Forlorn.

The Seer opened his mouth. Fen and Brenton leaned in awaiting to hear his first words after being redeemed from insanity.

Locrian whispered into the caved room. "There is a scroll I must find. I need to leave for Noriden immediately."

CHAPTER THIRTY-SIX

NO LONGER FREE

The wheels of the cage bumped and rattled against the dirt floor, waking Kaldon. As his eyes groggily opened, he peered through the iron bars. Crouched over, he laid in the small-iron box feeling heat sweltering his skin. Even though the sky was husked over, the sun's heat still prevailed. He ached from days of travel.

"Look who's awake. Welcome to your new home," the Dark Bishop said mockingly.

With a Dark Bishop on each side of the cage, Kaldon moaned as he was carried in the portable prison. The two men, Dias and Berk, had kept him captive since leaving Forin Woods.

They approached a city of magnificent stature. The city was encased by a black wall; a shield for the residents. Growing up in Rundle, he'd never seen anything like it. Even the Peak of Lore looked minuscule in comparison. An onyx tower stretched up to the skies, ending in a straight point. He had seen the tower in his vision; however, to see it with his own eyes pained him. His stomach turned. It was a tower so brazen that it was as though the mighty piece of architecture looked down upon the rest of Agadin.

The cage rattled onward closer to Gorath.

His body cramping from the confinement, he longed to be at the Peak of Lore again; safe behind the mountain walls. Beyond the squeaking of wheels carrying him onward, he could hear what sounded like powerful crashes in the distance. They came in swells, like a deep rumbling roar. Strangely, the crashes soothed him.

"What's that noise?" Kaldon asked, testing his voice as he lifted his head.

The cage stopped to a halt. Immediately, he felt his foresight beginning to clang throughout his nerves. Alarm gripped him. Even though his foresight made him aware of what was coming, in such a tight cage there was nowhere for him to go. He instinctively reached for *Humility* before remembering that both his swords were left behind at Orin's home.

He heard one of the Bishops pull out a weapon. The wooden handle of a spear jabbed between the cell bars, striking his side. Kaldon grabbed is ribs on impact, grunting. He could swear he heard a snap.

"You don't speak, unless we say otherwise!" Dias snarled into the cage.

The other Bishop muttered under his breath. "This fool doesn't even know the sound of the ocean."

The ocean, he thought.

Holding his hands over several ribs that he was sure were broken, he listened to the crashing swells of water. He had never heard the ocean before.

The Bishops began conversing, muffling the comforting sound of water crashing against stone. "Have you heard that the Sovereign has a new weapon?" Dias asked Berk.

"A new weapon?" Berk asked. "I heard Marradus doesn't respond to the Sovereign of Shadow."

"Marradus doesn't listen to anyone," Dias laughed in a gruff voice. "No, I've heard rumours that the Sovereign has a new weapon; something dreadful."

"What is it?" the Bishop asked curiously.

With seriousness in his tone, Dias said, "They call him, the *Wind of the Abyss.*"

"The Wind of the Abyss," Berk said in thought. "That's an odd name."

"I thought so as well," Dias replied. "I've heard he is called that because he can command the wind. He is its master."

Kaldon let out a disgusted sigh. He cringed at the thought of Tymas Droll now holding power over a Dark Roek. He had seen what Orin was capable of as a *Roek of Earth*. He didn't want to know what one who could command the wind was capable of.

He listened to the two warriors prattle on as he was carted past the black walls encasing Gorath. Upon entering, he could feel the wheels beneath him transitioning from bumpy to smooth. His captors pushed his iron box down a road throughout the Sovereign's hometown. Looking out, he saw what he did not expect; people lived their lives. Families moseyed about. Children played and vendors ran businesses. There were homes, buildings, taverns, and markets. The place was abuzz with happenings; however, one thing differed. Upon each individual's face, he could see that their lives were not their own. The Dominion of Shadow enslaved each resident.

"I never knew it was possible for someone to command the wind," Berk said as they made their way throughout the city.

"Our Sovereign is never short of surprises," Dias responded. "I heard the Sovereign wanted to overthrow one of the smaller cities only a few days away from here. He sent the Wind of the Abyss, and he called the wind to whirl into the city. Houses were destroyed. Buildings capsized. Hundreds were killed. I've heard he is merciless."

"That sounds even better than the Kreel," the Bishop said in excitement.

Dias laughed. "Apparently the Sovereign is quite pleased with his new weapon."

Delving deeper into the city, Kaldon shook his head in revulsion. Past buildings, homes, and residents he saw them nearing a tower overlooking a cliff. The closer they came to the isolated tower, the louder the ocean's roar became. The tower wasn't nearly as tall as the primary tower of the city; still it loomed over much of Gorath.

Closer to the tower, cries and wails began ascending above the ocean's call. Thousands of voices cried out, forcing themselves through the barrier of the stone walls. His eyes resting on guards standing around the tower's circumference, he immediately knew what the tower was.

The cart stopped at a halt. The caged door swung open. "Get out," Berk said aggressively.

Kaldon slowly moved his legs out from the cage, planting his feet onto the solid ground. It was the first time in days he'd had enough room to stretch. The Bishop grabbed the back of his cloak, forcing him to his feet. Regret surged through him as his eyes took in the prison, wishing he had his swords with him. He had killed Dark Bishops before; with his foresight, he believed he could do it again. However, he was at a drastic disadvantage without a weapon. Not only were there two Bishops, but there were dozens of guards watching the prison.

He looked to the arched doorway that he knew would hold his more permanent cell.

"Move!" Dias said, kicking Kaldon's back. In a jolt, he stumbled through the tower door managing to stay standing. His broken ribs throbbed.

Two Bishops beaconing him onward, he was consumed by the darkness of the prison. Guards scoured through every hall. Shouts and hollers raged, echoing through the sinister jail. He saw the nearly countless prison cells secured with iron bars. Hundreds of gangly arms writhed past the bars, trying to grasp at freedom.

"Let us out!"

"Please, help!"

Each cry cut into his soul. His eyes began watering at the futile pleas, knowing he had no way to free them.

"Who are all of these people?" he asked wide eyed, hardly noticing he even spoke.

Letting it slide this time that he spoke, Berk said, "These are those who refused to embrace the Sovereign's teachings. To reject his teachings is to give up your freedom and your life."

Kaldon stayed quiet at the words.

The Bishops led him up the tower, and he peered into each cell as he passed by. He saw men, women, and children. In each cell were those imprisoned for standing for life and truth. All wept, calling out for freedom they feared they would never see again. He was one of them now.

He looked down to the stone floor, no longer having the courage to look into the eyes of those begging for their lives. He marched onward, waiting for the Bishops to throw him into one of the dank cells. Climbing higher into the treacherous tower, he was surprised as they led him past where all of the other prisoners were held. His legs began to burn as they surged up the tower.

Finally, the three stopped before a solid-steel door. To Kaldon, it simply looked like a common door that led to another section in the prison; however, he dreaded it to be something far worse.

"This is your cell. You get one of the special ones. It was a request from the Sovereign himself," Dias said with a smile stretched over his burly face.

He could feel his heart racing, fearing what was on the other side of the door. Berk pulled it open with a heave. Kaldon's breath left his lungs at the sight. The room looked like a regular prison cell, consisting of stone walls; however, there was no back wall to the prison cell. Instead, the small room overlooked a cliff. Its drop from the cell's edge would have been several thousand feet. Beyond the edge of the cell, all he could see was the blue of the ocean. Waves roared in the distance. His eyes were wet at the realization that the first time he had seen the ocean with his own eyes was in the prison he would likely die in.

"The Sovereign created these cells for those not worthy of shelter from the natural elements," Dias said, smirking. "Don't worry, there is an advantage to these cells. When you grow too weary — which prisoners often do — you can always jump. Prisoners rarely last long in these cells. All eventually decide take *the plunge.*"

As the Bishops nudged Kaldon to step into the cell, he instinctively resisted, fearing being so close to the fatal fall. He could feel his breaths quickening.

"Move!" Dias shouted, shoving him.

Kaldon flew to the ground, his broken ribs colliding upon the stone floor. He grimaced upon impact, wincing at the pain.

Panting, he inhaled the dirt from the floor knowing the drop of thousands of feet was only a few inches away from him. He saw the jagged rocks engulfed in water beyond the cliff. He shut his eyes at the sight. The heights unnerved him. Panic hit him like a kick to the stomach. He heard the Dark Bishops laughing behind him as the door creaked eerily.

At the sound of waves crashing upon jagged stone, the steel door shut.

CHAPTER THIRTY-SEVEN

THE WAIT

K aldon awoke to dark clouds drifting before him. He slowly stood testing his ribs, realizing the pain had stilled to a numb. As each day passed, he attempted calling forth the Kingdom of Light to heal the wounds. He was thankful the pain was subsiding.

He walked to the edge of his cell looking over into the roaring ocean. Allowing the toes of his boots to hang over the cell's edge, he watched as dust crumbled from the ledge, fizzling downward.

His eyes wandering down, he remembered the stories his mother told him as a child of those who could Command Creation. In one story, a man was being chased by an entire army. To escape, he jumped from the ledge of a cliff, commanding the wind to catch him. He rolled upon the wind, causing him to drift to safety. He mused about the small flicker of flame he summoned from Orin's fireplace. His ability to Command Creation was far too undeveloped for him to try something so reckless.

He breathed in the humid air. The sun had set and risen twelve times since the cell door shut him in. Twelve days, he'd endured the fear-inducing cell. Even though during the day, the sun blared upon him providing him little comfort, the mornings did the opposite. Accompanying each sunrise, was the feel of wet dew coating his body, chilling him. Stepping away from the ledge, he rubbed his arms for warmth. At his movement, he felt the imprint of his father's book press into his skin. He was thankful they hadn't found it. It was the only thing keeping his mind alert during the countless hours of isolation. It reminded him of his mission. It reminded him of Anneya.

He pulled it out, reading aloud.

"There may be times when it feels as though trials crash upon you like a waterfall, pounding you into submission. Your circumstances may masquerade as mountainous obstacles looming before you in an attempt to intimidate you into cowering. However, never allow yourself to falter under seemingly impossible odds. You were not fashioned for defeat. To give up, is to settle; to dwell in lack. Lift your head. The sun shall rise again."

- Dolan Thain
Heart of the Brave

He looked around the empty cell. As much as his father's words stirred him, he could feel discouragement settling within him. He gently closed the book, flicking a stone with his foot off the jail room's cliff. The small rock descending through Agadin's skies, he laid upon his stomach, leaning over the edge again. He supposed he had done so hundreds of times already, yet hoped he had overlooked a detail that could benefit him. He reached over the edge, tracing his hand over the face of the rocky wall. It was smooth, providing no place to attempt a climb downward. There was only one way out from the cell, to take the plunge. The option promised escape, yet it wasn't the freedom he wanted. It was an option he vowed not to entertain.

"Hello?" a voice called faintly, gliding upon the wind.

Kaldon jumped in a startle. He looked around the empty cell, wondering if his mind was playing with him. If it were real, he assumed it was a prisoner in a nearby cell. He tilted his head to the sky, waiting to see if the voice would emerge again.

When nothing came, his curiosity gnawed at him. "Is someone there?" he spoke from the still prison.

The voice let out a tired laugh. "It's good to finally hear someone's voice."

Based on the sound of the voice, he knew it was a man; his cell a far distance away from his own. His tone sounded raspy, although he knew it wasn't due to age. It was hoarse, worn by continual cries. He turned to the direction of the voice.

"Why are you in here?" Kaldon asked.

After a lingered pause, the man spoke. "I am likely here for the same reason you are. I've denied embracing the Shadow."

Kaldon leaned against the stone wall.

"Is that why you are here as well?" the distant prisoner asked.

He surprised himself as a light laugh fell from his mouth, thankful to get to talk to someone other than himself. "In a simplified answer, yes, that's why I'm here."

His eyes looked out to the expanse of sky husked over by Shadow. He missed his freedom. "How long have you been here?" Kaldon asked.

The prisoner quieted briefly before responding. "Almost three months, but I've been a prisoner for much longer. I was transitioned from another prison to this one. I nearly escaped but was then recaptured and brought here. It seems that it is my fate."

He listened as the man prattled on in his lamentations. He couldn't imagine being locked in such a prison for three months. He would usually grow tired of those who were unnecessarily talkative; however, after twelve days of speaking with no one, he found the voice of another comforting. It made him feel as though he weren't alone.

Unexpectedly, the man slowly pattered off.

Kaldon lifted his head from the cold wall. "Tell me, where is it that you came from before being imprisoned here?" he asked, not wanting to be left alone in the silence of his cell.

The voice was quiet; unresponsive.

Kaldon readjusted himself on the hard floor, not understanding why the man would quiet so abruptly. "Where did you come from?" he pressed.

"They're coming. Stay quiet," the man said in a forced whisper.

Kaldon barely heard the vague voice from such a distance. Still, he could discern the fear in his tone. He quieted. Focusing his attention, he began hearing muffled footsteps ascending in sound. Guards visited the prisoners once per day, bringing water and gruel. However, they always came midday; never in the morning.

Listening, he felt his foresight beginning to stir. He cursed himself. If he hadn't been so distracted by the prisoner, he would have been able to sense it sooner. Something was wrong.

He listened as the boots stopped at his cell door. The bolt securing the door unlocked. He feared what awaited him on the other side. Over and over again he ran the words of his father through his head, trying to summon courage.

"Never allow yourself to falter under seemingly impossible odds. You were not fashioned for defeat."

The door swinging wide, standing outside his cell were five Dark Bishops; Dias was amongst them. At the sight, he felt helpless without a weapon. He was fatigued and weak due to limited food and water.

Dias took a step forward. In a gruff tone, the Bishop said, "Kaldon Thain, we have been sent by the Sovereign of Shadow to share with you your punishment for resisting the Dominion of Shadow and for taking the life of the Dark Paladin, Geran Rule. Your punishment will be hastened, since an army approaches Gorath."

Kaldon couldn't help but smile. He didn't know who would send an army to Gorath's door, but he was thankful for those who made the decision to stand for life.

Before the Bishop could continue, he spoke up, pushing words past his fear. "It was an honour for me to kill Geran; one that I would gladly do again. If I had a weapon, you five would be joining your beloved General in death."

Waiting for the Bishop to respond, he watched as a smile spread over Dias' face.

"You are making it even more satisfying for me to share with you your punishment," the Bishop said in a violent tone.

Dias continued, "The Sovereign has ordered a public execution for you at the central courtyard of Gorath. The residents will be invited to watch the death of the son of Dolan Thain. Your punishment will be conducted this evening, at the fall of the sun. The Sovereign himself will be there to perform the act. He says it will be an event talked about for generations to come. The first Paragon born in thousands of years, slain helplessly before the masses; by his own hand. The buzz of your execution is already making its way throughout Gorath. We are expecting quite the attendance."

At Dias' words, Kaldon felt his head beginning to spin. He stared blankly at the Dark Bishop.

Dias lifted his finger pointing to Kaldon. "Look boys! He isn't so bold now, is he?"

As all five Bishops laughed, he remained quiet. He was speechless, knowing that his life would be taken by Tymas Droll before the masses.

"Let's let this pathetic man enjoy his final hours alone," Dias mocked. The Bishop looked at Kaldon. "Don't worry, you will be seeing me again later. I wouldn't miss this for anything."

The Bishops laughed again. As the iron door clicked shut, he stood alone in the terrifying cell; his holding place until his inevitable doom. Through the stillness, he heard the mysterious voice rise in a sympathetic tone.

"Kaldon Thain... Dolan's son. I've heard of you," the voice whispered.

Kaldon didn't care. His life was going to be forfeited. He simply wanted to be free. He wanted to see Agadin safe; to see his friends and Anneya again. He knew there was no chance of escape. Slouching into the wall, he shut his eyes.

"I'm sorry to hear about your sentence, Kaldon," the voice said. "However, there is a way out of this."

Kaldon's pressed his eyelids tightly together. "What do you mean?"

The man cleared his throat. "Well, if you don't want to follow through with the execution, you could always take the plunge. There would be no shame in it. It would be a greater death than to be killed as entertainment."

He looked down the cliff's edge to the crashing waters below. The waves called to him, luring him to take an easier way out. He tried to hold back his tears.

"I refuse to take the plunge," he finally said. "I won't allow word to spread throughout Agadin that the son of Dolan Thain took his own life because he was afraid of what the Dominion of Shadow could do to him. I will take a stand for life, even if it means my own will be taken from me."

"Then you are far braver than I," the voice said quietly. "I wouldn't be able to bear the wait for this evening."

Kaldon could hear the prisoner's emotion, genuinely mourning his condition with him. He could feel his own emotions rising at the frustration of not being in control of his own fate.

"You may very well be the last friendly person I will ever speak to," Kaldon said hopelessly. "Tell me, what is your name?"

After a long pause, the voice spoke. "I was at one point the Chief Messenger of Stone Hedge. My name is Glaric."

Chapter Thirty-Eight

Open War

A nneya stood at the front of the two thousand person army with the remaining Paladins. After several weeks of travel, they had finally arrived. Her eyes rose, looking onward to the horrifying scene unfolded before them.

From outside of the walls of Gorath, she saw the onyx tower ascending into the skies. Multitudes of the Sovereign's army were planted upon the rocky land. Weapons in hand, all were stationed to protect their hometown from the dragon's flames if need be. Even though the masses were stretched before her, this was but a fraction of his army. Thousands upon thousands of the Army of Shadow watched the nightmare in the sky looming above them. As unnerving as the army was, it paled before the demon dragon thrashing through the dreary skies. A bolt of lightning cracked through the skies, Marradus blew wrathful fires through the fog. Soldiers flinched at the sight.

The army taking in the imposing sight, all awaited Tolek's command to head into battle. The Paladin stood far off, gazing onward to the impossible obstacle before them. Yet, Anneya knew that if she were to follow anyone into impossible odds, it would be him. Their objective was to kill Marradus, yet here an entire army, drastically outnumbering their own, stood between them and the dragon.

She clenched her hand over her bow, knowing that the army must be defeated. She knew Marradus wasn't only a threat to the single cities it devoured; all of Agadin was falling by its fire. Over time, she knew that all of the land would be reduced to ash. This was their time of opportunity to attack, knowing there may not be another.

She wrapped her fingers around the Legacy that hung from her neck. She wondered if Kaldon were somewhere in the city before her; if he had actually made it to Gorath. At the sight of the dragon hanging over the enemy army, part of her hoped he never made it this far, that he would be spared.

In the still before war, Henry leaned over to gaze at the Legacy she held in her fist. "It's in times like these when I am thankful that we have a Philosopher with us," he smiled.

Still holding the Legacy, she looked over to the enormous Paladin. She had grown quite fond of him over their travels. He began to feel to her like a big brother of sorts, giving her someone to joke and bicker with. It was a distraction she thankfully embraced.

She gulped, taking in the mighty force standing before her. "Henry, considering we will likely die this day, I have a confession to make."

He furrowed his distinct brows. "A confession?"

She nodded, lowering her voice so no one else would hear. "I am not a Philosopher. I am only a Blade."

Henry's gaze grew.

She looked from side to side, making sure no one heard. "Don't tell the others. They will have a fit if they find out I entered the Courts of Light without having been mantled as a Protector of Agadin."

Henry balked out a laugh, a sound that felt out of place under such horrible times. "You played the part well! You had me completely fooled!"

She looked over to Henry with a smirk. "That, my friend, is not a hard thing to accomplish."

He held a hand over his mouth, holding himself back from letting loose another savage laugh. "I should have known. You are far too feisty to be a Philosopher."

Anneya smiled, thinking of Fen. "Believe me, I know of a Philosopher who makes my feisty tongue sound sweet."

Henry rubbed his chin. "Sounds like my type of woman."

Anneya and Henry laughed aloud into the tense still before battle.

Tolek took a step forward before the army. She saw the onyx scale of Marradus strapped to his back; the impenetrable shield. He eyed the army, taking account of their forces.

"I still can't believe what Tolek did back at Flank," she said, the words falling from her mouth.

Without shifting his gaze from him, Henry said, "Tolek may be the bravest person I've ever met."

"Braver than the King of Paladins?" she asked.

Anneya couldn't help but be fascinated by the mysterious man. Since Tolek was a vault concerning their former mentor, anytime she and Henry were alone, she would ask him questions about the War Lord.

Henry went quiet. He finally said, "Rederick is another story. As a warrior, he is like nothing either of us have ever seen. That said, even though he trained Tolek, they are very different men."

"Tolek doesn't care for him, does he?"

"I wouldn't say Tolek doesn't care for him." Henry looked over at her. "He hates the man."

She gulped. "Why is that?"

"There must be hundreds of reasons," Henry said. "I would assume a main one is likely how their relationship first began. A long time ago, the War Lord was passing through a town and spotted a young boy, no older than nine years old. Immediately, he spotted the calling over his life; the mark of a Paladin."

Henry continued, "The War Lord took Tolek from his father and mother. He took him from his family, stealing his childhood from him for the purpose of making him a weapon. Rule was a harsh man; harsher to Tolek than a child should have to endure. In my opinion, Tolek has every right to hate him."

"That's terrible…" she muttered.

Looking at Tolek, she saw him in a light she hadn't seen before. Knowing what he had overcome, she respected him as a leader even more. Before she could ask more questions, Tolek lifted his sword, demanding the attention of the army.

Henry leaned closer to her. "Stay close, Anneya. I will protect you," he said, watching the army before them.

She smiled at his gesture.

A hush quieted over the army. She wasn't surprised at how quickly warriors quieted when they saw the valiant Paladin awaiting their attention.

"Today we will shape history together!" the lead Paladin spoke loudly into the night, his tone infused with authority. He pointed to the multitudes of enemy soldiers before the walls of Gorath. "This army seems great in number; but they are small in heart.

We will win this day, not only because we are skilled and well-trained; but because we fight for something greater than they do. We fight for the freedom of Agadin! We fight for the Kingdom of Light!"

The army soaked in every word. Anneya lifted her head, gleaning from her mentor's unwavering determination.

He pointed his sword towards the dragon. "Many of you have lost loved ones to the creature you see before you. We have the opportunity to fight for those we love, whether they still live or have fallen by the flames of Marradus. The creature you see before you will cower and fall! It will take no more lives! If need be, we will break its wings, so it can no longer fly! We will snuff its flames so it can no longer burn! It will go back to the bowels of the Dominion of Shadow where it came from!"

The army resounded in shouts and cheers. Henry lifted his war-hammer in a deep shout. Anneya lifted her bow, bellowing a battle cry.

Tolek lifted his sword into the sky. "Follow me into battle! Today, we advance the Kingdom of Light!"

With a shout, he turned and ran towards their enemy, an army of two thousand fast behind him. With a fierce shout, Anneya charged with passion. Her feet pounded upon the tough terrain. She wasn't surprised to see all the Paladins gaining more ground than the others. The soldiers scattered outside of Gorath turned to face them.

The two armies collided.

Anneya watched as Dianne rushed towards three emerging Dark Blades. She came in swiftly, cutting them down in mere seconds. Henry spun his war-hammer like a metallic tornado, taking lives immediately upon impact. Platius drew his bow, mid-gait, shooting soldiers from impossible distances.

Before her, Anneya saw a Dark Blade watching her with a double-edged axe. She decided that he would be her first kill.

From under his thick brow, the Dark Blade shouted to her. "Did you get lost, little girl?!" the man snarled at her.

As metal clanged around her, Anneya clenched her fists.

The man was much larger than her. She knew his barreling arms were more than capable of wielding the axe he carried. She knew she couldn't simply fire an arrow; he would find a way to dodge it. She needed to first put him off guard. In a dash, she ran at him.

When she reached the Dark Blade, he swung his axe low, aiming for her midsection. She leapt into the air, scaling the swing. Bringing a leg up, she planted a foot into his barreled chest. From the look on his face, he didn't expect her to be able to deliver such staggering impact. He stepped back to regain his balance. Still in mid-air, she pulled forth an arrow, firing it into the Dark Blade's chest. He fell onto the ground in a *thud*.

Pulling the arrow from the warrior's chest, she looked up to see two Dark Bishops running toward her. Anneya's gaze grew at the sight, knowing their skill in combat would be beyond her own. Before she could even nock an arrow on her bow, she saw Henry's war-hammer twisting through the air toward one of the Bishops. As it hit its target, she heard bones break. The sound made her cringe.

Henry barreled in reclaiming his weapon. The remaining Dark Bishop attacking, the large Paladin seemed to know what strike would come before it was even made. She knew Henry was using foresight, an ability that all Paladins were trained in. In moments, both Dark Bishops were slain at Henry's feet.

Anneya nodded her thanks. Henry smiled as he charged onward. Her attention turned to the enemy warriors skirting throughout the rocky floor. Arrow after arrow she fired.

Looking around, she saw their own beginning to fall. Their army was beginning to fold under the enemy's forces. Cries of agony filled her ears, chipping away at her tenacity. The Paladins fought tirelessly, killing an unfathomable number of soldiers, yet the enemy still pressed. There were simply far too many. She knew they would need to eliminate the army before they could attempt tackling Marradus, yet it seemed as though they had only taken out a small fraction of the soldiers. Many still lingered close to the city wall, their weapons not yet even tasting battle. How many would they have left after fighting such a force, if any?

She heard a shriek of another one of their own being killed. Watching another one of their warriors fall to their death, she breathed deeply. She could feel her hair filled with dirt and sweat, the gold strands sticking to her skin. Her body was stiff from travel and war. She was growing tired and weary.

Then she felt the rumble.

From beneath her feet, she began feeling the earth quaking. She looked around, seeing if others had noticed. Warriors scattered throughout the tough land paused, looking around in confusion. What began as a low tremble, quickly rose into a wild tremor.

With a sudden jolt from the earth beneath her, Anneya flipped onto her back. The earth shook in violence. In the distance, she heard a loud crack, followed by the shouts of the enemy soldiers. Cracks spiderwebbed up the city walls of Gorath. Close to the city, in a violent rupture, stone popped and spasmed from the earth.

"Pull back!" Tolek commanded. The army complied, distancing themselves from the enemy army at the sudden shift.

Anneya's breath almost stopped as she watched the earth open up like the jaws of a mighty beast. The rocky ground split like a chasm. Enemy warriors shouted and cried as they fell into the black abyss. They tried to run, but the earth would fall away, the hole widening its bite. One after another they fell.

She looked around to the confused faces that surrounded her. "What in the name of Divinity is going on?" she voiced to herself in stunned shock.

A generous portion of the enemy army was eaten up by the manipulated earth. While everyone's eyes were locked on the violence before them, Anneya's suspicion grew. Rising to her feet, her eyes darted around trying to find the source of the timely occurrence.

In the near distance, a frail man stood upon a weighty boulder. Past the hood of his hazel robe, she saw he was an older man; likely in his eighties in age. Holding his staff forwards, he wore a concentrated gaze. As his hands slowly moved, so did the earth, consuming those who served the Dominion of Shadow.

In the faintest of whispers, Anneya said, "Great Divinity, it's a Roek."

CHAPTER THIRTY-NINE

WEAPONS SPEAK

"Who are you?" Tolek's voice boomed through the battlefield, commanding an answer from the old man.

Anneya watched the elderly man atop the boulder as he lifted his hands. Pulling his brown hood back, he looked out upon the approaching warriors.

"My name is Orin. I am a Roek of Earth," he said. Even though his voice was raspy and tired, his tone held undeniable weight.

She watched in wonder. Kaldon had told her that a Roek still lived; she simply didn't know if she believed it to be true. Following Tolek's lead, they closed the distance between themselves and the Roek.

"We appreciate you saving us," Tolek said, with some perplexity. "Where did you come from?"

The Roek stood slightly hunched, with his staff pressed into the boulder on which he was standing. "Even though I have been in hiding for many years, in the past I had an important role to play in the Great War. I have stopped many armies that threatened the peace of Agadin. A friend of mine reminded me that I cannot spend the rest of my days in hiding. He reminded me that I need to rise. That is why I am here."

Anneya felt chills glide over her skin as Kaldon's prophecy whispered through her mind. *"The Roek must rise."*

In a gruff voice, Henry said, "And what friend would that be?"

Orin's eyes shifted from person to person. "His name is Kaldon Thain."

Henry's gaze widened from underneath his distinct brow. "It can't be…"

"Kaldon?!" Tolek exclaimed, slamming his sword in its sheath.

With tears in her eyes, Anneya took a step toward the old Roek. "You saw Kaldon?"

A smile swept over his gentle face. "Let me guess, you are Anneya."

Tears fell down her face. "I am."

"He spoke a great deal about you. He cared deeply for you," the Roek said.

"Cared?" Tolek asked hesitantly.

Anneya looked up with terrified eyes, her heart pounding. "Is he safe? Is he alive?" she demanded.

The old man's face turned sad. Through the sound of war around them he shifted his weight, reaching for a long slate-coloured satchel that was strapped across his shoulder. It was the first time Anneya noticed it. Holding it before them, he began untying the cloth.

She held her breath as he unraveled the cloth. What she saw made her want to crumble to the ground. She forced herself to stand, her eyes resting upon *Humility* and *Integrity.*

Bringing her hands up, she covered her mouth letting out a cry. "No… Please, no." She felt Henry's hand lay upon her shoulder in an attempt to comfort her.

Tolek's face was set in stone; yet the hollow in his voice betrayed his emotion. "Tell me what happened to him," he said.

Tears began brooking down the old man's face. "My cowardice betrayed him. Kaldon was at my home. I taught him, training him to Command Creation. One night, several Dark Bishops came to take him."

Orin paused, as he held back a sob, his face straining in emotion. "I let them take him because I was afraid of them seeing my ability; afraid of them seeing what I can do. He was weaponless, yet I did nothing to protect him. It is the greatest regret of my life."

The old man held out the two swords, his frail arms trembling. "He left these behind."

"Do you know where they took him?" she asked, her voice shaking.

The Roek shook his head in remorse. "I don't know for certain. I would assume a prison of sorts — if they allowed him to live."

Tolek turned his head to the side, clenching his jaw. She knew the Paladin was doing everything he could to prevent himself from ending the Roek's life right there.

Tolek spoke sharply to the Roek. "You may have put to death one of the few chances that Agadin has to survive!" the Paladin unsheathed his sword, heaving it into the distance. The weapon clanging upon stone.

Orin flinched at the sound.

Tolek reached out. He pulled *Humility* and *Integrity* from Orin's grip; swords that belonged to his lost pupil. He held *Integrity* before his eyes for a moment, taking in its golden glow. He strapped the sword to his side, where it once rested.

"This now belongs to you," the Paladin said, handing *Humility* over to Anneya.

Holding the hilt of Kaldon's childhood weapon, she knew her hand was where his had rested time and time again. "No, this doesn't belong to me. It belongs to Kaldon," she said definitively.

She strapped the short-sword upon her back. "I will keep it safe for him until we find him. I will not give up on him," she said, trying to hold herself together.

Tolek gave her a sad nod.

Looking upon the Roek, she winced as another quake trembled throughout the ground. The surprised look that shot over Orin's face told her that he didn't cause it. Slowly turning around, she knew such a quake could only be made from one thing. Marradus had thundered to the ground, ready to fight.

The dragon stood upon ground, glaring at those remaining of the armies. Marradus swung its scaled tail, swiping nearly thirty soldiers at once. Shouting, they were toppled over by the mighty blow; many lives immediately ended by the sudden strike. She could still see the arrow protruding from the dragon's eye.

Something caught her sight in the periphery of her vision. Looking over, she saw two of the Paladins rushing throughout the army. At first confused, her eyes widened when she realized what they were trying to do. They were trying to approach Marradus on their own.

She knew that the two Paladins, Sil and Tamil, had a reputation for running ahead of the others. They both implied it was their courage that led them; however, to her it seemed like unbridled passion, a dangerous compulsion in war. Marradus' eyes shifted from the army masses to the two Paladins.

"Stop! Not yet!" Tolek shouted.

The two Paladins were already out of ear shot, targeting the dragon. Anneya shook her head as she watched the Paladins prematurely engaging the demon dragon.

Sill and Tamil cut through soldiers as they approached the dragon. Marradus' reptilian gaze took in the two. It let out a heavy snort. Tamil fired several arrows and Sill brought forth his sword. Before Sill even reached the dragon, Marradus opened its cave-like mouth, revealing its deathly teeth. A spark ignited at the back of the dragon's mouth, fire shooting forth. Sill and Tamil tried to dodge the hungry flames, yet as reds and yellows flew forth, the Paladins were caught by its bite.

Anneya squinted at the bright flames, losing sight of Sill and Tamil for a moment. As the fire slowly died down, nothing remained of the two Paladins. Just like that, two of the finest warriors in all of Agadin were gone due to reckless zeal.

Marradus spread its colossal wings.

"Tolek, we can't allow Marradus to attack from the skies! We need to do something, fast!" she shouted.

Tolek, turned to Orin. "Roek, now is the time to redeem yourself."

The Roek nodded adamantly. "Just tell me what to do."

"Don't let that dragon fly," he commanded.

Orin nodded in compliance. As the gargantuan creature was about to launch from the ground, he lifted his staff. As he did, a strip of rocky ground ripped from the floor. Pebbles and small shrubs dropped from the hovering piece of earth, descending back to the ground. Anneya was shocked at how large the piece of earth was that Orin commanded. The mound swung around, forcefully dropping on top of the demon dragon. Marradus let out a grunt at the blow, roaring in frustration. Before it could try flying again, the Roek hurled several boulders at the demon dragon to prevent it from taking flight.

Tolek smirked at the sight. "Keep that up for as long as you can. We need that dragon on the ground floor in order for my plan to work."

The Paladin looked to Anneya and Platius. "You two, cover me with arrows." He then turned to the large Paladin. "Henry, come with me."

"What are you two going to do?" Anneya asked hesitantly.

Tolek looked at her with a serious gaze. "Something *stupidly outrageous.*"

Henry pulled forth his war-hammer. He let out a hardy laugh. "Perfect, let's go then!"

Chapter Fourty

Lightning and Thunder

With *Integrity* drawn, Tolek thought about how good it felt to have the ancient blade in his grip again.

As an enemy soldier came near, the Paladin cut him down effortlessly. Beside him, Henry — his friend since his youth — spun his war-hammer in wrath. Together, they slayed whoever came near. Tolek cut at unfathomable speeds and Henry smashed with incomprehensible strength. They were a duo of death; like lightning and thunder come in the flesh.

Drawing closer to Marradus, Tolek watched another strip of earth rip from the ground floor before him. Looking back, he saw the Roek wielding his staff, commanding the earth to obey him. Like a vicious wave of stone, the strip crashed onto Marradus' back, refusing it flight. The dragon let out a deafening roar.

Fire whirled from the creature's mouth. The flames were so scorching that only a demon dragon could conjure them. Tolek knew it was growing weary under the Roek's incessant pummels of stone.

"Henry!" he bellowed, his voice cutting through the sounds of war. "Are you ready?"

A determined sneer spread over the enormous Paladin's face. "Always."

Henry darted to the side of the dragon; Tolek ran head on toward it. With Tolek in plain sight, Marradus cocked its head back, creating wretched flames. The Paladin smiled, knowing that he had the dragon's attention. He needed to allow Henry to get close enough.

Fire shot at him. The Paladin reached behind his back pulling forth the dragon's scale; the impenetrable shield. Flame crashed against the onyx scale. The blaze bounced from the shield, leaving it unmarred. Flames flicking from the shield, Tolek could feel its touch.

"Come on!" he yelled at the creature with his shield poised against the flames.

With each step he took, his sword's tip dragged through the dry land.

With a crack, Henry's war-hammer came up, slamming against the dragon. Marradus didn't even flinch at the futile attempt to bring it harm, keeping its attention on Tolek. As flames exploded against his shield, he listened to Henry's powerful strikes. He was so close to the creature that he could see the dragon's chest heaving as it breathed. He looked upon the body adorned in flawless scales. All except in one place; the greyed stretch of exposed skin where Tolek's shield once laid.

Henry swung his mighty war-hammer with greater force, pulling at the dragon's attention. The dragon distracted, Tolek quickly strapped his shield onto his back. It was time to let *Integrity* loose to do what it did so well. While dodging the dragon's menacing claws, he dove forward with staggering speed. He didn't bother trying to penetrate the scales, doubting such a thing were even possible. His eyes locked onto the stretch of naked skin. He brought forth *Integrity*.

The Paladin slashed ravenously. From every angle he could think of he attacked, thrusted, and sliced. The barred plot of skin was left unscathed. Not even a scratch was seen.

Tolek growled in dissatisfaction. He leaned back to regain his strength. He needed to use the force of his whole body if he wanted to penetrate the skin. In a shout, he brought in *Integrity* with all his might. The sword soared at the belly of Marradus; yet, it simply skipped off its skin.

The Paladin panted, sweat glistening from his face.

"No!" From behind him, the blood curdling cry sliced through the intensity of battle.

He knew the voice. It was Anneya.

Tolek, a man used to the effects of war, was unsurprised by the unpredictability of it. Yet, when he turned towards her scream, his heart sank. He watched her run towards Orin. With an arrow sticking out from the Roek's stomach, red sprayed from his mouth.

"Orin! Please! No!" she wept, holding the Roek as he slouched in her arms.

Tolek knew he wouldn't live long from such a wound, especially at his age.

With the absence of the Roek hurling rocks upon the dragon, Marradus' wings shot outward. Several warriors flew to the ground at the force of the dragon's wings colliding into them. Tolek knew that with Orin not being capable of preventing the dragon's flight, their opportunity would be lost.

He looked up to the dragon's patch of skin. He gripped *Integrity* in his fist.

"Henry, we need to end this, now!" he shouted.

Without delay, the large Paladin ran over. His thick legs moved as fast as they could. Tolek looked up to where the dragon's scale was missing from its reptilian body. With any other sword, he knew what he was about to try would make the metal bend or shatter; however, he knew that if any sword could prove the impossible, it was *Integrity*.

In a flash, he brought up the sword. Placing its point against the skin of the dragon's stomach, he held it in place.

"Henry! Swing!" Tolek shouted.

Henry gripped the hilt of his war-hammer as he let out a barreling shout. With unfathomable force, he swung. The hammer came in, impacting with the hilt of *Integrity*. With a loud *rip*, the sword pierced the dragon's stomach. With *Integrity's* golden blade hidden within the creature's body, all that stuck out was the hilt of the ancient sword.

Marradus let out a howl that sounded like one thousand roars. Tolek and Henry held their ears at the sharp wail. Tolek watched the wounded creature writhing in pain. He knew one thing for certain; he wasn't finished with the dragon.

CHAPTER FORTY-ONE

OLD FRIEND

T
he ground beneath him shook as a roar echoed throughout Gorath. Only one creature could make such a wretched sound.

It was Marradus.

Birds shoeing away in the distance from the mighty roar, Kaldon knew night was drawing near. His eyes took in the murky air. He listened to the sound of battle in the distance. He didn't know who was at war, but he prayed the army of Gorath would fall. Amongst the clamour, he heard something different; something that made chills glide over his whole body. He heard chanting.

Chants rose up from Gorath. Even though war was taking place, residents of the city were joined together in synchronized shouts. The cries blended together, making the utterances indistinguishable. Much of the city was roused for his execution. He surmised they were chanting in excited anticipation. They wanted to watch the death of Dolan Thain's son.

His eyes watched the golden sun kiss the ocean-line. His execution was to take place at sunset. It was almost time. Just as the sun went to rest, so would he. The exception was that the sun would surely rise again.

Kaldon missed Glaric's voice. The former Chief Messenger had been speaking out encouragements to him throughout the day, inspiring him to persevere. Guards passing by heard his words and moved him to a different cell. Even though he was in no mood to talk, he missed the kind words. He missed not feeling alone. It didn't matter anymore. The Sovereign of Shadow had defeated him.

He ran through the vision he had been given back at the Peak of Lore over and over again. Was he really guided by the River of Time simply to be killed in such a horrific way? He watched the ocean as it rolled and toiled. He muttered the words from his vision. They were a mystery that he would never know the answer to.

"The Roek must rise. The Seer will fall. The Paladin needs to obtain the impenetrable shield. The Paragon must soar."

Slouching deeper into the iron door behind him, he knew it would open any minute. "I have to endure one night of torture; several hours of agonizing pain, then it will be done. I can rest for eternity," he said to himself, anxiety rampaging through his entire body.

As the fear-gripping images stormed through his mind of what he would likely be forced to endure, he knew he needed to distract himself. Closing his eyes, he allowed the noise of war and chants to fall from his ears. He focused on the sounds of crashing waves beyond his cell; beyond his fears.

In his mind, he envisioned his friends, allowing their faces to float through his consciousness. He thought of Fen, the Philosopher who was once sour and hardened; yet had become his close friend. There was a kindness and gentleness to her that was rare. He thought of Brenton, Flor, and their three girls. He respected Brenton's love for his family and how intentional he was as a husband and father. He thought of Anneya.

The image of her face growing in his mind, the light of her smile flooded through him. It gave him the willpower to continue on. Memories of her laugh gave him the courage he needed to endure.

He opened his eyes and saw that the sun had sunk behind the ocean-line. It was time.

He stood, taking in the private cell that he would never again see. Turning to face the door, he held his hands at his back. He waited for the door to open and for the Dark Bishops to escort him to ruin. He already made the decision that he wouldn't plead for his life. He would be brave. He would die in honour. With his eyes fixed on the iron door, he waited.

Divinity, give me courage, he thought.

As he lingered in the wait, stillness was interrupted. The ground shifted beneath his feet. The sound of a *thud* filled his ears. He shifted, then held out his arms to regain his balance. His eyes remained upon the iron door as he twisted his face.

He knew the source wasn't from beyond the door. The jolt rumbled from behind him. Looking down, he watched as pebbles trembled on the ground, then settled from the unexpected rouse. With his back turned to the open expanse of air, he listened to the steady breathes that now inhaled and exhaled from behind him.

His stomach knotted when he felt heat, like swells of fire beaming against his back. His breaths quickened.

"Marradus…" he whispered in dread.

Without even a sword in hand, he slowly turned around. His nerves blared in alarm.

The sight before him astonished him. The demon dragon was nowhere to be seen. Perched on the cliff of his cell, about the size of a man and a half in height, stood a bird clothed in scorching flames. It was the same bird he'd once seen as a child.

The majestic creature stood elegantly. Its mighty talons rested upon the ground beneath it. Its round face gazed upon him. Through the filter of his tears, he took in the eternal bird, the Owl; a bird from the Golden Land.

His mouth agape, he tried to speak, but all that spilled out were cries. Tears cascading down his face, he took a cautious step forward. He slowly approached the bird clothed in tumbling reds, yellows, and oranges. With each step he took, he could feel the heat's intensity pressing upon his body. Unmoving, the Owl's two golden eyes watched him approach.

He stretched out a trembling hand, reaching for the fiery Owl. His hand nearing, the flames agitated his skin. His lightning bolt scars itched. He watched as flames flicked from the bird and licked his hand.

He breathed in deeply. Summoning his courage and denying his pain, he thrust his hand forward, placing it upon the bird's head between its medallion-like eyes. As his hand rested, he watched the fire across the bird's frame dissipate into nothingness.

He flinched at the sudden change. As his hand rested upon the silky feathers, he felt them quickly cool. He was surprised to see the feathers weren't charred or burned. They were wondrous. The large feathers were magnified in stark white and silver. Intricate patterns and markings were sketched into them in adornment. He had never seen anything so majestic in all his life.

"Have you come to rescue me?" he whispered to the legendary bird.

The Owl turned around. It stretched its wings. The girth of its wingspan was wider than the cell. Kaldon was stunned at the sight. He knew the outstretched wings were an invitation to mount onto its back. Looking past the cliff-line, he felt nauseous at the sight. The staggering heights made his head spin.

He could hear the chants ascending from the residents of Gorath. His time was running out. The Dark Bishops would be there any moment to usher him to the Sovereign at the central court of Gorath.

Click.

"Great Divinity, no…" he whispered into the cell.

At the sound of the bolt unlocking, he watched the iron door swing open.

"Are you ready for your demise, Kal…" Dias stopped as he opened the door.

With four other Bishops around him, Dias stuttered. "What is that?!"

Kaldon was stunned, not knowing what to do. He didn't want the Sovereign's men to harm the legendary bird. The Owl lowered its wings, its eyes penetrating the five warriors. Before Kaldon could respond, the Owl was already on the move. Immediately, it darted around him towards Dias. The eternal bird let out a shriek as it lit into an inferno.

Dias' eyes went wide.

The Owl's talons pierced the Bishop's chest. At Dias' screams of agonizing pain, the large bird wrapped its flaming wings around him, lighting him aflame. The large bird violently jerked as it thrashed against Dias.

Metal clanged as he saw Dias' sword chime upon the cell floor. Reaching down, Kaldon picked up the unfamiliar weapon. It felt awkward in his grip. He tucked the weapon into his belt to keep it secure.

In a sudden jolt, he watched as the Owl threw Dias to the other side of the cell, launching him over the cliff. The Dark Bishop's wails echoed throughout the skies. His burning body lit up the dusk as it rushed to the ocean below to be swallowed by hungry waves.

As the Owl made its way back to the cliff's edge, the flames dissipated from its body once again; waiting for Kaldon to mount. He placed a hand upon the bird's glossy feathers, climbing atop its firm back. The hold on the bird felt uncomfortable and unnatural to him. At the feel of its body between his thighs, he knew it was constructed of solid muscle. It had strength he hadn't expected. Looking back, he saw the deathly cell that would no longer hold him. Beyond the iron doorframe, the remaining Bishops stared, transfixed by the sight.

Turning his gaze from the cell that imprisoned him, he looked onward to the open expanse of sky set before him.

"The Paragon must soar," he whispered into the open skies.

The Owl stretched its ivory wings. The legendary bird pushed off from the rocky floor. Launching into flight, it let out an unearthly caw that pierced the darkness.

"As evils ascend and demise draws near, every warrior is confronted with a choice. This choice is one of the most defining tests one will ever face; revealing what has been shaped and forged inside the core of a heart. The question churns like a raging fire. The question is this: 'Will I cower or will I rise?'"

- Dolan Thain
Heart of the Brave

CHAPTER FOURTY-TWO

GORATH

Clenching the Owl's feathers in his fists, Kaldon held on with all his might. The mighty bird soared, the wind pressing against them as they sailed over Gorath. With a daunting gap between them and the ground beneath, homes and buildings were beneath him. He didn't permit himself to look down. He kept his eyes forward as he listened to the sound of chanting echoing through the city. He was finally free from the Sovereign's hand.

Every time the Owl used its wings to stroke the wind or re-adjust from a mighty gust, his nerves would lurch and turn within him. He felt awkward upon the bird, as though he could fall at any moment. Thankfulness rose from within him as he looked at the marking of the Owl's feathers. The very bird that he once saw as a troubled youth, now carried him to safety.

He ran a hand over its feathered mane. "Thank you for saving me," he spoke aloud, feeling foolish speaking to the bird.

The Owl released a gentle coo into the skies, as though it was responding to him. He hoped he would grow accustomed to the foreign flight; however, his nerves ceaselessly stormed through him. Feeling nausea rise once again, he looked to the sight behind him to distract himself from the heights.

He heard a wild roar once again. Marradus' bellow sounded like an avalanche. In the distance, past the black gates of Gorath, he could still hear the sounds of war. Even though he was free from the shackles of his cell, his mind kept turning back to the state Agadin was in. Corruption reigned throughout the land. The demon dragon was still alive; Tymas Droll still controlled. He may be free, but Agadin was not. It was bound in the chains of the Dominion of Shadow. It was bound by chaos and death.

He could feel the lightness upon his back where *Integrity* would usually sit. He'd grown comfortable with its weight. It was a symbol of the fact that he was mantled a Protector of Agadin and a symbol of the responsibility he carried to stand for life.

As they soared, one thought clouded his mind. He was distancing himself from the man who threatened the existence of Agadin.

Kaldon loosened a hand from the bird's ivory feathers and ran it through his hair. He was without his swords. He still felt unseasoned in his gift to Command Creation. He was still finding his bearing with his foresight. What chance did he have against such a man as Tymas Droll? The Sovereign of Shadow would still be expecting him; waiting for him at the central court of Gorath.

Insecurity shooting through him, he thought of words that Orin once spoke to him.

"Learning your gift is important; however, a frail heart cannot properly wield a weighty gift. Only a confident and whole heart can. If you believe you are not capable without your ability, then you don't deserve to have it."

He allowed the words to course through him as the air ran over his face. He could still hear the chants in the distance. It wasn't too late.

"I need to turn around," he said, hearing his words without even realizing he spoke.

The bird turned its head and looked into him with penetrating eyes.

"I need to follow the chants. Please, take me there," he stated.

Without hesitation, the Owl tilted its wings changing the course of direction. As the eternal bird adjusted its wings, Kaldon did as well to stay well balanced upon the graceful bird.

Gliding past the onyx tower of Gorath, he felt small amongst the emblem of the hometown of Tymas Droll. The city was grand; however, the streets were vacant. Business owners were nowhere to be seen. Families weren't shopping for food. Children no longer frolicked in the streets. He knew they were all gathered in one place.

The sounds increased as he neared the city's centre. The chants rumbled throughout his body. In an open field of green, he saw the central courts of Gorath. The entire city was assembled around the grand centre stage. Multitudes chanted in wait. Behind the stage, the ocean roared, rolling over itself in waves.

On the marble stage, he saw a lonely tree standing, void of life. Its pale trunk was fitting in the corrupt city. Beside the woeful tree, the Sovereign of Shadow waited for him.

As the Owl hung over the somber city, Kaldon looked down to the Sovereign. He watched as Tymas turned his sinister face upwards, making eye contact with him. The crowds surrounding the stage looked up as well. Many pointed at the legendary bird in amazement.

"Take me down there," he said.

In immediate obedience, the Owl whirled downwards toward the white-stone stage. Kaldon felt lightness in his head at the decline.

Upon the grand stage, the bird landed. Slowly loosening his grip from the bird of eternity, he began to unmount. His body adjusted to being on land again. He was thankful to no longer be in the air.

The Owl lit into flame. The crowd gasped at the sight of the eternal bird being clothed in inferno. The Owl launched from the stage, flying to a nearby building, perching on a statue to watch the scene unfold. He was thankful to have the bird of fire watching over him.

He looked to the faces that surrounded the stage. Each appeared stunned at what they just witnessed. There must have been thousands; many being common warriors, Knights, Blades, and Bishops. Scattered among the soldiers were many of the city folk of Gorath. He saw men, women, and children. He saw blacksmiths, farmers, and bakers. All were suppressed under the rule of Tymas Droll. Amidst them, stood several Nahmen. Their grey-like appearance still unsettled him. Kreel snarled at him with teeth clenched. Their beaded eyes watched him, zealous for blood.

"Kal Wendal, I must say, this isn't how I expected you to arrive," the Sovereign muttered, looking up at the Owl lit in flames. "However, I'm glad you still chose to attend your execution. Where is Dias?"

"Dias is dead," he replied as a threat.

Tymas slowly shook his head. "Oh, what a pity. He was a good warrior," he said, waving his hand in dismissal. "No worries; I suppose I have enough servants for disposal if need be."

Kaldon breathed heavily as he took in the man who was the reason for so much chaos and death.

Tymas looked the young man up and down. "And so, you have come to take me on yourself then. Is that correct?" He scoffed out a laugh. "Your arrogance has ushered you to your death. You would have been wise to escape when you had the chance."

Kaldon felt his jaw tightening. "I am here to hold you accountable for the death of my father and mother, as well as for the multitude of lives you have stolen throughout Agadin."

"Is that so?" Tymas Droll mocked. "So, the sewer rat has become a judge, then? Your fantasies are entertaining."

The silence of the crowd was tangible; tense.

"I assure you, you will not live through this day," the Sovereign said. "Do you have any final words before your life will be taken from you?"

Kaldon looked around at the multitude. He saw many men who were likely fathers and husbands; women who were mothers and wives. His gaze rested upon a mother and child. The young boy, likely only three years of age, burrowed his face into his mother's shoulder. As he peeked out, Kaldon looked into his round eyes. A child so young shouldn't have to endure such times.

He kept his gaze upon the people. "I do have something to say."

Many in the crowd leaned in to hear what they presumed would be the final words of the son of Dolan Thain.

Kaldon began. "Some of you have fully given your heart to the Shadow. You are corrupt and unwilling to change. Others of you are simply suppressed under the Sovereign's hand and rule. Today you have the opportunity to make a choice. You have the choice to either cower or rise."

Many in the crowd looked around to one another, spilling forth in whispers.

He waited for the mutterings to still. He looked into the crowd, making eye contact with many of them. "Today you can take your life into your own hands. Under the Sovereign's rule, your sons will be recruited for war, forced to take the lives of innocents. Your daughters will be made slaves and the wives of brutes. However, you can make a choice now to live your *own* life, rather than following the will of the tyrant now among us."

Through the stunned silence that filled Gorath, a man spoke up. "If we leave now, we will be killed!"

"Maybe," Kaldon replied. "But at least you will have stood for something. At least you will have died with your life in your own hands. You will have died as free people, rather than as slaves to death."

He could see tears glistening in the eyes of many of the listeners. He took a step forward. "You have your own will. Now is the time to take a stand against evil. Claim back what should never have been taken from you. Reclaim your lives and your freedom!"

At the words of the Paragon, not a voice was heard. All listened intently as Kaldon Thain spoke.

"I assure you; Light will Reign again in Agadin. Rise today! Take your life into your own hands once again. Reject the Shadow that surrounds you. The choice is yours."

He watched the crowd, wordlessly awaiting their reply. Thousands of eyes rested upon him. Still. Unmoving. He noticed a man in the back of the crowd who bore conviction in his eyes. The man suddenly dropped his head. He grabbed the hand of his wife and eight-year-old daughter. Together, they turned from the stage. Together, they walked away from the crowd.

Kaldon felt a smile grow upon his face as he saw the family reclaiming their lives. He was surprised when a female Knight who served the Sovereign, dropped her sword to the ground. She followed behind the family, thus forsaking Shadow and choosing life. One after another, men, women, and children turned their faces from the stage. Each turned away from the Sovereign of Shadow.

With families and warriors walking away, the remaining of the Sovereign's soldiers looked around to one another not knowing what to do. The drastic numbers of people who rejected the Sovereign's reign were too many to count; there were too many to prevent from leaving.

Kaldon could feel emotion rising as he watched the brave ones making their exodus. His eyes scoured the remaining crowd, thankful to see that no more children were amongst them. If he were to die that day, he knew their young eyes wouldn't need to see his fall. Only the Sovereign's soldiers, Nahmen, and Kreel remained.

From underneath the dead tree, the Sovereign of Shadow spoke. "They will not make it far, Kal. Haven't you heard the sounds of war? I have an army stationed outside the walls of Gorath. You literally sent these people marching to their deaths. They will pay with their lives for their foolish choice of listening to you."

Kaldon allowed a faint smile to grow upon his face. "Divinity will reward them for choosing life." He turned to Tymas Droll. "As for you, I believe you are afraid."

Tymas let out a laugh. "Afraid?" He held out his hand to the warriors, Nahmen, and Kreel surrounding the stage. "What do I have to be afraid of? I wield the most powerful force in all of Agadin!"

He stepped towards the Sovereign. "I think you're afraid because I just proved to you that you have far less control than you thought you did. Even if I die today, there will always be someone to stand against you. There will be those who will refuse you. You aren't as powerful as you think you are."

"I will show you how powerful I am!" the Sovereign replied, giving him a grim gaze. "It is time for your execution, Kal Wendal. I will show you how much control I have by killing you myself. All these warriors are about to watch the son of Dolan Thain beg for his pathetic life!"

Kaldon pulled forth the rusty sword from the belt he'd retrieved from his prison cell. He gripped his hand over the black hilt. He swayed the sword from side to side feeling that it wasn't balanced to his liking. It would have to do.

At the sound of ringing steel, his eyes traced the Sovereign's elongated sword.

Tymas Droll pointed his sword towards his opponent, saying, "Now is the time for the son of Dolan Thain to fall!"

The Sovereign of Shadow bared his teeth while charging toward him.

"'Impossibility' is just a word. Never allow it to threaten or intimidate you. Rage against your ceilings. Overcome your limitations. The word 'impossibility' is a lie. Your mandate is to prove it false."

- Dolan Thain
Heart of the Brave

CHAPTER FOURTY-THREE

THE FALLEN

The Sovereign charged towards him. Staring into the tyrant's eyes, Kaldon saw the madness that gripped him. Darkness possessed his soul. His foresight ignited, an advantage he would need against such a foe. Refusing to take the defence, he instead pressed in toward the Sovereign, meeting him in battle.

In a crash, their swords met one another. As metal collided, the Sovereign spun. He brought an elbow to Kaldon's head. Upon seeing the attack moments before in a vision in his mind, Kaldon ducked, dodging the attempt.

The crowd of warriors cheered and hollered for their leader. Kaldon refused the rousing, instead fixing his ears on the ocean behind them. The sound of soothing crashes comforted him, championing him onwards.

Tymas Droll's sword curved down toward his head. Stepping aside, the Sovereign's sword clashed against the marble stage. As quickly as the sword fell, it rose again. He came in raging with wrath. His weapon was a blur at such speed. The man was far quicker in combat than Kaldon expected him to be. Tymas was no Paladin; yet, he didn't doubt that with his ability to heal, he could be a threat to one.

Using his sword as defence against the speedy attacks, the visions spinning throughout his mind overwhelmed him. His foresight came so fast he was having troubles keeping up.

The Sovereign shouted, swiping in at him again. Kaldon lifted his sword to block, but the force was stronger than he expected. Kaldon felt his sword loose from his grip. The blade flew through the air and skidded across the stage. Before Tymas could cut in again, he dove for his blade. He slid across the stage while grasping for the stern weapon once again — before it was too late. Gripping the hilt in his fist, he quickly rose to his feet. Tymas' cocky smile reminded him that he couldn't make such a foolish mistake again.

Visions spun throughout his mind as he watched the Sovereign stepping in to slice his sword sideways. The Sovereign was placing far too much of his weight on his right foot, which forced him into an awkward position. He knew that this was his chance.

Just as he'd seen with his foresight, the Sovereign cut in sideways. Stepping back, Kaldon watched the blade slice by him. He watched as the Sovereign placed too much weight on his right leg. He took the opportunity to drive in by bringing a knee into the Sovereign's ribs. Upon hearing a *pop,* he knew he broke several ribs upon impact. The Sovereign grunted as he drove his sword into his side, feeling it pierce the flesh. From the blood staining the Sovereign's beige robe, he knew he'd punctured fatal organs.

Kaldon breathed heavily in exhaustion.

"You have grown to be quite gifted," the Sovereign said, holding his side. "But, not nearly gifted enough."

Light began growing over Tymas Droll's wound, stitching his skin back together.

The Sovereign stood tall with not an ounce of pain or fatigue showing on his face. "You cannot win, Kal Wendal. You could cut me one thousand times and I would not die. Your attempts are futile."

He knew it would be difficult to fight a man who could not be harmed by iron or steel. He shouted while charging in with his blade toward the Sovereign of Shadow. Tymas used his sword to deflect the attempt by bringing his hand to Kaldon's face. As the Sovereign's hand rested before his eyes, he watched as light began to grow from his palm. Tymas summoned the Kingdom of Light.

The glow grew brighter and brighter, making Kaldon's head spin. He fumbled back, holding his eyes. His eyes weren't adjusted to such bright light. He blinked to test his sight. All he could see was the brightness. Realizing it stunned his ability to see, panic began flooding into him.

"What's the matter, Kal Wendal? Don't you like my little trick?" the Sovereign snarled.

He grimaced at the sound of Droll's mockery. Before he could respond, he felt the Sovereign's knee crash into his stomach. He grunted upon impact, crouching over in gasps.

"Over and over again, I have bested you," Tymas said. "Today will be the last time. This day, you will hand over your life to me!" the shrill voice said.

Kaldon knew he needed to find his bearing, or he would lose his life. He thought to his training sessions with Brenton back at the Peak of Lore; of how he would fight blindfolded, being guided by nothing but his foresight.

Allowing his mind to go blank, he summoned the gift to rise again. With his natural eyes all he saw was the sun-like glare, yet in his mind he saw much more. He saw the attacks and strategies the Sovereign would impose upon him. In his visions, he saw the Sovereign slowing in pace, the temporary blindness causing the tyrant to underestimate him. Tymas didn't strike as adamantly. His thrusts were more careless. He needed to act quickly.

In his mind, he watched the Sovereign's sword descending toward his shoulder. He listened as the blade whistled in the wind. Responding to the vision, he side-stepped the threatening slice. Quickly, he reached out, grabbing the hair of Tymas Droll. Pulling his head down, he brought his knee up. It exploded into the Sovereign's face.

Due to the impact, Kaldon heard Tymas crash onto the stone floor. Not giving the Sovereign the chance to catch his breath, he was already on the move, sword in hand. In the vision in his mind, he watched the Sovereign rise into a defensive posture. Kaldon would have to make sure he stayed that way.

Slice after slice, he cut, following the instruction of his foresight. While the Sovereign was able to deflect several of the blows, over and over again he felt his blade connecting with the tyrant's flesh. His blade craved the blood of the madman. The gasps and pants of the Sovereign let him know he was growing fatigued. That was what he wanted. He knew the Shan-Rafa would be healing as every cut came; however, that would cost him energy.

As his temporal blindness slowly began lifting, he was beginning to see the Sovereign's outline. He could faintly read the features upon his child-like face. He wore strain. With his elongated sword before him, Kaldon swiped his own against the Sovereign's. The curved sword shot from Tymas' grasp.

"No!" he shouted aloud as it flew into the crowd of warriors.

The Sovereign was now weaponless. Kaldon brought a foot up, crashing it into his chest. Tymas lost his footing, landing on his back.

He held out his sword at the Sovereign as he laid upon the ground. Through staggered breathes, he said, "Tymas Droll, I now hold you accountable for the death of my mother, and for the death of my father. I hold you accountable for the multitude of lives you have stolen throughout Agadin."

"Who are you to speak to me this way?!" Tymas Droll spat, sitting up. "I am the Sovereign of Shadow! I was chosen by Furion herself!"

"You are nothing!" Kaldon cut in. His voice rang throughout the central courts of Gorath.

Tymas Droll faltered under the words.

"You cannot kill a Shan-Rafa," he muttered. "Besides, do you think I don't have a multitude of plans in place? I have many who do my bidding; many who will advance the Dominion of Shadow. I have limitless armies of individuals who serve me with powers you couldn't comprehend!"

"Like who?! Your new puppet, the Wind of the Abyss?" Kaldon snapped.

Tymas' brows lifted. "Oh dear, you don't know do you?"

Kaldon's face twisted in confusion as he silently watched the Sovereign.

"Oh, this is priceless." The Sovereign let out a laugh. "Even for you, this is pathetic, Kal Wendal. Pathetic, indeed."

"What are you talking about?" he asked, pointing his sword at the Sovereign.

In response, Tymas laughed upon the marble floor as if relishing in the moment.

"Tell me!" Kaldon shouted, growing tired of games.

The Sovereign looked deep into him, speaking in a loud tone. "Wind of the Abyss! Come forward!"

Looking over, Kaldon watched as those in the crowd moved aside to make room for one passing through. Wearing a pale blue robe that stretched to the floor, the man's head and face were cloaked in a hood. Slowly, he walked up the steps onto the stage.

Kaldon could feel his anger rising with each step the Wind of the Abyss took. He was another murderer, just like the Sovereign of Shadow. Another who would need to answer to justice.

The hooded figure stood before him, looking to the floor instead of at him. His robe blew in the wind.

"Show your face, you coward!" Kaldon spat.

The man lifted his hands, pulling back the hood to reveal a clean-shaven head. The Wind of the Abyss slowly lifted his gaze, making eye contact with him.

Kaldon took a step back. "No… It can't be…"

As much as he wanted his eyes to be deceiving him, the trickery in the man's eyes were all the confirmation he needed.

It was Mikiel.

"No… You were lost in the Mountains of D'aal. It can't be you…" he pleaded.

Mikiel stood silently; expressionless. Tymas Droll rose, standing beside the young man. "Oh, I assure you it is. The young man embraced the Shadow as he took the life of the old Seer, Alden. Mikiel has become my weapon. He is a murderer of the people; my apprentice," the Sovereign hissed.

Kaldon looked back to the young man. "Mikiel, this isn't you. You are better than this! You once said that you knew you had a part to play in the Great War. Remember yourself!"

For the first time, Mikiel spoke. "I have remembered, Kaldon. This is who I am. This is who I've always been."

Mikiel stretched out his hands, a wild wind coursing toward him. Like a boulder to his chest, Kaldon plummeted to the floor. Upon impact, he felt all air leave his lungs. Mikiel stood over him, his face twisting in anger as he commanded the wind to crush him.

Looking into the eyes of the young man who was once his friend, he realized Mikiel was no more. He was now the Wind of the Abyss. Kaldon waited, expecting to hear the bones in his chest shatter. He tried to shout, yet nothing came out.

"Kill him!" the Sovereign growled.

Kaldon cringed under the words of the one who took everything from him. Now, he had taken Mikiel, his friend, as well. At the thought, he spilled over in tears.

Tymas leaned over him shaking his head. "As much as I hated your father, he at least had my respect. He deserved his title as a Warrior General. *You* on the other hand, are unfitting for a title. You are weak."

He barely heard the man, Mikiel's betrayal cutting into his soul.

Behind the mad laughter of the Sovereign of Shadow, Kaldon heard the waves of the ocean crash. In the distance, he could see the endless blue, like boundless sapphire.

Tears blurred his sight as he fought the wind. He stretched his fists out. The madness of the Sovereign needed to be put to an end for good. Unfortunately, so did Mikiel. With all his might, he released a shout. Through the agonizing cry, he called the ocean to obey him.

Beyond the Sovereign, the ocean swayed in a rhythmic flow. Waters rose in quakes and crashes. As Kaldon yelled, waters ascended into the sky.

Tymas Droll looked back at the rising waters. "No, it isn't possible..."

Waters advanced toward the stage, tearing through the black clouds that hung in the air. Mikiel's attention was stolen. The winds against Kaldon's chest loosened.

By Kaldon's adamant shout, blues collided into one another. At staggering speeds, the mighty wave approached. Shade from the waters draped over him, the Sovereign, and his followers. Every eye took in the mighty wave looming over them. Warriors shouted in panic. Kreel shrieked, attempting to flee. The Sovereign stood still; his eyes wide. There was no stopping such a force.

As he Commanded Creation, water spat upon Kaldon's face. It would all be over so soon.

Another mighty gust of wind suddenly coursed between them and the quickly emerging ocean. He looked up at Mikiel, seeing trickery in his eyes. The Wind of the Abyss smiled slyly.

"Farewell, my brother," the Dark Roek said in a whisper.

"No!" he shouted, watching Mikiel being caught up in the carry of wind.

Just like that, the Wind of the Abyss was gone.

"No!!!" Kaldon shouted.

The swell of ocean arching over the stage, Kaldon looked into the pale eyes of Tymas Droll. He didn't take joy in the Roek's escape. Under the shade of impending doom, the Sovereign wore no look of arrogance, nor of confidence. He was afraid; terrified, knowing that the weight of the ocean water would crush him, killing him instantly. Even a Shan-Rafa couldn't survive something so dreadful.

Kaldon took a deep breath, knowing he was about to die with the Sovereign of Shadow and his soldiers.

The water descending in fury upon them, he heard a caw break through the sound of waters. He saw the white Owl soaring under the crest of the falling wave. Talons gripped his arms, lifting him from the marble ground.

Once the Owl had him in its grasp, it jolted into the skies. The bird's talons prevented him from falling into the watery blue. He looked down, seeing Tymas Droll watching him through the sprays of water. The Sovereign grimaced as the weight of the ocean crashed upon him, crushing him. The mad ruler swept away into nothingness.

In mid-flight Kaldon struggled to climb up upon the Owl's back. His eyes scoured through the skies, but Mikiel was nowhere to be seen. Looking down, he saw that the waters covered the face of Gorath. Buildings and the black tower poked out from the layer of liquid.

The Sovereign of Shadow was no more.

"Though darkness presses, we need to hold on, because every so often there is a moment when everything undefined pulls together. This is when clarity is birthed. It is where confidence takes shape. It is in these moments that light shines upon our identity, revealing who we are."

- Dolan Thain
Heart of the Brave

Chapter Fourty-Four

Demon Dragon

Kaldon soared, clasping the Owl's feathers. In the open expanse of air, he tried to comprehend what just occurred. Tymas Droll was finally gone; his body lost in the boundless ocean. The moment should have felt triumphant, yet it didn't. Somewhere, hidden within the vastness of Agadin, was Mikiel. At the thought, he could feel tears threatening to sting his eyes once again. He steeled himself against it, hardening his emotions.

From the great heights, he saw the battlefield below. The numbers were thinned. Marradus must have had quite the feast. From the combat zone came a mournful roar that made him cringe.

From the ground damp with waters, he watched as Marradus launched into the sky. Narrowing his sight on the dragon, he furrowed his brow. In the past when he saw the dreadful beast, it was the embodiment of power; like a mountain in the air. Now, its movements were delayed; sluggish.

Realization struck him. The dragon was wounded.

Lagging throughout the gloomy skies, the dragon slowly made its way to a mountain beside Gorath, landing upon a stony cliff. It released such a loud grunt that he could hear it despite the distance.

Kaldon watched as the dragon sat still upon the mountain, attempting to rest from battle. He weighed his next move. He wanted to fly far away, escaping danger; curiosity also pulled at him to head below to where the armies fought. He wanted to see who could have been powerful enough to wound the monstrosity. However, as he looked upon the faltering dragon slouched atop the mountain, he knew this was an opportunity he couldn't waste.

Feeling the Owl's feathers woven between his fingers, he had a continuously evolving thankfulness for the wondrous bird. Already, it had saved his life on several occasions. Patting its side, he spoke to the legendary bird.

"I know that neither of us want to do this, but we need to go to the dragon. We can't delay."

Knowing that Marradus must have been one thousand times its size, he expected the Owl to fear such a supreme creature. Instead of objecting, the bird responded in immediate obedience. The Owl shifted its direction toward the jagged mountain where Marradus lay. Kaldon saw the dragon's merciless eyes watching him as he neared. He was surprised to see it sitting unmoved; like a tree firmly planted. It simply watched, apathetically.

Kaldon's body jolted at the sudden impact of the Owl's talons landing on the solid rock. He tensed being so close to the gargantuan creature yet again. The burn on his arm from Marradus' flames began tingling again in the dragon's presence, a reminder of what it was capable of.

He swallowed his nerves, dismounting the bird of fire. As his feet dropped onto the ground below, he heard the whistle of the wind swooning around him. Surrounded by dreary stone, he was nearly at the mountain's peak.

With the dragon's eyes on him, he unsheathed his rusty blade. Just as in his previous encounter with the dragon, he began hearing echoes swelling throughout his mind, like a legion of murmurs and screams. Amongst the array of voices, one emerged through the others. It boomed into his core.

"Only the bravest would follow one as mighty as I to such a high peak."

The dragon lifted its neck, arching it towards Kaldon. Even though everything within him wanted to run, he forced himself to stand.

"You are wounded. Who did this to you?" he asked, forcing words past his lips.

The dragon lingered in a pause before responding, fighting to admit that someone had achieved wounding it.

"Paladins."

Even though Marradus' response quickly drummed through Kaldon's mind, its body moved slowly; weakly. *Paladins,* he thought. He saw an arrow protruding from one of its eyes. Tolek had found the dragon.

"You cannot stop her."

The dragon's words wretched through his conscious, cutting through his thoughts.

"Can't stop who?" he asked.

"Furion."

Kaldon gripped his sword at the mention of the name. Regarding the fading dragon, he was astounded at how it still carried such arrogance, considering the state it was in. He wondered if he could turn that flaw against the creature.

"I bet you aren't even smart enough to know why Furion is a threat," he piped up.

Marradus let out a frustrated snort.

Kaldon was surprised how quickly the air warmed around him. He knew the dragon could consume him in flames in a split moment if it chose. Marradus brought its face closer to him, close enough for it to quickly make a meal of him.

"I have fed on thousands of years of knowledge. Besides, the Entity has confided in me time and time again. She has plans that would make you faint in fear."

"Prove it," he tested the dragon.

Marradus curled back its scaled lips, revealing its fangs, like a sinister smile. It let out an abrupt grunt, as though it were attempting to laugh.

"You think I'm a fool, that I would betray Furion's strategy?"

Kaldon pressed his lips together in frustration. He hoped the dragon would be eager to defend its pride. Before he could respond, Marradus spoke up again.

"One thing I can tell you is this: she has shared something with me that will be catastrophic to Agadin. She is so cunning to think up such a scheme."

He took a step forward, listening. "Tell me."

The dragon sneered.

"The plans are already in effect. They are unstoppable. She told me that Death's Snow is coming. It will fall as a sign."

Kaldon had never heard of the term *Death's Snow* before. Even though he didn't know what it was, the words unsettled him.

"What is Death's Snow?" he pressed.

"A sign of he who is coming. He will come with wrath and fury."

Kaldon grew uncomfortable at hearing the dark prophecy. Mikiel's face passed through his mind.

"I know very well who is coming," he said, hiding his emotion. "I have already seen Mikiel… The Wind of the Abyss. You are telling me nothing I don't already know."

Marradus brought its head closer again.

"The Wind of the Abyss may be vile, but he is not the threat I'm referring to. A greater judgement is coming; a wielder of death like no other. Under the banner of Death's Snow, the most ruthless throughout the face of Agadin will rise."

"If it's not Mikiel, then who is it? Who is coming?" he prodded.

"You will see soon enough. And then, there will be nothing left of Agadin."

"You are wrong!" Kaldon said with finality.

Marradus let out a mocking snort, shifting its weight.

Kaldon caught a glimpse of the creature's stomach. One of the dragon's scales was missing. Protruding from the exposed patch of skin was an unmistakable sight. The night-black hilt of *Integrity* stuck out. The last he saw the ancient blade was at Orin's home.

Words crashed into Kaldon's mind.

"I am never wrong."

The dragon stretched its mighty wings, arching its head to the shadow-filled skies. He knew he couldn't let the dragon flee. Too many lives had been stolen already by its fire. His eyes fixed upon the onyx hilt of *Integrity*.

The demon dragon gathered its strength to leap into the skies. The mountain peak quaked. Kaldon saw its staggered movements. If the dragon weren't wounded, it would have already been out of sight. He knew he could keep up with it.

"Divinity, be with me…" he whispered in dread.

Moving as fast as he could, he mounted the Owl's back. With a jolt, the eternal bird soared after Marradus. At such speeds he felt nerves tumbling throughout his abdomen. He gripped onto the Owl's ivory feathers.

Vertically ascending, he watched as Marradus reached the foggy cloud-line of the skies; the boundary created from the essence of the Dominion of Shadow. In a puff, the dragon was lost behind the veil of shadows. As the Owl soared closer to the cloud-line, the drastic increase in height made it harder to breathe. The air was thinning as they climbed. None-the-less, he shouted aloud, summoning the courage to persevere.

He followed the dragon into the shadowy fog. Dreary cloud smothered him. He gasped as he penetrated the fog, reaching the other side. Free from the shadowy veil, his eyes watered at the sight before him. Stars as far as his eyes could see shone like torches in the sky. He couldn't remember the last time he'd seen the skies without the taint of the Dominion of Shadow.

At the wondrous sight, his nerves suddenly began to toil. In the centre of the flawless canvas of night skies was a distinct blotch of darkness. Marradus hovered, waiting.

Upon the Owl's back, he looked down toward the shadowy floor beneath him. It was so thick he couldn't see the ground below. One slipup and he would plummet to his death; yet, he knew he couldn't turn back.

Without warning, fires raged.

Inferno painting the skies, the Owl dodged out of their way. He wasn't surprised by the bird's quick response. Marradus may have been an authority in power; however, with it wounded, the eternal Owl outmatched it in speed.

In a rush, the Owl propelled them closer to the dragon. Its colossal tail swung toward them. The Owl ducked out of the way, dodging every threat that came. Nearing the onyx dragon, he knew the Owl was darting toward the hilt of *Integrity* projecting from Marradus' core. He fixed his eyes on the blade. With stars shimmering around him like distant gems, the Owl brought him closer to the dragon's stomach. He flew close to the sword's hilt. Reaching up from the Owl, his fingers were still several feet away. The Owl struggled to bring him as close as he needed. He knew what he needed to do, instantly sweating at the realization. His heart hammered against his rib cage. Adrenaline screamed throughout him.

The words that he once declared over himself as a young boy crashed through his mind like an avalanche rampaging from his memories; like a wildfire swelling throughout his heart.

"I was created for more than the depths of the sewers. One day I will soar with the stars. One day I will be someone great."

Casting aside his fear, Kaldon rose, attempting to stand upon the Owl's back. Wind crashing against him, he kept his eyes upon the onyx hilt.

Reaching up, he felt the solid hilt of *Integrity* at his grasp. Kaldon concentrated on the Kingdom of Light — the flawless paradise of eternity. He threw his belief into the heavenly world he longed to see reign in Agadin.

In a flash, light shone from his hand and lit up the hilt of *Integrity*. The power of the Golden Land coursed through the ancient blade intruding into the demon dragon's scaled body. Marradus let out a wild howl into the night. Kaldon shook, never before channeling such a significant portion of the Kingdom of

Light. His whole body strained under the perfect sensation. The radiance shone throughout the skies, seemingly deposing the night like paradise invading Agadin.

Using his last bit of strength, his fist tightened around the hilt. In a shout, he pulled forth *Integrity,* freeing it from the dragon's form.

In a *bang,* he crashed atop the eternal bird.

Upon the Owl's back he looked up, watching the demon dragon jerk and writhe under the power of the Kingdom of Light. He could see the brilliance of light shining through the cracks between Marradus' scales. The dragon's organs were being disintegrated by the stellar force. It jerked and writhed under a power and force greater than itself. Its reptilian eyes were agape in the horror of its demise.

What was a terrifying sight — seeing something so massive contorting at such quick speeds — all stopped in a flash. All that was chaotic halted, as the demon dragon went limp mid-flight, its heart giving out.

Kaldon watched as the lifeless body of Marradus slowly began to fall. The massive corpse descended toward the shadowy cloud line. With a poof, the creature crashed through the fogged floor, falling from impossible heights.

Through the hole in the dark haze, Kaldon watched as Marradus fell. Swirling downward, he saw it falling toward the city of Gorath. The demon dragon neared the dark tower that stood in the proud city; the tower that was once Tymas Droll's seat of power as a tyrant over Agadin.

The sword-like tower that pierced into the skies now awaited, prepared to pierce the body of Marradus.

CHAPTER FOURTY-FIVE

DESCENT

<hr />

Anneya rummaged through shrubs and plants trying to find something to ease the pain of Orin's wound. Gorath was a dry land; however, water had unexpectedly rolled in from the ocean, coating the ground. Kneeling in the salty blue, she was thankful to find a small section of plant-life clustered amongst a small array of trees.

"Spikeweed, trailsbur, leafspire…" the Blade murmured to herself as she shuffled through the greenery.

"None of these will do," she said, looking aside in frustration.

She tried to heal the Roek, but the arrow penetrated far too deep. Several internal organs were ruptured, and she simply wasn't skilled enough to save him. Tolek did everything he could to save the Roek. She'd watched the Paladin work. He was more gifted than any healer she had ever met; even Master Healers didn't possess the Paladin's skill. She watched as his hands glowed wondrously. Light shone along the arrow into the Roek's body, touching what even eyes couldn't see.

Tolek sadly told her that Orin had bled too much internally. His organs were beyond repair. It was only a matter of time before he would be lost. Considering all the man had done for them, the least she could do was to help make his passing more comfortable.

Looking through the herbed plants, she watched as one of her teardrops fell, splashing into the watery floor.

The Blade let out a sarcastic laugh as she wiped away her tears. Marradus had escaped into the skies. She knew that Tolek and Henry had wounded the dragon; however, it was likely far from them by now. It was gone, and so was Kaldon.

She felt the Legacy hanging from her neck. *Humility* was strapped to her back. She wanted to hope for him, to believe he was alive. However, she knew Tymas Droll wouldn't have been merciful to the son of Dolan Thain. She needed to accept that Kaldon was gone.

The Legacy and sword were reminders of who he was; of who she lost. Her worst fear had become her reality. She was alone.

Through branches and leaves, she looked out to Agadin's skies. Death reigned in thick fog.

Suddenly, the stillness of the shadowed skies over Gorath was disrupted. Clouds shifted, as something massive plummeted through the dark clouds. Squinting, she tried to distinguish what it was. Then she saw plainly; Marradus was falling limp and lifeless. She couldn't believe her eyes.

She gasped, bringing her hands to her mouth. Marradus was falling toward the tower of Gorath. In a tremendous cut, the demon dragon landed upon the sword-like tower. Impaled. The defeated dragon corps slowly slid down the shaft.

"What could kill such a creature?" she whispered to herself as she looked back up into the skies from whence the dragon fell.

From the hole in the shadowed veil of the skies, she saw something emerge. Her eyes looked upon what she was certain she would never see again. The bird from eternity stroked the air with its elegant wings. She had never seen the Owl when it wasn't clothed in fire. The stark white feathers were stunning, befitting the heavenly bird.

Tears brimmed in her eyes as she saw that someone sat atop it, soaring toward the battlefield below. Her breath quickened. Unable to hold back, Anneya dropped to her knees in sobs.

She wept with abandon, words falling from her mouth.

"It's him."

CHAPTER FORTY-SIX

LIGHT SHALL REIGN

K aldon descended to the battlefield below. Warriors gawked, their eyes stuck on him and the Owl. He was thankful that the battle had completely simmered. There were also many civilians scattered within the scope of soldiers. He recognized many from the central court of Gorath: those who rejected the Sovereign's reign. His heart felt light at their presence. He felt encouraged at seeing those who risked their lives for taking a stand for freedom. As his eyes scoured through the multitudes, he saw the familiar amongst the aftereffects of calamity. Leaning against a boulder, kneeling next to a fallen man, was a Paladin. With his maroon jacket and white cape, his identity was undeniable.

The Owl landed before the Paladin.

At the sound, Tolek's head rose as he took in the sight. "It can't be," he said, rising to his feet.

Kaldon stepped down from the Owl. He patted the bird's ivory feathers in gratitude. The Paladin approached; his thumb hooked over his sword-less hilt.

"I can't believe it's you," Tolek said bewildered. "How are you still alive?"

He smiled in a silent response, reaching out grasping the Paladin's muscular forearm. Tolek's gaze scaled up the mighty bird before him. "I've only heard rumours of the legendary Owl from eternity. It is quite the sight."

"Well, the rumours were true," Kaldon replied.

"How did you come across it — let alone convince it to let you ride it?" he asked perplexed.

Kaldon couldn't hide the smirk from his face. It wasn't often that he did something that could impress the renowned Paladin. He looked over towards the Owl as it stretched its sturdy wings. Such a creature quickly grew discontent with the ground. The legendary bird launched into the air, exploding into flames. Instead of distancing itself, it remained in Kaldon's vicinity. Tolek watched the wondrous sight.

"It rescued me from prison. It saved me from my execution," he responded.

Tolek's eyes grew. "Your what?!"

"My execution," he said, holding back an amused laugh. "Never mind… It's a long story for another time."

The Paladin grunted, clearly not satisfied. He nodded towards Marradus' corpse spiked onto the tower of Gorath. "I suppose you are the one responsible for that, am I right?"

He looked down at *Integrity,* the sword that pierced the demon dragon. He knew that he only played a small part in Marradus' demise.

"We are responsible," Kaldon stated.

Tolek nodded in a smile. "Indeed."

"Tolek, how did you get ahold of *Integrity?*" he asked, knowing it was left in Orin's home.

At his question, the Paladin's face grew somber. "I'm sorry, Kaldon," he said dolefully, stepping aside. "He saved all of our lives. I tried everything I could to heal him, but there's nothing more I can do."

For the first time, he saw the identity of the hooded man propped up against the boulder behind the Paladin.

"No!" Kaldon shouted, rushing to the side of the wounded Roek, kneeling on the ground before him.

Orin let out a violent cough. The Roek's face was paled. Blood stained his robe.

"Orin, you came," he said, gripping one of the old man's leathery hands. "I'm so sorry. I didn't know it would end this way..."

A smile spread over Orin's wrinkled face. His voice coming out in staggered breaths, he said, "Don't worry about me, my boy. I helped save Agadin today. I have no regrets in leaving my home to come here."

"It's true," the Paladin said. "Without Orin, we wouldn't have been able to wound Marradus."

He was silent, watching the Roek slowly wither.

Orin continued, "Kaldon, I'm sorry for not protecting you. I should have prevented you being captured, but I behaved as a coward."

"I hold nothing against you," he said, pushing words past the lump in his throat. "And you, my friend, are no coward."

Orin smiled at the affirmation. His glazed eyes looked deep into the young man. "I met Anneya," he said.

The words pierced his heart. He hadn't seen Anneya for nearly three quarters of a year. He ached to see her; to hold her.

"She is wonderful, Kaldon," the old man said in a gentle tone.

He felt a tear tumble down his face. "Save your energy, Orin. I'm going to try to heal you."

He was exhausted from summoning the Kingdom of Light, but he needed to try. He wouldn't allow Orin's life to be lost.

"No," Orin said, letting out weak coughs. "Let me go. It's too late."

Kaldon shook his head. "Why would you choose death?"

"Because I want to be with Mary," the Roek said fearlessly.

Even years after her passing, he cherished her. Kaldon remembered the words the old man spoke back at his quaint home. He spoke them aloud, reciting them to the Roek.

"One of the marks of a true man is his ability to keep the heart of a woman for a lifetime."

"Wise words," Orin said with a smile. "Mary was worth it, Kaldon. I assure you, so is Anneya."

The truth of Orin's words warmed him. Kaldon clenched the man's hand in his own.

"Stay true, Kaldon Thain," Orin said.

Kaldon forced a smile as tears marked his face.

Orin breathed out a final wheeze, his life gone from him.

Kaldon bowed his head knowing that he had gone to be with Mary. As he leaned over the faded Roek, he mourned the loss of a friend; the man who taught him to Command Creation. The man whose lessons empowered him to take the life of Tymas Droll.

"Your legacy will not be forgotten, my friend," he whispered over the Roek.

Through the silence of mourning, a voice rose from behind him.

"Kaldon?"

The soft voice soothed his soul. It made him feel both weak and strong. He slowly stood, turning to see the woman his heart longed for; the woman who was more than a Blade to him.

In the customary armour of a Blade, she stood with her nervous hands entwined before her. Her golden hair shawled her perfect shoulders. By the look of her, he could see new confidence shaped within her. She seemed more secure; more certain of who she was. As his eyes lingered upon her, he noticed something difference about her face. The teardrop scar was gone; the mark of abuse washed away.

Wordlessly he approached her. Reaching a hand up, he stroked her cheek where her scar once stained her. "Your scar..."

"It's a long story," she replied, lost in the sight of him.

He understood. He had accumulated his fair share of *long stories,* himself.

"Kaldon..." she stuttered. "Did you kill Marradus? I saw it fall from the sky. How did you escape Tymas Droll's hand? How did you find the Owl?"

He didn't hear her words. He simply watched her. Orin was right; she was worth it. She was one worthy of spending a lifetime with.

In the moment, standing before her, there was only one thing running through his mind; only one thing that he desired to speak.

With a timber in his tone, he spoke. "Marry me."

Anneya's eyes widened. "What did you say?"

He reached out, grabbing her soft hand. "Please, I need you to marry me. I never want to be apart from you. I want to hold your heart for a lifetime."

Even though warriors darted around them and victory was being celebrated, the moment was still between them.

Her eyes glistened. She looked into the eyes of the one who made her feel safe; made her feel complete. He was the one who made her know undeniably that she belonged; that she was never alone.

Under her rosy cheeks, a smile grew. "Of course."

Kaldon came in, pressing his lips against hers. He could feel the wetness of her tears upon her face. He finally had her in his arms; finally felt her warmth once again. Amidst the mighty army, they embraced one another. Pulling away from her, her smile shone as vibrant as the sun.

They watched one another as the sound of someone clearing their throat pulled their attention away. Anneya still in his arms, he looked over to see Tolek with a proud smile etched onto his face. Gratitude washed over him at seeing the Paladin's joy for them.

His focus was pulled from the Paladin, seeing an enormous man watching them from beside Tolek. The man's eyes were glossed with tears. He had never seen someone so large in all his life.

Loosening her grip from Kaldon's hands, Anneya spoke. "Oh, Henry, you big softy!" the Blade shouted. She looked to Kaldon. "You need to meet Henry!"

The large Paladin walked closer, gripping his wrist in a lock of greeting. The man's hand and arm were so large that Kaldon felt like a child in comparison.

"It is an honour to meet the son of Dolan Thain; the soon-to-be husband of the feistiest Philosopher I have ever met." Henry looked to Anneya, giving her a wink.

She balked out a laugh.

Kaldon laughed along, even though their inside joke was lost to him. "The honour is mine," he replied.

Tolek stepped in. "I don't mean to break up the celebration. But, Kaldon, have you seen any trace of Tymas Droll? Do you know if he is here in Gorath?"

"The Sovereign of Shadow is dead," Kaldon said seriously.

"You killed a Shan-Rafa?" Henry asked, his voice coloured with wonder. "How did you accomplish such a thing?"

Kaldon's gaze was solemn. "I dropped an ocean wave on him."

He watched the three look down to the damp floor beneath them, soaking their boots.

"*You* did this?!" Anneya asked in near disbelief.

"What?! You Commanded Creation?!" Tolek stuttered — something Kaldon had never heard the Paladin do before.

The three looked at him in shock, not only that he had accomplished an unimaginable feat, but that the Sovereign of Shadow was actually gone.

The sudden sound of footsteps rose in their ears.

Kaldon, Anneya, and the two Paladins shifted their attention to the sound. Clothed in dirtied rags with a frazzled beard and hair, a man approached.

"You must be Kaldon Thain," the man said in a hoarse voice.

"What is it to you?" Henry said, stepping forward with his war-hammer held in front of him.

Kaldon recognized the man's voice. He motioned for the large Paladin to lower his weapon. "This man isn't a threat," he said.

"You're Glaric, aren't you?" he asked the timid man.

The man brought a cordial hand before him, bowing. The formal gesture looked unfitting considering his apparel. "I am," he stated.

Kaldon shook his head in a faint laugh. "How did you escape?!"

Anneya and the Paladins watched the scenario unfolding, confused at his sudden laughter.

Her brow tensed. "Wait a minute — Glaric? You're Ceanne Brimnas' Chief Messenger that she mentioned back at the Peak of Lore?"

Kaldon nodded, placing a hand on his shoulder. "Yes. Glaric, here, was my prison companion."

A sly smile spread over the Chief Messenger's face. "Thankfully, I'm not a prisoner anymore. When one of the guards came to bring me my meal, I was able to surprise him, taking him out."

Kaldon crossed his arms. "But the prison was brimming with guards. You couldn't have just left."

"You're right," he said, shaking his head. "I couldn't just leave. I waited until most of the guards left to watch your *supposed* execution. The guards left us prisoners unattended. This permitted me to free the other prisoners who were locked away for denying the Dominion of Shadow."

The Chief Messenger motioned to a nearby group of people filled with men, women, and children. All were dirtied, covered in filth from their time spent in prison.

At the sight of children freed, no longer imprisoned, Anneya took a step forward. "You freed all these people?"

"I did," Glaric responded. "But now I'm left without a mandate. I desire to advance the Kingdom of Light throughout Agadin. What do you suggest I do?" he asked, looking to Kaldon.

Kaldon reached to his hip, pulling forth the rusty sword that he used to fight Tymas Droll, offering it to Glaric. "If you need a new mandate, then take this. You will need it."

Glaric eyed the weapon, feeling its weight. "I am no warrior. I am only a messenger."

"I'm aware," Kaldon said. "You will need this for protection. I have a message that needs to be proclaimed across Agadin to cities and towns; to kings and queens. It's a message so important that only a Chief Messenger could be entrusted with it."

Glaric lifted his head. Even though he was clothed in dirt and wasn't groomed, dignity rose within him. "Tell me the message."

Kaldon looked the adamant man in the eyes. "Tell all cities, towns, kings, and queens alike, this message: The Sovereign of Shadow is dead. His rule has crumbled. The demon dragon, Marradus, is slain and terrorizes no more. We need those across Agadin to rise, to stand for freedom and life. Tell them that Light shall reign once again throughout Agadin."

Glaric smiled, nodding. "It will by my greatest honour to deliver such a message."

"What about us?" Henry asked. "Many throughout Agadin have embraced the Shadow. Armies of darkness will not stop simply because Tymas Droll is gone."

Kaldon looked upon his friends; those devoted to making an impact in the Great War. Looking up to the skies that remained stolen by the Dominion of Shadow, his eyes turned sad. He knew what their next objective needed to be. As much as he despised it, he knew it wasn't a task that could be avoided.

With both sorrow and surety in his tone, he said, "We need to find the Wind of the Abyss."

Chapter Fourty-Seven

The Children Play

Walking down stone halls, Locrian's charcoal robe trailed behind him. Past the beige archways, shrubbery, and trees dressing the ancient abode of Philosophers. In the distance, he could hear a waterfall crashing into crystal waters. It was simply one of many scattered throughout the wondrous place. Noriden was a paradise; a dwelling place for some of the greatest thinkers alive. His reason for coming wasn't for his own growth. It wasn't for him to linger, nor to rest; he needed to find the scroll he saw in the River of Time. That feat was proving to be more difficult than he would have hoped.

A smile grew upon the Seer's face as he watched children running throughout the stone halls, their feet pattering upon the rough ground. Their laughter filled the halls as they chased one another. He saw Hayley, Haddy, and Honey with the other children. He couldn't help but laugh aloud at seeing them enjoying themselves. He was thankful Brenton, Flor, and their girls came with him. After hearing what he saw in his vision concerning the scroll, Brenton insisted on joining him on the journey to Noriden. The journey all the way from the Peak of

Lore with three young girls made for an interesting venture. It was trying at times, but he was thankful for the company none-the-less. He found there was a place in his heart for the three young ones.

Looking through the linen archways, the smile fell from his face. Black and purples covered the face of the sky, thwarting its vibrance. The skies over Agadin grew darker each day. He was becoming tired of his search. He assumed he had likely searched through at least fifty rooms brimming with writings throughout Noriden.

The abode of Philosophers was constructed quite obscurely. Noriden was widely spread out, providing numerous places for Philosophers to study and muse. How the multitude of books were stored was similar, in a spread-out fashion. In the Peak of Lore, all books were held within a large library; whereas Noriden consisted of rooms scattered across the expansive place, like separate houses to function as homes for the wells of knowledge. Each of the home-like rooms brimmed with an assortment of books and scrolls. It was like an entire city built of knowledge. The Seer assumed one could spend a lifetime and only make it through a fraction of the writings stored there. He knew the ancient scroll was somewhere amidst the mass of collected wisdom. He vowed to find it.

He stepped into one of the enclosed hallways, thankful to be rid of the sight of the dreadful skies. At the end of the hallway, he saw one of the simpler home-like rooms. The room looked tarnished by time; the paint was chipping and worn. He'd given up searching the elite rooms. If the scroll was in one of those rooms, any Philosopher in the city would have read it hundreds of times over. Instead, he searched through places where something could become not only lost, but forgotten.

He found himself searching through storage rooms.

The Seer placed his hand upon the loose doorframe that shifted under his grip. As he stepped into the storage space, he felt spider webs pressing against his body, betraying how long it had been since someone was actually in the quaint room.

Looking inside, Locrian saw old and tired furniture piled on top of each other. He squinted. The only light in the room was the faded sunlight poking through wooden boards placed over windows. The room was so dark he could only make out the outline of the back wall. Trying to force his way deeper into the room with his hands stretched outward for guidance, he shimmied his feet forward. He grew agitated at how many times he bumped into objects sprawled about.

He paused as he saw in his peripheral vision a flash of light coming from behind him.

"Seer, is that you in there?" the raspy voice called.

He jumped at the startling interruption. His heart was racing. Looking back, he saw a woman standing behind him, her frizzy hair outlined by light. Holding a torch before her, he saw that it was Fen.

"Great Divinity! Don't sneak up on me like that," Locrian scowled.

Fen let out an amused laugh. "You are quite jumpy for one who can see the future."

He couldn't help but smile at the Philosopher as he shook his head. He was thankful she chose to come with him and the others. She had outgrown the Depths. It seemed as though she had been already been befriending many of the other Philosophers throughout Noriden. Considering her extensive knowledge, he knew the resident Philosophers were likely taking advantage of her experience to learn from her.

Locrian couldn't hide his grin. "Can you bring that torch over here?"

She walked over, the light of her torch casting upon the forgotten room.

"Have you asked the Philosophers here about the scroll you saw in your vision?" she asked inquisitively.

"Every one of them," he admitted. "None have heard of a scroll written by Dawntan Forlorn. It's as though it doesn't even exist."

Fen nodded in thought.

"Come this way," he said, motioning to the back wall.

Fen stepped toward the back. They saw an ancient bookcase that was illuminated in light. Resting upon it were dozens of scrolls, matted in cobwebs that had clearly been accumulating for decades.

"Do you think the scroll is here?" she asked.

He could feel her stare pressing into him. "I hope."

Reaching out his hand, he began wiping away the aged cobwebs. His eyes took in the richly scrolls revealed beneath.

The Philosopher piped up. "These can't be them, Locrian. They are in too good of condition to have been written by Dawntan Forlorn. They aren't aged enough."

He knew she was right. As his eyes scaled up and down the dark-wooden bookshelf, he reached out pushing the scrolls aside. As each tumbled from the shelf hitting the ground, their eyes rested upon a remaining scroll that was tucked away, leaning against the back of one of the shelves.

Wrapping his fingers around the ancient scroll, it felt fragile. He slowly opened the four-thousand-year-old script being careful not to tear it.

"This is it…" Lorcian muttered aloud in astonishment.

Fen quickly leaned in.

As the Seer's eyes ran over the words, he read them aloud.

"I have accomplished what others deem as remarkable. I have dethroned corrupt kings and queens. I have dismantled armies. As I continue to understand the Great War, I fear that my feats do not matter, for I have mistaken my enemy.

"It is true that many have embraced the Shadow. Corruption reigns within many hearts, but there is a far greater evil. I have known about her for quite some time, yet I underestimated her involvement. She not only plays a part in the evil taking place; she is its source. She is the mother of evil. Furion is the one who wields the Dominion of Shadow. If a corrupt ruler is defeated, she will simply raise up a dozen more. If a ravenous creature is slain, she has hundreds of other plans already in place. She is death; and desires for Agadin to be in the palm of her hand."

Locrian paused, letting the words sink in.

"Keep reading, Seer," Fen encouraged.

"Once I came to this conclusion, I had a vision. This was not just a vision by foresight; I saw as a Seer sees. Like an explosion in my mind, I saw death coming to Agadin. I do not know when this will take place; however, I believe it will occur long after my days run out. Furion's goal is both grand and terrible. She doesn't only desire death to cover Agadin; she longs for nothingness to take it. It will all begin when the Door of the Dominion opens."

Locrian felt chills glide across his skin, like ice running over his body.

"There are several occurrences that will take place when this door opens. The first, is that the Dominion of Shadow will drape over the skies of Agadin, blinding the sun. This will result in Furion sending Death's Snow to cloak the land, draping it in death. Heat will be dethroned. Crops will die. Famine and plagues will spread. I have seen Death's Snow in my vision. It is terrible. Death's Snow falling is a sign of Agadin coming to its end. If the snow falls, then I fear it may be too late, for it is a sign of he who is coming.

Locrian and Fen looked to one another in wonder. Who was Dawntan was referring to?

"He will rise, a warrior like no other. Furion has corrupted even the deepest places of his soul; his heart is as dark as Shadow itself. He will rouse a tremendous army; one that I doubt anything could stop. This army will be able to demolish kingdoms in a single day. This man will ignite a war that could very well cause the end of Agadin. Under the kiss of Death's Snow, the most ruthless man on the face of Agadin will wield unparalleled rage. Furion will summon the King of Paladins.

"The War Lord will rise."

"Great Divinity, not him: not Rederick Rule..." Fen whispered, shaking her head.

Locrian shuttered at the thought of the War Lord's heart being corrupted by the Shadow; stolen by Furion. The Seer read the final words of the prophecy.

"I fear for the ones who must endure such times. I wish I could offer counsel on how to overthrow Furion; however, the feat seems hopeless, for they do not battle against flesh and blood. They battle against an Entity."

- Dawntan Forlorn

Locrian and Fen stood in silence at the morbid words. They had received word that Tymas Droll and Marradus were killed. Gone. However, it seemed like it no longer mattered. If Dawntan Forlorn's words were true, far more terrible things were coming; things more dreadful than even a demon dragon or a fascist tyrant.

As the two felt the weight of the revelation, from outside the house they heard the sound of someone running.

"Locrian! Locrian!" the small voice called.

Looking to the door of the room, he saw a tiny head pop into the house. It was Hayley, Brenton's oldest daughter. At the sight of them, Hayley rushed into the house, stepping over old furniture that draped the dusty floor.

"Locrian. Fen. Come quick! I need to show you something!" she said excitedly, nearly out of breath.

He forced a smile. "Not now, my dear, we have work ahead of us."

Hayley propped her fists on her hips. "If you wait, you are going to miss it!" The young girl pouted, popping out her bottom lip.

Locrian sighed, "What will we miss?"

"I'm not telling. You'll see when you come with me," Hayley said, raising her eyebrows as she leaned in.

He smiled at the young girl's blissful naivety. Here, the world was falling apart around her, yet she was caught up in the wonder of child's play. How he wished for a peaceful world for her to live in.

Fen looked to him with a smile. "Maybe we should tag along, Seer. It seems like we both need some lightening up."

He allowed a fabricated smile to creep onto his face. "Alright, my dear, we will come with you. Show us the way."

Pulling their sleeves, Hayley ushered Locrian and Fen out from the forgotten room.

"What is it that you have to show us Hayley?" Locrian asked, as he walked down the stoney hall.

Turning her head with a wide grin, the young girl spoke. "Oh, you'll see! I'm sure everyone here is watching."

Letting out a tired laugh, he allowed the young girl to guide him.

Rounding the corner, Locrian stepped into the grassy garden. He watched as hundreds of residents of Noriden looked up.

"No, it can't be," Fen spoke aloud, her voice fading.

In the middle of the field, children danced and played. Hayley let go of the Seer's sleeve and ran to play with them. "Locrian! Locrian! Do you see it? It's snowing! It's snowing!"

Black ash rained down from the sky as Locrian pushed words past the lump in his throat. "Yes, my dear, I see it."

Children ran playing throughout the yard. Their hands were held up in the air trying to catch cinders. Their laughs contrasted the looks of dread cast upon the faces of those mature enough to recognize something was terribly wrong. The specks of black char fell upon the men, women, and children; marking them. It stained the ground with death.

Locrian felt a hand rest upon his shoulder. Looking over, he saw it was Brenton.

"Locrian, what is going on? What is this?" Brenton asked with hopelessness glistening in his eyes.

The Seer took in the man's stone face. The Blade was afraid, just as he was.

Locrian looked back to what laid before him. His gaze rested upon the children playing in the charcoal-flakes of ash. "My friend, I fear it is Agadin coming to its end." He paused before his next words.

"The War Lord is coming."

Story Continues In...

The Golden Land

RISE OF SHADOW · REIGN OF LIGHT

VOLUME III

L.R. Knight lives in Alberta, Canada with his wife of many years. He is the author of several books which have been published in multiple languages. His works include writing on behalf of acclaimed motivational speakers and for the arts and entertainment industry; his works have also been adapted to theatre.

L.R. Knight believes in the power of storytelling.

"Stories can speak to the hidden places of our souls. They encourage us to lay aside the complexities of adulthood; to once again embrace childhood wonder." - L.R. Knight

Manufactured by Amazon.ca
Bolton, ON